The author is a nuclear physicist who leverages software developments, mathematical representations, computer simulations, and engineering judgement to enable *practical* nuclear reactor plants, inspired by the no-nonsense approach of Admiral Rickover. His experience spans reactor core design, manufacturability, safety, performance, transport, and waste management.

The author is a proud father of two daughters. In his spare time, he is a keen bodybuilder, software developer, studier of history and inspirational figures, DIY enthusiast, and creative writer.

Exploitation is his first novel.

To my dear children,

You'll blow us all away—just you wait.

Jeffrey J. Jordan

EXPLOITATION

AUSTIN MACAULEY PUBLISHERS™

LONDON ∗ CAMBRIDGE ∗ NEW YORK ∗ SHARJAH

A CIP catalogue record for this title is available from the British Library.

ISBN 9781398426788 (Paperback)
ISBN 9781398426795 (Hardback)
ISBN 9781398426801 (ePub e-book)

www.austinmacauley.com

First Published 2023
Austin Macauley Publishers Ltd®
1 Canada Square
Canary Wharf
London
E14 5AA

Chapter 1
Normal Business

Toby Beaumont-Knight's bright white headlights finally materialise from around the street corner. I maintain a tight grip on the steering wheel and stare unremittingly into the wing mirror. Their rapidly increasing brightness progressively intensifies my already throbbing headache until I am forced to close my eyes.

Several days ago, Toby voluntarily positioned himself in the Harkov crime family's crosshairs for the final time. On the previous occasions, the prospect of financial gain temporarily restrained the members of this typically trigger-happy family from exerting pressure on their triggers. However, on this latest occasion, he heedlessly exerted the pressure himself when he attempted to physically assault Mikhail Harkov, the head of the Harkov crime family. That level of arrogance and stupidity marked the culmination of his privileged, yet neglected, upbringing. Whilst his extremely wealthy father, Lord Alfred Beaumont-Knight, personally ensured that his pecuniary needs were always catered for, he was emotionally and physically unavailable. He always shipped his son off to public school for the full boarding experience at the first opportunity every term, and kept him there until the very last.

Lord Beaumont-Knight is this city's most well-placed mediator. He leverages his family, professional, and personal connections, including members of his old boys' network, to bend laws and regulations to mediate lucrative, yet mostly immoral and outright illicit, business deals. Many of these business deals involve international clients with questionably derived sources of wealth and power.

Until relatively recently, Toby—now a tricenarian—relied wholly on the monthly allowance provided by his father. This afforded him the ability to not only sustain the lifestyle of a socialite, but to also sustain the upkeep of an extensive harem of live-in prostitutes and social media influencers. For the last couple of years, Toby has fervently pursued his entrepreneurial calling—well, at least fervently pursued ways to ensure his place at the centre of attention at all social gatherings. Naturally, many of his business ventures failed, some at great expense to the Beaumont-Knight family estate, which was also suffering from several of Lord Beaumont-Knight's own poor investment decisions. Despite this situation, neither father nor son could bring themselves to face the ensuing embarrassment if they changed their lifestyles to reflect the required retrenchment of their outgoings.

Before any tough financial decisions were required, Toby was surprised to find out that his exclusive gentlemen's club, 'Handsome Knights', was beginning to thrive. Handsome Knights is currently in vogue for well-off, ostentatious, and frivolous bachelors, many of whom had formed friendships with him at the various boarding schools he briefly attended before being expelled—or, as officially stated on his student record, rusticated—and shipped to the next.

It wasn't long before Handsome Knights' success, and, most importantly, profit caught the attention of Lord Beaumont-Knight. He was horrified when he found out. He first demanded, and then he begged, Toby to shut it down; Toby remained steadfast in his refusal to shut it down. Thus, he was forced to turn to his own circle of corrupt associates. However, despite him paying them a fortune out of his own pocket, even they failed him on this occasion.

To make the situation much worse, and despite his father's increasingly aggressive protestations, Toby had convinced himself that he should continue to ride the wave of success so decided to add two larger, more mainstream, gentlemen's clubs to his business empire. To guarantee the popularity of these establishments, especially with the hoi polloi, as well as to outstrip the competition, he knew that he had to overload them with exceptionally beautiful women. His now financially challenged father pretended to let it slip during a family meal that Mikhail was the only person in the city, possibly even the country, who could deliver his required quantity and quality of product.

Toby invited Mikhail to one of the handful of restaurants still owned by the Beaumont-Knight family to negotiate a deal. Lord Beaumont-Knight had forewarned him about the consequences of not treating Mikhail with the utmost respect at all times. He was also informed that Mikhail would only respect him if he held a firm, but fair, position; Mikhail would lose respect for him immediately, and probably forever, if he attempted to be greedy.

It is now evident that respect and deal-making are qualities that Toby neither inherited nor acquired. From the introductory handshake, he mistakenly thought that he was in control of the situation; he treated Mikhail as a simple Russian pleb who should be eternally grateful to even be considered by a member of the aristocracy for such a business opportunity.

Mikhail quickly concluded that Toby was the arrogant prick he was expecting as he watched him, through half-closed eyes, describe a business enterprise that he already knew intimately. He owns nearly all of the strip clubs and nightclubs in the city, and has, on many occasions, gone to extreme lengths to ensure their success. He only chose to let Handsome Knights flourish due to the value of an enduring relationship with Lord Beaumont-Knight being significantly higher than the cost of the reduced profits inflicted by Handsome Knights; however, he was not willing to let Toby increase his market share further without his close involvement—as Lord Beaumont-Knight had rightly predicted.

It had been a long time since Mikhail had been spoken to in this tone and manner. He later told me that he had to immediately order two double shots of vodka in an attempt to calm himself down and disguise any external manifestations of the rage that fermented inside of him; unfortunately, the disgusting, poor-quality vodka, which had been relabelled as a premium Russian vodka brand, only compounded his rage. If there wasn't a substantial amount of money on the metaphorical table then this sin alone would have resulted in Toby's face being smashed into the physical table.

Toby commenced the negotiations by demanding a supply of women in exchange for Mikhail being given a five percent stake in the new establishments; Mikhail made it very clear that he would require at least a fifty-one percent stake. In reality, it was at least a fifty-one percent stake or Toby wouldn't have made it home without having a 'serious accident'—such would be the cost of his disrespect. Mikhail continued to explain the other non-negotiable terms of their deal before softening them with the benefits he would bring to their partnership, including the free advertisement their new establishments to all his associates and customers, as well as the deployment of his own 'muscle' to protect them.

Toby began to panic and struggle like a trapped animal. He realised for the first time in his life that he wasn't going to get what he wanted; he was no longer in control. Contrary to his father's advice, he greedily continued to try and insert his own demands into the negotiations. Both parties deliberately didn't mention his flagship club. Unbeknownst to him, Mikhail had already made moves to secure Handsome Knights, as well as several other businesses owned by the Beaumont-Knight family.

Mikhail is a skilled and experienced predator. Despite the interpersonal conflict between them both, he remained professional and expertly manipulated his prey into submission—like he has done many times before. He administered the coup de grâce when he unlocked his phone and showed Toby the photographs of all the women that he had 'in stock'. Toby couldn't swipe through them fast enough. Even before he had finished viewing them all, he verbally agreed to Mikhail's terms and thrust his hand into Mikhail's. The handshake alone was worth more than any legal document, at least to Mikhail.

As promised, Mikhail delivered the women and the 'muscle', who, in turn, were responsible for controlling the internal distribution of Mikhail's designer narcotics. Both clubs were an instant success. Inevitably, it did not take long for greed to take over; Toby began stuffing his own pockets with a portion of Mikhail's share of the profits. Mikhail knew that this would happen. It always happens—although, possibly not in such a short time period as it played out on this occasion. His trusted foot soldiers on the clubs' payroll kept a close eye on Toby and the accounts for him. In the interest of retaining a profitable partnership, and the continued use of Lord Beaumont-Knight's 'services', he grudgingly made the unprecedented decision to offer him temporary absolution in exchange for a confession.

Three nights ago, with neither a reservation nor an invitation, Mikhail and his personal bodyguard, Valentin, entered one of the Beaumont-Knight family-owned restaurants whilst Toby was entertaining a large entourage of friends. Toby sprung from his chair and stormed angrily over to Mikhail, heading him off before he reached the dining area. Mikhail stretch out his hand to shake Toby's hand and exchange pleasantries, but Toby had other ideas: he tried to sucker punch Mikhail. Mikhail nonchalantly stepped back, avoiding the uncontrolled fist easily. If Toby had instantly fallen to his knees and offered Mikhail the opportunity to flay a large portion of his flesh, prune several of his digits, and dictate the amount of financial compensation, then there was an incredibly small chance that all this would have placated Mikhail's bloodlust;

however, he opted for insisting that he and his friends take the two Russians 'outside'.

Toby screamed disjointed battle cries as the cold winter air hit his lungs. He shadowboxed whilst he waited for everyone to join him outside. Mikhail had barely stepped out of the restaurant when he launched another uncontrolled swing. Again, he failed to make contact. Instead, a return blow sledgehammered into his abdomen. With the wind knocked out of him, his knees landed on the hard, damp paving slabs. Both Mikhail and Valentin are very able, experienced, and deadly fighters. Even though they were outnumbered and only used their fists, they were untouchable. Toby, through showers of blood, watched his friends fall to the floor all around him, some of them never to get up again.

Alerted by the loud screams, Toby's bodyguard, who had been waiting in the car, managed to sneak up behind the Russians and take them by surprise. With his handgun pointed at Mikhail's face, he hoisted Toby up off the floor and they both retreated to their car. Despite the gun being pointed at Mikhail's face, neither he nor Valentin was prepared to let Toby escape; they matched their pace step for step. The frightened bodyguard turned his aim and fired one shot at Valentin, who silently dropped to the ground.

Undisturbed, Mikhail continued to advance. Toby was terrified; he shouted louder and louder for his bodyguard to also shoot Mikhail as he steadily closed the gap between them. When they reached their car, the bodyguard had no choice other than to fire at Mikhail. The shot winged him, giving them just enough time to get in their car and escape.

Mikhail's elite, brutal, and loyal team of henchmen—the 'Murder Squad'—were quickly on the crime scene to 'remind' the restaurant's employees and customers that they hadn't seen anything. The corrupt police officers knew their lives depended on them dawdling to the crime scene and then either removing or tampering with any evidence that even remotely suggested Russian involvement. This resulted in a misleading, conflicting, incomplete, and essentially worthless investigation report. Only a couple of loose ends remain.

Toby has since been ordered by his father to go into hiding and stay there whilst he tries to broker a pardon for him by assisting Mikhail with numerous business deals. Now his son's life hangs in the balance, there is no law he is not willing to break and no financial expense he is not willing to pay. In some respects, his efforts are noble, but they are completely hopeless all the same. Mikhail now has him where he wants him—whether his son is alive or not.

I am sitting in an old, grey Ford Focus. I don't stand out; I can't afford to be noticed. The car's clock suggests that it is nearing one o'clock in the morning; my body clock suggests it is much later. It is bitterly cold, raining, and pitch black. This can be a relatively busy part of the city; however, in these conditions, not many people are out and the ones that are around are too distracted and in too much of a hurry to notice what anyone else is doing. Perfect. The weather is my ally tonight.

I've sat still for the last three hours. I should be cold, but the predatory instinct stirring in my gut keeps me warm. Despite my incessantly throbbing headache, I am fully prepared for the task at hand. I am deathly still; my breathing is steady. This is the part of my job that I love: the stalking. I do not particularly care for the killing itself; however, that sentiment is client dependent.

I am parked down the street from a nightclub that is known in socialite circles as 'The Underground'. It does not have an official name as it is not a legal enterprise. Mikhail's latest rivals, the Albanians, have been allowed to operate it after they came to an arrangement with the city's officials and police force in exchange for halting the bloodshed that followed them to this city.

This club goes to extreme lengths to guarantee that its customers can openly indulge in their various poisons without them having to worry about tactical flashlights and tabloid camera flashes—the latter being potentially more harmful. There are three main policies that the club employs to minimise their customers' risk of exposure: no phones or cameras; drugs and drug paraphernalia are not allowed to enter or leave the premises; and attendance by invitation only. The guest list is populated with prospective customers selected from an extensive list of vetted individuals. A physical token is anonymously delivered to these prospective customers during the morning on the day that they have been invited to attend.

I do not recognise the two well-dressed doormen who frame the club's entrance. My friends do not work at such exclusive establishments. I become momentarily distracted when I allow myself to think of the lengths Mikhail went to in order to not only find out that Toby would be in attendance at this club tonight, but also to obtain me an entry token.

The roaring engine of a brand-new BMW X6 suppresses the bile rising in my throat and brings all my senses back to the hunt. Despite the car's speed, weather conditions, and deliberately poor public lighting in this area, I catch enough of the licence plate to know this car belongs to my target. The car is parked several cars ahead of me—people are not allowed to park or be dropped off directly outside of the club.

Toby leaves his car and heads towards the club, dragging a young lady, eyes rolled back and chewing vigorously on her gum, behind him. His bodyguard stays in the car: he is on lookout duty tonight. Despite the Albanians not allowing it, I still wait a couple of minutes after Toby has entered the club to confirm that none of his other security personnel follow him in. I have been sitting here for long enough to categorically confirm that none of them are already waiting for him inside. I suspect he is relying on the Albanians for his protection tonight. The fact that the Albanians have allowed him in their club suggests that they are unaware of his recent disagreement with Mikhail. They do not want Mikhail anywhere near their club. Even if he has somehow managed to employ the Albanians to protect him from Mikhail, it wouldn't particularly matter to me—I would still achieve my objective.

My car has been running for the past hour, so I simply check my wing mirror before pulling out into the deserted road. As I drive past the BMW, I see Toby's bodyguard sitting in the driver's seat. His face is lit up by his phone. There is plenty of room for me to reverse-park in front of him. The Underground is still quite a distance away on the other side of the road. The two doormen are facing the other direction; their attention is on the drunken group of scantily clad women who've just arrived at the club.

I take a deep breath and exhale whilst reversing. My lungs are empty when I collide with the BMW. The airbags are disabled to avoid the distraction of them exploding in my face. I flip open my boot and roll the car forward about a metre. As I grab the beer can out of the passenger footwell, I resist my body's sudden urge to collapse and fall asleep. I open the beer can and drop it onto the road when I open the driver's door. I stumble out of the car and dedicate one hundred percent of my attention to rescuing my beer can as the beer glugs out. I grab the can with my left hand and pretend to drink its contents whilst discreetly thrusting my right hand into my inside jacket pocket and taking a secure hold of my knuckleduster.

The bodyguard gets out of his car, stroking his forehead; I act as though I am oblivious to the crash. He says something to me as he inserts his phone into his right trouser pocket. I cannot hear him over the rain, which begins to fall harder. When he gets within striking range, I stumble forward and to the right. He is quicker than expected and tries to move out of my way; however, before gravity takes full control of my fall, I stamp my right leg down and use this movement to initiate the swing of my right knuckleduster-wielding fist. To avoid killing him, I prioritise precision over power. I strike him squarely on his lower jaw with just enough force behind it. He is instantly knocked out. Using the momentum of his collapsing body, I bundle him effortlessly into the boot of the car.

I lift his legs up, forcing him into the foetal position. I throw the now half-full beer can into the boot alongside him before grabbing the duct tape and securely fastening his hands and feet together behind his back. I check to make sure that he is still alive by putting my finger under his nose and feeling his faint, hot breath against it. Good. Mikhail would be very upset with me if I killed him before giving him chance to. After sticking a piece of duct tape over his mouth, I have to slap it a couple of times to encourage it to remain stuck to his wet face. I pull his wallet and phone out of his pockets, close the boot, and walk around to the BMW's open driver's door.

I pocket his phone, fling his wallet onto the front passenger's seat, flick off the interior light, and push the driver's door shut until it sits ajar. I check that there are no cars or people around before jumping back into the Ford and pulling out into the deserted road. After driving down the road for only two-hundred metres or so, I turn right and park in a deserted dead end.

I send the text message, *Done.*

I stare pensively into the blackness for what seems like twenty minutes before my phone vibrates and lights up with the repeated text, *Done.* The wait was only five minutes.

This message means that a close associate of mine has taken the BMW away to be crushed and disposed of. No loose ends. I secure my phone and knuckleduster in the glove compartment. I get out of the car, open my plain black umbrella, and head to the club, taking several painkillers on the way. When I reach the main street, I manage, through the heavy rain and darkness, to glimpse the taillights of Toby's BMW before they disappear behind a building.

With the umbrella covering my face, I approach the two doormen, who would not look out of place down the road in the financial district. Whilst they are of relatively normal stature, the outlines of their suits suggest that they have large, well-defined muscles—I find them non-threatening as my experience suggests they are for aesthetic, rather than functional, purposes. This club obviously does not call for the type of doormen required in a regular nightclub

My blood boils with rage; I want to snap his hands off. She spins from his grip, and her short, frilly skirt lifts, revealing the full length of her long and slightly muscular legs. I am violently thrown back into the room when she faces my direction: she isn't who I thought she was. She throws her arms around her girlfriend, and the rejected man retreats into the crowd.

"You want to buy some coke, big man?" someone says behind me, poking my lower back. I slowly turn around and look down at someone who I instinctively presume is the infamous Richie. His accent and expensive, but very tacky, suit clearly inform me that he is not a member of the privately educated elite like most of the other people in this room. The fact that he is employed to operate here suggests the customers value having an authentic drug-buying experience; it probably causes them to reminisce about their school days. He has two large, amateur bodybuilders standing either side of him. They both wear equally tasteless suits, but theirs are a couple of sizes too small for them. They both present tough-guy personas, although I can tell from their stance that neither of them is ready to engage in combat; in fact, I suspect neither of them even know how to fight. If I was a normal person, I would probably be intimidated by their presence; however, unbeknownst to them, I could kill all three of them without even being touched.

I look deeply, but respectfully, into Richie's eyes.

"Not tonight, my friend. I am taking it easy," I say politely, with a relaxed posture.

"OK, not to worry," he says, frowning and nodding his head. As he turns to walk away, he catches a woman clicking her fingers in his direction. He responds by blowing her a kiss before turning back to face me. "I know what you want." He digs his right index finger into my chest. "You want a couple of eighteen-year-old virgins, don't you?" The two men either side of him nod their heads in agreement.

"Like I said, not tonight, my friend. I am waiting for my girlfriend to get back from the little girl's room," I lie.

"Well, if you're sure you're not interested." He shrugs his shoulders.

"I am sure. Thank you. Maybe another time." I look in the direction of the ladies' toilets. He doesn't leave. He reaches up and puts his hand on my shoulder. He starts to really irritate me.

"Well, I can get you really beautiful girls who will do anything you want." He raises one eyebrow.

"I said, I'm not interested. Anyway, thanks for the offer." He removes his hand from my shoulder.

"Or maybe I could get you a couple of little boys to play with." He looks at his mates, who both raise their eyebrows and shrug their shoulders simultaneously. "It doesn't matter if you do—we don't judge here." They all shake their heads; smirks spread across their faces.

"You can?" I ask the question not for personal pleasure, but out of professional interest.

"I knew he likes little boys," he says smugly to his friends. "Go on then, what would you like, my friend?" A maliciously large grin spreads across his face.

"What can you get me?" I continue to play along as I'm interested to find out if he is bluffing. If he is being serious then I'll need to make sure that I pay him a visit after tonight.

"I can get you any age and any colour you want." He nods his head and tilts it to one side. The woman clicking her fingers becomes desperate and frantically waves her arms to catch his attention, which is all currently directed on me. "Obviously, if the price is right."

I straighten my back, causing my overly developed chest to bulge out. He is taken aback by my full dimensions as I tower over him. I instantly regret my actions and force myself to remember why I am here. I have a job to do; I cannot let this interaction distract me any further. Instead of saying what my gut is telling me to say, I go with my head's recommendation and say, "Please leave me alone. My girlfriend will be back any second." I glance over at the ladies' toilets again. The little prick is momentarily speechless at my sudden change of attitude. He obviously thought that he was going to make a lot of money out of me tonight.

"Well, you know where I am if you change your mind, my friend," he says with a cruel smile. Much to the woman's relief, all three lads rush over to take her order. I'll have to actively avoid him from now on: I might not be able to control myself next time.

Toby's girlfriend gets off his lap and tries to pull him to the dance floor with her. After much fuss, he reluctantly stands up. Whilst continuing his conversation with his friends, he slowly picks up his wallet and his phone token off the table, storing them in his left-hand inner jacket pocket. She grabs his hand and seductively leads him onto the dance floor. None of his friends follow them.

Now's my chance. I put my full bottle of beer on an empty table next to the dance floor and pocket the napkin.

Now that I need to make my way across the pulsating dance floor, it seems significantly busier and more energetic than it was several moments ago. It appears to be one single organism that moves harmoniously to the beat of the music. If I manage to walk in a straight line, I will walk by the side of Toby on my way to the exit on the other side.

I commence my journey but quickly come to a halt as I struggle to wade through the dancers. Each dancer appears to be in an intoxicated trance; everyone is either oblivious or ignorant to the people tightly packed around them. A woman swings her arms around and hits me in the face. Undisturbed, she continues swinging her arms around and nearly hits me again. No one takes any notice of me so I continue to push through the crowd. I tire quickly so decide to change my tactic by trying to act like I am also in an intoxicated trance. Despite my lack of animation, it takes much less effort and time to reach Toby.

I slide up next to the lovely couple and continue my lame attempt at dancing whilst studying his breathing pattern. He is breathing hard to fuel his over-enthusiastic dancing and singing. He extends his arms into the air and tilts his head back with his eyes closed, preparing himself for the chorus. Moments before the chorus starts, I kick his girlfriend in the shins, causing her to go to ground. I take a deep breath. When she is a safe distance away, I thrust my inhaler between his parted lips and spray multiple puffs in quick succession with one hand, whilst exchanging his phone token for mine with the other. I am satisfied that more than a fatal dose has entered his lungs. I've disappeared into the crowd before his body hits the floor.

As soon as I open the exit door, a high-pitched scream flows with the river of music and laps against my eardrum. The two bouncers, each with a hand against an ear, turn and push me out their way as they search for the source of the scream. I put my head down and walk past the new arrivals approaching the dance hall.

The woman in the cashier's cage continues staring at her phone and texting with one hand when I hand her Toby's phone token. It has the number nineteen on it. She doesn't speak or look up as she exchanges it for Toby's phone. A rowdy group of men enter the club, causing her to prepare herself to pretend to revel in their distasteful flirtations. I take this as my cue to slip away. I grab my umbrella and begin opening it before I step back across the threshold. As I exit the club, I keep my head down and act like I am on the phone. I say the first thing that comes into my head: "OK, baby. I am just leaving the office—I'll be home soon."

My acting goes unnoticed: the doormen are distracted by what is being said to them into their earpieces. I take the opportunity to covertly photograph the doorman that recommended Richie to me earlier. I doubt he is involved in human trafficking, but I need to be sure. I cross the road and walk in the shadows. I send the doorman's photograph to my only true friend, Emma. This also gives her Toby's number, which she will use to interrogate his phone records for further information relating to Mikhail and his human trafficking network.

A sustained explosion of shouting and commotion originates from the club. Two men power walk past me. One of them says to the other, "What happened?"

Already out of breath, the other replies, "It looked like several people were overdosing in the seating area. We need to get out of here before the police arrive." They step up their pace into a gentle jog. Despite having seen their faces before on a TV advert, I can neither remember their names nor what they were trying to sell me.

I spot the Richie and his two mates walking on the other side of the road. They are walking fast, trying to get away from the crime scene. Richie pours something from a vial onto his index finger and sniffs it off. That batch of drugs must be superior in quality to what he sold to Hattie and the other unsuspecting partygoers.

I cross back over the road and follow them behind a young couple holding hands, who, I suspect from not viewing such shabby clothing tonight, haven't come from the club. We all walk for another minute or two before the three men turn right down an alleyway. The couple keep walking; they do not pay them or me any attention. I stop and check that no one is watching before cutting down the alleyway after them. There are streetlights but they are placed far enough apart to provide shadows for me to hide in. I pry a relatively loose brick off a wall as I wait for them to cross a reasonably well lit bridge over a loud, fast-running stream. I continue waiting until the distance between us obscures the extra visibility provided by the bridge's lights before continuing the pursuit.

I steadily and silently close the gap between us with my umbrella covering most of my body. I stop and place my umbrella open on the ground. As they step into the shadows between two streetlights, I sprint to them. I throw the brick at the back of Richie's head. A corner of it hits him square on the back of his head and he collapses to the floor. As the man on my left starts to turn, I elbow him in the side of the head with my right elbow. His head hits the wall and bounces off it. This time, I target his nose with the same elbow. His nose breaks, spraying blood in my face. My elbow smashes his head back into the wall. This time, his body sticks to the wall and remains attached as he slides down it.

The man on my right just stares at me, petrified. The look on his face reminds me of the look that the first man I ever killed had on his face after I had thrust my shank into this neck. His face still appears in my dreams to this day. I lower my body and punch him in the stomach with my left. The air is forced out of his lungs and he doubles over. I lift my body up and pull my right arm back. I am using nowhere near my full power when my fist connects with his jaw. My knuckles feel it slide out of place. His whole body is forced sideways and he trips over Richie.

All three men are lying unconscious in a heap on the floor. I raid their pockets and take all their wallets and phones, as well as a clear bag containing two dozen pills from Richie. I take a photograph of all their driving licences and send them to Emma. I take the half-full vial of white powder out of Richie's pocket and smash it on the pavement before heading back to my car.

I retrieve my umbrella and when I pass over the bridge, I throw their wallets and phones into the turbulent stream below. I hold Richie's bag of pills up to the streetlight. All the pills are engraved with a brown Russian bear on each side. Observing this trademark confuses me: why are Mikhail's drugs available for purchase in Albanian territory? I take a photograph of the bag and send it to Emma. I pour the bag's contents into the stream and pocket the bag.

When I reach the main street, several police cars and ambulances are now parked outside the club. I remember that I still have blood on my face, I wipe it off with my wet sleeve. I duck behind a car when a siren-less police car hurtles past me towards the club.

Muffled groans from Toby's bodyguard are audible as I approach the boot of the car. I grab my knuckleduster out of the glove compartment and secure it tightly in my right hand. I open the boot with my left hand, and, before Toby's bodyguard's eyes have time to focus on me, I strike him hard in the temple. His head hits the back of the back seats; he is knocked out cold, again.

I close the car door behind me and wipe my wet hair and forehead with the back of my hand. I grab my phone from the glove compartment and call Mikhail.

I struggle to hear the sound of the ringing tone over the heavy rain hitting the car. I deliberately terminate the call when I hear the third ring.

Chapter 2
The Drop-Off

I drive southwards out of the city through a recently declared brownfield site. This district used to be a thriving industrial estate until all the businesses were forced to sell their properties cheaply to Mikhail after being hit by the economic downturn and/or by his targeted strong-arming. I slow down as I approach what appear to be open, unguarded entrance gates to an old facility that once supported some kind of heavy industrial work. I flash my headlights three times so that Mikhail's security team, who are hidden in the darkness, know that it is me approaching. From now on, my head will remain securely fixed in the crosshairs of at least one battle-hardened sniper.

The heavy rain reduces my visibility, making it difficult to successfully navigate the potholes in the gravel carpark. I misjudge the position of the front tyre on the passenger's side and end up driving over one, which is much deeper than expected. The car's suspension groans from the impact and is quickly followed up by a loud thud from the boot. I park one space further along from Mikhail's Maybach. The light from my headlights reflects off the factory wall into his car. His chauffeur looks at me with his usual unwelcoming expression. I nod my head at him, and he slowly returns the gesture. He doesn't have his hands on the steering wheel because his gun will be pointed at me through the driver's door. I turn my lights off and the chauffeur disappears into the darkness.

As the sound of the engine dies, the noise of my captive trying to kick his way out of the boot can be heard. I get out of the car and head around to its rear. As soon as I open the boot, the fumes of shit offend my nostrils. He flaps around and repeatedly bangs his head against the back seats. I partially open the boot so that Mikhail's men cannot see what I plan to do next.

I grab him under his chin and force him to make eye contact with me.

"You're going to die very soon," I tell him bluntly. His eyes are already aware; he has accepted his fate. "I appreciate that you were a relatively small and insignificant cog in the human trafficking machine; nonetheless, you were cognisant of this fact, and you accepted the risk. If it wasn't me that brought you here, it would have been someone else."

The wind changes direction violently and sprays rain hard into his face.

"You now cannot escape imminent death. You shot Mikhail in the leg and put one of his men—one of his close friends, in fact—in intensive care. You should have pulled the trigger with the intention of killing. Mikhail isn't going to repay you with such leniency. His Murder Squad are well-practised torturers; they are infamous for inflicting extreme pain for long durations. You shot their boss, so they are going to set all kinds of new records with you. Whilst I want to help you escape this particular fate, I can assure you that there is nothing else I can do."

I reconvince myself that he is a sacrifice worth making. I've done a background check on him: he doesn't have any family or friends that will particularly miss him. This comforts me, slightly.

I tuck his gold crucifix necklace back into his t-shirt.

"There isn't anything he can do to help you now, I'm afraid. Anyway, here we go." I hoist him out of the car easily and position him on his feet. Childishly, I close the boot as loudly as I can to give Mikhail's security team and chauffeur a little scare. I reach down and cut the duct tape binding his legs together with a key. His legs shake violently. I hold him in an upright position by the back of his collar. "Come on then, let's get this over with." He tries to walk forward, but his legs have turned to jelly. I force the back of his neck towards the entrance of the factory to give him some momentum. He begins to cry; he doesn't try to escape. As I push him hard, face first, into the steel front door, I whisper "sorry" into his ear.

The door swings back and bangs against the wall, causing an echo to ring through the huge, abandoned factory. I don't know what type of factory it was; I would guess from the rust-covered machinery that it was some type of printing business. Mikhail and Yosef are about ten metres in front of us, stood between two rows of huge machines. Yosef is Mikhail's best friend from childhood and the leader of the Murder Squad. I have had several dealings with him, but I've never been in the presence of any other member of the Murder Squad.

They are both lit up by several portable work lights. The rest of the factory is dimly lit by the cast of weak moonlight shining through the surrounding high windows, which are mostly partially smashed. They do not register us as they continue their argument. I cannot hear what is being said over the sound of the rain hitting the corrugated asbestos cement panel roofing.

They continue their argument as we walk towards them. Mikhail keeps pointing his finger at Yosef. I try to lip read and understand what they are saying; however, unfortunately, they are talking fast and my command of the Russian language isn't good enough to follow. I can see in Yosef's eyes, and from his posture, that he wants to lash out, but he is restraining himself. When we reach a couple of metres away from them, I stop and kick my captive behind his knees harder than necessary. His knees crack loudly when they hit the rough, bare concrete floor. Mikhail abruptly stops shouting at Yosef and turns his head to face us. He awkwardly spins around on the spot and walks over to us. He is limping and I resist the temptation to look down at the responsible gunshot wound. His expressionless gaze turns deadly as he approaches; I feel him already sucking the life out of my captive.

"Step back," he orders me with a thick Russian accent. I instantly follow his command. In these situations, image and reputation are everything. "You've fucked up, my friend. My associate here," he points his finger at Yosef, "and our friends, including Valentin, the person you put into intensive care, are very experienced at causing intolerable pain—and making it last a very, very long time." He pauses for a couple of seconds. Then, out of nowhere, he kicks him hard in the face with the sole of his left foot. My captive's head snaps back, narrowly missing my groin.

"I'll meet you in hell, my friend," he says, smirking to himself as my captive falls forward, landing on his face. I take another step back as Yosef starts walking over to him. Without hesitation, Yosef bends down and grabs his right ankle. His scared eyes remain fixed on me as he lets himself be dragged away without putting up a fight.

Before Yosef reaches the fire exit door, it is flung open for him by someone on the other side. I am startled to see Toothless, a member of the Murder Squad, on the other side. He holds the door open, allowing Yosef and his captive to pass through without stopping. On the other side of the door is a white transit van. The van's side door slides open and the interior light shines brightly, revealing Viktor and Yuri inside of it. Yuri jumps out of the van and places a black bag over their captive's head. Yuri and Yosef get an armpit each and launch him in the van. Yuri jumps back into the van and helps Viktor to tie him up. Yosef opens the front passenger's door and the interior light exposes Boris in the driver's seat. Yosef gets in the van. Toothless forces a sinister, gummy smile at me as the door closes behind him.

I try to hide my shock at seeing, and understanding the subtle message being sent to me by allowing me to see, all the members of Mikhail's infamous Murder Squad in person—but I am fairly sure I am unsuccessful. These men are amongst the most vicious and savage men to have ever walked on this planet. They are a pack of insatiably bloodthirsty wolves—Mikhail is their alpha. As such, they obey all of Mikhail's commands; they would even kill themselves if he asked. They work out of the Chop Shop, the nickname given to their pawnshop, which is situated in one of the least desirable areas of the city. I know how to put names to their faces because I've had their Chop Shop under surveillance for quite a while now. Considering the amount of people that I've seen being dragged in, and the timing, amount, shape, and size of the black bin bags being carried out, I can confirm the rumour that there is a very well equipped torture chamber in the basement of their aptly nicknamed shop.

If brutal assignments or torture need to be carried out, then Mikhail uses his Murder Squad; I am used for the more specialised and discreet assignments, especially ones requiring either no attention or misdirection of attention.

The fire door slams shut. The resultant echo ricochets around the factory. Mikhail uses the distracting echoes to sneak up next to me and throw his arm around me. He tightens his hold and turns me back towards the front door.

"You've done a good job, as expected," he says calmly, like he's talking to an old friend. His English has improved greatly since he reluctantly accepted that it's the world's lingua franca. To the extent that he is now trying to also rid himself of his Russian accent. He desperately wants to move up the social ladder and mingle with this city's bourgeois; but his Russian accent is hindering his integration and, hence, advancement. Obviously, he resorts to a strong Russian accent when the occasion calls for it. "Are you feeling better, my friend?"

I do a good job of hiding my surprise after being ask that question.

"There is nothing wrong with me. I feel really good," I reply casually, ignoring the fact that I am most likely dying.

"OK. It's just you didn't look too good when I saw you last," he says insincerely, whilst continuing to grasp my shoulder. His demeanour and attempt at showing compassion grates on me; however, I cannot afford to provoke him by insulting his intelligence.

"Ah, a couple of hours before I saw you last, I'd been through a couple of rounds of boxing with one of my friends."

"Actually, you may have mentioned that; it probably just escaped my mind. Perhaps I forgot because I can't imagine you being challenged in a boxing match. Your friend must be a beast. I could use more people like him." I do not take the bait. The silence quickly becomes awkward. I want to ask him why Richie had his drugs on him in the club tonight, although I think better of it. Even though he tries to make me feel like I am alone with him, I sense a small army moving with us in the shadows.

"Anyway," he says, "as we agreed, this hit is worth two hundred thousand." I nod my head in agreement. "But I've kept the standard twenty percent for investment."

"How much of my money do I have invested with you now?" I ask, despite already knowing the answer.

"My investment portfolio has been growing very well lately, so I think it must be coming up to one million. The one hundred and sixty thousand is waiting for you in your car. I've got another job coming up, which I think will be difficult—even for you." He winks at me. "So, I'll be in contact with you soon, my friend." He pats my shoulder twice before he removes his arm and releases me.

"I look forward to it," I say, grinning. "As always, I am at your disposal." As I open the door, he swiftly manoeuvres himself closely behind me to hold it open. His quick movements put me on full alert and my right fist automatically clenches. The taillights of the Murder Squad's van disappear around the side of a building. "Goodnight." I jog out of the building into the wall of intense rainfall.

I dive into the car. Its suspension creaks unforgivingly under my weight. My mission has gone as well as expected and it has temporarily rid me of my headache. Although, as the adrenaline begins to rapidly wear off, I can feel it coming back with a vengeance. The loud noise of the bullet-like raindrops hitting the car's roof become more and more unbearable. I start feeling weak and exposed again.

My hands begin to shake uncontrollably; I have just seen the Murder Squad, which is equivalent to seeing the Grim Reaper. Mikhail must be on to me and have plans in motion to put me out of my misery earlier than expected.

A black holdall has appeared on the passenger's seat. I am one-hundred percent sure that there isn't a bomb in it—especially as Mikhail would have known that I would have parked as close as possible to his precious Maybach. Even so, I slowly pull back the zip. It looks like it contains the right amount; I am too tired to check properly. Plus, I haven't worked tonight because of the money—I've already got plenty of that. My body jerks violently, stopping itself from falling asleep. I desperately need to get into bed.

I have accepted that I'll never see the forty thousand: it is the unnegotiable cost of dealing with Mikhail. He always protects his investments, no matter the cost. One of the ways he ensures that he keeps hold of the money he has 'earned' is to never have it in his possession. He widely publicises this, moulding it into his reputation. This is because it significantly reduces his chances of being robbed by friends, family, foes, and, most importantly, the police. He also regularly puts himself out to ensure that the police on his payroll are paid generously and promptly. This is because many of his associates, especially those who thought they had escaped the reaches of the law, are now serving multiple life sentences and have had their cash and assets stripped from them— with much of this stripping done before they'd even stepped foot inside the police station.

Chapter 3
Stolen Goods

I was visiting a friend in the hospital several weeks ago when I overheard the owners of this Ford Focus arguing about money. Their daughter was receiving chemotherapy and they were concerned that she would not have a home to return to after completing her latest round of treatment. They had this concern because the father had just been sacked from work, both for taking too much time off and for being too distracted when he was at work. When I found out that their daughter was called Katie, I didn't stick around to listen to the remainder of their conversation as it was truly heartbreaking.

With this information, my friend 'Hero' hacked into the hospital records database and found me their address. I also had Hero access the parents' bank accounts. Their financial situation wasn't as bad as I had expected; they were good people who had simply fallen on hard times. To give them some breathing space, I anonymously paid off their mortgage and creditors. Additionally, I bribed and threatened the father's former manager to apologise and re-employ him.

I followed Katie's treatment via the information provided to me by Hero; unfortunately, her sad situation only grew worse. I couldn't sit back and do nothing so I called in a favour and got her enrolled in an experimental drug trial. She is now on the path to full recovery—hopefully. Katie 'won' a competition that I created just for her, so, at this moment in time, she and her parents are currently enjoying an all-expenses-paid holiday at Disney World.

I park the family's car back on their driveway, keeping it fair distance away from their house. I get out of the car, taking with me the bag of money. I walk up to their partially rotten front door, which anyone could easily kick open, and post the one hundred and sixty thousand through the letterbox. They are decent people and I trust that they will spend the money wisely; however, for Katie's sake, I'll be keeping an eye on them just to make sure. I remove all my possessions from the car before starting a fire on the passenger's seat using lighter fluid and a box of matches, both having been stored in the glove compartment. I leave the passenger's door ajar, walk casually across the road, and get into my car—another Ford.

I collapse into my armchair, fully dressed, as my clock changes to 04:00. I set my custom-made house alarm via a remote control that resides on the coffee table next to me. Again, I become concerned that tonight is the first time that I have been allowed in the presence of Mikhail's Murder Squad. The thought of Mikhail overwhelms the forefront of my mind; for weeks, he has been the only topic that my brain wants to entertain. This thought, the throbbing in my head, and the gentle hum of the extractor fan in the kitchen, all combine to make it very difficult to even relax, let alone fall asleep.

There are a myriad of rumours surrounding Mikhail's life prior to his ascent to power. I am sure he creates and peddles many of these rumours himself, particularly those that directly conflict with one another in order to obfuscate his true past whilst fuelling his notoriety. I have personally followed Yosef on several occasions and I believe I have been relatively successful in obtaining information on both Mikhail and Yosef's current operations. I have also found out a fair amount about their personal histories from overhearing the stories that he regales when he inducts his new recruits.

Supposedly, the father of Mikhail and his older brother, Vitali, had an illustrious career in the Soviet Army before his sudden disappearance. It is unknown whether he was killed in action, recruited into a secret division, blacklisted as a deserter, etc.; nevertheless, after his disappearance their mother, Ekaterine, was forced to work gruellingly long hours in a factory to put the poorest of excuses for meals on the table. Unfortunately, not long into her employment, a chemical spillage occurred at her work and she, along with many of her colleagues, never made it home. With no living relatives, the authorities marched both boys to one of Leningrad's many overcrowded and rat-infested orphanages that catered solely for boys.

Their mutual friend, Yosef, was marched along with them to this orphanage as his mother had died alongside their mother. Yosef was quickly embraced as the third brother as all three boys knew their chances of survival greatly increased if they all stuck together.

It doesn't take much imagination to appreciate the difficulties they all faced growing up in an orphanage in Leningrad. Like all the other orphanages in the city, theirs was used as a hunting ground for the local mafia outfits whose business model was underpinned by a constant supply of desperate, malleable, and expendable adolescent boys. In order to keep the orphanage operational, the overstretched Russian Orthodox nuns in charge of running it had no other option than to regularly sell boys or their services to the encircling mafia outfits. The authorities were grateful to the nuns for voluntarily keeping the majority of the boys out of the cold and out of a life of crime, so they gave them a wide berth. In fact, it was a wide enough berth that they were essentially allowed to operate with impunity.

The three boys were the first ones from their age group to be purchased by the mafia. As soon as they walked out of the orphanage, and without being given any training or guidance, they were forced to undertake the criminal activities with the largest prison sentences attached. These activities included stealing government assets, such as post-war military equipment and weapons out of the many poorly guarded—or completely forgotten about—warehouses, as well as paperwork from the homes of government officials.

It inevitably did not take long until one of their illicit involvements was noticed by the entity that was even more cruel, ruthless, and unforgiving than the mafia: the criminal justice system. Mikhail and Vitali were caught in the act of selling stolen grain—a very serious crime. They had stolen this grain from a train carriage the previous night whilst Yosef had kept the train stationary from the comfort of a signalling station. To make their predicament astronomically worse, supposedly a consignment of Nazi gold being transported by train, hidden under a pile of grain, had also been stolen the previous night.

Without due process or hesitation, the KGB operatives apprehended them and tortured them mercilessly; however, the level of pain that was inflicted on them couldn't possibly reach the level that they would eternally be subjected to if they let down their sibling. Neither brother faltered; speaking out was not an option. The KGB operatives did what they needed to do in order to satisfy themselves that the brothers hadn't stolen the gold; nevertheless, the state had zero tolerance for grain thieves. The brothers were dispatched to a distant and extremely remote Siberian forced-labour camp to work until they died.

Yosef was (and still is) indebted to his 'brothers' for never embroiling him. This feeling of indebtedness caused him to become possessed with a relentless dedication to rescue them. He elevated his position within the mafia's ranks by making his superiors obscenely wealthy, which he achieved by bribing, threatening, and killing anyone who got in his way. Once he reached the required rank, he leveraged the associated power, money, and loyal soldiers to break his brothers out of the camp.

Approximately two years after the jailbreak, Emma and her colleagues were taken by surprise when all three brothers just seemed to materialise out of nowhere as the most feared, deadly, and pre-eminent gangsters in this city. They rapidly acquired, inter alia, properties, people, businesses, and governmental departments like they had an infinite amount of money and muscle at their disposal. The city quickly had to adjust to dealing with a high daily number of bodies of murdered people from all walks of life being found all over the city at all times of the day. Both Emma and I have risked exposure several times, and I have spent what feels to me like an infinite amount of money, but—frustratingly—we still haven't managed to gather any trustworthy information on their activities or whereabouts during this two-year chronological gap.

When I undertake investigations, I always start by following the money. I did manage to find a bullion dealer who claimed to have physical proof that vast quantities of Nazi gold began to circulate on the black market shortly before their materialisation; however, he disappeared before I could collect this proof from him.

Chapter 4
The Diagnosis

My symptoms are always at their worst when I first wake up and this morning was no exception. I have arrived slightly early for my doctor's appointment at 14:00. I am in the waiting room of one of the world's most expensive private medical centres. The receptionist informed me moments ago that Dr Black is on schedule. I have run several errands already today, giving myself enough of a distraction to provide temporary respite from these symptoms. My heavy head makes it difficult for me to balance myself. I strategically collapse in the seat closest to the fire exit. I am sensitive to the bright fluorescent lights but I can make my headache slightly less unbearable by squinting. With half-opened eyes, I begin the process of studying my surroundings; however, I cannot concentrate well enough to take in all the details, let alone play out certain emergency scenarios in my head.

This medical centre mainly caters for royals, business elites, celebrities, and other wealthy individuals who all come here to receive the best health care, five-star accommodation, and luxury food, as well as to hide from the public, their employees, and the media. After some heavy-handed persuasion, the Harkov crime family also has unrestricted access to this centre. Mikhail ensures that he and his family, associates, and footmen are all taken care of at this centre, away from the prying eyes of the law and his enemies. I have used this centre on several occasions myself mainly because I do not have any official medical records and I am extremely exposed in public places. Plus, I do not want to put vulnerable people at unnecessary risk.

I lean forward and pick up one of the newspapers off the coffee table. Most of the front page is covered by a photograph of Sheikh Latif joyfully smashing a bottle of champagne against the hull of his next-generation super-yacht. At the back of the crowd of people standing behind him is Lord Beaumont-Knight, who looks like he is trying to push his way into a more prominent position in the photographer's shot. Through blurry vision, I scan-read the associated article.

The article portrays Sheikh Latif as a humble, sincere, and virtuous philanthropist who works tirelessly to grow the prosperity of his home country whilst, at the same time, suggesting that he sanctions controversial—bordering on criminal—activities and does not let small matters, such as human rights, get in the way of economic progression. It also claims the only reason he has just purchased the yacht company, 'Tranquillity', was simply due to the fact that he liked working with their world-leading designers and engineers during the construction of his super-yacht.

I flick through the rest of the newspaper, scanning only the headlines to see if there is a story that covers the death of Toby: there isn't. The Albanians will have either moved or disposed of the body for me; they will not risk bad publicity and the law getting close to their operations. I am sure Mikhail has already taken care of Toby's business affairs.

The receptionist sighs loudly when the phone starts to ring. She reluctantly drags herself away from her computer monitor and mutters several curse words under her breath before she answers it. A door clicks open in the distance. I make out the fuzzy outline of Dr Black—a small, grey-haired, and grey-bearded man—poking his head out into the corridor. He shouts louder than necessary, "Mr Smith."

Before I even get the chance to nod my head in acknowledgment, he has retreated back into his office. My right knee pops awkwardly as I stand. I return the newspaper to the coffee table, straighten my back, and shrug my shoulders tightly before making my way to his office. Through squinting eyes, the clock behind the receptionist shows me that it is 13:55. As I pass close by her, her shrill voice causes my brain to push much harder against my skull. I find it difficult to hide my frustration.

I reach the threshold to his office just as he flops down on his big leather chair. A grand oak desk, which would be better suited to a study or library in a country mansion, separates us. All the walls are featureless and painted in brilliant white, except for the wall behind him, which is wholly covered by bookshelves fully laden with leather-bound books. His hands are noticeably shaking. He tries to type quickly on his keyboard, but he keeps mistyping, so must continually interrupt his flow by hitting the backspace.

me to the library, where speaking is strictly forbidden, the games room, and the restaurant. My hands start shaking nervously at the thought of seeing Nataliya.

I open the door at the top of the staircase and cross the threshold. I stand still and scan the room whilst taking deep breaths. A large stage snakes its way down the centre of the room with dancing poles positioned at regular intervals. The booths are positioned irregularly around the stage and have high backs so that the members have difficulty seeing one another. Visibility is reduced further by the dim lighting and thick cigar smoke that lingers in the air like smog. It is busier than I expected for this time of day.

Each occupied booth tends to have at least one dancer providing entertainment. I continue to scan the room until I notice Nataliya in the far corner. She is sitting on a very old gentlemen's lap. Despite having conversed with this gentleman on multiple occasions, I cannot recall his name. I am too angry to think. They both laugh; hers is fake. She flicks her hair back and drowns his nostrils in her feminine scent. It breaks my heart seeing her doing this. I take one step towards her when the DJ stops the music and announces, "Now gentleman, let me present to you, three of the most beautiful ladies in the world. Could Shyla, Isabella, and the especially beautiful Nataliya, please make your way to the stage?" Simultaneously, they all pop up out of the sea of booths. Swinging their hips seductively, they all walk confidently in their heels, which seem excessively high, to the stage. I step back against the wall, out of sight from Nataliya. My eyes are solely on Nataliya; her graceful movements never fail to impress me. She slides effortlessly up, down, and around the pole to the rhythm of the music. Her moisturiser, or oil, or whatever covers her skin, sparkles under the spotlights, adding a diamond-like quality to her skin. I start to shake nervously again; a bead sweat runs down my face. My heart beats uncontrollably—but I manage to get a handle on it before it translates into an anxiety attack.

A member's cash-loaded hand reaches out from the darkness of his booth. She swings her derrière in his direction so that he can attach his cash to her thong. She blows him a kiss and swiftly moves over to the next outreached, cash-loaded hand. After the next hand has secured its cash, it gently strokes her left buttock. I am thrown back against the wall in shock; my arms tense as I visualise them in my head ripping the member's arm away from his body. I am even more shocked when I realise that the only bouncer in the room is not one of my men. He looks significantly more threatening than Graham, who usually works this shift, and his face does not suit the image of this club. He is sat on a stool guarding the curtains that covers the corridor to all the private dance rooms as well as the changing room provided for the dancers. He even notices the member touch her but chooses to ignore the indiscretion.

I am slightly relieved as the bartender, Kyle, who is one of my men, is still here. Although, I am angry with him for not informing me about the employment of this bouncer. I am also upset with Franco because a non-negotiable condition of me becoming a silent partner was that a strict 'no touching' policy had to be enforced—even if the dancer wanted to be touched. The bouncer's smug face causes my rage to explode into an urge to kill every man in this room. I scan the room and quickly work out how I would most efficiently satisfy this urge.

When the music ends, the three dancers head for the changing room. They all closely guard their cash, despite not having to worry about a member trying to take it from them at this venue. I rush after Nataliya but am impeded by the room's layout. Before I reach her, she discreetly hands the bouncer several notes as she steps through the curtains. I storm up to him, resisting the urge to snap his neck. He doesn't initially notice me as he is too preoccupied with securing her money in his inside jacket pocket. He looks up at me and throws his arm out to stop me going through the curtains. His arm is huge; nearly as big as my own.

"Why did Nataliya give you money?" I growl, glaring at him.

"This is a private area, you are not allowed through without a dancer's permission," he says with a very strong Eastern European accent. This startles me. I can't place the exact origin of his accent, but I know that it isn't Russian—much to my relief. Although, it could be Albanian. I will kill Franco if he has put Nataliya's life in danger; he knows that he can only use my men for security. For the time being, I ignore his place of origin, and the fact that he hasn't answered my previous question, and ask him, "Graham usually works this shift. Where is he?"

"Ah, Graham no longer works here; I work here now." He looks over my shoulder.

"Excuse me, Steve," says a woman with a husky voice. As I turn, Shyla tries to squeeze past me.

"My apologies, Shyla." I take a wider than necessary step to the right to demonstrate how sorry I am.

"Not a problem, Steve. Are you waiting for Nataliya?" She unintentionally grazes her arm against mine.

"Yes, I was too slow to catch her after her routine. Can you please tell her that I need to talk to her?"

"Of course. She might have gone on her break though." She also hands the bouncer several notes, "there you go, Stefan."

"Thank you; I would greatly appreciate that." I say as she disappears through the curtains.

The bouncer struggles to cram the money into his already full inside jacket pocket before turning his attention back to me.

"You need to give me twenty if you want to talk to Nataliya." He holds out his hand.

The situation instantly becomes tense. There is movement in my peripheral vision, so I turn and watch two men enter the room. One of them is Henry Morley, who works at Gladstone Wealth Management, which is a private bank a couple of doors down from here. Our paths have crossed several times, and he owes me several large favours. This is not a good time to talk to anyone, especially him as he is a 'talker'. I face Stefan again, thrusting a twenty into his hand.

"Nataliya, Steve is here to see you," he shouts, but is not loud enough for her to hear from the changing room. He remains seated, rolling the twenty between his fingers. As expected, there is no response. He looks at me with a face that says, 'I've done all that I can'. I sigh and wave my hand forward in a gesture that says, 'go and find her'. He sighs loudly. "OK, I'll get her. You wait here though!" he growls, pushing his index finger against my solid chest.

I wait patiently for about thirty seconds before sounds of raised voices and commotion can be heard from behind the curtains. Nataliya flies through the curtains, struggling to keep her balance in her high heels. Her long hair slaps my face after I catch her in my arms. When I breathe in, I accidentally smell her hair. I am horrified by my actions; I have violated her trust. She directs her Russian curses at Stefan; he looks at her with a deathly scowl. He has physically hurt her and is now trying to frighten her. I will have to deal with him later; I don't want to scare her—or worse, scare her away from me.

"Steve, please can you not wait? I'm about to go on my break," she says in a tone that conveys her annoyance with me. Her command of the English language has improved greatly since I last saw her.

"Unfortunately, I can't, Nataliya. I need to talk to you and to give you this." I hold up the holdall, but she ignores it.

"OK." She lightly takes hold of my free hand and leads me through the curtains. I avoid looking at her exposed buttocks when I glance down to make sure that I do not clip her high heels with my feet as we walk in silence.

She pulls back the curtain of a private dance room and ushers me through first. I fall back on the soft, relaxing sofa with the holdall placed on my lap. She, however, remains standing in front of me with one hand placed on her hip. She bites her lips nervously, staring down at me. She must be the most intimidating person that I've ever met.

"Would you like a quick dance?" she asks, teasingly.

"No, no, don't be silly. You know that I am not here for that." I answer, apologetically. My facial expression and body language notify her that I found her question insulting. I take her hand and she doesn't resist as I gently pull her down next to me. "I'm afraid I won't be able to see you ever again." Her eyes do not reveal any change in her emotional state. "My doctor has diagnosed me with a terminal brain tumour; he thinks that I only have several weeks, possibly a couple of months, left to live."

She doesn't say anything; instead, she puts her arm around me, and tries to pull me close to her. My emotions start to get the better of me. I quickly pull myself away from her. "As you know, I care for you very dearly and I want you to have the happiest life possible," I stop speaking abruptly to prevent myself from crying. I place the holdall on her lap.

"Oh, sweetheart, you didn't need to get me anything." She cautiously unzips the holdall. She flicks her hair back, unintentionally revealing her failed attempt at disguising the bruising around her right cheek with a heavy layer of makeup. I start tapping the floor with my right foot to calm myself down. I inhale twice through the nose and exhale through my mouth. Her eyes spring open and her jaw drops when she lays eyes on its contents. She remains motionless for several seconds before leaping to her feet in anger. The holdall falls onto the floor and two bundles of cash spill out.

"This a joke?" She shouts, angrily.

I am left flabbergasted by her reaction.

"No. Of course not." I stare into her eyes, trying to maintain a sense of innocence and naivety to keep her relaxed. She begins pacing around the booth. She stops suddenly and engages me in eye contact again. Moments later, her upper body relaxes and relief washes over her. Her body brushes down the side of mine as she sits down next to me. I take hold of her hand again, and, despite being a bit too close for comfort, I look deep into her big blue eyes. "In this holdall," I scoop the two bundles of cash back into it, pick it up off the floor, and place it back on her lap, "is approximately three hundred thousand." Her eyes open wide and her jaw drops.

"But why give this money to me?" She is genuinely puzzled. She pulls the zipper back towards her, revealing all the bundles of cash. I cannot stop looking at the bruising on her face; I truly hope there is an innocent reason for it.

"I've told you many times before that I have several people searching for Lilyana; you just never believed me." I still feel hurt by her distrust, despite finding it understandable—I would certainly be more distrusting if our roles were reversed. Lilyana was Nataliya's best friend growing up, but she was trafficked here from their home country several years ago and Nataliya has been trying to track her down ever since.

"Oh, Steve, I didn't think you were being serious. All my life, men have promised me everything, promised me that they would take care of me. But they always disappear after they've been with me." She looks down, ashamed. "I knew you were different; I just couldn't risk getting hurt again."

"It's OK." I squeeze her hand gently. "I am sorry for this personal intrusion. I have to ask: Why is there bruising on your face?" My fists automatically clench; I brace myself for her response. She grimaces in pain when she gently presses her hand against the bruising.

"Ah." She looks at the curtain and converses sotto voce. "The new bouncers have been threatening and roughing us up, demanding we hand over a share of our earnings to them. Don't worry, it is nothing that the girls and I have not experienced before." She chews on her bottom lip and shrugs her shoulders.

"When did this start?" I momentarily disappear into a trance, thinking about the horribly gruesome ways that I am going to torture anyone that has laid their hand on her.

"Only a few days ago. Stefan, who is the bouncer on tonight, is particularly rough. He pushed my head against a cubicle door in the ladies' bathroom because I refused to give him any of my money." I am furious; I will kill him. "I've also got a bruise on my thigh from a separate occasion. He grabbed hold of me as I tried to sneak through the curtains when he was distracted and I hit it against his stool." I force myself to look at her thigh; she has also failed to completely disguise that bruise with makeup.

"I need you to leave with me right now." I squeeze her hand tightly. She looks at me nervously from the corner of her eye.

"Steve, I cannot leave. I've got a job to do. Also, Stefan will not allow it." Tears well up in her eyes.

"Do not worry about Stefan, or your job. Inside the holdall, in the side pocket, is your new identity and a piece of paper. The piece of paper contains all the information that you need to find and access the storage areas and safety deposit boxes, which contain at least ten million in total, all in cash." I try to sound as though I am not trying to impress her. She goes white and looks like she is on the verge of fainting. I squeeze her hand tightly again to bring her attention back to me. "I wish that I could hand over more of my money to you, but there is not enough time."

"I don't know what to say, Steve. This is crazy. I cannot leave with you because I think I am now getting really close to finding Lilyana." Her eyes are transfixed on the holdall.

"As I've said before, I have people searching very hard for her as we speak; I promise you. They tell me that they are also very close to finding her." I find it difficult lying to her. I doubt she would believe me; however, if she did, then she would probably kill me if I told her that not only had I already found Lilyana and her new-born, Talia, but that I am also actively helping them recover from their drug addictions whilst trying to build up their general health. I am hoping that in the not-too-distant future they will both be fit enough to meet her.

"DO NOT LIE," she erupts. On autopilot, I slap my hand against her mouth to stop her from shouting, but I exert too much force. Her eyes instantly change to the same eyes that everyone has when they realise that they are about to be killed. I quickly release my hand and jump up off the sofa away from her.

"I'm so sorry." I squeeze my hands together tightly behind my back. She continues to tightly hold the holdall whilst shaking violently. She looks at me forgivingly. A tear rolls down her face.

"Please do not play with my emotions. Are you sure that you can find Lilyana?" She leans forward.

"I promise you," I say with absolute certainty. Before I can continue talking, Stefan throws the curtain to one side and storms into the room. He thrusts himself forward and tries to grab me; I knock his hands away.

"You must leave now; you've upset the girl," he says, aggressively. He attempts to grab me again, but I step back and remain out of reach. He positions himself between Nataliya and me whilst trying to usher me towards the exit.

"What the fuck are you doing?" I spit in his face.

He thrusts himself forward again; this time, I also step forward. I let him grab me so that I can, in turn, grab his throat with one hand. His eyes nearly pop out of his head in shock as soon as I start crushing his throat. He releases his grip and frantically claws at my forearm to free himself from my vice-like grip. He throws his head and body from side to side to try and rip himself away from me. He steps back as Nataliya tries to stand. I try to move him out of her way but am unsuccessful and he knocks her back down onto the sofa. As she falls, she loses her grip of the holdall, causing many bundles of cash to spill onto the floor. I manage to keep his head up so that he doesn't see the cash.

"I am so sorry," I say apologetically to her as she scoops the last bundle of cash back into the holdall. Before Stefan passes out, another unknown bouncer gets me into a headlock from the side. I voluntarily release Stefan's throat and allow myself to be taken. I cannot kill someone in Nataliya's presence. Instead of being dragged out via the fire exit—as I had hoped—I am dragged back through the curtains into the main room of the club. I am lucky that no member, especially Henry, notices me; their tailored entertainment absorbs all their attention.

I am taken down the staircase when Nataliya materialises through the curtains, clutching the holdall, which she has zipped back up. I look across at the bar area and Kyle is nowhere to be seen; Emma will have to speak to him and find out what has been going on here. I comply with the bouncer's guidance as he drives me down the staircase. She reaches the top of the staircase the instant I am dragged off the bottom step. I could break free from his amateur grip and kill him in seconds; however, I don't want the police knowing about Nataliya. As I am dragged past Aliysa, I say, "Goodbye Aliysa. Have a good day!"

Her hand covers her mouth in shock. The bouncer throws me back across the threshold of the club; I narrowly avoid knocking one of the valets down the staircase.

"I don't want to see your fucking face ever again," he manages to bellow, even though he is out of breath. He has the same accent as Stefan. As he closes the big wooden door, Nataliya shouts after me. The door slams shut and is immediately locked.

The two valets look at me, unfazed. I give my ticket to the one who took my car earlier. He slowly picks up his phone and calls another valet to retrieve it from carpark. I'll try and catch up with Nataliya later after she has had time to calm down and think about my offer—or Emma may have to do it for me. The sun's rays heat my face and gently calm me down. The second I allow myself to enjoy this heat, a cold breeze blows it away.

I stand at the bottom of the staircase for several minutes, waiting for my car to arrive. The valet parks my car next to me; I hand him the first couple of notes that I pull out of my pocket. His facial expression suggests that I have given him too much. Today, my car is a Range Rover Sport SVR 'Ultimate', which blends in well with my current environment and complements the character that I am trying to portray at this club. I drive to the end of the club's building—a distance of just over ten metres—when movement in my peripheral vision catches my attention.

To my utter disbelief, Nataliya and Stefan briefly play tug of war with her holdall before he slaps her to the ground with the back of his hand. I am electrified with rage and feel as though I could rip my steering wheel off. I drive forward a bit further before reversing down the alleyway and stopping within a couple of metres of Stefan, who now has his back to me. I quickly scan the walls either side of the alleyway to confirm that there are still no cameras around here.

I know that he will not simply let me walk away with her and the holdall. I flip open my boot before jumping out of my car. As he turns to face me, a cruel smile spreads across his face. He is still holding onto one of the holdall's straps. When Nataliya, who is still lying on the floor, yanks on the other strap. This pulls his arm back, forcing him to face her.

He doesn't hear me over her squeaks as I swiftly position myself right behind him. I kick him hard behind the knees. His legs buckle and I grab hold of his head tightly.

"Quick, Nataliya, get in the car."

She ignores me and keeps pulling on the strap. I start to crush his head, forcing him to release the strap and concentrate on prising himself free. She takes custody of the holdall. Whilst she gets to her feet, he tries to kick her, but I pull him back just in time. She runs to my car with the holdall dragging behind her and jumps in the back. With my right foot placed in front of my left, I manoeuvre my right hand over his mouth and my left hand over the back of his head.

A savage monster surges up from deep inside of me, forcing every muscle in my upper body to scream in white-hot pain under the self-generated tension. I feel his neck muscles and tendons move over one another as I rotate his head clockwise. He gargles loudly in pain during the final tectonic shift in head movement. When I have finished with him, his head is barely attached to his neck. The monster inside of me promptly evaporates and my muscles relax to their normal state—like nothing had ever happened.

I grab him under his arms and launch him into the boot of my car. I glare at him and angrily think 'look what you made me do' before closing the boot and forgetting about him. Before exiting the blind alley, I take one look at Nataliya in my rear-view mirror. Despite my heavily tinted back windows, she holds her head down—her survival instincts have kicked in. The valets on my right are too distracted by two dancers stepping out of their taxi to notice me turn left onto the main road.

Nataliya starts crying, which makes me become all emotional. I struggle to hold back my tears. There is no time to play the gentleman; I must quickly get her to safety. I am conscious of the time, but I need to head away from the golf course. I am never late; so, if I am late on this occasion, then Mikhail will be even more suspicious of me, and my intentions. I pull into an old, run-down self-storage unit and drive up to unit twenty-four. I get out the car and undo the combination lock. I open the door, revealing a whole host of equipment and tools that Emma and I use for reconnaissance work. In the centre of this unit is Emma's Vauxhall Corsa.

Nataliya wipes the tears off her face and lets herself out of the car. Her legs are shaking and she is visibly confused. I grab the satellite navigation system off the Corsa's dashboard and begin entering the address of the new Hilton Garden Inn at the airport.

"Right, this is your new car," I say, struggling to type the address into the satnav with my large fingers. "The keys are on the passenger's seat. You need to follow the satnav to the new Hilton hotel at the airport." I finish typing the hotel address and hand it over to her whilst it calculates the route. "Check into a room using your new identification and wait there. My friend Emma will get you as soon as she can; she will keep you safe until she finds Lilyana." I hated lying to her before about Lilyana, as well as not telling her about Talia; however, keeping this information away from her is now paramount to maintaining her safety. "Afterwards, she'll help you retrieve the rest of my money that I want you to have. You can both use it disappear and start a whole new life together, far away from here."

"Where are you going? Please do not leave me!" She starts to panic. I hug her delicately.

"I trust Emma with my life. You should with yours too—especially as she will be risking her life to protect you. Please do whatever she tells you to do. She'll keep you far away from me, which will be the safest place for you. Also, knowing that you are safe will allow me to do what I now need to do." I manage to pull myself away from her; it is the hardest struggle I've ever faced. As I walk away, I let her grab my right arm momentarily before I rip it from her grip—I just wanted to feel her touch one last time.

I jump back in my car and lock the doors. She bangs and claws on the driver's window; ignoring her is unbearably painful. I accelerate hard and do not look back. Tears pour down my face as I force myself to focus on the task ahead.

Chapter 6
Operation Endgame

"Hi James, sorry about the delay. I've been questioning a suspect. Is everything OK?" Emma says, on my fourth attempt at getting through to her.

"Yes, everything is OK, I suppose. Thank you." I enter the carpark at the golf course.

"I've run the names you sent me last night through the system. They're only small-time drug dealers and troublemakers. I've tried, but I cannot find any connections to any big-league players. Do you want me to add them to the 'to-be-monitored' list?"

"Yes, please. I believe that they're part of Mikhail's drug, and, possibly, human trafficking operations. It is worth finding a way to bring them in; I don't think it'll be too difficult to get them to talk. They are definitely informant material."

"Jesus, it seems that for every scumbag we catch, two more take their place. I know a couple of officers that desperately need to get back in the captain's good books after they recently only avoided suspension by the skin of their teeth. I'll give them a heads up. Anyway, how was your doctor's appointment?" She asks, genuinely concerned. In fact, it was her concern—and nagging—that persuaded me to make the appointment in the first place.

"Erm, yes, well. It didn't quite go as well as I had hoped for," I splutter.

"Oh, no." She starts panicking because she knows I am greatly downplaying the situation.

"Let's just say that I've been given a fairly short deadline to finish what needs to be done. I'm sorry, but I'm already on my way to commence 'Operation Endgame'—or at least a version of it." I scan the carpark for Mikhail's car.

"Nooo!" she screams.

"Don't worry, we're well-prepared for this situation—I am confident you'll easily carry on our good work in my absence. The only difference my diagnosis has made is that I'm guaranteed to die soon; you now don't need to worry every time I do a job."

"Please don't do this, not now!" she cries.

"I have no choice. I need to do it now whilst I'm still physically able. Nataliya should currently be driving your Vauxhall Corsa to the new Hilton hotel at the airport. I've instructed her to check-in and wait for you there." I am forced to slam on my brakes as a golfer, who is oblivious to me, probably because he has consumed several alcoholic beverages, reverses out of a parking space on my right-hand side. He speeds off and nearly hits two golfers as they try crossing the road. The vacant parking space reveals Mikhail's car parked on the row behind it. I continue forwards and see that there is an available space next to his car.

"But—" she tries to start talking, but I cut her off.

"Please listen—there isn't much time. You need to hurry; Nataliya will be waiting for you and I'm not confident she'll wait around for you. Your priority is to either get her out of this country or to one of our safe houses as soon as possible. She has her new identification and about three hundred thousand in cash. You'll have to retrieve and send the share of my money that I've set aside for her later. She still doesn't know that we've rescued Lilyana and Talia. Please do not mention that you've got them until you have first gotten her to safety.

"Actually, I've not visited them for a couple of days, so you'll need to ensure that Lilyana is sticking to her rehab programme and that both of their recoveries are on track. Once they're strong enough, I want it to be you who takes them to Nataliya. Please don't tell Nataliya anything about me. I don't want her knowing anything that could jeopardise her safety."

"Yes, I know." She grows impatient as I explain my wishes to her for the umpteenth time. "Where are you now?"

"I'm literally about to park next to Mikhail's car. Thank you for everything—and good luck!" I promptly end the call. I don't have time for an emotional farewell; I am nearly running late due to my friend, Guy, who works at the crematorium, having to finish incinerating someone else first before he could incinerate Stefan. I park next to Mikhail's car and look across at his chauffeur.

He mouths the words, "He's here," into the microphone attached to his lapel.

I smile at him; he doesn't reciprocate. I get out of my car and, with my right knuckle, tap on the Maybach's front passenger's window. He presses the electronic window switch down on the driver's door. The window descends slowly. His other hand remains steadfast under a newspaper on the passenger's seat. When the window is halfway down, I ask politely, "Where is he?"

"Teeing off on the third hole." He flicks the electronic window switch up.

I walk around the outside of the clubhouse and am taken aback by the magnificent golf course; however, its lushness cannot be fully appreciated due to the sheer number of golfers that are playing on it. There are even several groups of golfers queuing in an orderly fashion to tee off on the first hole. The outside seating area is overflowing with rowdy golfers. There are no women around except for those squeezing through the gaps between in the tables, chairs, and bodies to deliver the food and drink.

Two Russian brutes, who have no chance of blending in, sit amidst all the golfers in the seating area. Not only are they considerably bigger and about twenty years younger than everyone else, they are also the only ones not enjoying themselves. I smile and nod at them. They ignore me. I study the golf course, and the golfers, to try and work out where the teeing ground is for the third hole. After a couple of seconds, it becomes obvious when I notice the entourage of men in black suits stood to the side of one group of golfers. I am only stood still for a moment, but it is long enough for people to start eyeing me with suspicion.

I head to the shadow of the tree line, which forms the edge of the golf course. The grass naturally springs up after each step as I effortlessly glide on it towards Mikhail. A golfer tees off on the first hole, but slices their golf ball, causing it to hurtle towards me. Panic sets in when I realise how dangerous it is being on a golf course, especially one full of drunk golfers. I quicken my pace. The golf ball bounces on the ground where I was when it was launched off the teeing ground before whizzing into the woods. There is a loud thud when it collides with a tree trunk. I keep an eye on the thicket behind the tree line, trying to spot Mikhail's sniper, who I suspect is hidden within.

When I am just over one hundred metres from the teeing ground for the third hole, it becomes apparent that both Mikhail's security detail and the accompanying group of business associates are larger the usual. Mikhail is on the far side of them all, lining up his shot. As I get a bit closer, I notice that four of these men are of Middle Eastern descent. Hidden within this group is a man dressed in a brilliant white thawb. It is Sheikh Latif from the front cover of the magazine I saw in the waiting room earlier. It does not surprise me that he is here with Mikhail and his group of business associates.

Whilst being surrounded by his own security detail probably makes him feel safe, in reality, they just provide a false sense of security. Mikhail's sniper would take all of them out before they could even draw their weapons. They are all well groomed and very smartly dressed; in fact, if they were not so solidly built, they could all pass for fashion models. One in particular stands out: he has a similar build to myself, or at least when I was in my prime. There is an air of authority—with a hint of savagery—about him.

Mikhail's group of business associates make the wealth of footballers, pop stars, and movie stars look unremarkable. Not only are they extremely rich, they are also extremely powerful and influential. They have their fat, murderous fingers in anything that makes money, from arms and ammunition to missile defence systems; from oil and timber to solar panels; from trafficking women and children to conserving rare species. I have even heard Mikhail seeking their advice on how best to transport spent radioactive material.

When I reach the group, I automatically raise my arms up to allow Yosef to commence his pat down. The rest of Mikhail's security detail do not pay me much attention as they know that I am not a threat; each member of Sheikh Latif's security detail shifts their stances slightly, making it even quicker to access their concealed weapons. Mikhail strikes the golf ball very powerfully, propelling it down the fairway. It hits the ground and bounces several times before entering into a roll. It comes to a halt in the centre of the fairway and, despite it being the closest one to the putting green, it is still quite far away. The people behind him over-enthusiastically clap their hands, trying to disguise their relief that he is in the lead. He turns to face the group behind him and says something to them. They all laugh, except Sheikh Latif and his men, who study me with intense suspicion.

Mikhail makes his way over to me; everyone else jumps in their golf carts, heading towards their golf balls. Sheikh Latif drives off in his golf cart; his security detail, who fill two of their own golf carts, are hot on his tail. Mikhail's security detail remains with us. He holds out his right hand to me, whilst handing over his golf club with his left to—who I believe is—his newest recruit. He looks the youngest; he is probably in his late twenties. The scars on his face suggest he is already battle-hardened. I get on one knee and kiss the huge gold ring on Mikhail's outstretched hand.

"Have you come to check on Toby's bodyguard? I've heard that he is still going strong." I ignore him.

"Thank you for seeing me," I say. He nods his head disinterestedly. "I know this is highly irregular, but I've got a little proposition for you—and it cannot wait." I wobble noticeably as I stand.

"It is not a problem, my dear friend. What can I do for you?" he says, looking in the direction of Sheikh Latif.

"Unfortunately, my doctor has given me some not very good news this afternoon. To cut a long and uninteresting story short, I only have a short time left to live." Mikhail doesn't even try to look concerned. My headache makes a painful return as I remind myself of my illness. "I don't want to curl up in a ball and wait to die. I certainly am not going to kill myself; I'm not a coward. That's why I want to play a little game." I scan the tree line and convince myself that a glint of sunlight has just reflected off his sniper's scope.

"Sorry to hear that. What do you need me for?" He barely pays me any attention, stepping one step closer to his golf cart.

"I want you to put a hit on someone for me. I want you to put the word out that the person who kills my target will receive all my money that I have invested with you." He nods his head several times, contemplating my proposal.

"That's a lot of money. Are you sure that you don't want more time to think about this?" I slowly move my head from side to side. "I would like to remind you that as soon as you shake my hand, there is *nothing* that I can do to call off the hit?"

"Yes, I fully understand."

"OK. As you wish. Go on then, tell me: who the hit is for?" His face turns stern as a group of rowdy golfers approaches us.

"Me," I state.

"God damn." He gives me his full attention—although, he doesn't look as surprised as I expected him to be. "You really are as cold as ice. Jesus." He nods his head to himself. "This is going to be fun," he laughs, confidently. I thrust my right hand out for him to shake that fast that it shocks all members of his security detail. They all instinctively react by diving into their suit jackets, grabbing hold of their weapons; Mikhail—unfazed—smashes his palm into mine and takes a firm hold.

Whilst I have a strong desire to painfully crush his hand, I keep my grip relaxed to avoid insulting him. I also have a strong desire to pull his body over to mine and rip his trachea out with my teeth. "If I were you, I would book myself into a penthouse suite in Vegas and surround myself with hookers, cocaine, and Cristal—go out having fun on my own terms."

"You know that's not me. I only have one wish: they must kill me quickly" My mind races towards my recurring dream of Nataliya and I holding hands whilst paddling along a Caribbean beach at sunset.

"OK, I'll tell you what I'll do for you." He goes quiet, lost in his own thoughts.

"What will you do?" I politely prompt him, bringing him back to me without being rude.

"In fact, you have caught me in a good mood. I'll do you two favours: I'll waver your commissioning fee and I'll round up the reward to the full one million." I nod my head, pretending to be impressed. "It has been a pleasure having you as my dirty little secret. You plan your jobs with amazing precision and no one has ever suspected I was involved, unless I wanted it that way." He laughs to himself. "For this, I thank you—I really do. I wonder how many people you've killed for me."

He shakes my hand again, but much more lightly than last time. I do not answer; I have also lost count. "I know that you hate my Murder Squad. But, I understand, and, in a small way, respect your reasons for doing so. I truly do." He holds his hands up in an 'I-am-guilty' gesture. "They're reckless, messy, and they have no problems killing innocent people. That is why I've kept you both apart. That said, if you've not been killed after twenty-four hours, I'll release them to finish the job."

His response does not surprise me; he has used the same tactic many times before. After twenty-four hours, the target is usually weak, tired, and easy pickings for them. Plus, it means that he gets to keep a larger share of the money.

"I understand." I act as though I am not too happy about this additional clause, but inside, I am ecstatic. It is what I have planned for—well, not quite, but close enough.

"I'll start the game at 21:00 tonight, whether you're ready or not!" On that ultimatum, we both hug each other tightly.

A golfer in the approaching group shouts something, but all I catch is, "Fucking Russians." He laughs loudly, trying to impress his friends.

The atmosphere instantly becomes hostile. Mikhail's newest recruit spins around and storms over to the golfer with a robot-like gait. In the blink of an eye, the golfer has an angry, ogre-looking Russian forcing his head back with the muzzle of a handgun. He holds the handgun in both hands with his back flared, stretching his suit jacket to its limits. He takes his responsibilities seriously; it's obvious that he wouldn't hesitate to pull the trigger. The golfer's facial expression and body language have changed from an ostentatious alpha male to a regretful child awaiting their punishment. All the other golfers in his group become petrified statues. I study the tree line and work out the quickest path to safety that I will immediately sprint down after he has pulled the trigger.

"Leonid," Mikhail shouts, playfully.

Leonid keeps the handgun remained fixed against the golfer's forehead. Smiling, Mikhail walks over to the Leonid and golfers. I take this disturbance as my cue to leave; I retreat into the shadow of the tree line.

Chapter 7
The Set-Up

My stomach churns painfully; I breathe deeply and push down on it to prevent it from regurgitating my final supper. As I place my steak knife on the plate, I get a mild urge to ram it into my temple to end the tension building up within. According to my kitchen clock, it's 20:55—but that means it's actually 20:50.

A hitman's lifespan is only as long as their employer wishes it to be. Once they have served their time, their employer will task the next up-and-coming recruits to kill them as risk mitigation, as well as to provide these recruits with an opportunity to prove their loyalty, commitment, and skill. Thus, I need to kill Mikhail before he has me killed; hence, the commencement of 'Operation Endgame'.

I could try and kill Mikhail but there is a good chance of failure. In the event of failure, he would retreat and go into hiding, giving himself the opportunity, time, and motivation to not only mobilise his full army, but also recruit additional soldiers against me. I would never see him again, let alone have an opportunity to kill him. To avoid failure, 'Operation Endgame' involves deliberately placing myself in danger to reduce the threat level I pose to him, all in the hope that this elevates his perceived position of power, control, and personal safety. Fortuitously, my terminal illness naturally elevates his perceived position further, albeit I need to move quickly before I become disadvantaged by it. This should provide me with the latitude to weaken the strength, size, and morale of his army in bite-sized chunks on my own terms, whilst he hopefully carries on like normal, remaining in the public arena until I am ready to strike.

Mikhail should now have put my assassination out to tender. This means that his non-Russian contract killers will race one another to be the first to kill me and claim the sizeable reward. It has only been relatively recently—ever since he tried to kill Private Hardy—that he has used non-Russians. This is because it makes it difficult to trace the murder(s) back to him, and, in the event of their capture, it will be impossible for them to disclose any incriminating evidence on him when under interrogation. He does have plenty of work to keep his Russian contract killers busy though. Such as two months ago when the Russian authorities gained evidence of a Russian businessman selling state assets for ludicrous profits, but he had fled the country before they could detain him. At the request of the Russian government, Mikhail ordered his Russian hitmen to find the businessman and publicly execute him and his family.

Mikhail only has three of his non-Russian contract killers available to him for this job. The most high profile being the notorious Private Hardy, who is AWOL from the United States Army. During his second deployment in Afghanistan, his unit was on a routine patrol when they were ambushed by rebel forces. The initial spray of bullets tore into his torso, incapacitating him. As his life was literally being drained from him, his unit was swiftly slaughtered. There had been a drone providing air surveillance; however, moments before the ambush, it was reassigned, at the request of the Natural Well Oil Corporation's CEO, Benjamin Devenish, to get footage of local oil wells that were at risk of being taken over by the rebel forces.

Later that night, when the rebel forces had returned to the mountains, the local villagers found him and carried him back to the closest home. They had adapted to living in a conflict zone, becoming self-taught experts at removing bullets from bullet-riddled bodies. It must have been a spectacle to witness the humble villagers, with only their primitive surgical knowledge, experience, and surgical tools, operate on him as he lay bleeding out on one of their dining tables.

Despite the village only having minimal resources, all its residents worked together to ensure his speedy recovery. He initially thought they were only keeping him alive so that they could use him as a bargaining chip with the rebels; however, it quickly became apparent that they viewed him as their potential saviour. Only one young boy—the only boy the village could afford to allow to hike the five miles to the school every day—knew rudimentary English, so he became his default interpreter.

Once the word spread of his presence, people from further and further away made the secret pilgrimage to his bedside. Many not only prayed, but also begged, for his help. He became very attached to them; they shared their heart-breaking stories of how their loved ones had been kidnapped, injured, mutilated, tortured, killed, or raped by the soldiers on both sides of the conflict. The conflict commenced shortly after the Natural Well Oil Corporation started drilling for oil on their land, both without their permission and without offering any compensation. They understood that the discovery of this oil under their feet had permanently changed not only the physical, but also the political, social, and economic landscape of their land. They just wanted a share of the profits to improve the quality of their lives.

A few weeks after the ambush, despite still being in debilitating physical pain himself, he could no longer take the pain and suffering that was being inflicted on the villagers—now his friends. To avoid soldiers fighting on either side of the conflict inflicting even greater pain and suffering on his friends by discovering his presence, he scarpered under the cover of darkness back to his military base without saying goodbye to anyone.

From his field hospital bed, his anger grew further everyday as he watched the western media only concentrate on the hostility shown, and destruction caused, by the locals, portraying them as terrorists, even though they were essentially only trying to protect their land, family, and friends. Increasing his anger further, it dawned on him how he and his unit had signed up to help people who could not help themselves, as well as to promote the American Dream around the world, but had basically been exploited to satisfy the whims, careers, and bank balances of politicians and war profiteers.

A week after returning to base, he became fully radicalised when one of the rebels' suicide drivers drove a heavily fortified car, loaded with explosives and lots of sharp shrapnel, into a US military convoy. Not only did it claim the lives of the targeted military personnel, but also many innocent civilians, including the English-speaking boy and several other villagers that had saved his life.

Once back on US soil, he turned himself into a one-man army against everyone he deemed responsible for creating and/or continuing the conflict. One by one, he hunted them down and killed them swiftly, without mercy; his weapon of choice was a crude homemade nail bomb.

The stories of Private Hardy were reported and repeated on mainstream media for many weeks until it became apparent that their reporting was increasing his popularity further because a large portion of the general public sympathised with his cause. When his killing rampage had claimed over fifty lives, Benjamin Devenish, who was already in hiding long before this point, knew that the police would never catch him, so he contracted Mikhail, via Lord Beaumont-Knight, to put an end to his killing rampage.

To put it bluntly, this resulted in an internationally publicised bloodbath of Mikhail's foot soldiers. He didn't care about the loss of his men, but he did care about the unwanted attention from the authorities and the media—anonymity and reputation are everything in his line of work. It took a fair while but he finally accepted that Private Hardy could not be taken down. On a slight aside, he must have had some admiration for Private Hardy, particularly on the speed that he was eliminating his foot soldiers. It is unknown what happened next, but based on the fact that they were both observed in the same hotel at around the same time, they likely struck a deal in-person.

This deal must have included providing Private Hardy with the location of Benjamin's hideout because the day after they were seen together, Private Hardy was caught on a traffic light camera rolling a nail bomb under Benjamin's stationary car. It is believed that he has been working for Mikhail ever since.

Emma tried hard to link the foot soldiers killed by Private Hardy back to Mikhail, but Private Hardy blew up the mortuary. As such, Mikhail now only uses Russians when they are absolutely required. I've tried to track Private Hardy down several times, but his army training serves him well. I am led to believe that there is evidence that Private Hardy has helped Mikhail gain control of the Natural Well Oil Corporation's board, but I haven't been given this evidence so haven't verified it.

The second contract killer is Lukas Danzl, who is well known to Emma and her team. He used to work for the Jordanov crime family, based in Germany. Without hesitation, he would carry out his orders; he would kill whomever he was told to kill and transport whatever he was told to transport.

About two years ago, whilst he was transporting a van full of unconscious Russian prostitutes late at night, he stopped at a service station to use the facilities. Surveillance footage shows him become beside himself with rage in the carpark on his way back to his car after a Jewish man innocently bumped into him. He is a practising Nazi and wasn't going to let what he saw as an insult go unpunished. He is seen punching his dashboard whilst he waited for his target to get back into his car. As soon as they both returned to the deserted autobahn, he overtook his target and sped away into the distance. Once he was far enough away, he swiftly turned around in a layby and headed back towards his target with his lights off.

Emma has given me a copy of the police report so I've seen the truly heart-breaking photographs of the wreckages. There were no brake marks at the scene;

his target never saw him coming. The man, his wife and their two children, as well as all the unconscious Russian women being trafficked, were killed upon impact. Somehow, the only survivor was Lukas.

He had been in such a rage that he had forgotten to wear his seatbelt, which resulted in him being launched from his van through the front windscreen. The police report shows photographs of blood, flesh, and clothing at intervals along tens of metres of the road leading to a small crater in the shrubbery at the side of the road. His body was never found; he somehow managed to escape from the crime scene. However, it wasn't long before his bosses tracked him down and severely punished him for killing all the women. These women were destined for Mikhail so he now finds himself in Mikhail's service.

The third contract killer is currently unknown to me. I have had no reason to put much energy into trying to find him because as far as I am aware he hasn't murdered anyone in this city, or anyone that I have been keeping tabs on. I only know that he exists because the Murder Squad have mentioned him briefly in passing on several occasions. My Russian interpreter tells me that they call him weak and pathetic because he employs stealth techniques. He also told me that they do not trust him and are unsure why Mikhail uses him.

My flat takes up a quarter of the third floor of a five-storey block of luxury apartments. Most of the apartments are so expensive that the type of people that can afford them only visit the city a couple of times a year, if at all. When this building was being renovated, I paid a lot of money for the contractors to install hidden cameras, for my use only, in the lifts, on the fire exit stairs, on the roof, in the lobby, and around the building. My front door is the only internal entrance to my apartment; it is secured with standard locks and reinforced with three heavy iron drop bars.

My curtains are still drawn from this morning, but it doesn't matter if anyone can see me through them as the contractors, at my request, installed bullet-resistant windows. With that thought, I head over to the kitchen window, throw the curtains back and take what could be my last observation of mankind. I am slightly envious of all the people scurrying around on the street below. Some are walking reluctantly to start their night shifts, whilst others stumble noisily and unsteadily to the next drinking establishment.

There are also numerous businessmen, with deeply bagged eyes from fourteen hours in the office staring at numbers on computer screens in order to barely keep financially afloat in this expensive city, making their way home to their neglected families. I catch a loving couple laughing and groping each other, which reminds me of what I could have had with Nataliya; I find it hard to override my urge to become upset. My eyes fall upon the white van parked directly below me. It is exactly where I left it.

I stroll into my living room, which is only illuminated by the array of monitors displaying all the hidden camera feeds. I notice nothing out of the ordinary; 21:00 comes and goes. As soon as I collapse into my armchair, my phone rings. I have difficulty retrieving my phone from my trouser pocket; by the time that I do, it has stopped ringing. I do not recognise the number. It is likely a poor attempt by one of the contract killers to locate my phone. A message appears on my screen stating that I have a voicemail. I call my voicemail and wait to hear the message.

"Hello, Mr Smith, this is Dr Black," he stutters. "You had an appointment with me this afternoon. I'll get straight to the point. I'm afraid what I told you earlier was a complete lie. Please ring me back urgently—your life is in danger." He ends the call.

Obviously, my life is in danger. What does he mean he lied to me? For fuck's sake, I haven't got time for this distraction. I decide to call him back. On the first ring, he picks up.

"Hello, Dr Black. This is Mr Smith. What are you talking about?" I let him hear the frustration in my voice.

"Erm," he says, followed by a long pause. "Well, well, I'm afraid there is a problem with the results that I gave you earlier." He struggles to get his words out.

"Go on, spit it out; I am in a rush," I say, impatiently.

"I am very sorry." The line goes eerily silent.

"Hello, are you still there?" I ask, desperately scanning the array of monitors.

"You have to understand that I have a family to provide for." He bursts out crying. I remain quiet whilst he pulls himself together. "You see, I perform private health checks on his women to make sure that they're healthy, and, most importantly, free from sexually transmitted diseases. Depending on the disease, I either treat them, or his men will remove them from my care. They are usually too drugged up to even notice me; however, this one woman started flirting with me." I already know where this is going but I let him continue. "She was the most beautiful woman that I had ever seen. Suffice it to say, she wasn't faced with much resistance when she started to rip my clothes off. Expectedly, Mikhail, the bastard, had it filmed and then threatened to show the footage to my wife if I didn't tell you what I told you."

"But—you showed me my scan?" My heart races. I am not angry with the doctor; I am furious at myself for being set-up.

"Ah, I simply used another patient's scan." He continues to sob.

"Why are you telling me this now?" I ask, even though the answer will not change my situation.

"Because, I have syphilis. And I suspect I have given it to my pregnant wife."

"So, what's wrong with me then?" I cut him off—I don't have time to listen to his domestic situation. I want to know why Mikhail honey trapped him.

"Well, Mr Smith, after Mikhail's men had briefed me about you and my mission, I was expecting you to arrive at the appointment in good health; however, as soon as I saw you in the waiting room, I knew something quite serious was wrong with you. I was ordered to throw your blood sample away without testing it, but my curious nature got the better of me so I tested it. The results showed that your carboxyhaemoglobin levels are elevated, but not elevated enough to kill you—I've seen worse.

"I presume that you are suffering from carbon monoxide poisoning. You need to find the source of the carbon monoxide and stop it before it causes you any further damage. I also need you to get yourself to a hospital; you'll need oxygen treatment. You are a big, strong, and determined guy, so it should not take you too long to fully recover." A cleansing wave of relief washes over me; I begin to feel much stronger already. "I am so sorry Mr Smith; please can you forgive me?"

My brain goes into overdrive. I quickly connect the start of my illness to the day after both my bathroom's extractor fan and air conditioning unit stopped working. I didn't think much of that strange consequence at the time; I am annoyed I didn't check. Whilst I have been too busy since to get them fixed, there hasn't been any urgency because I have been removing the moisture out of my apartment using my cooker hood, which has been on a low setting continuously ever since. I tune into its faint hum, which I've now become accustomed to. By sheer luck, I have adverted being iller than I already am—or worse.

"Yes, of course I can forgive you. Mikhail feeds off good, honest, and hard-working people like yourself before destroying them without mercy." I try to comfort him, whilst walking into my bathroom.

"Well, he has certainly destroyed my life. My wife will go ballistic when she finds out what I've done." I do not reply; he should have known better. Although, I can sympathise with him as he was placed in a situation that I doubt many men could have gotten themselves out of. The doctor starts crying loudly. I am in no position to comfort him further, so I put down the phone.

In one fluid motion, I step up onto the side of the bath, which creaks loudly under my weight, and smash my fist into the extractor fan's plastic casing. It takes two punches to obliterate the casing. The plastic shards tinkle as they rain down on the bath's enamel. Encased within the metal flexible ducting hose, nearly out of sight, is a hosepipe. I try to grab the hosepipe, but I cannot get a good enough grip on it to pull it. Mikhail, the fucking bastard. I take my towel off the towel radiator and use it to bung up the ducting hose. I close the bathroom door behind me and block the gap at the bottom with the throw off the back of the sofa.

Mikhail must have somehow found out about me. A surge of anxiety paralyses me momentarily at the thought of him potentially also finding out about Nataliya and Emma. He must have only kept me alive, albeit in a weakened state, so that he could find out what I know about him, and, possibly, who I've been working with and any other weaknesses that I have got. Oh, the irony—that is what I have been doing to him. I convince myself that he doesn't know about Nataliya or Emma.

I deeply regret allowing Emma's involvement now. I slap myself hard in the face and scream loudly. I take deep breaths to try and calm myself down. I suddenly remember that there will still be high levels of carbon monoxide in the air. I storm over to the cooker hood and turn it up to full speed. Mikhail must have found out that none of the apartments have carbon monoxide detectors because this building is not connected to the gas mains.

I clench my fists tightly and storm back into the living room screaming, "Fuck you, Mikhail. Fuck you! I am going to kill you!"

Chapter 8
The Challengers

It is 21:30. I would have expected at least one of them to have been picked up by one of my cameras by now. I reach down the side of the armchair and pick up my M4 carbine assault rifle off the floor. In addition to this, I have two fully loaded Walther P99's, including several extra magazines, strapped to my sides; two grenades attached to my belt; and a leg sheath containing a dagger.

With every passing second, I grow more vigilant, scrutinising my monitors more intensely. There is nothing suspicious; nothing out of the ordinary. Whilst keeping my eyes on the monitors, I grab my phone and call Emma. She answers before the first ring.

"She wasn't there. Neither was my Corsa."

My whole body, including my heart, goes still. I am petrified; I've failed Nataliya.

Bang. BANG. I am deafened by the explosions originating from the floor above. The whole building shakes; I am nearly rocked out of my armchair. Sprinkles of dust fall from the newly formed fissures in my concrete ceiling. There is another, but much longer, series of explosions in quick succession; every explosion momentarily paralyses my body, pinning me to my armchair. All my monitors vibrate off the table, cracking their screens as they land on top of one another. The room falls into near darkness; the only light comes through the gap in the kitchen door. A square piece of ceiling falls onto the pile of monitors a couple of metres in front of me. A beam of light from the room above infiltrates through the darkness. A round, football-sized object descends into my living room in the centre of this light beam.

Instinctively, I spring up out of my seat, dropping my M4 in the process, and sprint and dive through the kitchen door. I slide painfully along the tiled floor until I stop myself under my oak kitchen table. I kick the underside of the table and turn it over so that it faces the direction of the living room. An almighty explosion slams into me, smashing my eardrums. Everything goes pitch black.

Even though I am completely disorientated and visionless, I can still sense the nails darting from the epicentre of the blast. They pierce everything around me. Both the explosion and the nails force my kitchen table back into me and together we are both pushed back towards my kitchen cabinets. Somehow, I manage to end the call to Emma and pocket my phone as I slide along the floor whilst also clinging to my table.

I am left stunned for what feels like ages, but it is probably only several seconds, before my consciousness starts to return to me. Whilst my ears ring loudly and my faculties reboot, I can sense, what I believe will be, Private Hardy making his way through the rubble. The place is a literally a bombsite. All the kitchen furniture and cabinets have been ripped to pieces; there are big holes in the now nail-studded walls and ceiling; the bullet-resistant window is severely cracked from all the nails that are embedded in it. My cooker hood's casing has been heavily damaged, but its fan still works; it loudly churns the concrete and plaster dust.

I reposition myself so that instead of lying on my side, I am crouched down, ready to pounce. I let out a quiet whine to give the impression that I'm wounded and not a threat. He stops moving and breathing momentarily before continuing to move forward; this time more cautiously. From the soft crunching of the rubble and shattered woodwork, which used to make up my kitchen cabinets, under his heavyweight, I try to triangulate his position and determine his stance. He must be at most eight feet away from me.

I let out a loud whine. This time, he doesn't stop advancing. Five feet. Four feet. As I let out another whine, I pounce with as much force as my shaking quadriceps can manage. My body is thrust upwards; I clear the table easily and head towards the ceiling. I startle my prey—I was right, it is Private Hardy—causing him to freeze with shock. I fall back down to earth with my hands stretched out. I wrap them around his throat and force him to the floor.

As we both land on the floor, I power my right knee into his crotch. The pain causes his whole body to turn into a solid block of stone; he releases his assault rifle, which is the same type as mine. With one hand, I throw it into the corner of the room before quickly securing my hand back around his throat. He doesn't try to say anything, but with nostrils flared wide, his eyes scream in rage. All my muscles contract as I try to keep him **pinned to the** floor. He squirms and shakes desperately under me. He punches my **ribs several** times, but I don't feel a thing.

A cold flow of water breaks through the ceiling and pours down onto the back of my neck. It streams down both of my sleeves, over my hands, and onto him. The water loosens my grip and I struggle to keep him pinned down. This change of circumstance gives him a new lease of life; he flaps even more aggressively. He manages to bring a knee up and push it against my chest. He takes his hands off my wrists and forces his thumbs into my eyes.

My grip breaks and the force from his knees launches me off him. I roll back and headbutt the backs of several nails that are embedded in my toaster. I desperately grab the back of his collar with one hand, but he rips himself out of my grip. He crawls through the rubble, obliterated furniture, and water to the corner of the kitchen. As he throws the remnants of a chair out of his way, I notice, through the gap between his right arm and body, that his weapon is lying in a pool of water. I jump to my feet and sprint towards my living room.

I jump over the remnants of my sofa, which is now blocking the doorway to my living room. My right ankle twists when my foot lands awkwardly on rubble; I ignore the pain. There are no gunshots so either I made it out before he could take aim or his weapon is water-damaged—I suspect the latter.

"Come on, Mr Smith, you are only delaying the inevitable. I promise that it will be over quickly," he shouts. I do not reply as I run through what can only be described as a waterfall in my living room. As I am bent over extracting my assault rifle out of the rubble, he pokes his head into the living room. I beat him to the draw and fire a quick burst of shots at him. I narrowly miss him; he retreats out of view.

An almighty force smashes into my body; the force feels the same as when a van once reversed into me at speed. I am lifted off the floor and flung backwards. I hit the living room wall a couple of metres away from where I was standing moments ago. My body hits the wall, but my head keeps moving back, penetrating the plasterboard before hitting the underlying concrete wall. My body is fixed to the wall momentarily before I slide down it onto the rubble and the remnants of the TV monitors, which are all embedded with many nails.

My front door has been obliterated; the three heavy iron drop bars remain fixed in place. The light from the corridor is mostly blocked by a newly formed dust cloud. Lukas sticks his head in the gap between two drop bars. He laughs cruelly when he sees that I am lying awkwardly in a heap on the floor, barely conscious. He replaces his head with possibly a Heckler & Koch MP5 and starts firing it before he even has me in its sights.

I do not waste even a nanosecond trying to defend myself as the spray of bullets meanders across the wall towards me. From a press-up position, I force myself upright and dart towards my living room window, which, like my kitchen window, has maintained its integrity despite being severely cracked from the embedded nails. I fire at a metal plate hidden between the plasterboard and the wall to the right-hand side of the window frame. It takes several bullets to hit my target, but when I do hit it, the uPVC frame is visibly released from the wall.

I rest my assault rifle on my right shoulder, with its magazine facing the ceiling, and fire blindly behind me to stop my attackers from shooting me in the back. My right ear is deafened again. Almost instantly, the magazine is spent, so I toss the assault rifle away. Lukas starts firing and his bullets meander across the wall again, homing in on my position. At nearly full speed, I dive at the window with my right shoulder leading the way. The whole window remains as a single unit as my shoulder forces it out into the abyss.

My fingertips briefly grab hold of the internal window-board in an unsuccessful attempt to reduce the speed that I exit my living room with. In the vastness of space, I look back at my annihilated living room. Private Hardy jumps over my sofa into my living room; I withdraw the handgun on my left-hand side with my right hand and, without aiming, I fire three times. His head snaps back a split second before I fall from view.

As I descend, bullets escape from my living room and smash the windows of the building on the opposite side of the street. I keep my eyes and weapon focused on my living room opening. I exhale all the air out of my lungs and completely relax my body. My van's roof crumples on impact, absorbing most of my energy as I designed too. In one smooth movement, I roll off my van and land on the tarmac, narrowly missing my window. I roll once more to ensure that all the gravitational potential energy has been consumed. I end up back on my feet and use the remaining angular momentum to power myself into a sprint; I head diagonally away from my window towards a side street.

Lukas's MP5 roars voraciously. His bullets pour down around me as I sprint for my life; they mercilessly strike many innocent bystanders. A taxi driver is shot through his windscreen. His taxi, which was not travelling very fast, mounts the pavement and clips a small boy's baggy coat, before ploughing into his mother, pinning her up against a streetlight. As Lukas pans across, her body is riddled with bullets but, luckily, the line of bullets passes over the small boy's head.

As I jump and slide over the taxi's bonnet, the driver gargles, "Help me," whilst choking on his own blood that has poured down his face from a crevice in his forehead. The back passenger is dazed as he pulls his face out of the front passenger's headrest. I think I recognise him, although I cannot put a name to the face. I ignore everyone and concentrate on saving the small boy; I grab his coat and fling him into the safety of the side street.

As soon as we are both protected behind a building, I grab his coat again and launch him further into the side street. I slightly regret his painful landing, but he is safe and momentarily distracted from the thought of running back to his mother. I pull out my other gun as Lukas' bullets sweep past the side street. I drop and roll sideways, fully committing myself. I fire both guns simultaneously at Lukas until they are spent. I don't think I managed to hit him, but at least he has retreated back into my apartment.

I quickly reload both of my guns before continuing to point them at my non-existent living room window. Crying, the small boy runs past me to the corpse of his recently deceased mother. This was one of the most beautiful and affluent areas of the city, but now it looks like a war zone. I cannot believe how many people are around tonight; it is usually never anywhere near this busy. Whilst I am glad that I have potentially taken out one assassin, it is a pyrrhic victory.

I scream in my head, '*What have you done!*'

The people that have survived the short burst of terror crawl out from their hideaways. The taxi driver's dead eyes stare at me, sending a shiver of shame down my spine. The approaching sirens from the emergency vehicles signal that my time is up. Before withdrawing into the side street, a tear forms in my eye as I take one last look at the small boy, who cries gut-wrenchingly as he hugs his mother's bloody corpse.

Chapter 9
Extra Arm

I have killed a countless number of bad people, and regrettably, heartbreakingly, and unavoidably several innocent people who have found themselves caught up in my firefights. I consider myself fully responsible for their deaths. In the aftermath of these tragedies—such as now—is when their collective deaths weigh most heavily upon my conscience. I am distracted by the thought of all those that have lost their lives tonight, and the long-lasting devastation that it will have on their surviving loved ones, as well as the generational trauma; I cannot get the imagine of the little boy hugging his mother's bloody corpse out of my mind. I also openly confess that I have inflicted pain, sometimes bordering on torture, on many innocent people, but, in my defence, I only pushed them far enough to save either their lives, or the lives of many others.

The strong, cold wind harshly cuts my throat with every breath; however, my core stays warm with the heat of rage and revenge that pulsates unquenchably around my body. Lukas has extremely infuriated me by how many innocent people he has needlessly killed tonight; I am literally shaking with the thought of ripping him apart with my bare hands. I make a vow to myself that I will never rest until I have killed him. This won't do much to satisfy my conscience, although it might provide a small amount of closure to the surviving loved ones of those he has killed tonight.

My phone screen is so severely cracked from tonight's events that it has been rendered nearly useless. Despite this, I keep my head down looking at it as a constant stream of emergency vehicles pass me as I walk to my boxing club. It's a strange feeling, but I can sense the city's collective grief, and its growing anger, over tonight's trauma. I can also sense the different authorities arming themselves with information, motivation, and weapons as they prepare to commence the relentless hunt. I now feel extremely vulnerable. I pick up my pace, but not enough to draw attention to myself. I remain vigilant and use a whole host of escape and evasive manoeuvres and tactics, such as looking at reflections in shop windows and crossing the road moments before a slug of oncoming traffic passes by, so that no one can follow me, or at least not without me knowing about it.

I peer through my boxing club's single glazed windows at the usual cohort inside, plus a couple of nervous-looking newbies. Everyone's attention is on the two boxers sparring in the boxing ring positioned in the centre of the room. One of the fighters is an angry-looking newbie; he is becoming increasingly infuriated by the taunting from his untouchable opponent, Big Stan.

I cannot, and do not necessarily want to, kill everyone involved in the world of human trafficking; therefore, one of my initiatives is to stem the flow of ex-convicts, especially those with valuable information on human trafficking operations, from re-joining criminal organisations.

Over many years, I have discreetly cultivated the reputation of my boxing club as a haven for ex-convicts who want to redeem themselves and pursue an honest life. Emma and I peddle this reputation to prisoners, particularly those that we deem potentially valuable to us. The only cost of this service is information; they've got to be willing to share with us every single detail from their previous employment with particular focus on the human trafficking aspects. Emma deals with all the other valuable information in a lawful manner.

The first time that ex-convicts step into my boxing club they must prove themselves in the boxing ring. It is only possible to see a person's true character, and how much that they are willing to sacrifice in the pursuit of redemption, when their life is in mortal danger—or at least perceived to be. It doesn't matter how good a fighter they are; they always get beaten. This also naturally creates a strong bond between the fighters.

I used to fight everyone until recently when I was particularly unwell and Big Carl capitalised on it. He caught me off guard, knocking me to the canvas, much to everyone's surprise—especially mine. Even though I have not had many opportunities to utilise my groundwork tactics for quite a while, I easily brought him down onto the canvas next to me and, much to my relief, he surrendered quickly in a skull-crushing headlock.

Big Stan was the first former human trafficker that Emma and I recruited into our cause. He started his working life as a bouncer at one of his local nightclubs, but it wasn't long before his huge frame and intimating presence caught the attention of his superiors, who promoted him into the more jeopardous, yet lucrative, prostitution game. As part of his 'promotion', he was made responsible for a group of high-earning prostitutes. He was sickened by what he was tasked with forcing them to do; however, his superiors made it very clear that either he controls them with a heavy hand, or one of his own hands would be removed.

Additional to this moral conflict, he fell deeply in love with one of women he was in charge of. He struggled more and more each day to direct her to perform unspeakable acts, many against her will. To make it more bearable for them both, and thus increase their chances of surviving their situation, he kept promising her that he would find a way to secure her freedom. They both knew that they could not run off together as they would be hunted down and killed; therefore, he inquired with his boss about the possibility of him buying her freedom.

Obviously, she was too valuable to be sold. Plus, his boss needed his employees to act objectively and setting this precedent would affect the power dynamic within his organisation. After his boss had made it clear that he would only consider selling her if she could no longer make money, he took great pleasure in reminding Big Stan that it was very difficult to not make money in this industry; hence, Big Stan should think again if he was thinking that disfigurement and/or mutilation would help his case. To aggravate an already bad situation, his cruel boss decided that he would use this opportunity to test Big Stan's loyalty. He did this by forcing Big Stan to watch him aggressively rape the beloved woman in her flat. With great difficulty, Big Stan managed to restrain himself, at least until his boss started strangling her.

Under the influence of uncontrollable anger and desperation, he stormed over and tried to attack his boss, who had a hidden dagger close at hand. His boss uninterruptedly continued to rape the woman whilst he expertly wielded his dagger. Before Big Stan knew what had happened, he was lying in a pool of his own blood, fighting for his life.

Fortunately for Big Stan, the prostitute living in the flat directly across the hallway heard her friend screaming and, through the spyhole in her front door, watched blood seep out from under her friend's door. Thinking the blood was from her friend, she put her own life on the line by calling the emergency services. Emma, and her elite task force, stormed the building ten minutes later.

The officers that Emma has recruited into her task force have the same attitude to human traffickers as Emma and I; therefore, there was a collective temptation to let Big Stan bleed out. However, professionalism prevailed, and they sent him to the hospital, albeit with little time left to spare. Eight prostitutes were rescued that day, including the woman that Big Stan had fallen in love with. Unfortunately, the boss managed to elude them by either getting away or hiding very well within the building. Emma provided each of the women a place in witness protection in return for providing valuable information. Luckily for us, they all opened up and provided us with a wealth of valuable information.

Even though none of Big Stan's vital organs were penetrated by the dagger, he still needed around-the-clock medical care due to the life-threatening amount of blood he had lost. He was placed in a private room on the intensive care unit and armed police officers were assigned bed-watching duty. The deployment of this armed precautionary measure is standard practice under the circumstances to protect the safety of the general public, as well as that of the prisoner. Big Stan needed this protection because he was viewed as a high-risk target after his altercation with his former boss, who was not only well known for using firearms in the public arena but was also the prime suspect in several ongoing murder investigations.

Emma saw great potential in Big Stan. She knew that he would become a great asset to our cause with the right training and guidance. Before he was transferred to the local prison's medical unit, she managed to sneak me into his private room in the guise of a doctor. We gained his respect and attention as soon as we made it clear that Emma had placed the love of his life in witness protection with her colleagues, and that they had all agreed to remain there at least until his former boss had been brought to justice. I explained that if he agreed to work with us then we would provide him with the training and wherewithal needed to track down and kill his former boss—as well as other people like him. In the couple of minutes available to us, we secured his agreement to come and join us after he had served his prison sentence. The combination of me providing him with a very good attorney and him officially supplying Emma with valuable human trafficking information, resulted in him receiving a relatively short prison sentence.

He kept his head down and he sailed through his prison sentence. As promised, I was waiting at the prison gates when he was released. I drove him straight to my boxing club and, without delay, threw him into my boxing ring. As his opponent, I directly witnessed his very average fighting ability, which comprised a basic arsenal of punches and moves that were most likely replicated from action movies. I never had this setback of having a false impression of fighting because I never really watched any TV shows, let alone an action movie, before I had been forced to fight for my survival. That said, I had seen several punch-ups during the live football matches that I had watched on a small, fuzzy TV through a forest of men's heads.

I have honed my own style of fighting from a young age; it is based primarily on survival. I would never have made it to adulthood if I hadn't quickly neutralised or, if the situation dictated, mercilessly killed my opponents. When you're a malnourished eight-year-old boy and you've got the hands of a grown man clamped around your neck, you simply must do whatever it takes to survive—you don't have the time to play around when your opponent is three or four times your size, and many more times stronger.

To break free from their holds, there wasn't—and still isn't—anything I wouldn't do. I would spit in their eyes, ram my fingers or any nearby object into their eyeballs, bite off their fingers, and bite chunks out of their arms, calves, faces, and throats. By the time I had reached puberty, I had killed a fair amount of people, with nearly all of them being a result of self-preservation, both reactive and proactive. All the killings were done in messy and gruesome ways and, on many occasions, I felt that I had come off worse.

During my first fight with Big Stan, I played with him, I taunted him—similar to how he is behaving with the newbie now. He swung his arms around wildly, but he found me untouchable; I knew every move that he was going to make, sometimes even before he did. After one swift and undefendable uppercut, he was knocked out on the canvas. Whilst I was equipping him with the skills that he needed to kill his former boss, Emma kept her task force out of my way so that I was free to track him down. It didn't take me long to find him. I kept him under observation until Big Stan was ready to face him.

Once he had proven himself to me, we both broke into his former boss' flat, but I left him to settle the score on his own terms. His former boss came at him with the same dagger that had nearly ended his life during their last encounter; but, this time, he was ready for it. He dodged the first thrust and grabbed hold of his wrist. As we had practised, he snapped his wrist back and took ownership of the dagger. The dagger was introduced to its owner's groin before slicing through his heart. He repeatedly stabbed him in the chest until long after he was dead. I didn't count exactly how times he stabbed his victim, but it was likely over fifty times.

That event was a while ago and ever since then I have dedicated tremendous time and effort into grooming him to be my successor. He has developed into a truly deadly fighter, possibly on a comparable level to me now—well, at least before Mikhail started poisoning me. I believe that I have his complete loyalty; however, I am not quite ready yet to share with him my innermost secrets like I have done with Emma. This is because he needs to turn his back on the love of his life in order to survive in this game. Whilst he claims that he is happy to do this, I remain unconvinced. Emma and I have made sure that the woman he loves is now as far away from him as she possibly can be, but there is nothing stopping her from returning to him—except her promise to us that she wouldn't return under any circumstance.

Even if he still harbours thoughts of being with her, they are not proving to be a distraction; he is working hard to excel in my brutal training programme. I have included him on several taster missions, such as stealing Toby's BMW X6, and on all occasions he has executed his role perfectly. He also dedicates a lot of energy to this boxing club, so I made him the manager, as well as the head trainer for the guys that represent the boxing club in the unlicensed boxing circuit. This gives me more time to concentrate on getting information from the ex-convicts and integrating them back into society.

I integrate the ex-convicts back into society by using my extensive list of people who owe me favours to either secure them a decent job or provide them with assistance in setting up their businesses. I also help them financially with interest-free loans from my treasury. This treasury is now quite substantial as all the previous ex-convicts voluntarily continue to provide me with a share of their income/profits after they've paid back their loans as a way of expressing their appreciation and to help me continue my integration programme.

No one notices me stepping into my boxing club as their attention is on Big Stan and the newbie. I keep watching the fight whilst stealthily walking behind everyone until I reach the fifth step on the rickety old staircase that leads up to my office. The newbie has taken a serious beating but continues to fight with his unruly style. His fist flies towards Big Stan's forehead, who teasingly moves out of the way at the last possible moment. I can tell by the stance he has now positioned himself into that that punch was a little bit too close for his comfort.

The newbie's guard is up, but it is weakly constructed. Big Stan throws a hard right, which easily blows his guard apart, and ploughs into the side of his face. The force jolts his head back violently. He is thrown off his feet and his whole body goes limp in mid-air. His body crumples up as it lands awkwardly on the canvas. The gym erupts as everyone, apart from the other newbies who have still yet to step into the ring, cheers and claps. This celebration is not directed at Big Stan, but at the newbie, who has given it his all and earned everyone's respect; he has taken his first step on the path to redemption.

I continue clapping as the cheering and clapping from everyone else dies down. One by one, everyone in the gym turns around to face me. I stop clapping once I have nearly everyone's attention. Nearly everyone looks shocked to see me, but I suspect that it is more to do with me being covered in cuts and blood with a nice coating of brick dust. Big Stan is the only person who doesn't look concerned: he has seen me in similar conditions before.

Once all the muttering quietens down, I shout, "Can I have your attention please?" However, it was not loud enough to capture the attention of the few people that are in the boxing ring, helping the unconscious newbie. I do feel slightly guilty for delaying aid to the newbie, but there isn't time to wait. Everyone else remains in a fixed position; some look at me with great anticipation, whilst others look at me with great fear. "I need everyone to be extremely vigilant tonight. If anyone sees anyone acting suspiciously outside this building then I need you to come and get me right away. Please be careful, they will be extremely dangerous. OK everyone, carry on. Except Big Stan and Big Carl: can you both come here please?" I wave them to me with my fingers.

They both make their way to me whilst the crowd disperses. First, I address Big Carl, who is a very good driver and is currently in possession of an impressive sports car, which I suspect he stole—but I have no evidence to confirm my suspicion. "Big Carl, I want you to go and wait in your car for me." Without question, he turns and sprints towards the exit. "Start your engine and keep it running," I shout after him. He throws a thumbs up above his head in acknowledgement of my command as he uninterruptedly continues running away from me.

"What do you want me to do, Boss?" Big Stan says with a straight back. He resembles a soldier who is waiting for the details of his mission. His shoulders and traps have grown noticeably since last week; I have told him to avoid steroids, but he clearly hasn't listened. Whilst I do not care about steroid usage per se, I care that it messes with one's mental clarity. I will address this issue when all this is over, assuming I survive.

"Get whatever weapons you've got at hand and then wait in the darkness of the alleyway across the road. If you see anyone suspicious spying on, or approaching the boxing club, then call my office phone. I'll give you instructions on how to proceed." He nods his head. "Only take them out yourself if they look like they're going to put someone's life in danger. Do you understand?" I ask knowing that he'll try and take them down on his own no matter what I say to him.

"Of course, Boss. What do you want me to do with the newbie?" He glances back at the unconscious newbie spread-eagled on the canvas.

"Leave him for now; let the others sort him out. I need to clean myself up and sort out a few things. I'll be out of here as soon as possible." He nods his head intensely before jogging to the changing rooms.

I shut my office door and immediately start throwing all the club's boxing trophies off the shelves. Once the trophies have been removed, I rip the shelves off the wall and then remove a few of the wooden wall panels, revealing my hidden safe. I expeditiously throw the safe's dial around, like I've practiced many times before; it takes me seconds to unlock it. I grab the safe's only contents, which is a small holdall, and throw it on my desk. I do not check its contents as I know that it comprises exactly two hundred thousand and a new phone. I slot my SIM card in my new phone and I throw my damaged phone into the safe and lock it.

As I put the wooden wall panels, shelves, and trophies back together, my left eye becomes irritated by the brick dust collecting in it. I start panicking that I'll go blind like I always do when something gets in my eyes. I throw my guns, magazines, grenade, leg sheath, and knife into the holdall. I strip off my clothes. I walk blindly into my personal bathroom and launch myself into a brutally cold shower.

I finish drying my hair and dab the towel around my left eye, which is now functioning properly again after I've rinsed out all the dirt. As soon as I finish zipping up my black hoodie, an explosion of shouting erupts in the boxing club. My office doesn't have any windows, but I can sense the movement and tension building up outside. I open my office door and John-Boy falls into me, headbutting my chest.

He is a weedy, scruffy man, who has ratty facial features and smells particularly bad tonight. He was a drug addict—and had been one from a very young age—who used to work for a local drug dealer. One of his responsibilities was to be a guinea pig, where sample doses from fresh batches of heroin would be injected into him and he would provide the feedback on the quality of the Product before his boss purchased it. Another one of his responsibilities was administrating heroin into his boss' prostitutes and ensuring that they were always kept 'topped up'. Part of his payment for these services was heroin for his own personal consumption. Unfortunately, his tolerance became too high, which resulted in the overdosing of numerous prostitutes. As punishment, he was forced to confess to a murder that was actually committed by his boss.

I was surprised when John-Boy arrived at my boxing club and was extremely reluctant to let him in. However, despite his appearance, and my tendency to avoid working with drug addicts, he convinced me that he had managed to kick his habit whilst in prison and that he was willing to give himself over to my cause. As such, I made what turns out to be the correct decision in giving him the benefit of the doubt. Although, I did initially have my doubts when I first got him into the boxing ring and he collapsed from exhaustion before I got a chance to knock him out.

He is probably one of the most physically inferior man that I've ever met; however, he makes up for it by his sheer determination to bring down drug dealers and human traffickers—which is only rivalled by my own. Even though his former boss, and several former colleagues, were all murdered during his imprisonment, his determination to bring down these types of people has not diminished. In fact, it remains as strong as ever because of all the suffering that they inflicted on him, as well as all the suffering that they manipulated him into inflicting on the innocent people that they trafficked. He cannot bear anyone else having to experience what he or his victims went through.

He has always done what I've asked him to do without hesitation. Plus, we've leveraged his extensive heroin distribution network to our advantage on numerous occasions and, on some of these occasions, it has been pivotal in rescuing trafficked people and bringing those responsible to 'justice'. However, I really do not fully trust him—and never will. It is nothing personal, I just do not trust any drug, or former drug, addicts. Despite this, there is a strange quality and usefulness about him, so I keep him close—probably closer than I should.

John-Boy says something, but I do not catch it; my attention is drawn to the swarm of people that start coalescing around something or someone. I leap down the stairs, three steps at a time, whilst holding onto both bannisters. When I reach the crowd, I forcefully pull back a couple of spectators to reveal a monster of a man in the centre. He slowly regains his consciousness. He rubs the side of his head at the source of the dripping blood. Big Stan is on the opposite side of the gathering to me, staring at me with the look of a loyal servant. He firmly holds a solid gold knuckleduster, which slowly drips blood from its spikes onto the floor.

"Is this who I think it is?" I direct my question at Big Stan, screwing my lips up in anger. I am angry because he has brought a very dangerous man into my boxing gym.

"Yes, it is Aleksandr 'Extra Arm' Kallinski," Big Stan says, now trying to avoid my eye contact as he is aware of my anger and his mistake. "In my defence, I didn't know who it was until I dragged his body into the light. I saw him crouched down and peering through that window over there," he points to the big window on the side of the building. "So, I snuck up behind him and cracked him on the side of his head." I shake my head disapprovingly.

Everyone is getting too close to Extra Arm, who will lash out like a wild beast as soon as he becomes aware of his surroundings. I shout, "Get back everyone. Get back." I push back the two people either side of me.

A minute or two later, his eyes come into focus. He isn't taken aback by the crowd of intimating looking men towering over him, which I was hoping to use to my advantage. I grab his jacket's collar with my left hand and slap him hard with my right hand. It doesn't shock him; in fact, he expects it and, for the time being, he accepts it.

"What the fuck are you doing here? Are you trying to kill me?" I accidentally spit in his face. He ignores me. He closes his eyes and tries to fall back down. I hold him tighter and lift him up higher. "Why are you here?" I demand. He starts talking in Russian then falls into broken English.

"I here to talk to Mr Smith." His eyes are closed as he pronounces each word slowly with a thick Russian accent. "I learn about his Nataliya." My whole world disintegrates at the sound of her name. My heartbeat quickens and becomes more intense. I struggle to stop myself from collapsing. His collar slips out of my grip and his head hits the hard concrete floor. With dead eyes, I look at all the concerned people surrounding me. Mostly everyone here refers to me as either 'Boss' or Mr Buchanan, so they are all curious to know who both Mr Smith and Nataliya are.

Trying not to be sick, I ask slowly, "Tell me what you know?"

He slowly opens his eyes; his lips part into a cruel smile. He knows he has information that I desperately want and will do anything to get. Even with all my friends surrounding him—ready to kill him—he knows that he is in control.

"OK, everyone. Let's give him some space," I command. Some people are slow to step back, so I spread out my arms to physically move them back. "John-Boy, can you please go and get that chair over there?" I point to the chair in the corner. "Also, can someone please get Mr Kallinski an ice pack?"

A couple of guys break away from the circle to get the ice pack. Two other guys pick him up and sit him on the chair that John-Boy places behind him. He seems over-relaxed and annoyingly nonchalant. I have zero patience and am desperate for answers. He is given some ice in a bag and he holds it against his head where Big Stan punched him.

"What do you know about Nataliya?" I glare at him.

He ignores me for several agonising seconds before he replies, "I know where Nataliya is!"

I struggle, but manage for Nataliya's sake, to fight the raging urge to rip off his head.

"Why were you spying on me?" I try to act as though I don't care about Nataliya in an attempt to reduce his leverage on the situation.

"I've been following you ever since you jumped over my taxi," he says this like it's obvious. I think back to the passenger in the back of the taxi outside my apartment. He is correct; I am disappointed in myself for not recognising him. "You very hard man to follow, Mr Smith. But I manage it." He smiles, enjoying his own story. I cannot hide my surprise or annoyance. I relive the journey quickly in my head; I conclude that there is no way he could have followed me here.

"Why the fuck would you, a former world heavyweight boxing champion, be following me?" I do not hide my frustration.

"I now work for Vitali." His pronunciation becomes sloppy as the pain in his head distracts him. He rubs his head with the ice pack in a circular motion.

"Why do you now work for Mikhail's brother?"

"I was a world heavyweight boxing champion. No one could defeat me. For my last fight, Mikhail uses my confidence against me and convinced me into betting all my money, plus more money I had borrowed from Vitali, on me winning." He clenches his jaw angrily before turning his attention back to me. "I didn't feel right when I started boxing; I started to feel very drunk. I quickly realised that I must have been poisoned. I fight as hard as I could, and I thought at one stage that I could possibly won—but the poison, with a little help from my opponent, eventually brought me down. Vitali now has my wife and son as his slaves, and he is going to keep them until I repay my debt." A tear falls down the side of his face as he is reminded of his family.

"So, Vitali has sent you here to kill me?" I speak loudly and clearly as the thought of his family distracts him.

"No, I overheard Vitali, Mikhail, and someone else, who I don't know, talking about the reward for you. I desperate to get my family back. I need to kill you to help get my family." He shuffles his body slightly and his eyes flick to attack mode. He is in a fight or flight situation—and he has chosen fight. I am already in a strong stance and prepared to defend against an attack. Even so, I need to be amicable to keep him calm until he at least told me where Nataliya is.

"Surely this situation could easily be resolved if I simply pay off your debt in exchange for information on her whereabouts?" I say, honestly. I will pay any price to rescue her. He naturally assumes that I am messing with him and disregards my olive branch. I scan the faces of all the men surrounding us; their concern, concerns me.

"Nataliya is where my family." His eyes flick to desperation so I take a quick deep breath.

Like a striking cobra, he shoots forward towards me with his hands stretched out, ready to grab me by the throat. I knock his hands to one side as I step backwards. Big Stan jumps on his back and wraps his arms around his throat. Several other brave men dive on him and help Big Stan wrestle him back down to the floor. He resists and tries to squirm his way free, but everyone manages to keep him restrained on the ground. Big Carl lightly pushes past me and places his knee on his temple, pinning his head to the ground. Slowly, as his energy depletes, he calms down. He completely gives up fighting when he realises that escape is futile.

I smile at him with sincere sympathy. His attack is not personal; my life is the only thing standing between him and his family.

"OK." I wipe away the saliva oozing from his mouth with my hoodie's sleeve. "We will get our loved ones back!" I promise. He closes his eyes and shakes his head in disbelief.

"Impossible. It can never be done. The only way for me to get my family back is to kill you." His eyes are drawn to the boxing ring. "We fight?" His eyes light up as his own idea surprises him.

There is no time to fight him, but he is a very strong man and torturing him will probably take a long time. After weighing up my options, I conclude that the quickest route to finding Nataliya's whereabouts is to fight him. Everyone looks at me with keen interest as they await my decision. Even though I view most of these men as friends, I can see in their eyes that they want to see how good of a fighter I really am, even if that places me at risk of a serious injury, or worse, as a result.

"Are there no other options, my friend?" My patience wears thin. "Every second we waste here will feel like a painful eternity to your family and Nataliya. I am literally begging you to reconsider." He tries to reply, but his lungs cannot draw in any air due to the pressure of all the men on top of him. I put my face closer to him, and he spits in it. "As you wish." I drop my head, shoulders, and voice in disappointment. He smiles at me even more cruelly than before whilst I wipe away his spit.

I flick off my shoes and socks before jumping into the boxing ring. I have fought over hundred different individuals in this boxing ring and this is the first time that I've not wanted to. I start jogging on the spot whilst windmilling my arms around and rolling my head from side to side in a lame attempt to loosen myself up. Some of my muscles and joints, particularly in my lower back, have already started to stiffen up from the ordeal that they've been through tonight.

In one fluid motion, he rolls sideways on the canvas and then up into an upright position, all six foot seven inches of him. He throws his jacket out of the boxing ring before effortlessly ripping off his t-shirt, revealing an intimidating amount of muscle mass. His body is covered in the usual tattoos donned by Russian criminals. These tattoos are new because he never had them during his boxing career. He throws his t-shirt at me and, as it flies towards me, I prepare for a follow-up attack. But there isn't one. I catch it and throw it in the direction of his jacket.

A pair of boxing gloves land in front of him and, as they bounce, he kicks one of them back out of the boxing ring. He wants to fight me with bare knuckles. This suits me fine; it is what I am used to. He shuffles his weight from side to side and starts jabbing the air furiously. I can feel the draught created by his jabs as he slowly dances his way over to me.

I start to dredge up very serious internal anger to pump up my adrenaline levels, whilst ensuring that I externally appear cool, calm, and collected. Everyone is deadly silent; the only noise comes from the canvas groaning under Extra Arm's shuffling weight. He stares at me with unwarranted evilness in his eyes. He has frustrated me greatly as we should be working together, not fighting each other. I need to make sure that this frustrating situation doesn't impact my judgement. We don't need to explain the ground rules of the fight as there are none. We need to keep fighting until one of us surrenders, or, in an extreme case, when one of us is killed—although, I am hoping Big Stan and my men would help me out before it got that far.

I slowly take off my own t-shirt to reveal a muscular body. It is not as impressive as his; nonetheless, it takes him by surprise. He slows down his shuffling and slouches a little bit, but just for a moment. I could try and dissuade him again, but he is a proud man and will not accept the peace offering. I cannot recall any of his noticeable weaknesses or fighting styles as I desperately attempt to remember his fights. The only thing I can remember is that his trademark is to go in strong from the start.

He charges at me and punches me hard with his left. I block the blow with my forearm, but it forces my whole body back. Immediately, he follows it up with his right. Again, I block, but barely. Then, out of nowhere, I receive a powerful, unexpected blow from his 'extra arm' to my lower abdomen; the wind is knocked right out of me. I desperately suck in air, but none enters my lungs; there isn't time to worry about oxygen. With all his strength, he keeps swinging wildly, out of control. I block most of his punches, but a couple to my abdomen get through.

This causes me to mistakenly lower my guard slightly. He takes advance of the situation with a hard right aimed at the side of my face, which I dodge, although as he pulls his fist back, he clips it. I know he is former world heavyweight boxing champion, but his speed, power, precision, and aggression has taken me by surprise.

He concentrates his next burst of attacks on my now extremely tender abdomen again. I keep my guard high even though I cannot take many more hits; it feels like all my ribs are about to break. He begins to tire and slowly moves his attention higher to my guarded face. His right hook demolished my guard and connects with my face with a force that I didn't think was possible. I try to stay on my feet, but my legs go limp and the canvas becomes ice-like.

In the blink of an eye, the side of my face becomes hot from sliding over the canvas. I am momentarily paralysed, sprawled out on the canvas. As I start to regain the use of my limbs, he stamps on the back of my head. My face ploughs back into the canvas; my nose pours with blood on impact. I lift my head up, leaving a bloody face print behind. Another stamp on the back of my head forces my face into the pool of blood.

Through tears and blood, I make out the blurry mixture of shock and concern displayed on all my friends' faces. Several of them climb up onto the boxing ring ropes, but I wave them back. He seizes the opportunity to boot my exposed ribs. He'll kill me soon if I don't move quickly. I desperately avoid allowing myself to embrace the comfort of the canvas.

I roll onto my back and my unconscious reactions stop most of the power from his next kick. He is slow to withdraw his foot, so I seize it with all my strength. I spin my body around and kick the side of his right knee with my heel. He collapses and awkwardly hits the canvas hard. I quickly perform a backwards roll to escape the danger zone. I get on my feet too quickly and feel faint for a couple of seconds. Blood drips from my nose, but there is no time to worry about it, let alone try to stem it.

His mouth foams angrily as he is unaccustomed to getting back to his feet. Once he is upright, his right knee buckles violently. He momentarily loses his balance but manages to remain upright. I have winged the beast. He stumbles around for a bit, trying to get his knee back under his control, which has given me a much-needed opportunity to get my breath back. His feeling of confidence transmutes to worry. It dawns on him that he has never fought anyone like me before and that he is ill prepared for the type of fight this fight is fast becoming.

He walks cautiously back over to me; I start jumping around in an attempt to reduce his confidence further. He releases a round of jabs, but they are not nearly as forceful or committed as before. I let one of his jabs hit my shoulder and follow his withdrawing arm with my own jab aimed at his face. He easily blocks it, but my audacity takes him by surprise.

He forces me into a corner where he unloads a round of solid punches in quick succession. This time, most of the punches hit the sides of my face as he desperately tries to further damage my nose. He unleashes a wild haymaker with his left, which I block by forcing my left elbow to his forearm. I response unpredictably by spinning around quickly and elbowing his right eye. As I withdraw my elbow, the fresh cut below his right eye leaks blood. His eye swells quickly, forcing it to close. I spin back around to my original position and follow up with a powerful right hook to his chin, knocking him back several steps. That must have hurt him; it certainly hurt my fist.

He lunges forward and attacks me; I try to move my face out of the path of one of his punches, but his knuckle digs deep into my cheek. Ignoring the pain in my cheek, I drop down on my right knee and punch his right knee with all my strength. His knee buckles and I narrowly avoid a wild kick that he throws as he collapses onto the canvas again.

I move to the opposite side of the boxing ring from him in order to catch my breath again. The damage I have caused him will not slow him down for long. The thought of his family will override any level of pain. The rate of blood rushing out of my nose has resided, so I wipe the residual blood away with the back of my hand. He presents a well-formed guard as he limps back over to me. I cannot take many more big hits from him; I need to stop him from getting too close. I step towards him and jab his face with my left, jab his abdomen with my right, and then, as he lowers his guard slightly, I swing my left violently at his face, but he blocks it completely.

He bombards me with another round of attacks, all of which I manage to defend against. When I think he has stopped, he smashes his right fist straight through my guard and I am too slow to withdraw my head. He clips my face causing a small cut above my left eye. Blood drips from the cut and I can feel it begin to swell. He swings a right hook, which I narrowly avoid and instantly respond with several rapid, hard punches to his ribs. My fists quickly become sore from punching his brick-wall-like abdomen. Out of nowhere, his fist skims the top of my head and I stumble back against the ropes. We both stop for a second, desperate for a break.

I do not have time to get away from the ropes before he steams over to me with another powerful barrage of attacks. He makes contact several times. As he slows down, I lower my guard and leave the left side of my head exposed. As predicted, he swings a right hook forcefully to the left side of my face. I duck just in time and punch the side of his right knee as hard as I can again with my right fist. The momentum of his missed punch and the power delivered to his injured right knee causes him to plough into the ropes and bounce off them.

I violently twist my body around and jump in the air. I kick him hard in the chest, causing him to stumble back into the ropes again. I land on my back, roll over and am immediately back to my feet again, ready to fight. He unsuccessfully tries to hold himself in the boxing ring as he falls through the ropes. He takes a couple of my friends down to the ground with him. He hits the floor with his forehead. He remains face down and motionless for several seconds. He looks like he is unconscious, but I have my doubts. A couple of my friends approach him; I wave them away again. Oxygen rushes to fill the alveoli in my lungs so I cannot shout them away.

After about thirty seconds, he starts rolling around on the floor before attempting to get back to his feet. His right knee is useless to him and greatly hinders his ability to stand. He thinks that is family depend on him getting into an upright position, so he adapts to the situation by balancing all his body weight on his left leg. My friends give him a wide berth as he hobbles back to the boxing ring.

Something stored underneath the boxing ring takes his attention away from me. He reaches down and pulls out a metal bar that was most likely being stored there by one of the guys. Some of them surround themselves with hidden weapons so that one is always within easy reach in the event of an emergency. This is a survival ritual they developed during their prison sentences.

He rolls back into the boxing ring under the bottom rope. He uses the metal bar as a crutch to assist himself getting back to his feet. He proudly waves the metal bar around, playfully swinging it near my face. My friends are now very concerned about my safety as he is not playing 'fair'. I can feel their tension building up. I say matter-of-factly, "Please put that down before one of us gets hurt."

"What you mean, before *one* of us gets hurt?" He holds the weapon confidently, acting puzzled. I try to hide my delight regarding the change of circumstances. He doesn't realise that he is far more dangerous in a fistfight. I am very experienced in both hand-to-hand and weapons combat. He had a good chance of beating me in a hand-to-hand combat situation, but the odds have now swung in my favour. He has a few practice swings like a baseball player warming up.

With his first committed swing, I wait until the metal bar gets close to me before pulling myself back. The metal bar skims over my abdomen. Once the metal bar has uninterruptedly been swung past my body, I follow up with a round of hard punches to his face. His granite-like jaw causes painful shockwaves to resonate up my arm after every blow. For the first time, I start forcing him back— but it feels too easy.

He doesn't even try to protect his head, instead, he accepts the hits. I quickly grow tired and cannot sustain the power and intensity of the punches. As soon as the period between my punches increases, he seizes on the opportunity and swings the metal bar at me with the power of a professional baseball player. This time it clips my left arm, rendering it useless. Using my remaining fist, I jab his face quickly, but the force is too weak to cause him any significant damage.

As he pulls back the metal bar again, I kick his right knee with the sole of my foot. His leg bends awkwardly out of place as I drive my foot forward until his knee snaps loudly. As he falls towards the canvas, I jump in the air, pull back my right arm as far as I can, and punch him in the face with of all the force I can muster. The side of his head smashes into the canvas first, swiftly followed by the rest of his body. He isn't knocked out, only severely dazed.

I carefully roll him onto his back with my foot, whilst being mindful that he could grab it and pull me down next to him. His arms lie lifelessly either side of him. Swelling slowly fills the craters where his eyes used to be. Blood gurgles in his throat as he struggles to breathe. I sway from side to side, trying to keep my balance. I take ownership of the metal bar and leave a trail of blood and sweat in my wake as I move to a safe distance away from him.

"Where is Nataliya?" I take deep breaths between each word.

"Vitali has handed them over to Mikhail in order to keep them out of my reach. I believe that Mikhail has stored them, along with other captives, in his captives' house, which next door to his house. This house also serves as his escape house." He exhales deeply; he is defeated.

"Do you mean his new riverside mansion?" I have recently become aware that Mikhail has bought a very large mansion next to the river, but I've been too ill to reconnoitre it.

"Da." He wipes a mixture of his and my blood away from his eyes.

"How do you know this?"

"Vitali bought the house next to his own and connected them with an underground tunnel." His eyes go heavy. "So, I suspect that Mikhail has employed the same system."

My mind races back several months ago when Emma found out that the police were following the Roldugin brothers, and their entourage, around the city. These people are experienced in tunnel warfare from their days in the Russian army. They are suspects in many European bank robberies and drug smuggling operations. The police informed all the banks in the city to prepare for a tunnel attack, but a couple of days after their arrival, they disappeared. Not a single bank was touched. I now suspect that they were here digging Mikhail's tunnel. I'll need to get Emma to find out if the police saw them with Mikhail, or Vitali, or any of their close associates.

"I also believe that my wife and children, and I assume Nataliya as well, carry out menial work for Mikhail during the day." He turns into a scared child right before my eyes. "Tomorrow night, there is a party at Mikhail's house, well on his yacht. That is when you rescue Nataliya." His voice fades away as he passes out. This draws me in and I crouch down closer to him so that I can better hear what he is saying.

Whilst I think about whether I will need his help to get our loved ones back, I lose concentration for only a split second, but it is enough time for him to try and take advantage of the situation. He thrusts himself forwards and attempts to grab my throat again. I simultaneously fall back so that I can use my whole-body weight to break free from his closing, and soon-to-be unbreakable, grip and swing the metal bar towards his temple. The metal bar 'dings' loudly when it connects with his temple.

His eyes roll into the back of his head and his unconscious body falls limply on top of me, pinning me down. I let the metal bar roll away so that I can put more energy into getting his body off mine. But it is useless: I am too weak. As my eyes close, several of my friends jump into the boxing ring to free me.

Chapter 10
Prescription Barbiturates

A shockwave pulsates through my body, which, for a split second, I mistake as a hypnic jerk; however, it is a result of Big Stan dropping me onto an old, knackered sofa, which cracks fatally as it embraces me. Its arm doesn't offer much padding; my head hits the internal woodchip board with a thump. This pain is immediately overridden by all my other aches and pains from the fight vying for my attention. I am extremely vexed at myself for exposing my body to this much pain and destruction this early on in my quest to retrieve Nataliya and destroy Mikhail.

I take fast, shallow breaths to fuel my recovering body, which is starting to seize up and become cemented by the build-up of lactic acid. I am exhausted and drift in and out of sleep as people busy themselves around me. Even with my eyes closed, I make out the blue flashing lights of an emergency vehicle pulling up outside.

Before I drift into an even deeper sleep, I am awoken by water dripping onto my face. I open my eyes slowly to express annoyance. Big Stan stands over me and hurriedly wipes sweat from his forehead with the back of his hand.

"We've got a bit of a situation, Boss," he says in a much-panicked tone. "Despite me trying to ban the use of phones in the boxing club, a newbie called an ambulance for the newbie that I knocked out before your fight.

"Well, tell them it was a false alarm."

"I have been trying to. We managed to hide the newbie and Extra Arm out of sight in the men's changing room, but, unfortunately, the paramedics saw you lying here covered in blood through the open front door. They're now threatening to call the police if we don't let them in to see you. What should we do? What if they're here to kill you?"

"OK, calm down. It's not a problem. I do not believe anyone else knows that I'm here. Here's what is going to happen. I want you to pick me up and carry me to the ambulance. That way the paramedics will be so concerned about helping me they will not question anything else going on in here. To cover ourselves, if questioned, you need to make it clear that it was only you that I was boxing. I expect that the paramedics will call the police to cover themselves when they leave, if they haven't done so already.

If the police come, you'll need to provide them with a statement, and, if necessary, go back to the police station with them." I grin widely. He momentarily looks scared at the thought of going back to a police station. "Don't worry, you won't go back to prison."

"I am not worried about that. I am more bothered about you suing me." He laughs awkwardly. "What do you want us to do with Extra Arm?"

"He is to remain in my office as my 'guest' until you hear back from me. If the police take you to the station, then I want John Boy to take charge of looking after him. Make sure that he is comfortable and keep reassuring him that I'll get his family back for him. Do not take any chances with him. As you've seen already tonight, he is a very dangerous man." The voices by the entrance start getting louder as the impatient paramedics start forcing their way into the boxing club. "Also, please inform Emma that Mikhail has Nataliya." He nods his head seriously.

"I'll call her as soon as I've dropped you off."

"OK then, mate—let's get on with this." My eyes close as I lose the fight to keep them open.

Big Stan puts his arms around me and effortlessly launches me into a fireman's lift. On our way to the ambulance, Big Carl runs up to me and grips my left arm, which is still dead from being hit by the metal bar.

"You are one motherfucking badass. I cannot believe it; you were incredible. That was the best fight I've ever seen. You were, you were so amazing! I also can't believe that I nearly beat you," he says like a child meeting their hero for the first time. "I could probably go professional." I force a laugh out to hide my annoyance that he should have been in the car waiting for me. Luckily for him, I do not have time to give him the bollocking he deserves.

"Big Carl, I need your help." He goes instantly quiet as he hears the annoyance and disappointment in my voice from him disobeying my order. As soon as we step outside, a cold wind blows my body's heat away. "I need you to get my holdall out of my office and **follow the ambulance**. I'll try and escape from it before we reach the hospital; **however, if** I don't manage to escape then you need to drive to Battersea Road, **which is opposite** the hospital's multi-storey carpark. You'll need to keep your **engine running** and lights on, I'll try not to keep you waiting too long."

Before Big Carl gets a chance to **either accept** or question my orders, I am thrown off Big Stan's shoulder and **dropped harshly** onto the stretcher. I begin to shiver uncontrollably; Big Stan **places his hoodie** over my upper body. A paramedic starts fussing over me and **asking me questions**, but I do not respond. Instead, I close my eyes and try to **fall asleep**.

The stretcher is slammed into the **back of the ambulance**, waking me up with a violent jerk. I open my eyes and see **an oxygen cylinder** in front of me, which, as Dr Black told me, would **be perfect** for further lowering my carboxyhaemoglobin levels. Before **I get a chance** to ask for it, I growl loudly like a captured lion when, without **warning, the paramedic** injects morphine into my already cannulated left arm. I **internally question** whether I qualify for morphine, but because of the aggression **he received** at the boxing club, he may want me sedated to keep me calm **until we reach** the hospital. Unethical, but understandable. I don't mind; I would **do the same** in his situation.

My whining goes unnoticed by **him. I think** about escaping from the ambulance, but a hot tantalising flow **enters my** vein and travels slowly up my arm. It works its way to my heart and **from there** it is pumped around my body. I love this feeling, and this is why, **under certain** circumstances, I can be sympathetic to drug, or former drug, **addicts. I lose** control of my body; my eyes roll around with the movement of the **ambulance**. Inner peace takes hold of me and removes the thought of escaping.

The ambulance's siren resonates **drowsily in my** ears as we meander around traffic. I am taken off the stretcher, **out of the** ambulance, and placed on an inflatable lilo, floating on the **Caribbean's gentle** crystal-clear sea. The sun's intense radiation softly browns my **young, unwrinkled** skin. The cool wind gently rolls newly formed beads of sweat off **my body**.

I begin to feel a little overheated so **I reach over** to the lilo's inbuilt cup holder and grab my large, brightly coloured, **and heavily** garnished cocktail drink. As I take a sip, the paper umbrella harshly **stabs my upper** lip. The local birds chirp softly in their native tongues. They **provide relaxing** background noise until they get interrupted by the sound of splashing water when Nataliya clumsily runs into the sea.

The ambulance abruptly comes to a halt, rocking me viciously out of my relaxing dream. The paramedic who was driving the ambulance opens the back doors and helps my attending paramedic roll me out of the ambulance. One of them pushes the stretcher from the back, whilst the other one steers it from the front towards what is an ugly, unwelcoming concrete behemoth of a hospital. Big Stan's hoodie has been replaced by a thin sheet, but it is my morphine coat that protects me from the cold, harsh night. I am exposed under the black cloudless night's sky until I pass under the intense heat from the electric heaters positioned above the A&E department's double doors.

The A&E department is typically busy, but Lukas' trigger-happy killing frenzy earlier is causing it to burst at the seams. The paramedics have great difficulty manoeuvring the stretcher through the crowds of impatient patients waiting to be seen. The rowdy drunks, who are battered and bruised from getting themselves into fights that they didn't have the faculties to win, are now looking for any excuse to kick-off and fight someone to redeem their pride and purpose. The audacious drug addicts are here to try and con the hospital staff into handing them any kind of drug to keep their unbearable addiction at bay throughout the night. Several homeless people try to hide in plain sight to stay warm. The genuinely ill and injured patients are sitting quietly, biding their time, whilst trying to cover up their symptoms and pain.

A particularly intoxicated patient, who is oblivious to us, staggers into our path and the stretcher hits him painfully on the side of his knee. This collision goes unnoticed as he is protected by his beer armour, but the force causes him to lose his balance and fall surprisingly graciously on the hard, cold, and what feels like a bacteria-ridden floor. Another intoxicated patient, maybe his friend, clumsily tries to help him up, but his good deed is mistaken as the instigation of a fight. He is pushed back against the stretcher; I take the opportunity to swipe a set of keys from his back pocket. There are several keys, so I take what appears to be the sharpest one and discreetly place it between my first and index finger, before enclosing the remaining keys in my fist.

My heartbeat starts to rise when I think about the danger that I am putting all these innocent people in; however, I cannot escape because the morphine keeps me fixed on the stretcher—I will have to wait for the morphine to wear off. The general layout of the hospital is already in my head, and as we make our way deeper into it, I update it with additional information, such as the locations of the fire escapes, toilets, storerooms, etc. In dangerous and life-threatening situations, one sometimes only manages to survive by knowing the immediate area and leveraging it to their advantage.

We enter a patient ward adjacent to the hectic A&E waiting room. It has a relatively subdued atmosphere. All the bays, except the one that I am pushed into, have their privacy curtains drawn. These curtains do nothing to muffle the sound of the pain and suffering being experienced behind them. As soon as the paramedics finish transferring me to a hospital bed, they get a call informing them of their next pick up. A very stressed and exhausted nurse appears at the end of my bed; she gets a quick brief from the paramedics before they have to rush to their next job.

From the nurse's appearance, it is safe to say that the kindness, empathy, and love provided by her has been very much taken for granted; but, despite the many undervalued, underpaid, and degrading years, she has not lost sight of her duty of care. The long, busy shifts, combined with unbearable stress and tragedy, have prematurely aged her complexion, and the disruption to her eating habits have made her vulnerable to weight issues—she looks after everyone apart from herself. She picks up the chart that has mysteriously appeared at the end of my bed.

She says with a strong local accent, "Sorry for the delay, love—it's chaos here tonight. It says here," she pointing at the chart, "that you've been in a fight." She looks up and scans my body. "I probably could have deduced that from your appearance." She smiles good-naturedly; I return the smile. "You wouldn't believe the number of people I've dealt with from fighting. Although, I've not seen many of them receiving such as good a going over as you've received."

I nod my head and let out a chuckle, but it gets cut short by the pain in my ribs. Before the nurse has a chance to read my notes any further, a high-pitched alarm beckons in the distance. This alarm is instantaneously accompanied by shouts and screams from all the hospital staff as they rush to the source of the noise. She looks at me and rolls her eyes.

"Jesus, not again. There was a shootout earlier tonight; there are so many gunshot victims. We've had two deaths and six in a critical condition, so far; and more are heading our way as we speak, I believe." She throws the chart onto the bottom of the bed before turning to leave. As she runs out of my bay, she uninterruptedly grabs the curtain and throws it across my bay. She doesn't throw it hard enough for it to fully close. Through the gap, I can see all the hospital staff undertaking their roles superbly; they are all working in complete harmony to rapidly address the emergency situation.

After several minutes, an East Asian doctor squeezes through the gap in the curtains and steps into my bay. I now know the identity of Mikhail's third non-Russian assassin. He pulls the curtain fully closed behind him, and we both nod our heads at each other in acknowledgement.

"You've not lived up to your reputation, Mr Smith. Or, should I say, Mr Kallinski?" Hiromi says, smiling sinisterly. Hiromi is not his real name; he is Chinese, not Japanese—as his name tries to suggest. He works for the Dragon Master—the boss of the Chinese Mafia—whom I have a good relationship with, or I thought I did at least. I shrug my shoulders nonchalantly. "This might be my easiest kill yet."

I stare at him in silence, pondering why one of the Dragon Master's assassins is here. "Do you want to know the story of your downfall, Mr Smith? How I came to your bedside?" He grabs my chart and acts as though he is interested in it. The formality in his approach does not faze me, although, I am curious why he didn't just shoot me as he walked past my bay.

"Does the Dragon Master know you're here?"

"He loaned me to Mikhail." I nod my head. The Dragon Master has been trying to build bridges with Mikhail in an attempt to reduce the bloodshed between both of their organisations. This must be why the members of the Murder Squad were unhappy and didn't trust him. "My orders from the Dragon Master were to subserviently carry out all of Mikhail's orders, unless they involved the harming of anyone of Chinese descent, both directly and indirectly. Despite you not meeting this caveat, I still sought his permission to go after you. I thought he would be interested in your assassination, especially considering all the trouble that you've caused his organisation."

"And what did he say?"

"He told me to proceed as I saw fit." He smiles sinisterly again.

"How did you find me?" I ask, trying to buy my liver as much time as possible.

"I didn't, not exactly. During the meeting I had with Mikhail to discuss your hit, he told me that he had already poisoned you, so the hit would be as easy as shooting a sedated bear caught in a bear trap. Before we had finished talking,

Vitali showed up. Extra Arm was lingering in the background, and I knew that he would do anything to get his family back.

"Therefore, I orchestrated it that my conversation with Mikhail got loud enough for Extra Arm to overhear it. I did this because I am not arrogant enough to assume that I can take you on solely by myself—even if Mikhail was telling the truth about your situation. So, I manipulated Extra Arm to do all the legwork in tracking you down and risk his own life to physically weaken you further before I considered going after you. I simply put a tracker on his phone and followed the signal until it settled on the boxing gym. I picked up the trail from there and, alas, here we are."

"A very good plan; it has worked very well for you."

He withdraws a curved blade from his inside coat pocket. I've seen this type of blade before in the Dragon Master's collection. I think he told me that this type of blade is typically infused with a poison, killing you with a single, minor cut. Even though I am in a hospital, I doubt anyone could stop the poison in time should it enter my bloodstream. Plus, it would be my luck that it would be some ancient Chinese recipe that this hospital doesn't have the equipment, knowledge, or antidote to deal with it.

He walks towards me, but only makes half the distance before he is interrupted mid-stride by an exhausted doctor entering my bay. This forces him to shuffle suspiciously to angle his body sideways in order to hide his blade from the genuine doctor.

The doctor speaks first, "Oh, sorry, doctor. I was informed that this is my patient. The nurse must have made a mistake," he says, yawning widely. He walks over to Hiromi with his left hand outstretched to shake hands whilst he places his stethoscope around his neck with his right hand. Hiromi is forced to put my chart down on my bed to shake his hand. "My name is Karl Jenkins, well Dr Jenkins." He looks over at me, remembering that he is in a professional setting. "This is only my second shift at this hospital." Hiromi looks down at his own name badge.

"My name is Dr Johnson; it is very nice to meet you." Dr Jenkins has a good poker face, but I can tell that he is discreetly taken aback by Hiromi's identify. "Yes, the nurse must have made a mistake; it is an easy mistake to make with all chaos tonight. It is despicable that people are still getting machine-gunned down in the streets in this day and age. We'll both be working solidly for the next twenty-four hours, at least."

"Yes, it is despicable. Bullets cause unbelievable damage, and the little bastards tend to reside in a different location to what their trajectory path would suggest after they have ricocheted around the inside of the body." He shakes his head in disgust. "And, to make matters worse, we've now also got firearms officers patrolling the hospital slowing us down further; they believe that if the shooter didn't finish the job, then they might come here to finish it." Hiromi also shakes his head. "Anyway, I best crack on, my waiting list is already ridiculously long—twenty-four hours will pass in no time at all. Nice to meet you anyway; give me a shout if you need any help. I'll see you around."

"Yes, nice to meet you too, Dr Jenkins. Good luck." They both shake hands again.

As Dr Jenkins turns to leave, he looks back at me. I smile and nod; he does the same. Hiromi repositions the blade enough in my peripheral vision for me to steal a look at it. Dr Jenkins follows my line of sight in the mirror positioned above the sink. His gaze settles on the blade for the smallest fraction of time before looking back at me. He looks me in the eyes; I cannot help but look anxious. I produce another quick smile that lets him know that he is OK to leave. He looks at Hiromi, who smiles back. His lingering causes the tension in the bay to grow noticeably. He remains motionless whilst he contemplates his next move.

"Please leave," I say in my head. "Forget about the Hippocratic Oath." I will not be able to save him before Hiromi rams the blade into his neck. I relax slightly when he grabs hold of the curtain to leave. He steps forward, then all of a sudden, he has a change of mind and releases the curtain. He spins around and walks back to me.

"Actually, Dr Johnson, I am sure that this is my patient; I'll just check the chart to put the matter to rest?" The chart is at the end of my bed, but he must pass Hiromi to get to it.

"I can assure you, Dr Jenkins—this is *my* patient. He is not in a critical condition, so your time would be better spent dealing with those out there that have been shot, instead of being here," Hiromi says, but it falls on deaf ears.

"That may be true, but I need to see that chart; otherwise, I could get prosecuted for negligence. You know that I need to see that chart." He straightens his back, preparing himself to become physically confrontational.

Dr Jenkins suddenly launches himself forward, attempting to snatch my patient chart off the bed, but Hiromi knocks his hand away. His posh shoes slip on the smooth floor, but that doesn't **stop him from** trying again; Hiromi easily blocks his second attempt. He seems **to have become** too preoccupied with getting my chart that he has forgotten about Hiromi's blade. He feigns a third attempt, before throwing himself at the panic alarm. Hiromi is fooled into trying to stop him from reaching the chart. Hiromi responds to the deception by swiping the blade over his face and neck just after he has pressed the panic alarm.

Dr Jenkins' blood sprays all over Hiromi and the curtain. He grabs his neck and staggers back towards me. Hiromi pushes him hard in my direction, and he falls along my midriff. He cries out in pain; the cut is not too deep and hasn't hit any arteries. He'll survive—unless the blade is infused with poison. Hiromi now turns his attention to me.

"Any last words, Mr Smith?"

"Nope, let's get on with it," I respond, impatiently.

"As you wish." He raises his blade high in the air. As the blade accelerates down towards my exposed neck, I stab the key fixed tightly in my knuckle into his abdomen. His blood sprays all over my face as I withdraw the key. He screams out in pain, surprise, and anger. I manage to stab the key into his abdomen once more before he steps back away from my bed. He drops his blade on the floor as he slams back into the wall. He wraps his arms awkwardly around himself to try and stop the bleeding from both puncture wounds. As I try to slip out from being pinned down by Dr Jenkins, he rolls under the curtain into the adjacent patient bay, leaving behind a trail of blood.

I lift Dr Jenkins up slightly, slowly slip my legs out from under him, and get out of bed. My body is slow, and I quickly get out of breath. I do not have time for my body to slow me down as I need to hunt for Hiromi whilst he is wounded. I throw on Big Stan's hoodie and fasten it up. I peel back my curtain, expecting to have to find a way to sneak past the hospital's staff; however, they are all completely focused on treating their own patients. A nurse materialises from behind the curtain of the patient bay opposite me. She is petrified when I grab her and pull her into my bay. She takes one look at Dr Jenkins flapping about on the bed and starts screaming and thrashing about uncontrollably. I manage to hold onto her, keeping her attention on him.

"Please calm down; I promise you that I'm not going to hurt you. I really need you to concentrate on saving Dr Jenkins' life." Her eyes are fixated on the blade on the floor; she is literally scared stiff. "I didn't do it by the way." I slowly release my hold on her, but instead of doing her duty, I allow her to rip herself from my weak grip and run away. Two armed security guards walk past the ward's exit doors as she runs screaming through the curtain. As the curtain swings back, I lock eyes with them both through the closing gap.

I leave my patient bay in the same fashion that Hiromi left it, following his trail of blood. The patient in the adjacent patient bay is attached to various drips and machines; he looks at me with lifeless eyes. Before I follow the path of blood into the patient bay on the opposite side, I do a double take. It is Extra Arm's taxi driver. I mouth the words, "I'm sorry," but they don't register with him.

The next patient bay is actually empty, and on its far side is the ward's external wall. This bay also contains a few droplets of blood. I peer through the front curtain as the two security guards steam into my assigned patient bay. I dive, roll, and stay low behind the nurse's station. No one is looking over at this area of the ward as everyone, apart from the two security guards, is either concentrating on staying alive, or keeping someone else alive.

One security guard looks very frightened as he scans around the ward searching for me whilst talking on his walkie-talkie. The other security guard rushes into the adjacent bay that contains the taxi driver; he is following the trail of blood. The ward doors open and two porters roll in another patient on a trolley. I crouch behind the moving trolley and dive through the closing doors, barely managing to squeeze through them before they close.

Several people notice me as I roll into the overcrowded A&E waiting room; however, they don't pay me any attention as they've got their own problems. I pick up the trail of blood and try to follow it through the waiting room, but, within a couple of steps, most of it has been trodden in and become very faint. Before I get into the range of the sensor for the double doors, four police cars screech to a halt about ten feet in front of me, forcing me to dive to one side and out of view. They'll be looking for someone who fits my description, and it is currently impossible to hide within plain sight, especially as my feet are bare. I turn and head to the opposite side of the waiting room.

I take a quick look over my shoulder and instantly recognise Lukas' wide, well-built frame hidden unsuccessfully underneath a large, black overcoat; he enters the waiting room, disguised as a homeless man. His conscience disregards the numerous people between us as he withdraws two submachine guns from his overcoat. He pulls back both triggers before his guns are pointed anywhere near me.

The sustained rapid fire from each gun home in on me using a pincer movement. The bullets mercilessly rip through everyone and everything in their path. Screams, blood, and concrete dust suffocate the waiting room. Patients and hospital staff push and fight one another, desperate to escape this horror. I take a deep breath and everything turns into slow motion. Before the two lines of bullets zippers through my midriff, I turn and clumsy launch myself over two rows of fully occupied benches positioned back-to-back.

I lie still on the floor as blood from my human shield rains down on me. Before I get a chance to wipe the blood out of my eyes, dead bodies start falling and piling up on top of me. The roaring guns go quiet. Whilst he reloads, I push the dead bodies off me. With a thin layer of blood and bodily fluid acting as a lubricant, I slide effortlessly between all the dead bodies and under the next two rows of benches behind me. The next round of bullets mows down all the petrified patients who were cemented in their seats on these rows. A porter half enters the waiting room pushing a patient lying on a trolley when they are both riddled with bullets. The trolley is wedged between the double doors, allowing bullets to leave the waiting room, and foment their chaos, destruction, and death in the corridor.

My adrenaline overpowers the morphine in my bloodstream, giving my muscles enough energy and power to launch myself towards the trolley. There is now nothing and no one between myself and his guns. They start roaring proudly again, and his bullets start hitting my shadow on the wall. I cannot propel myself up onto the trolley as the floor is too slippery. A person in my path tries to push themselves up. I regret even having the thought, but I have no other chance of escaping this bloodbath alive than to put my blood-covered foot onto their blood-drenched denim jacket.

I soar through the air a distance of about two metres before crash landing on the murdered patient lying on the trolley. The force of my impact causes the trolley to move back out through the double doors into the corridor. I jerk forward on top of the deceased patient when the trolley collides with a parked, patientless trolley. The infinitely long corridor contains many people, and they all scramble past one another in order to hastily escape the forthcoming carnage.

Warm blood oozing from the deceased patient's bullet wounds is absorbed by Big Stan's hoodie, making my skin feel uncomfortable. Lukas keeps firing at the double doors. The bullets that hit the doors are stopped by them, but several of them manage to slip through gap, which diminishes every time they swing past each other as they draw to a close, and hit the wall next to me.

I roll off the deceased patient as Lukas pushes both double doors open with the barrels of his guns. Before he starts firing again, I kick open the door in front of me, and throw myself into the stairwell. He keeps his fingers on the triggers as I travel up the first flight of stairs. I head towards the roof; I need to draw him away from all these innocent people and give myself enough time to think of a plan to take him down.

As I leave the platform between the first and second floors, he fires a burst of bullets at me. I throw my body against the back wall, keeping out of his direct line of sight. I grab hold of the bannister and thrust myself up the next flight of stairs. My feet feel the vibrations from his bullets hitting the underside of the concrete staircase. I barely make it off the next floor before he starts firing again. Third floor, fourth floor, fifth floor. Even though he is carrying two guns, he is hot on my tail. I am quickly running out of breath and energy, and there are still four more floors left until I reach the roof. For the first time in many years, a stitch burns hot on the side of my stomach; I won't make it to the roof.

On the staircase leading to the sixth floor, the walls are plastered with copies of the same poster. As I continue my ascension, I read a snippet of information from each one. They inform me that the whole of the sixth floor has been vacated for renovation purposes. When I reach the sixth floor, I pull back the plastic sheet that covers the double doors. These doors are locked, but I easily shoulder barge them open.

Lukas releases another round of bullets as I step across the threshold. I smash a fire alarm on the wall to evacuate the hospital now that he will soon be clear of the stairwell. I cannot see or hear him behind me, so I have to weave in and out of the bare concrete pillars to avoid him having a clear shot at me. I run past several side rooms before darting into one of them; I barely avoid tripping over some reels of electrical cable in the process. I slam the door shut behind me.

This room is a patient ward that is undergoing renovation. The far wall is completely made of glass and the only way out of the room is through the door that I came in through. The ground below is the hospital's small communal garden, and to the right is the multi-storey carpark that is attached to the side of the hospital's tower. On the road at a tangent to the far side of the multi-storey carpark is a row of parked cars. The car parked at the end of the row closest to me is the only one with its lights on—that must be Big Carl.

I assess the room for items that I can use to my advantage; there are builders' tools and building material messily lying around, as well as several original items that have not been cleared out yet, such as a couple of patient beds—I suspect the builders find them useful during break times.

I should still have a small amount of time whilst he searches for me in the rooms that I ran past. I dash to a patient bed at the back of the room and release its brakes. I spin the bed around with one hand and position it so that it is in between the window and myself. My bare feet are now dry and grip well to the dusty floor as I push the bed forward. I pick up speed quickly, but it difficult to keep the bed moving forward in a straight line towards a corner of the glass because the wheels cause it to violently wobble all over the place.

I ram the bed into the window with great force, causing the glass to crack severely and detach itself from the hospital building in the corner that I hit it. Despite my best effort, the glass remains as one sheet. I pull the bed back a couple of metres before thrusting it back towards the window; this time, I aim for the far corner. I do not achieve as much speed as I did in the previous attempt, so when the bed hits the glass, I engage the muscles in my chest, shoulders, and triceps to exert additional force.

The glass still remains as one sheet as it springs from its fixings. It falls towards the communal garden, and the bed tries to follow it. I lean back, counteracting the weight of it that I've mistakenly allowed to protrude over the ledge. My feet stick to the floor, providing me with a solid foundation to pull it back into the room in one clean movement. I manoeuvre the bed back into its original position but struggle to come to a halt as the wind pushes me hard into the room. I grab a hammer and slouch down against the wall behind the door— the only hiding spot available to me.

He takes longer than expected. A couple of minutes pass before he apprehensively opens the door. Once he has fully committed himself to the room, the wind seizes hold of the door and smashes it back against me. He tries the light switch, but it doesn't work; the cable for the lights has been removed. The window draws his attention first, but he quickly turns and scans the room in search of me with military vigilance and speed, before stepping forward. He slowly makes his way towards the open space where the window used to be.

He scans the room one final time before looking out of the window. I dash out from behind the door and grab hold of the bed. I place my right heel on the wall and push off to overcome the initial inertia. I engage all of my muscles to power the bed at him; this time, the wheels do not try to push me off track.

After I have covered half the distance, he starts to turn around. When he is half facing the room, he notices me and the bed approaching him in the corner of his eye; he spins himself and his machine guns around earlier than I had hoped for. His face remains emotionless when we lock eyes. He drops the machine gun in his left hand to take hold of the other end of the bed; he starts firing with his right machine gun when it is pointed forty-five degrees away from me. He doesn't even try to move out of the bed's way; he is too preoccupied with killing me. He continues to swing his gun toward me as he is pushed out of the building.

I am slow to release the trolley and duck out of the way of the bullets, but, luckily, the bed deflects them upwards out of my way as it follows him over the ledge. I slide on my left side and come to a halt with a good foot between myself and the ledge. He continues firing in my general direction during his descent; a handful of bullets pulverise the ceiling above me and the rest of them either hit the building's windows or the night sky.

I crawl to the ledge and peer over it. I can see the bed but cannot see his body in the dimly lit garden; he has either fallen into one of the trees, or the bed has landed on top of him. Several speeding police cars scream past Big Carl. I pick up the machine gun and check its magazine; there are plenty of bullets left. To leave the hospital, I am going to have to get past many firearms officers. I will try not to kill any of them, but if they force me into a corner then I will not hesitate to seriously wing them. I set the gun to single-burst mode and head for the exit.

A group of firearms officers enter the floor from the stairwell, but they do not notice me. I bend down on one knee and fire a bullet into the thigh of the leading officer. He drops to the ground, clutching his thigh; I cannot hear him scream over the sound of the alarm. The second officer spots me and starts firing in my direction. The third officer grabs the back of the first officer's bulletproof vest, and they all retreat to the stairwell. I trip over some loose electrical cable, which sparks an idea. I backtrack to the room I was just in. I take the end of the electrical cable, feed it through the gap between the room's door and the door frame, and wrap itself around itself several times before manipulating the stiff material into a knot.

I kick the cable roll and it unravels as it rolls towards the window ledge. It rolls over the window ledge and out of sight. I poke my head around the door again; there are now more than ten firearms officers on this floorplate heading towards me. As a warning, I fire several bullets at different concrete pillars, but they go noticed due to the fire alarm covering their sound. There is a large fire extinguisher between myself and the officers; I fire at it causing it to explode and fill the air with dense smoke. I drop my gun in the centre of the room, and sprint towards the window ledge.

When I am one metre away from the ledge, I drop onto the ground, and slide on my side alongside the cable. Before I slide out into the abyss, I loosely grab the cable in my left hand. As I slide over the window ledge, I believe that a firearms officer has me in his crosshairs, but he doesn't take the shot.

I fall about two to three metres before I start to tighten my grip on the cable. It painfully burns my palm but does little to slow my fall. I realise that my left arm is not in a great condition. After a fall of about four metres, I clamp the cable with my right hand and quickly come to a stop. It looks like the cable goes all the way to the ground. I think about sliding down to the ground until several police cars screech to a halt on the other side of hospital's garden. Even though the temperature is very cold, my hands sweat from all the burning, making it difficult to maintain my grip on the cable.

Instead of lowering myself to the ground, I opt for the multi-storey carpark's open top roof, which is about five metres to the right of me. I place my bare feet against the hospital's glass windows and push myself in the direction of the multi-storey carpark. My feet slip and slide on the cold damp glass as I walk sideways like a crab.

Gravity forces me back to my nominal position after several steps. I use gravity to my advantage and move my feet as fast as I can in the opposite direction of the multi-storey carpark. Once I've reached the maximum height of that swing, I spin my body around and turn my attention to the multi-storey carpark. On the descent, my bare feet continue to slip and slide on the glass as I sprint nearly perpendicular to the glass. At the peak of the swing, I push myself away from the glass.

For a split second, it feels exhilarating to be flying through the air, especially as it brings back some memories of the more impressive, death-defying stunts that I pulled when I was younger. I land on a car windscreen; my back takes most of the impact, with my legs, arms, and head taking the remainder shortly after. The windscreen cracks severely, but it remains intact as I bounce straight off it, hitting the adjacent parked car with my shoulder. I rebound off this car, and my fall finally comes to an end when I half hit the tarmac and half hit the wheel of the car that I originally landed on. I feel like I've just endured a rematch with Extra Arm. I imagine a referee stood next to me counting whilst I lie motionless. After five seconds, I jump to my feet. I wobble enough when I get on my feet that any decent referee would stop the fight.

The firearms officers are grouped together on the ledge; their facial expressions contain different degrees of amusement, admiration, bewilderment, and respect. They have all lowered their weapons; they will not risk firing at me from this distance in a public space. None of them even considers trying to follow my route out of the building. They all retreat into the hospital to continue the pursuit.

When I reach the bottom of the car ramp on the second floor, three firearms officers exit the stairwell on the far side of the floorplate on my right. I guess that the officers have spread themselves across all floors; I'll be trapped very shortly. A car between myself and the officers leaves its parking bay and heads towards the officers. I dive out of view between two parked cars.

One of the officers stops the car whilst the other two search inside of it— much to the distress of the driver. I grab hold of the carpark's concrete wall and jump over it. I keep hold of the wall as my legs dangle and my face rubs against the rough concrete surface. I try to stretch my legs out to reach the top of the concrete wall on the floor below, but it is futile: I am several feet off. To stop the officers on the first floor from seeing my dangling legs, I have no choice other than to release my grip.

My right foot twists on a discarded bottle of beer when I land in the bushes below. To stop myself from screaming, I squeeze my fists together and grit my teeth. It is painful to move my foot around, but my ankle doesn't appear to be broken. The branches rustle loudly as they continue to move past one another; the wind then picks up and makes them rustle even louder. A few seconds later an officer peers over the wall on the first floor. He uses the torch on his gun as a searchlight to scan through the darkness; I crouch down, hiding in the darkness of the bushes. His light passes over me several times; he cannot see me under the cover of the bushes. He continues to scan the area until he's satisfied that I am not here.

A helicopter—I must anticipate it being police helicopter—appears in the distance, heading in the hospital's direction. The traffic lights are about twenty yards in front of me. Despite the road being previously quite quiet, a slug of traffic is forced to queue when the traffic lights change to red. As a bus approaches the back of the queue, its brakes squeal loudly. Branches rub and cut my face as I force my way out of the bush. Ignoring my aching ankle, I sprint as fast as possible down the slippery grass verge. I run around the back of the bus so that it is between myself and the multi-storey carpark and continue run alongside it as it slows down.

There is now a significant amount of police activity in the multi-storey carpark. A stream of police cars race towards the hospital along the road that forms the crossroads with the road that the bus and I are on. The police helicopter begins to circle around the hospital, so I dive under the bus to hide from view, including from any thermal imaging cameras. The traffic lights change to green but all the vehicles have to wait a couple more seconds for all the remaining police cars to pass before any of their accelerators are pressed. At the last possible moment, I roll out from under the bus and run flat out towards Big Carl's car. I run diagonally across the crossroad so that the bus provides me with cover for the longest possible time.

Before I get a chance to sit down properly, Big Carl puts his pedal to the metal, forcing his car to wheel spin forward. The sudden lurch forward presses me into the seat and closes the door for me. Looking through the rear windscreen, it is clear that the firearms officers have confirmed that I am no longer in the multi-storey carpark: they are now searching its local vicinity, including the bushes that I fell into. The police helicopter circles overhead again, but it does not follow us.

Chapter 11
Lilyana

Big Carl drops me off on a deserted side street now we have travelled a safe enough distance away from the hospital and I have ascertained that no one has followed us. I head towards my flat that is currently being used to house Lilyana whilst she gets back on her feet. This will give me a safe place to rest my head for the night. I will assess Lilyana's condition in the morning; hopefully, her and Talia are well enough for Emma to get them both to Nataliya.

The streetlights and endless neon advertising signs above the shops and eateries, as well as the headlights from the continuous stream of traffic, illuminate the street. It is raining heavily; I do not look out of place walking with my hood up and face down. Unfortunately, trying to remain unnoticed severely limits my peripheral vision from noticing potential foes; consequently, I grip the gun that Big Carl gave me even more tightly under my hoodie. I walk with difficulty wearing Big Carl's shoes. They are uncomfortably too big for me; there is plenty of space between my ankle and the shoe's collar. When I step in a deep puddle, water washes over my bare ankle and pours into the shoe. The smells from all the kitchens are blown out onto the street; I suddenly realise that I am very hungry and thirsty.

I enter the river of bodies and become what feels like a free-floating organism. This artificial waterway meanders down the pavement and flows around manmade obstacles, such as lampposts and dog muck. Regrettably, one obstacle is a legless Romanian lady, who resides in the doorway of a foreclosed shop. She holds up a sign asking for change; this sign would most certainly have been written for her by her handlers. Everyone fixes their gaze on either the floor or something insignificant straight ahead; no one wants to look in her desperate, pleading eyes.

I continue walking with the crowd for several minutes before branching off into a deserted alleyway that I know doesn't contain any surveillance cameras. I sprint into its dark depths and hide in the porch of a shop's side door. My gun is firmly fixed on the entrance of the alleyway. Everyone walks past; no one even looks in my direction. After several minutes of waiting, I continue deeper into alleyway until I reach the rear entrance of a block of flats. I type the access code into the keypad; it flashes green before the electromagnet releases the lock. The lift has a camera so I have to quickly make my way up the dimly lit, and rarely used, stairwell; my tired, abused legs scream in pain with every step.

Once I reach my flat's floor, I open the door to the corridor, but I do not pass through it. Instead, I close it loudly. I take a step back and look down the stairwell, performing one last check to confirm that no one has followed me.

I knock firmly on Lilyana's door five times in a certain rhythm so she knows it's me at the door. The sound of muffled voices comes from behind the door; it sounds they originate from the television. The hairs on the back of my neck stand up; I sense someone watching me. I tune out the muffled voices and hear someone shuffling behind the door of the flat directly behind me. I consciously only turn my head slightly so that they cannot see my full face through their spyhole. Their shadow moves in the light shining through the gap under their door. I turn back to face Lilyana's door, ignoring the nosey neighbour. Despite me telling her many times that she needs to ensure that her front door is locked at all times, I push the door gently and it opens slightly.

I gently close the door behind me. I flick the deadlatch on so that the door is locked; I cannot use the deadlock because the key is not in it. Litter and a whole host of other items hide the floor. I edge my way down the dark corridor towards the flickering light from the television. I step on Lilyana's hairbrush and nearly slip over as my foot slides with it along the laminate flooring.

I peer into the open-plan living area, which comprises the living room, dining room and kitchen. Lilyana is wrapped up in a thick throw on the sofa and is fast asleep. I step sideways into the living room, keeping my back against the wall so that I can survey the room. The bedroom and bathroom are on the far side; both of their doors are open, but I cannot see inside of them as their lights are turned off.

The kitchen comprises a small row of cabinets, a sink, a fridge, and a washing machine. The chipboard worktops and sink support a host of dirty plates, pans, etc. The bin is overflowing with, and surrounded by, garbage comprising mostly take-away containers. Even from this side of the room, the unpleasant odour of organic material decaying abuses my nostrils. It looks like Lilyana has had trouble looking after the place; I don't judge her on this because it is difficult looking after a baby, especially when one is trying to maintain sobriety.

I know it is immoral, but I struggle to not look at her face as I make my way around the edge of the living room. Despite the many years of drug, alcohol, and sexual abuse, she is still beautiful. Her stubborn beauty is possibly the only reason she is still alive today.

Nataliya told me that she grew up with Lilyana in an isolated, access-restricted Russian city dedicated to progressing Russia's naval nuclear ambitions. Lilyana was the most beautiful girl in their friendship group, which resulted in her receiving a lot of attention from the older boys in their school and men—sometimes, very old men—when walking through the streets. In fact, Nataliya believes it was one of these old men, possibly one who worked for the local mafia outfit, that kidnapped her and forced her into prostitution after he had killed her mother and father following a dispute.

Nataliya informed the authorities of Lilyana's disappearance, and the old man who she suspected was responsible for it, but it fell on deaf ears; the authorities were in the Mafia's pocket. After her disappearance, the old man promptly moved to Moscow so she followed him there. She continued her search for Lilyana in Moscow, but she needed contacts, and money to persuade these contacts, to give her the information she required; as such, she got a job as an exotic dancer. After searching for a while, she was informed that Lilyana had been in Moscow, but had already been moved on; like with all mafia-owned prostitutes, she was constantly moved around and sold to different families. So, she packed up her stuff, and followed the scent. After many years of Lilyana being traded between Russian mafia families, Nataliya found out that Lilyana had ended up in Mikhail's possession.

After Nataliya reluctantly told me about Lilyana, it did not take me long to track her down. Unfortunately, when I found her, it looked like she had been in a heroin-induced stupor for quite a long time; she was on the verge of dying. The staff at the private hospital told me that I had managed to get her, and her seven-month-old unborn baby, to the hospital just in time to save them both.

Once Lilyana was released from the hospital, I checked her straight into the most expensive rehab facility in the city. Due to her poor health and the length of abuse, the rehab facility recommended that she had her baby in their care where they could support her. This was because looking after a newborn baby is a big stress initiator that would likely lead to relapse.

Of course, I was happy for her to stay in rehab for as long as she needed—they had carte blanche as far as I was concerned. She has been living in my flat ever since she got out of rehab a couple of months ago. In hindsight, I have been incredibly selfish keeping her away from Nataliya: I wanted her to be in such a good condition, both mentally and physically, that Nataliya wouldn't have had to spend all her time with her when I reunited them.

It suddenly occurs to me…*Where is Talia?*

I quietly make my way over to Lilyana's bedroom door. At the side of her bed is Talia's cot. The smell is as bad in the bedroom as in the living room. I shuffle my feet along the floor in order to not trip over any of the clothes or rubbish that lie on it as I head to the cot. I can only see the outline of Talia; I pull back the blackout curtains just enough to be able to gaze at her sleeping peacefully—she has her mother's beauty. She looks very healthy, which brings me great relief. I get an urge to pick her up, but I restrain myself as Lilyana will probably kill me if I woke her.

I make my way back to the living area, and instantly become fixated on Lilyana's beautiful face again. It makes me feel sick when I think of how many men have taken advantage of her, especially when she was in a forced heroin-induced stupor. Images of various torture techniques flash by quickly in my head as I conjure up ways of killing all the people that have taken advantage of her.

I close the bathroom door quietly behind me. It is significantly cleaner in here than the rest of the flat. I pull the bath panel away and grab the two bags stored under the bath. One bag contains a fresh set of clothes and a pair of shoes; the other bag contains money and several handguns, plus plenty of ammunition. I throw the clothes out of the bag and place them on the towel rail. After pouring the water out of my shoes into the sink, I rip off my clothes and put them in the now empty bag. I throw this bag back under the bath and slot the bath panel back in place. I set the shower to the coldest setting and turn it on. A cold shiver runs down my spine when the ice-cold water catches my withdrawing arm.

My body experiences great pain now that the morphine has mostly worn off. The injuries that I have sustained thus far will take a long time to heal without the cumulation of others that it will undoubtedly receive shortly. I stretch my leg over the side of the bath and dip my foot into the pool of freezing water. My body tells itself that it would prefer to have a nice relaxing soak in a hot bath;

however, my brain is more practical and convinces itself that my body needs a cold shower to help reduce swelling, better preparing itself for the upcoming battles.

The bath creaks loudly as it acclimatises to bearing my full weight; I brace myself for the cold shock as I shuffle forwards. The cold, heavy water takes my breath away when it hits the top of my head and shoulders. I keep gasping for air as the coldness washing over my body penetrates my inner core. My body stiffens; I close my eyes and meditate to block out the pain.

After several minutes, I cannot stand much more, so I quickly wash my body all over with a luxurious, floral-smelling shampoo. I turn the shower off and stand still for several seconds, frozen stiff. A peculiar grunting noise originates from the living room, which I dismiss as a strange TV advert. I grab Lilyana's warm towel off the hot towel rail.

I am forced to accept when getting dressed that I have to take a deep breath in order to tighten the last button on my jeans. I leave my redundant belt on the towel rail. I open the bathroom door and become momentarily thunderstruck.

One man has pulled Lilyana's throw off her naked body, and is attempting to climb on top of her, whilst another man is frying something on the cooker. Both men look like drug addicts, and I instantly realise the tragedy that has befallen her. My left arm smashes the bathroom door open against the wall as I sprint into the open-plan living area. I am not thinking. My body is overtaken by the pure rage that pumps through my veins. I feel like a bull being released into the bullring; the guy on top of Lilyana is my unsuspecting matador.

I am several feet away from my matador when an almighty surge of energy is delivered to my left calf and quadriceps. I fly through the air and clear the back of the sofa with ease. Before my matador has a chance to look up, my shoulder slams into his upper chest. His body provides no resistance to my momentum. I keep my shoulder planted in his chest, putting all my weight behind it, and use him to cushion my fall. Before he has a chance to scream, I grab his throat and my thumbs quickly crush the life out of him. Fluid in his throat gargles before his eyes roll into the back of his head.

I let go of my matador and am enraged further when I notice that his pants are down, exposing his small, limp penis. I spin around and see the sofa throw that once covered Lilyana is now lying crumpled up on the floor. She remains motionless, face down and exposed; a syringe hangs loosely, still attached to her right foot, which dangles off the edge of the sofa. Tears stream down my face.

The guy cooking yelps loudly, which pulls me away from my mourning. He has cut himself trying to open a tin of baked beans with a steak knife.

I spring up off the floor to my feet before jumping back over Lilyana and the sofa—this time I have to use one hand to provide extra leverage. The guy doesn't even know that I exist as all his attention is on futilely trying to get to his food. I grab hold of the back of his head and smash his face through several ceramic plates that lie on top of each other on the worktop. His head bounces off the smashed plates and he collapses onto the floor. Pieces from the broken plates slide off the kitchen worktop and smash loudly into smaller pieces when they hit the tiled floor around him.

Blood oozes out of various crevices in the guy's face onto the floor tiles, flowing away from him along the brilliant white grouted channels. The keys to this flat fall out of his trouser pocket and dam the flow of blood down one channel. His eyes are bloodshot and glazed over. I still don't think he evens notices that I am in the room, let alone what I have done to him. I am disgusted by this low-life; he physically makes me feel sick. His eyes focus on the tin of baked beans that is now butted up against the fridge, about one metre from where he lies. He awkwardly twists his body around and crawls towards them.

I grab my belt off the towel rail in the bathroom. On my way back to the kitchen area, I accidentally glance at Lilyana's naked body—I shake my head, disgusted at myself. I place my thumb on my belt approximately twelve inches away from the buckle, grab a dirty fork out of the washing up bowl, and stab my belt near my thumb with one of the fork's outer prongs. The hole produced is very small but I easily manage to put the belt prong through it when I wrap the belt around the guy's throat. Even though the belt is suffocating him, he keeps hold of the tin of baked beans in one hand whilst he claws at the belt with his other hand.

A couple of fresh needle marks, several painful-looking red scars, and a small Russian bear tattoo—a sign that she is Mikhail's property—encircle the syringe embedded in Lilyana's right foot. It is common practice for the 'owners' of prostitutes to brand them like cattle. Before a prostitute is sold, the existing branding is removed, typically using either a hot iron rod or battery acid. It looks like she has been the property of at least three owners.

I pull the syringe out of her foot and throw it in the general direction of the dead guy; the needle penetrates and sticks into his groin, a few centimetres along from the end of his shrivelled-up penis. Remaining optimistic, I check her neck for a pulse. I immediately try to convince myself that I have found it—but I haven't. The cushion next to her mouth is a little bit damp where the white staining is. I bend down, grab the sofa throw, and cover her with it.

The guy being strangled by the belt on the kitchen floor flaps around like a fish out of water. He has now released the tin of baked beans; he frantically claws at the belt with both hands. The thought of Talia causes me to sprint like a madman towards the bedroom. I press the bedroom's light switch, but the filament does not light up. I trip over the clothes and rubbish on the floor, but miraculously manage not to fall over as I head to the cot. I lean over the cot to check that she is alive by putting my finger under her nose. I feel a gentle, intermittent, and hot breeze against my finger. Thank God for that.

I sit in the armchair facing Lilyana and shake uncontrollably with anger. I blame myself for her death. I think of all the things that I could have done differently to avoid this sad ending, as well as all the ways that I will punish myself to pay for this mistake. Nataliya is going to kill me when I tell her—or worse, she'll never want to see me again. The guy being strangled to death relaxes me slightly; I yawn widely.

I think I had momentarily drifted off to sleep when the front door slams shut. Two guys are talking and making their way towards the open-plan living area. Instinctively, I slide off the armchair and roll on the floor to hide behind the door. I clench my fists, the only weapons available to me. My guns are still in the bathroom. Two big guys enter the room; they are laughing and joking. It takes a couple of seconds before they both cry out simultaneously, "What the fuck is this?"

"Elijah, get over here. Joe-Joe has a belt around his neck; he's being strangled by it," the bigger guy says. Elijah puts his rucksack on the back of the sofa and makes his way over to Joe-Joe. The rucksack topples over and falls on top of Lilyana—he will pay for the disrespect.

"What the fuck. He can't die: he owes us money!" says Elijah. He tries to release the belt but makes the strangulation much worse. "Fucking hell, someone may have tried to kill him. Shit, they might still be here, Jacko." They both cautiously stand and scan the room for threats, leaving Joe-Joe to fend for himself.

I push the door softly to a close. They both jump out of their skins when I step out of the darkness. I lift my head up and straighten my back in a slow and intimidating manner. They both step back like cornered animals; each guy tries to position himself so they can use the other as a human shield. They both come to their senses after a couple of seconds when they realise that they outnumber me.

"Who the fuck is you?" Elijah shouts at me.

"Why are you here?" I say in a demanding tone.

Elijah looks over the sofa and sees the guy that I crushed the life out of on the floor. He elbows Jacko, "Fucking hell, he has killed Kenny also." Jacko looks over the sofa at Kenny then back at me.

"This fool better not think he's going to take us on," Jacko says, pulling a small machete out of his jeans whilst positioning himself into a fighting stance. Elijah swiftly follows by pulling out a similar machete, but he doesn't look as experienced at handling it.

"Answer the question. This will not end well for you if you think you're going to kill me," I state, unfazed. I step across to cover the doorway so that they cannot escape without first going through me.

"Come on then, old man—let's see what you've got. We are drug dealers from the streets; we are very experienced at dealing with people like you," Jacko says, boldly. Elijah nervously takes another look at Joe-Joe. A battle plan has already formed in my head; they will not be leaving this room alive.

"I don't doubt you," I smirk. "My patience is running thin; I am not going to ask you again." I take two steps forward.

"We also have weapons, old man," Jacko enjoys explaining the obvious as he waves his machete around. Elijah's machete-holding arm shakes nervously.

Eight feet remains between us after I take another step forward. Jacko brings his machete up high over his head; he takes an obvious striking pose. I continue walking slowly. Seven feet, six feet, five feet. At four feet, Jacko lunges forward whilst bringing down his machete; I respond by also lunging forward. I grab his wrist with my left hand. I ram my right palm hard into his eye socket, causing his head to snap back. As he steps backwards, I rip the machete from his grip, taking ownership of it.

Elijah takes a slow swing at me; I smash my machete down onto his machete-wielding wrist. His hand continues to grip the machete as they both fall to the floor. He screams in pain as he clutches his handless arm, which squirts blood all over me. I kick him in the side of the knee; he collapses onto Joe-Joe. He covers both Jacko and Joe-Joe in blood. Jacko tries to escape but as soon as he runs past me, I swipe the machete across his right Achilles tendon.

When he puts his right foot down, his ankle twists painfully and he falls onto the floor. He slides along the floor until the closed door brings him to a halt. He becomes stiff with fear as he turns to face me.

"Please don't, I'll—" Before I allow him to finish his sentence, I bring my machete down on the centre of his forehead. The machete is quite blunt and doesn't sink far enough into his skull to satisfy my killing urge; nevertheless, it kills him instantly. I pull the machete out of his skull and slam it back into it with as much force as I can muster. This time, I smile widely as the machete sinks to a satisfying depth in his skull.

Elijah witnesses me murder Jacko and drops his head back onto Joe-Joe; he is already defeated. The machete is lodged in Jacko's skull, so I place my foot on his body and heave it out. I lift the machete up high and walk over to Elijah and Joe-Joe. Elijah closes his eyes and screws up his face as I bring the machete down. I slam the machete down onto Joe-Joe's throat slightly above where my belt is. It passes straight through his neck and smashes into the floor tiles. His head comes clean off and rolls onto its side, facing the kitchen units. As I grab my bloody belt, my face gets sprayed with blood that has spurted from Elijah's amputated arm.

"Did I not warn you? Were the other two bodies not enough proof that I would kill you?"

I bend down and wrap my belt around his amputated arm. He tries to respond, but it comes out as mumbo jumbo; he is panicking too much to make any sense. Without looking at Lilyana, I pick up his bag that has fallen on her. The front section of the bag contains a lot of cash; the back section contains syringes, like the one I pulled out of Lilyana. The bag doesn't contain any drugs; their runners must have dropped off the drugs earlier. They were only here to collect the money.

"Right, my friend, if you make this quick, I'll drive you straight to the hospital myself," I lie.

"Anything, get me to the hospital now. I am bleeding out," he panics. He is starting to lose consciousness from all the blood loss.

"First off, why are you here?" I believe that I already know the answer, but I try to waste time to make him more desperate, and thus, more likely tell me what I need to know.

"To collect what is owed." I can sense that he is thinking of ways to kill me.

"When was the last time you were here?" I step back away from the growing pool of thick blood that oozes out of Joe-Joe's neck.

"Three nights ago. Kenny was bragging that he had robbed some old ladies' house and found lots of cash stuffed under her bed. He wanted to celebrate his windfall, so we brought a large quantity of heroin around here. However, when we got here, he didn't have the money on him; he claimed he had stashed it somewhere while the heat died down. That's why we are here now: to collect the money." He looks in the direction of Kenny, but the sofa blocks his view.

"Who do you work for? I had a deal with the local drug lord that no drugs are to be sold in this building."

"We—well I," he corrects himself, "work for a new and very aggressive crew, who will find you and kill you for what you've done here. Trust me, brother, they will kill you if you don't get me to the hospital!"

"Answer the question, who do you work for?" I act as though I am loosening the belt. He doesn't have the energy to fight me off. He doesn't respond. "Don't make me ask you again!"

"Alright, alright. I've heard rumours that the guy who calls the shots is known as the 'General'." I am taken aback by this, but I do let my surprise be seen. Ralph Boyd, or as he prefers, the General, is a former SAS soldier, who now works for Mikhail—he never reached the rank of General in the British Army though. There is an agreement between the Russians and the Chinese that the Chinese own the rights to sell narcotics in this area of town. So, either Mikhail has been trying to take over Chinese territory, or the General has broken away from Mikhail and thinks that he can take them both on. "Come on man, you need to get me to the hospital."

"One more question: How long has your outfit been selling narcotics in this area?" He starts to go very white. Even if I had the intention of getting him to the hospital, he is probably too far gone to survive the journey now.

"Probably about a month now." He struggles to keep himself conscious. "I know your type. Wait until I tell your wife that you've been fucking Lily like the rest of us punks." He takes me completely by surprise.

"What did you say?" I stumble to find the words as I am left speechless.

"I know your type, mate. You've fallen in love with Lily; you want to keep her for yourself. I can't blame you: Lily's a fine piece of meat." He closes his eyes and a wide smile stretches across his face. He has raped Lilyana and now he is reminiscing about it, I convince myself.

"Do not talk about Lilyana like that. She got clean. SHE WAS CLEAN!" I shout, infuriated by his words and his thoughts. My heart starts beating out of control and my anger levels rise to a height that I've rarely experienced.

"Those that try to get clean too quickly usually end up being my most loyal customers, my friend. Once they've experienced my free, high purity samples, they are hooked for life. Lily became desperate after her first hit; she would let me do whatever I wanted to her just so that she could relive that first hit." He opens one eye. "I remember my first time with her, I—"

Before he has a chance to boast about what he has done to her, I stamp on his face with my right foot. His nose is crushed into his face whilst his head is forced into Joe-Joe's chest cavity. I continue stamping on his face until his skull is severely deformed. I am out of breath and my heart feels like it is about to pump itself out of my chest. As I take a step back, all the brain matter stuck in the tread of my shoe nearly causes me to slip on the floor; I stumble but I recover the situation.

I collapse in the armchair facing Lilyana. I am exhausted. Talia has a brief outburst, which makes me jump out of my skin; however, she goes quiet again before I have a chance to stand up. I look at Lilyana; I am too distraught to form any tears.

Chapter 12
The Deadly Awakening

"Think fast," Nataliya screams over the sound of gentle waves lapping the beach. I turn my gaze from the clear, blue sea and quickly raise both hands to catch the foxtail ball before it collides with my face. As I lower the foxtail ball, she puts her hands up, covering her open jaw. My relaxed smile removes her fear, bringing a smile back to her face. We are on a tropical beach surrounded by families playing and having fun.

I lose awareness of my surroundings as I become solely focused on Nataliya. I grab the tail of the foxtail ball and swing it around. At the perfect point, I release it; it rockets up high—very high, in fact—into the sky. She looks up but has to shield her eyes from the sun with one hand to allow her to track its trajectory. My right foot sinks deep into the sand as I thrust myself forwards; I sprint towards her using the full pumping power of my arms.

Before I reach her, my feet splash loudly through the seawater that an untypically large wave has just pushed over the sand. She looks down at me as I make contact, tackling her softly to the ground. I use my body to shield her from the falling foxtail ball; it lands a foot to the right of my head, forming a mini crater in the sand. As we look into each other eyes, a bad case of butterflies grips my stomach; I have never been happier. When her soft lips touch mine, another untypically large wave comes in, blasting a mixture of sand and cool, foamy water in our faces. Under the influence of the returning seawater, we roll down the beach, clinging onto each other. The sea releases us and we both lie next to each other laughing.

Before we get chance to get back on our feet, an even larger wave hits us. Some seawater washes down my throat, causing me to choke temporarily. As the seawater returns to the sea, it grabs hold of us again, pulling us with it. Its grip on us gets progressively stronger. I desperately try to keep hold of Nataliya, but she gets ripped away from me. I try to touch the seabed to spring myself to the surface, but it has disappeared; the harder I try to swim to the surface, the deeper I am pulled down. Desperation kicks in; I use all my strength to overcome the sea's overpowering embrace—but it is no use. I clench my jaw as hard as possible to stop water ingress into my lungs. The pressure in my ears and head becomes intolerable; its feel like my head is going to implode.

"Donnie, DONNIE. Stop it—you're going to kill him," someone shouts with a Chinese accent. Despite my blurry vision, I make out the outline of three men stood in front of me. I believe that I recognise the outline of one of them. As they run towards me, Kevin's face comes into focus. I grab hold of Donnie's arm around my throat and easily prise it away. I yank it forward, causing him to be thrown over my head. He lands on the floor in front of Kevin, who tries to avoid him, but ends up tripping over him. Kevin's face first falls onto my knee, quickly followed by the floor. I try to stand but am too weak and dizzy from the oxygen deprivation. I slump back down into my chair. The two remaining goons try to pin me down, but I kick one of them in the shins, causing him to collapse onto the armrest, and I grab the other by the throat.

I keep hold of the man's throat whilst he keeps trying to punch me. He is wasting his time though because my arm is longer than his; he only hits my flexed bicep. The man on the armrest weakly punches me in my abdomen, causing me no pain. I respond by elbowing him in the face, forcing him off the armrest and onto the floor next to Kevin. I use the man's throat to pull myself upright. As soon as I am upright, there is a sharp pain in my calf.

I look down and see that Kevin has forced a syringe into my calf. It falls out as I lift my leg up and smash my heel into his nose, causing it to erupt with blood. A hot burning sensation works its way up my leg, distracting me from feeling the punches to my bicep. My knee fails, and I bring down the person I am strangling with me as I collapse onto the floor. The room starts spinning and my whole body feels like it is becoming lined with lead.

Donnie crawls over to me on his hands and knees before punching me hard in the face. The punch forces my head to the side and releases my grip on the man's throat. As I lose consciousness, I get one last look at the beautiful—yet heartbreaking—sight of Lilyana.

Chapter 13
The Diversion

Nataliya cheers loudly when my lead pellet knocks down the fifth and final target. The operator of the Wild West Air Rifle Range reluctantly unhooks an oversized, sun-worn teddy bear and places it on the counter. Before I get a chance to put down the 1950's air rifle, Nataliya hoists it off the counter, taking custodianship of it.

"Thank you, baby," she says to me whilst looking into its eyes. Even though it completely dwarfs her, she hugs it tightly, determined to keep hold of it. She manoeuvres it to one side and leans in to kiss me. Our lips barely touch before a group of overexcited children knocks me away from her as they rush to the Mad Mouse Roller Coaster. I am momentarily distracted by the thought of how planning permission was granted for such a large roller coaster on this relatively small pier. The smiling parents wait patiently as their carefree children are violently thrown around. Whilst their smiles suggest that they are happy, their eyes give away their nervousness, as well as their desperation, to get their children back into the safety of their arms.

I put my right arm around Nataliya's back and under her right arm; I bring her close to me and bear all of her teddy bear's weight. As we head to the end of the pier, there is no more shade to protect us from the sun's intense radiation. Panic sets in when I become conscious that my armpit is close to her face and will quickly become malodorous. I try to prise the teddy bear away from her, but she hugs it even more tightly.

Another group of children scream and laugh as they run around us, shooting one another with water pistols. We both welcome the cool water hitting our skin in return for briefly serving them as human shields. The group of people in front of us are not quite as open to the idea of being human shields: the oldest lady in the group shrieks loudly—too loudly—causing the children to concentrate all their spray on her. We both look at each other and laugh. We wipe the excess water off each other's face.

We reach the end of the pier and Nataliya rests her teddy bear on the railings. I hug her tightly as we look out over the sea. This is heaven. Several seconds later, black clouds begin coalescing in the sky. A huge swell appears on the horizon; I know instantly that an enormous tsunami is headed in our direction. I jerk Nataliya around, causing her to lose grip of her teddy bear; it falls over the railings and plunges into the sea. We are already running at Nataliya's top speed when other people begin to take notice of the tsunami.

An old lady, who is oblivious to what is going on, steps back into Nataliya's path. I am left with no other choice than to force her painfully out of the way with my left palm. I look back and someone stops to try and help her up, but they both get mercilessly trampled on by the forming stampede.

The roaring tsunami hits the pier and greedily consumes everything in its path. I look over my shoulder as the tsunami washes over us both. The ice-cold water only blasts the top half of my body, with my face taking most of the force. I try to shudder, but my body is pinned back against a hard object.

Everything goes pitch black; I blindly swing my arms around to try and grab hold of Nataliya. I try to resist breathing in, but it is futile. My mouth and lungs autonomously open, attempting to suck the oxygen molecules away from their polyamorous relationships. Much to my surprise and relief, oxygen floods my lungs with only a small amount of water trickling into my mouth. The oxygen electrifies my central nervous system, forcing my eyes open and my body to become animated. Whilst my eyes adjust to the bright light, a smoky silhouette emerges in front of me.

It takes several seconds for the silhouette to materialise into the Dragon Master. He sits in front of me, sucking on his signature big, fat cigar. There is a large oak desk separating us; the only thing on it is a half-filled crystal ashtray. It takes a few more seconds for my eyes to handle the light pouring into his office through the large window behind him.

The guy whom I elbowed in the face earlier stands to my right, holding an empty water jug in his hands. His mouth curls up at the edges, displaying a small sense of pleasure at the payback; his eyes reveal a hunger for complete revenge. Large ice cubes rest on my lap, melting into my groin. Goosebumps spring up all over my body; I fail to resist a cold shiver, causing him to smile even wider. I successfully resist an urge to shout "*bastard*" at him.

My shoulders start to burn under the strain of my wrists being tightly tied together behind the back of the chair. My feet are also bound, but I can feel that this knot has been weakly tied. Kevin and Donnie try to cradle machine guns menacingly in their arms either side of me, but it comes across quite comically. The door behind me—the only exit—is closed. I lean back in my chair and stretch my legs out, giving the impression that I am relaxed.

"Good morning, Mr Kulikov." The Dragon Master pronounces each word slowly and softly in flawless English. This is not the name he knows me by; for some reason, he is making his foot soldiers think that I am Russian. "From all your cuts and bruises, as well as the tiredness in your eyes, one can easily deduce that you are having a bit of a rough time." I smile and nod my head in agreement—which he reciprocates. "I'll not insult you by pretending that you are our captive, Mr Kulikov."

"Thank you for your kind hospitality, sir," I say sternly, bowing my head. "You are correct—I am having a bit of a rough time of it. I must politely warn you that you are all in grave danger from simply being in my presence right now." He and I share a fair amount of history and we have a lot of respect for each other, but we have only dealt with each other in secret. None of his men know about our relationship, so I play along, pretending not to know him.

"Mr Kulikov." He relights his cigar. "Apologies for being blunt, but I have a non-negotiable proposition for you." My face remains expressionless. "As you probably know, the Chinese and the Russians have a mutual understanding: the Chinese have the sole rights for all 'activities' in and around Chinatown, while the Russians have free rein across the rest of the city. That is how it has always been—well, until recently. Have you heard of the General?"

"It is funny that you should mention him because I've recently discovered that he was ultimately responsible for my friend's death. He either works for Mikhail or has recently left his employment—I suspect the latter."

"Correct. About one month ago, he started dealing drugs on the outskirts of Chinatown. Initially, we dismissed this transgression as confusion over our respective borders; however, about a week ago, he stepped across the line when he intercepted a large heroin shipment. Mikhail and I have been on very good terms for a long time." I know that this is true because he has made many sacrifices to maintain a good working relationship with Mikhail. He needs a strong relationship with him because he potentially has something that he desperately wants or could at least help him secure it more easily. "I suspect the

124

General has started running his own, independent operation; but I am currently not in a position to broach the subject with Mikhail, so I cannot categorically confirm my suspicion."

"Why don't you just set a trap for the General?"

"There is no time. We have another very large shipment of heroin arriving this afternoon. I do not care about any financial losses, but this shipment has buyers—including Mikhail and his brother—that I am keen not to anger. I am especially concerned about losing this shipment because it is going to be while before I receive next one." His eyes dart to the guy that I elbowed in the face and then back at me. This intentional look informs me that he is a loose cannon and cannot be trusted.

"I understand. For what it is worth, I don't believe that Mikhail is behind it; he is currently working on several highly lucrative deals to help him and his organisation expand their portfolio of legal operations."

I turn my head perpendicularly to face full-length mirror; damn, I do look like I'm having a rough time of it. This mirror is a relatively new addition to his office; I presume that there is a man standing behind it with a gun pointed at my head. This is a fairly common practice for people like the Dragon Master. I quickly scan for signs that there is a secret room behind it, but there are none. You could not tell that there is a secret room hidden behind it unless you have been in the room before its installation.

"The alternative is that the General now either works for or commands a new, upcoming, and ambitious criminal organisation that is not afraid of stepping on toes. Either way, both scenarios are unacceptable. We are solely responsible for Chinatown and its residents. We will not tolerate this behaviour; we will never give up *even one inch* of territory."

Donnie and Kevin become distracted by the Dragon Master's patriotism, so I use the opportunity to twist my wrists around and lever them apart. My shoulders burn painfully as I stretch the bondage binding my wrists together until it snaps. As the Dragon Master starts his next sentence, I launch myself up, reaching for their machine guns. Before they can react, I have relieved each of them of their weapons—which feel lighter than I was expecting.

In a synchronised movement, I drive the butts of their guns into their thighs. I swing the gun in my right hand across my body to hit the Donnie on my left-hand side in the face; he falls to the floor clutching his face. I ram the butt of the gun in my right hand into the thigh of the Kevin on my right-hand side again before smashing the butt of the gun in my left hand as hard as I can into his face. The force drives his head back and he collapses.

The remaining guy throws his bucket at me in an attempt to give himself time to withdraw his own weapon. I don't even attempt to block the bucket; it hits my chest as I drive my foot into his groin. I quickly manoeuvre myself behind him so that he shields me from the gun behind the large mirror. I drop the gun in my left hand and get him in a headlock with my free left arm. The gun's safety is turned off, so I fire at the bottom corner of the mirror—but no bullets are released.

My hostage stops trying to rip himself out of my grip; instead, he reaches for my gun. As soon as I release him, I elbow him in the back of the head. I snatch the Dragon Master's ashtray off his desk, turn, dive, and roll to decrease the amount of exposure I have to the mirror as my former hostage provides less and less shielding as he ungracefully falls to the floor. When I end up back on my feet, I launch the ashtray towards the mirror. I sprint the three remaining feet in the open before I am protected by the bookcase.

Looking at the reflection of the room provided by the clock on the wall, the ashtray bounces off the mirror and knocks some books off the shelf behind the desk. The mirror quivers but remains intact. I unclip my gun's magazine; it is empty. I throw them both on the floor and walk out from behind the bookcase with my hands up.

The Dragon Master has not moved, or even acted slightly surprised, the entire time; in fact, he looks like he is enjoying the show, nonchalantly sucking on his cigar. All three guys remain on the floor. The guy that I elbowed—again—is the only one not flapping around. The mirror swings open and a guy steps out of the secret room. He looks at the Dragon Master then back at me. He throws his magazine at me, drops his gun on the floor, and makes his way over to me. I walk towards him, stepping over Kevin.

Like with many of my confrontations, my opposition leads the fight with a big wild right hook, which my forearm deflects. As he pulls back his right arm in preparation for a repeat strike, he attempts to kick me in the ribs with his left foot. My elbow strikes his left shinbone, sending a painfully judder up my arm. When his left foot touches the floor and bears some weight, his shinbone snaps. This sudden and unexpected shock causes him to look down; this provides enough of a distraction for me to grab hold of his lapel with both hands unchallenged. I lift him up off the floor and towards me with ease. His fingers futilely claw at my arms. I drive my head forward for the headbutt. My head barely recoils, but his head is knocked back hard upon contact. I let go of him and the force propels him across the room.

The Dragon Master knocks his cigar ash into an old-fashioned whiskey glass that he has just pulled out of his drawers. I step back over Kevin and sit down.

"Right, now that's sorted, where were we?" I say, cordially.

"Very impressive, my friend," he says, stroking his chin whilst nodding his head a little. In the blink of an eye, he brings a handgun up from under his desk and points it at my forehead. "I can assure you this one is loaded."

"Naturally."

I make a stupid face and close my eyes when his index finger applies pressure to the trigger. It releases one of the loudest gunshots I have ever heard. Warm liquid splashes over, and runs down, the left-hand side of my face. I slowly open my eyes. His face is expressionless as he moves the gun across my body and fires another single gunshot. This time, the gunshot is much quieter as my senses have relaxed; I do not get covered in blood.

Blood oozes out of the bullet hole in the centre of Donnie's forehead. The guy that has received a couple of elbows from me has been shot in his right eye; his left eye remains open, staring at me with malice. I face the Dragon Master, but he is already out of his seat and walking around his desk to the guy who was hiding in the secret room. He stops abruptly, takes aim, and fires a bullet into the side of the guy's head. He turns, walks slowly back to his seat, and takes a long puff from his cigar. He sits down elegantly in his leather chair and places his gun on the desk next to his glass. He looks me in the eyes.

"I thought I'd trial the professionalism of my personal guards. When I ordered them to bring you in, I made sure that they didn't take their guns with them for their own safety. I used this opportunity to remove the bullets from all their magazines."

"Why?"

"Because they're my personal guards, and I wanted to test whether they provide me with the highest degree of protection that I demand. Not one of them checked their weapons when they got back here." He becomes visibly frustrated. "The only chance they'd have of protecting me from you would've been to shoot you. With compromised weaponry, they were effectively putting my life in mortal danger. They failed me and have paid the price. My remaining personal guards will never repeat their mistake."

I gaze at the handgun in his hand. I've never seen one like it before; it looks like it's from the future. There is a green LED band around the back of it between his grip and its barrel. He follows my gaze to his gun, but he ignores my hint for an explanation.

"What is this non-negotiable proposition that you've got for me then, my friend?" I release a polite smile. Kevin starts to squirm about on the floor, and the Dragon Master catches this movement in the corner of his eye.

"Despite the fact that you've interrupted several of our operations, and killed many of our men, we recognise—and I'd go so far as to say, admire—your talents, and know that with the right leverage you could potentially become a valuable asset to us," he says for the benefit of Kevin. Kevin sits up and wipes the blood off his face, some of it drops onto his lap. "Our organisation is rationale and doesn't deviate from the path required to satisfy our long-term strategy. This is what separates us from the barbarous Russians."

I nod my head in agreement.

"Frankly, I would like you to find out if the General still works for Mikhail, and what designs either he or Mikhail has on Chinatown. I need you to do this without anyone else finding out that he has been approached. I must make myself crystal clear though: under no circumstances are you allowed to kill him. First, we need to understand the situation before planning the subsequent course of action. That said, if you need to severely torture him to get the information then I'll default to your expert judgement on how to proceed in that case." He deeply inhales smoke from his cigar as Kevin gets to his feet.

"Why do you need me for this? You have hundreds of guys desperate to prove themselves to you." Kevin looks at him confused. He turns his attention to Kevin.

"Kevin, please go and get May-ling." Kevin bows, ashamed that I got the better of him. He looks at me with disgust as he steps over his deceased friend. I grab his arm as he walks by.

"Where is the baby?" He jumps out of his skin and looks at the Dragon Master, petrified.

"Excuse me?" the Dragon Master says, perplexed.

"Your men picked me up in a flat where I was looking after a baby girl because her mother had recently overdosed."

"And you left her there?" he explodes. Kevin does not respond. "We are not fucking animals! Get May-ling then the both of you go and bring the baby back here, immediately. For your own sake, I hope nothing bad has happened to her." As Kevin sprints to the door, he turns his head back to me; he wants me dead. "I cannot apologise enough. I promise you that once this is done, he'll be severely punished for his actions." I nod my head and grin.

"If he doesn't come back with the baby then I'll kill him myself."

He chooses to ignore me. "We need to be discreet. Even though we're fully prepared for an all-out war, it is not currently in our interests to go down that path." He smoothly knocks his cigar ash into the glass. "Also, now I know that you are OK, I'll call Hiromi back."

"Excuse me?"

"Yes, well, I should've said something earlier. I loaned Hiromi to Mikhail recently for several jobs that were of mutual benefit. When Mikhail asked for him to take part in the competition to kill you, I had no plausible excuse to decline his request." I move about uncomfortably in my chair. He glances at his gun. "In my defence, I was told that you were dying and had put the hit out on yourself."

"Well, yes—that is technically true. Long story short, Mikhail had me convinced that I was dying of natural causes when I made that arrangement with him."

"Ah. You can tell me all about it when this is all over then." He smiles with a 'you-know-you-can't-trust-Mikhail-so-what-did-you-expect' smile. "Anyway, I cannot apologise enough. As we are good friends, I will admit that I could not help but think that using your death to help restore peace between our two organisations would have been what you would have wanted?"

"Don't worry, my friend." I emphasise the words, 'my friend'. "I would've done the same if I were in your position. Anyway, I'll do whatever you require me to do in order to resolve the situation with the General. Well, as long as you do something for me in return."

"I'm listening."

"I need to borrow six of your men. They don't have to be your best men; in fact, any will do as long as they know how to fire a gun in a general direction."

"I potentially have some men that will suit your needs. When and where?"

"Spread out, discreetly surrounding Mikhail's estate at twenty-three hundred hours tonight." He frowns. "Don't worry, the Russians will not find out that the Chinese were even there. Your men should pop up at the perimeter of his estate and discharge a full magazine. They should then wait exactly twenty seconds, discharge another full magazine, and then disappear into the night. I should point out that your men are only there to provide a distraction—under no circumstance is anyone innocent to be injured.

"Some of your men should fire at his house, which I'll make sure is empty, whilst the others should concentrate on the vacant parked cars, etc. If any of your men are good shots, then to make my life easier, they should try to kill any of the men that fire back at them. If a couple of grenades could be thrown during the twenty-second break, then that would be welcomed."

"If you take care of the situation with the General then my men will carry out your plan."

"OK. It looks like we have a deal. Ah, one more thing. To protect your organisation, you may want to get your men to use the same weaponry that the Albanians use. They have been causing Mikhail quite a bit of trouble lately." He nods his head gently, but confidently, and places his cigar between his upturned lips.

He lets go of his gun and as soon as his palm leaves its grip, the green LED band changes to red. He pulls a photograph out of his top drawer and reluctantly shows it to me. It is an old photograph of his sister, Changying, which Emma and I have seen many times. It was taken a couple of months before she was abducted from their home village back in China.

"We will find her." I stare at her, struggling to hold back my emotions.

"We need to. I still have faith that we can track her down."

"I promised you we would. We can still do this and other great things together." I place my hand on his hand that is holding the photograph.

"I wouldn't put this extra burden on you if I had a choice. The situation with the General has the potential to cause an all-out war, which would greatly hinder the search for Changying." I take my hand off his and look into his eyes. His eyes expose a man who will never be stopped, distracted, or defeated. "You are the only one who I can trust to discreetly resolve this situation."

"Thank you for your kind words. After I've finished with Mikhail, I'll continue searching for Changying."

I extend my hand to him. He shakes it with an overly tight grip for an uncomfortably long time. He pulls his phone out of his inside jacket pocket. Within five seconds of ringing, the respondent answers.

"Plan C. Return to my office." He ends the call and places it on the desk next to his gun.

The office door is swung open, making me jump. The Dragon Master doesn't move. May-ling is stood at the threshold, beaming at me. She scowls briefly at the Dragon Master as she closes the door. Once the door is closed, she runs up to me, and embraces me.

"You're still alive, Patrick." She holds me tightly. "I never wanted Hiromi to go after you."

"I know. The Dragon Master made the right call—although, I wish he had at least tried to inform me of his decision."

"I am just so happy that you're still alive." She squeezes me even more tightly before releasing me.

"Did you think that he could kill me?" She laughs loudly, wiping a tear from her eye.

"May-ling, for sakes of appearances, please always refer to Patrick as Mr Kulikov. We can never be sure who is listening. And get yourself together. Have you seen Kevin?"

"No." She shakes her head.

"Can you please take Mr Kulikov to Madame Grace and her team of healers for a strong course of traditional Chinese physiotherapy and medicine. Also, tell the chefs to start preparing a feast for him. No expense is to be spared. I want him back here in a few hours, and I want him to be fighting fit again.

"Yes, Dragon Master." She bows her head low.

"Thank you, that is very generous of you."

"You are my guest; you shall be treated like an Emperor." His cigar hangs loosely between his lips. "One more thing, May-ling. I sent Kevin to fetch you as I need you both to retrieve a baby for Mr Kulikov." She looks at me shocked but doesn't question her orders. "Can you please inform and prepare the wet nurses: the baby is likely to be very hungry when you bring her back here. Also, please can you order Doctor Chiang to come here at once to give her a health check?"

"Yes, Dragon Master." She squeezes my shoulder before helping me up off the chair. We link our arms together.

"Relax, Mr Kulikov, we'll take of you."

Simultaneously, we both bow our heads low at the Dragon Master before turning to exit. As she opens the door for me, I whisper, "If I don't make it, can you please ensure that baby Talia is given to Emma?"

"Of course—I was going to ask if that was your wish."

Chapter 14
The Dragon Master

I am lying naked, face down on the rickety massage table—which I am possibly a couple of stone too heavy for. My hands are placed under my legs to hold up my arms because they hang over the sides of the table. It felt uncomfortable at first, but my face has quickly become accustomed to being squished into the headrest. Madame Grace's dainty feet appear underneath me then she places what looks, and smells, like incense directly under my face. The smoke attacks my face, mildly irritating my eyes.

"Take deep breaths, Mr Kulikov. Very deep breaths," she says, rubbing her hands over my back.

I close my eyes and start inhaling large volumes of the incense smoke. It becomes increasingly difficult to breathe as I start wincing in pain once she homes in on one of my many large, well-established knots. After a couple of minutes, my concerns, stresses, and body pains begin to evaporate and I become light-headed. With each breath, I succumb to a deeper and deeper sleep.

Weird shapes, objects, and colours start flashing violently in front of me until they become more stable images and footages of events that have occurred in my life. The footage of when Emma and I were sat in our surveillance van monitoring the camera feeds of a container port begins to play. That night we were reconnoitring the container port to develop a greater understanding of the Chinese Mafia's human trafficking network.

We were observing the foot soldiers unloading a consignment of slaves out from a shipping container through several infrared cameras that we had set up many weeks earlier. Once they had unloaded everyone that had survived the journey into one van, they started unloading everyone that hadn't into a separate one. Whilst the foot soldiers were in the container collecting another dead body, a 'dead' woman jumped out of the van and ran into the maze of shipping containers.

She probably would have escaped too, if it wasn't for the Dragon Master—who was unknown to us at the time—overseeing the operations from the comfort of his Porsche Cayenne. He leapt out of his car, gun in hand, and pursued his prey. She quickly escaped our surveillance range and he was hot on her tail. I sprinted after them with no other intention than to observe the outcome; I could not interfere with their operation without highlighting that it was under surveillance.

In the shadows of the surrounding shipping containers, I observed the woman collapse from exhaustion; however, he caught her before she hit the tarmac. As she lay in his arms, I had my gun pointed at his temple, fighting the temptation to pull the trigger. He spent several seconds whispering into her ear, which seemed to bring her back to life. Unexpectedly, he then released her and watched her whilst she stumbled away into the darkness. On his return journey, he casually fired one bullet into the sea.

I remember debating with myself whether to catch the slave or follow him—I chose the latter. I followed him back to his crew, who had finished unloading everyone and were waiting nervously for his return. The gunshot had asserted his dominance; instilling order, and, more importantly, fear in the new slaves. It also restored order and fear in his men, especially those that were rebellious and overly ambitious.

The Dragon Master waved one hand forward once, and everyone jumped into their vans and disappeared into the night. With my gun still pointed at his head, I watched him for several minutes from the shadows whilst he did nothing other than look at his phone. Afterwards, he calmly got back into his car and drove away.

The original plan was for Emma and I to follow the van containing the living slaves. She would drive the surveillance van; I would drive my car. This would have allowed her to demonstrate the tailing techniques that I had taught her. But, by the time that I got to where the surveillance van had been, Emma had already left; she was not willing to risk losing the tail of the van containing the living slaves. I ran to my car and raced after them.

I quickly caught up with the Dragon Master. After a short distance, he pulled into a layby along the container port's external fencing. As he turned, his headlights panned across the fencing and I glimpsed the escaped slave waiting on the other side of it as I drove past. I had no choice other than to put my foot down on the accelerator pedal and speed into the dark, deserted stretch of road in front of me.

Once I reached the next village, I pulled into a side road and waited for him. After waiting for roughly ten minutes, I thought that he must have taken another route back to the city. As I was about to drive off and catch up with Emma, he casually drove past me. He was laughing with the slave, who was sat next to him in the front passenger's seat. Somewhat relieved, but now even more curious, I waited for a short amount of time before following him again.

I became very unsettled by the image of him laughing with the slave as I followed him back towards the city. We were headed towards Chinatown when he unexpectedly turned down a very respectable, well-to-do street. He indicated momentarily before his brake lights lit up my car. This forced me to duck down out of sight behind my steering wheel. He turned into the driveway of what looked like the most expensive house on the street.

Once I had driven by, I immediately turned off my lights and pulled over. Before I came to a halt, I simultaneously turned off the ignition and pulled up the handbrake. I fell out of my car and sprinted back to his house. His driveway was poorly lit, so I didn't hesitate in getting low and diving behind his car. I remained hidden behind his car, getting blasted by strong diesel fumes, as he slowly rolled it forwards into his garage. As soon as he stopped, I awkwardly crawled under his car.

They both silently got out of the car and left the garage via an internal door. The garage door closed shortly afterwards, leaving me lying in complete darkness. The car's lights momentarily lit up the garage when it locked itself.

I waited for approximately thirty minutes before rolling out from under the car. I withdrew my gun and surveyed the garage and car with my phone's light. There was nothing out of the ordinary. I also egressed the garage through the internal door. I climbed the steep stairs, which were under the house's main staircase, towards the source of the light streaming through the gap under the door at the top.

I opened the door and stood at the threshold, listening to the slave joyously singing a Chinese song in the shower upstairs, and the ringing of cutlery behind the door on my right. I entered the hallway and was momentarily distracted by the pair of beautifully crafted Chinese porcelain vases supported by a modern oak table. I kept my gun pointed at the origin of the banging behind what I deduced was the kitchen door.

The kitchen door was already ajar, so I slowly pushed it open until it revealed him standing in front of me with his back facing me. He threw the contents of the wok into the air and caught it all again like a master chef. Before I fully committed myself to enter the immaculate kitchen, I made sure that he could not see me in any reflections from any shiny surfaces or the windows. My heart rate spiked when I saw that the table had been set for three people. I spun around to make sure that no one had snuck up on me from behind; the hallway was deserted. The slave continued to sing after she turned off the shower.

As soon as my heart rate settled, it peaked again when he casually said, "I hope you're hungry, my friend." He continued to cook undisturbed with his back facing me. I did not reply. "I would greatly appreciate it if you would put your gun away; you'll scare my other guest when she comes downstairs." He lifted the wok off the cooker and turned around with it to face me. I recognised his face, but I couldn't place where I had seen it before. He smiled at me but didn't say anything as he carried the wok to the dining room table. Both of his hands were on its handle, so I tucked my gun back into my belt.

He turned to face me with a beaming smile. "Where would you like to sit, my friend?" After I'd finished assessing the situation, I concluded that there was no immediate threat; I nodded at the chair with its back to the wall, facing the room. He continued to smile. "Of course." He waited for me to take my seat before he piled the food onto my plate. As he leaned into me, I scanned his face and eyes to spot any telltale signs that he was going to escape or attack me, but there were none. In fact, he was genuinely very calm and relaxed.

Over his shoulder, on the wall next to the kitchen door, was a TV that displayed an infrared camera feed of his garage. I let out a deep sigh; I was more embarrassed than annoyed. His smile spread even wider across his face. "Your dinner would've been ruined if you had stayed under my car much longer."

The girl walked timidly into the kitchen. He stood up straight and turned to face her. I followed his lead. She stopped in her tracks when she saw me, internally questioning who I was and why I was here. He noticed this. He walked around to the chair on my right-hand side and released one hand from the wok so that he could pull it out from under the table.

This wasn't enough to relax her, so he whispered something to her in Chinese. After she took another look at me, her shoulders and demeanour relaxed. It was obvious that she was very malnourished, even under the oversized male dressing gown. Prior to sitting down, she bowed to him and hesitated momentarily before bowing to me. Once she was sat down, I sat down.

She was disappointed when she was only served a small portion of food, but she didn't question it. She had been starved for about a month so, despite the massive temptation, she needed to slowly reintroduce food into her system. He served himself a standard portion of food. The girl stared at my food when he returned to the kitchen to put the empty wok in the sink. I kept a discreet eye on his hands to make sure that he didn't pick up anything on his way back to attack me with. His knife block remained fully populated—which I suspected was a decoy to comfort me.

The girl and I sat in silence whilst we were both poured a glass of ice-cold water. As soon as her glass was full, she picked it up and started to down it. After several deep gulps, the glass was pulled from her grasp and placed on the table. Her hands shook due to a mixture of low blood sugar and nerves. She became too afraid to look at me; she still had reservations about my purpose at this table.

He joined us at the table and said a few words in Chinese before picking up his chopsticks. The girl and I followed his lead. As I struggled to get the first piece of beef secured firmly between the chopsticks, he said, "My name is Lee Huang, and this is May-ling." May-ling was too busy eating to look up at the sound of her name. "And how do we address you, my friend?"

"Call me, Patrick," I said, calling out the first name that popped into my head.

"Patrick. I've been working hard recently to ensure that our paths crossed." The piece of beef slipped out of my grasp halfway to my mouth and fell back on my plate. I internally questioned if he has set me up, but I did not display any concern.

"Have you really?" I continued looking down at the elusive piece of beef that I was determined to get it in my mouth. It had been a long time since I had eaten such a good meal. The girl was shovelling the food into her mouth until she caught his gaze. He turned his attention back to me.

"We both hate human trafficking and will do whatever we can to put an end to it." I could tell that he had a well-toned body hidden underneath his clothes. This, combined with his mannerisms and calm nature, led me to believe that he had either good hand-to-hand combat skills, or a weapon close at hand. I felt under the table for a weapon, but to no avail. I decided to take the bait.

"I find your sentiment a little contradictory, considering that I witnessed you unloading a consignment of trafficked slaves from a shipping container tonight." I said, victoriously placing the delicious piece of beef into my mouth.

"Ah, yes. I suppose that does appear a bit contradictory on the face of it. As you may be aware, I've recently been made the Head of Human Trafficking Operations for the Chinese Mafia in this city. I achieved this rank by staying one step ahead of the 'vigilante', or should I say, you! Can you remember the shootout that took place between the police and the Chinese foot soldiers approximately seven years ago at that same container port where we were earlier?"

"Vaguely. You'll have to remind me of the specifics though?" I replied, knowing full well the event that he is referring to.

"Well, I arrived on these shores in a shipping container from China. I was bundled into a minibus, and a couple of minutes later a shootout broke out. The foot soldiers were significantly better armed than the police, who, in turn, were better organised and managed to corner several of them near the other minibus that was loaded with slaves. The police blew out the tyres of that minibus whilst mine sped away.

"The cornered foot soldiers knew that they could not escape, especially with the slaves. So, they set the fully loaded minibus on fire, hoping that it would provide a big enough distraction for them to escape. Even though many of my new friends were being burnt alive, I could barely keep my eyes open long enough to watch. That was until you jumped out of the black sea, like Poseidon himself. Without hesitation, you punched through the glass in the back door of the minibus, opened it and dived straight in."

I glanced at the scar that runs a good length of my left index finger, which still sometimes hinders its movement, especially when it is cold.

"Moments before my minibus disappeared behind a shipping container, I saw you throw three slaves, who were on fire, over four metres into the sea from inside the back of the minibus."

"I couldn't stand by and watch." He leaned forward, taking in every word that I said.

My right shoulder blade hurts painfully from where the flames licked it, and I didn't know if it is imaginary pain, or it is Madame Grace is being particularly rough with a knot.

"It was like watching a superhero movie." He threw his hands up in the air. I laughed out loud whilst trying to slurp way too many noodles into my mouth.

"In the movies, everyone would've been saved. Unfortunately, the minibus was overcome by flames and I couldn't save everyone." He nodded his head respectfully.

"I cannot thank you enough for what you did that night. Especially, as you gave me the inspiration and drive to get to where I am today. That said, I'm now in a position where I need your help?"

"I'm sorry, but I'll not stop until your organisation has ceased all human trafficking operations." I contemplated blowing his brain out. He looked at the girl then back at me.

"She reminds me of my younger sister, Changying." He handed me the same photograph of her that he showed me earlier. I picked up the photograph; they did look like siblings. He held out his hand and I handed him back the photograph. "I'll do whatever it takes to find Changying. Whatever!"

He smashed his chopsticks on the table. He scared May-ling but didn't apologise. "I needed to get involved in all aspects of the human trafficking operation to keep her trail alive. The people who have her must be buying other slaves. My search has been slow, especially as I am forced to be very discreet and cautious. Also, you've disturbed many of our operations, and have affected our relationships with many buyers, one of which may already have her.

"I've greatly improved the conditions in which my people are being trafficked. The survival rate for the journey is now ninety percent." He was stating facts, he wasn't boasting. Plus, I was not impressed. "I've also saved many people from the clutches of the buyers." There was sorrow in his eyes when he glanced at May-ling, who by now was struggling to eat all her food. "Every time I save someone, it feels like I've saved a part of Changying." He then changed the conversation before he upset himself too much. "You've already helped me greatly." It was then that I released where I had seen his face before.

"With your predecessor?" I interrupted.

"Precisely."

I tracked a consignment of slaves being transported in a lorry from one holding house to another. Later that night, I broke into the holding house and started taking down all the foot soldiers. Unfortunately, several of them managed to escape, but his predecessor got locked a room with me. It was the Dragon Master's face that I saw through the glass on the other side of the locked door. I severely beat up his predecessor before breaking out of the room and setting the freed slaves on him. They were vicious creatures; they ripped his skin off using only their fingernails and started eating it whilst he was alive.

I was only halfway through eating when he finished eating his meal. He placed his chopsticks next to his plate. He then proceeded to tell me his story.

"Nearly everyone in my home village back in China was a farmer, including everyone in my family. We farmed to feed ourselves mainly, making little money from any surplus we could hide from the local crime lord, who demanded 'security payments'. My dad had the biggest farm in the village and he worked hard enough on it to not require my hands to help out—or that is what he told me. This gave me the freedom to attend the medical school at the 'local' university.

"During my final year, where I was on course to finish at the top of my class, there was a particularly brutal heat wave. This, and the consequential drought, resulted in a poor harvest. The small yield that managed to grow was stolen by the local crime lord's goons to feed their own families. They did not leave much for everyone else to eat, let alone sell. In a short space of time, the heat, drought, and lack of food caused the village's population to plummet. My mother died from exhaustion whilst working the ground.

"To make matters worse, the local crime lord had debts with an even more powerful and deadly regional crime lord, which he couldn't fulfil due to the villagers defaulting on their security payments to him. To pay off his debts, him and his goons swooped into the village one night and kidnapped as many of the surviving girls and young women as they could get their hands on. The local crime lord personally fought and killed my father, who tried to protect Changying." He wiped the tears away from his face. May-ling didn't understand what he was saying but grew very concerned.

"I was obviously beside myself with rage and thought of nothing other than finding Changying, and killing the local crime lord and all his goons. Several days later, as fate would have it, he was rushed to my hospital due to an infection originating from several of my father's bite marks. I knew that the corrupt police force would never do anything about the crimes that he and his goons had committed; I had to take matters into my own hands. Especially, as I knew that this could be the last opportunity that I'd have had to locate her before she potentially disappeared forever.

"During the night, as the activity in the hospital died down, I snuck onto his ward. He was big and had a reputation for beating very experienced fighters, so I safeguarded myself by tying his arms and legs to the trolley before waking him. The ward was very understaffed, and he was heavily sedated, so I managed to push his trolley to a private room unnoticed with ease. I started off trying to strangle him for information, but it was fruitless—he was such a strong man.

"Therefore, I was forced to use the scalpel that I had stored in my pocket for extra protection. Suffice it to say, it didn't take long until he told him that she had been sold to the regional crime lord to pay his debt, and that she would most likely have been dispatched to this country in a shipping container along with the rest of those taken from my village.

"I ensured that he received a quick, but very painful death, before locking his corpse in the private room. Private rooms were rarely used, so it would have been a while—possibly days—before anyone knew about the murder, especially as I stuck a handwritten 'Do Not Enter – Renovations in Progress' sign on the door. This gave me maximum time to flee from the authorities, and possibly his goons; if they still cared about him enough to seek vengeance without being paid. I withdrew my meagre savings and headed straight to the dockyard where Changying had been sent. The dockyard was run by the Chinese Mafia, and they didn't hesitate to take all my money and launch me into an already overcrowded shipping container.

"We were all locked in the container for over a month, and only saw daylight once a week when the container was being hosed down. Most of the people in my container were there by choice, each having their own reasons to escape our home country. Despite the lack of food and water, they were determined that they would survive the journey, which is why all, except a small handful, did. Those that died were simply weighed down and tossed overboard.

"I was never under the impression that I would be set free once the ship docked. Although, I was shocked by how badly humans can treat one another. As soon as the shipping container's doors opened, I was hoisted out of it and thrown into the back of a minibus. There was then the drama with the police and you, but after that, we didn't stop until we reached the safety of Chinatown. I was given a couple of days to rest and recover, before I was forced to work inhumanely long hours for free as a modern slave in the kitchen of one of Chinatown's less hygiene conscious All-You-Can-Eat restaurants.

"Every second I spent slaving away in the hot and hectic kitchen, the colder Changying's trail became. To make matters worse, I was forced to work eighteen hours a day; the only time I had out of the kitchen I actually needed for sleep. I quickly mastered how to operate in a kitchen environment, which wasn't too dissimilar to working in an operating theatre. I worked harder than anyone else to gain my handler's trust. Although, it took several weeks—which felt like a lifetime—for my handler to trust me enough to let me escape for short periods during the restaurant's quiet hours to follow up leads on Changying's whereabouts.

"Unfortunately, on one occasion, the bus I was returning on broke down. This resulted in me making it back to the restaurant a lot later than I had agreed with my handler. Insubordination of the slaves is not tolerated, so my handler sent everyone else home when the kitchen had stopped serving, leaving me to finish cleaning it on my own as punishment. Well, I thought that was the only punishment until I realised that he had ordered three new recruits to rough me up as part of their initiation into the Chinese mafia.

"First, they started throwing me around the kitchen. At the time, I thought they were going to kill me, or at least injure me enough to impact on my ability to find Changying. I grabbed a recently sharpened kitchen knife and, because of my medical background, I knew the places where to stab it for a quick, unstoppable death.

"The first guy to approach me was unaware of my knife until I stabbed it into his jugular. Blood sprayed everywhere and when the next guy tried to grab me, he slipped on it, cracking his head open on the floor. The final guy grabbed his own knife and charged at me. I knew that I wouldn't be able to fight him, so I seized the handle of a saucepan that I was 'soaking' with boiling water and threw its contents at his face.

"Afterwards, I slouched on the floor next to the kitchen units drenched in blood, trying to catch my breath whilst contemplating my next move. I thought someone was looking at me; I looked up and saw one of the top bosses peering at me through the circular window in the kitchen door. This is that same boss, that with my help, worked his way up to become my predecessor, whom I locked in that room with you." He smiled nervously, but I ignored him.

"My handler must not have known that the boss was having a family meal in the restaurant—his restaurant—that night. He had seen the three men enter the kitchen and was concerned about what was going to happen on his premises. He left his family meal to investigate. He said that he watched everything in amazement from the kitchen window.

"Luckily for me, instead of being angry that I had killed what were essentially his men, he was in fact impressed by my determination, grit, and audacity. The level of incompetence of people in the lower ranks used to be appalling. That is why when he looked at me, he not only saw a caged animal desperate to get out, but also a man who would be a very valuable asset to his organisation with the right guidance, direction, and grooming.

"I had now made it onto my boss' radar and it didn't take me long to further impress him. It turns out that I had the skills, intelligence, and entrepreneurship needed to survive in this world and, above all, make them all a lot of money. No one worked harder than me; I was desperate to be initiated so I could gain the freedom to properly start looking for Changying. Being uninitiated was like being lost in the wildness without a map. Eventually, after killing, manipulating, and bribing people, I have managed to become the Head of Human Trafficking Operations. Unfortunately, even in this position, certain paths on the map still need to be unlocked." His face turned serious. "Will you help me find Changying?"

"Of course, I will," I responded instantly. A wide smile spread across his face like he had won the lottery.

"As I've already said, I'll do anything to find Changying. What is your price?" he said.

"I do not have a price," I replied. The smile diminished noticeably on his face. "I appreciate what you've been doing, but we cannot risk you freeing any more slaves. Whilst it is noble, if your bosses found out, they would kill you and possibly replace you with someone who is extremely callous; therefore, I'll help you find Changying and help you get to the top of your organisation as long as when you get there, you promise to abide by the following conditions: first, you'll only transport people here if it is for their own safety; second, you'll greatly improve the conditions that are endured during transport and once they are here; third, you'll pay everyone at least a living wage and, where possible, you'll give them contracts of employment to put an end slavery; fourth, no one will be forced into prostitution; fifth, you'll provide free transport back to China for those that were removed without their permission; sixth, you'll help those who want to stay here become citizens, if possible; and seventh, you'll allow me to discreetly oversee all human trafficking operations."

"If you help me get to the top, I promise to abide by those conditions, and more, even if we haven't found Changying by then. Having been through the current process myself, I am keen to ensure that no one else ever experiences such brutality," he said, with his hand held out. I reached across the table and firmly shook his hand.

Chapter 15
The Alliance

Five hours later, I feel fully revitalised. The massage, the Chinese medicine, the full meal, and the quick nap have given me a new lease of life. Madame Grace opens the Dragon Master's office door, which catches on the carpet, and hands me a small, clear bag of white powder.

"One pea-sized amount for mild pain, double the amount for bad pain, triple the amount for serious pain. Don't take more than this if you've still got a fight ahead," she says, quietly.

"Thank you, I am sure that this will be very handy," I say, bowing whilst continuing to walk. She reciprocates the bow. I stuff the bag into my new jeans, which are uncomfortably tight, but they are very stretchy, giving me a full range of movement.

I re-enter the Dragon Master's office, which is now packed full of people and a hive of activity. The room falls quiet as everyone turns to face me. They all shuffle awkwardly, ensuring access to their weapons is even easier. I survey the room looking for potential weapons should I need them, but they are all out of easy reach. I eye up the foot soldiers and quickly decide which ones I would attack first and by what means.

All the foot soldiers are positioned in a rough semi-circle around Hiromi, who is sat in the seat I was held hostage in earlier. Kevin leans on the wall on the other side of the Dragon Master; from his body language, it is obvious that his testicles still hurt him. The fact that Kevin is still in the room means that he is very valuable to the Dragon Master. The Dragon Master doesn't even look at me as he speaks, "Mr Kulikov, welcome back. Everyone, this is our new friend. You need to extend to him all the courtesies that you extend to me." They all hate me even more now; everyone in this room would kill everyone in their family to be addressed like this by the Dragon Master. Hiromi stands up and gestures with his hands that I take the now vacant seat. I reject his offering by waving my hands out and shaking my head. I stay at the back, positioned nearest to the door. He shrugs his shoulders and sits back down on the chair. There is no sign of blood on the carpet around the chair. This, combined with the desk now being slightly closer to the window and the catching of the door on the carpet, means that the carpet has already been replaced.

I study all the faces in the room and try to remember each of them. The Dragon Master looks me in the eyes and without showing any facial expressions, I know that he knows what I am thinking. I am thinking why has he shown and introduced me to all these people? He knows that I will have to kill everyone in this room now as I cannot afford for them to remember my face. I will have to be careful working with these people as they are likely to be very junior and/or untrustworthy foot soldiers.

"You all know your roles; do not fuck up," the Dragon Master says intimidatingly. "Everyone, go to your vehicles. Everyone except for Mr Kulikov and Mr Li, please remain here." Without a word or even a mumble, everyone leaves apart from Kevin.

As Hiromi glides past me, he whispers, "If the Dragon Master hadn't called me off, you would be dead already." I do not reply; instead, I stare menacingly at him until he leaves the room. The last guy out of the room closes the door behind himself.

"Right gentlemen, before we start, shake hands," the Dragon Master demands.

I look at Kevin with disgust, but I do not hold a grudge. He was only doing his job and, fair play to him, he got the upper hand on me. If anything, I am annoyed at myself; I will make sure that it doesn't happen again. I notice the full-length mirror and am positive that the guy behind it this time will have a fully loaded machine gun.

Kevin struggles walking to me, and I spitefully do not move to make his journey that little bit more painful. He nervously reaches out with his right hand whilst his left hand unconsciously moves to cover his testicles. When my palm contacts his sweaty palm, he squeezes as hard as he can. I assert my dominance by having a limp grip, forcing him to adjust his grip to also be limp.

"I know that you two will not be best of friends, but I can assure you that Kevin does not hold any grudges."

"That is true. I do not." Kevin's head slumps forward. He does, but the Dragon Master has forewarned him that revenge is not an option, at least not whilst our assignment is in progress.

"And I do not hold a grudge against you for injecting me with whatever poison you injected me with and holding me hostage at gunpoint." I maintain a stern face. This takes them both back a little bit as this was not part of their rehearsal earlier. Kevin looks at the Dragon Master, who averts his gaze.

"That is good." I stop the Dragon Master from proceeding to his next sentence by asking, "How is Talia?" He sits back and smiles; this time he welcomes my interruption. We both look at Kevin.

"She is very well. I left her with May-ling and the wet nurses. The doctor should be with them shortly," he says, proudly. I nod my head and keep it lowered just in case tears start to well up in my eyes—but they don't.

"Thank you for doing that. That is a big weight off my shoulders. I know she is in good hands if May-Ling has got her." The Dragon Master goes straight back to business.

"Kevin is one of my promising new recruits, and I am hoping that if he proves himself worthy, he'll soon be promoted to the Head of Human Trafficking Operations."

I stop him from proceeding to his next sentence again.

"Has he been fully briefed?" I am mad that he hasn't briefed this to me before. Kevin is taken aback, and visibly frustrated by how I am talking to the Dragon Master.

"Yes, I have," Kevin says, but the Dragon Master cuts him off.

"No, not all. Being trafficked here himself as a slave, he knows what we are trying to achieve." Without knowing more about Kevin's background, I suddenly have a lot more respect for him. "However, he does not know the full extent of your involvement, and I've explained that he may never know—which he has accepted. He appreciates any help that you can provide. He also appreciates your need for complete discretion so, for this assignment, he has chosen our, somewhat, more expendable members." He smiles, sinisterly. "Upon completion of the assignment, he will kill everyone else involved."

"Even Hiromi?" I say, abruptly.

"Well, we've talked about this and Kevin is happy to take care of Hiromi—unless you disagree or would like the challenge yourself?" He smiles, teasingly. I just return a noncommittal smile. "It is worth me pointing out that Hiromi has

146

recently been working hard to prove himself; he is desperate to be my deputy. To be truthful, he has gone above and beyond what anyone else has done for this organisation, but he is not the type of person that we need in a position of authority." I nod my head, understanding what he is avoiding saying. "Additionally, I do not trust him, certainly not as much as I trust Kevin." He smiles at Kevin.

"OK, I'll be keeping a close eye on them both anyway," I say in a successful attempt at scaring Kevin. He knows that he is no match for me, especially as I am nearly three times his weight. "Anyway, let's move away from this subject, and onto the assignment in hand."

"Very well. Kevin will be your assistant until you return back to me."

"Why? You know I work best when I am alone."

"I want him to learn from you. Also, if you're not as fully recovered as you think you are, then you may need someone to watch your back. He'll not slow you down. If he does, and/or compromises the assignment, then you have my permission to leave him behind or kill him—whatever is needed. OK?" He is deadly serious. Kevin looks at me proudly.

"It doesn't look like I have a choice. As long as he doesn't get too close. All I ask is that if I give him a command then he follows that command, no questions asked."

"You have my word, Mr Kulikov," Kevin says confidently with a straight back.

"We've confirmed that the General is currently staying in the flat where he has been keeping his slaveboy. His slaveboy is a Russian boy, possibly as young as fourteen, who has been kept captive in the flat for over a month now," the Dragon Master says, lighting half a cigar. "We don't know anything else about him, not even his name."

"How have you even got that information?" I question, concerned that the General has set a trap for us.

"We got it from our contact who lives on the same floor as him," the Dragon Master smiles. "We have eyes everywhere." I smile back.

"So, that is how you found me. The person in the flat opposite my flat is also one of your contacts?" He nods, deeply inhaling his cigar. After he exhales, he says, "Like I said, we have eyes everywhere."

"Does Mikhail know about the slaveboy?" I ask, suspecting that I already know the answer.

"I highly doubt it. You need to act fast because the best time to question the General will be when he is with his slaveboy."

"Why?" Kevin interrupts. The look that the Dragon Master gives Kevin shows that he is not impressed with his naïve question.

"Mikhail and his men do not tolerate homosexual behaviour, especially homosexual behaviour with minors—possibly reminds them of their own experiences growing up. Therefore, it is highly unlikely that he'll have any homosexually sympathetic bodyguards protecting him. Hopefully, his bodyguards do not even know where he is."

Kevin reaches inside his jacket, pulls out a gun, and offers it to me. It is a strange-looking modern gun. It is not as elegant, nor as sophisticated, as the one that the Dragon Master had earlier. It has an especially long magazine and I can tell from its weight that it is not loaded.

"This is a new close-range pistol; it was designed for the Russian Secret Service," he explains. "These guns have recently started to appear on the streets. We view them as a smaller, and somewhat friendlier, handgun version of the Kalashnikov. It will look more like a Russian hit if we use these weapons." I hold the gun to my face. "I am sorry, Mr Kulikov, but the bullets are in the minibus." He is relieved by his own statement. "It is a protocol that uninitiated members do not have weapons in the presence of the Dragon Master."

"Do not worry, sometimes I can be deadlier without a weapon," I state matter-of-factly.

Chapter 16
The General

Kevin and I step out of the lift onto the lowest level of the underground carpark and walk towards the two minibuses. These are the only two vehicles on this level, except for the fleet of black G-Class Mercedes-Benz that are lined up on the left-hand side. This fleet is the Dragon Master's pride and joy. Kevin guides me to the front minibus, which only contains a driver. The other minibus contains all the foot soldiers, who have changed their appearances to give the impression that they are a group of Chinese tourists; they certainly look very nonthreatening. Hiromi sits in the front passenger's seat. His body language suggests that he is bitter and revengeful.

We reach the front minibus. Kevin jumps in the front; I jump in the back. Before I can shut the sliding side door, our driver accelerates forward. He negotiates the concrete pillars and narrow ramps with the skill of a professional racing driver. We reach the ground level and the cars on the road immediately give way, allowing both minibuses to seamlessly enter the flowing stream of traffic.

The Dragon Master's office is strategically placed at the heart of Chinatown's business district. The residential and tourist districts that surround the business district act as a moat. Any police entering the surrounding areas are quickly reported to the local foot soldiers, who are quick to forward on the message. The Dragon Master ensures that very generous gifts are given to anyone providing his foot soldiers with useful information, or putting themselves in danger, to ensure the ultimate survival of the Chinese Mafia and Chinatown.

After approximately twenty minutes, we arrive at a council estate, which has an ugly-looking concrete tower block in its centre. Both minibuses drive into the estate and park on a quiet side road. I lean forward and tell my driver, "Please tell the other driver to park behind that black Volkswagen up the road. You'll then park behind it, but not too close."

Our driver looks at Kevin, who nods without looking at him. He picks up his walkie-talkie and relays my request to the other driver in very quick Chinese. As soon as the other minibus parks behind the Volkswagen, all the foot soldiers jump out of it and disperse. As they spread out, a brand-new BMW drives slowly past us. The two occupants draw my attention further because they are too smartly dressed for either of them to be residents, or have business interests, in this area. Also, no one would be stupid enough to park such as a nice car around here. I put my hands up to cover my face and look at them through my fingers. All their attention is on the driver until they notice Kevin and me. The driver and Kevin do not even notice them pass by as they both seem too preoccupied dealing with their nerves.

I lean forward again and whisper, "Kevin, I would appreciate it if all communication was in English from now on."

"But some of the guys don't even speak English," he whispers back.

"Then only communicate with those that can." I end the conversation. My brain cannot stop analysing the two people who drove past in the BMW. I feel like I am a sitting duck; the longer I sit here, the more trapped I feel. Kevin turns and holds up a balaclava.

"Do you require a balaclava, Mr Kulikov?"

"No, thank you." I lower my eyebrows. "Please make sure that no one else wears one either. It will attract too much attention." A fat youth walks across the road, heading away from the tower block. I tap on the driver's shoulder and say, "Go and buy that youth's hoodie and cap off him, please."

He looks at Kevin, who looks at me and then turns back to him and nods. He reluctantly gets out of the minibus and jogs over to him. They barely have time to exchange any words before the youth pushes him out into the road. The few people that are around momentarily look at what is going on before looking back down at their phones.

"Kevin, please go and assist him. I wasn't expecting such a scene."

I position myself to jump into the driver's seat so that I can follow the BMW if it drives past again. Kevin huffs in annoyance but gets out of the car and jogs over to them. He has already withdrawn a bundle of cash from his pocket by the time he reaches them. The young man snatches the money out of his hand. He takes his garments off quickly and hands them to him. The exchange is over in seconds.

Kevin is on his phone as he walks back to the minibus; I can hear him talking in Chinese. He doesn't look at me as puts the phone in his pocket before opening the front passenger's door.

"We are clear to go, Mr Kulikov. The General is with his slaveboy and my men have confirmed that the area is clear." He closes his door. I barely register his words as I am in deep thought.

"Pass me the hoodie," I say, ripping it out of his grip. "You can wear the cap."

Something in my gut tells me not to go through the main entrance of the tower block. I assess the available options in my head, and I agree with myself that I am not willing to risk my life based on information from this incompetent group of people, even if they are unequivocally loyal to the Dragon Master. I think it is Hiromi that is tormenting my subconsciousness; he has tried to kill me once already, and I don't think he will hesitate to try again, especially if he knew he could get away with it. I put the hoodie on and it stretches well to accommodate my body. I put up the hood to complete my outfit.

Kevin puts his cap on, opens the glove compartment, takes out a long magazine, and passes it to me. I eject the current empty magazine, insert the new one, and check that the gun's safety is still on before tucking it into my trousers and hiding the exposed magazine under my hoodie.

"Do I only get one magazine?"

"That's all we brought for you; you shouldn't need anymore because you'll be well-protected if a firefight breaks out." I am annoyed, but I don't let my face reveal it. Kevin and his men are just protecting themselves from me.

I lean forward as the driver gets back into his seat and closes his door.

"I need you to drive very slow and as close as you can to the tower block. After Kevin and I leave the vehicle, I want you to spin around and come directly back to this spot, facing the tower block with the engine running. Do you understand?" I know he understands, but I want confirmation. He looks slightly confused but nods his heads. "I want you to wait here until you see us leaving the flat then come and collect us. Do you understand?" Again, he looks confused but nods his head anyway. "When I signal you, I need you to drive as quickly as possible to pick us. Once you have us, take us straight back to the Dragon Master, and do not stop for anyone or anything." I turn to face Kevin, who gives me his undivided attention.

"If you insist on following me then please step out of the minibus." He looks at me suspiciously but does as I ask. He follows me to the rear of the minibus; I scan the area, making sure no one is around.

"What are you planning, Mr Kulikov?" He keeps his distance from me.

"Pass me your foot." I cup my hands together slightly above his knee height. "We are getting on top of the minibus." I sigh. "The deal was that you do not ask questions!" He smiles, placing his right foot in my hands. With ease, I launch him on top of the minibus. I place my left foot on the rear step and launch myself up after him. As soon as my foot leaves the step, my hands slap against the roof. I lift myself up until my arms are fully extended, swing my left leg up, and roll onto the roof.

I lie down and check that the coast is still clear before banging on the roof with my right knuckle. The driver immediately jerks us forwards and it is more aggressive than either Kevin or I had expected. Kevin loses his balance and would have fallen off the minibus if I hadn't of grabbed his trouser leg and pulled him down next to me. We both adopt a low crouching position.

"Are you sure that you still want to go through with this." I concentration on the approaching first-floor balcony. He does not reply as he is also concentrating on the approaching balcony. Something about his demeanour suggests that he has transformed into the soldier that I need him to be. As we get closer, the driver is going faster than I would like him to; I bang my fist on the roof to signal that he needs to slow down. After a couple of seconds, he hasn't responded to my cue, so I smash my fist into the roof—denting it badly. This time, he gets the cue straight away and slows down, but it isn't slow enough. He isn't exposed to the elements so he probably feels like he is travelling at an appropriate speed.

Moments before we make the jump, a young family drives past us; all the members of the family are engrossed in an argument, distracting any of them from noticing at us. There are no other cars on the road and only people that around now are the Dragon Master's men. Once we are within a metre of the middle first-floor balcony, Kevin jumps first swiftly followed by me. I judge the distance well and get a good grip on the top of the balcony wall. Kevin is up and over first. As I pull myself up, he attempts to grab hold of my wrist to help me up.

"What do you think you are doing?" I demand, launching myself up onto the balcony.

"I was only trying to help you, Mr Kulikov." His head drops like a misbehaved dog when it knows it is in trouble.

"Well, don't."

"Many apologies, sir."

"If you want to be of assistance then check that no one in this flat has seen us," I instruct. He spins around and gets out his gun before looking through the patio doors.

"Clear."

"Put your gun away. Imagine if someone had seen it—the police would be here in no time." He hesitates before putting his gun away, so I grab hold of his wrist. "No one innocent gets killed, OK?" He shrugs his shoulders. This angers me, so I tighten my grip on his wrist. "Do you understand?"

"Yes, yes—of course."

"Good. Can you get your men to confirm that no one saw us?" I ask. He pulls his phone out of his pocket and presses one button before putting it to his ear.

"Are we clear?" The respondent barely has time to answer before he puts the phone back into his pocket. He looks at me. "Yes, we are clear."

He looks back into the flat whilst I study the balcony above and work out if it is better to break into the flat and walk up the internal stairwell or scale the outside of the building. After several seconds, I announce, "Let's crack on then, we climb up the outside of the building." I decide that the risk to the public is too great to go up the internal stairwell. Without hesitation, he walks over to the balcony wall. Like a machine, he steps onto it and effortlessly jumps up and grabs hold of the balcony wall above. He hoists himself up with impressive speed and athleticism.

A couple are looking down at their phones as they walk underneath me. I put my left foot on the balcony wall and lift myself up. I place my left hand on the balcony wall above to balance myself. I extend my right arm, but I am still a foot—maybe a foot and a half—away from the top of the wall. Kevin is a lot smaller than me, which makes his feat even more impressive. However, I do weigh an awful lot more than he does. The fall wouldn't kill me, but I would be seriously hurt.

I bend both of my knees and, still using my left hand to balance myself, I launch myself up. My right hand grabs hold of the top of the balcony wall above.

I swing my body slightly and bring my left hand up to also grip the top of the wall. With both hands, I easily lift myself up. Once my chest is on the wall, I turn my hands around and push myself up using my triceps. I swing my left foot onto the wall, which helps me lift up my trailing body parts.

"Clear," he says as both of my feet land on the second-floor balcony floor. I rest on the wall for a second whilst he walks over to the wall on the other side. He springs up on top of it with both feet before jumping up to the third-floor balcony and out of sight. Damn, he is showing off now. I am determined to keep up with him. Using the same process as before, I jump up to the next balcony.

This time he doesn't even wait for me to get on the balcony before jumping up to the fourth-floor balcony. I look down and realise that we've quickly gained some serious height. I can hear Kevin's and a female's muffled voices coming from the balcony above whilst I pause to catch my breath. The voices grow louder, but I cannot make out any words. They abruptly both go silent, and I worry that he has hurt her, or maybe killed her—his promise means nothing to me.

I reach the fourth-floor balcony as he attempts to go up to the slaveboy's balcony on the fifth floor. I put my hand on his shoulder in time to stop him jumping onto the wall.

"Hold on a second." I balance myself on him whilst trying to not give away that I am a little out of breath. He smirks like he has beaten me when, in fact, I may have just saved his life. Standing at the threshold of the flat is a young lady, who is counting a roll of money awkwardly as she cradles a can of cider. She doesn't even notice that I am there. A baby starts crying and she disappears inside her flat. I turn around and confirm that our driver has parked the minibus exactly where it was before. I wave at him and he sticks his arm out of his window, waving back—good, he is paying attention.

"OK, Kevin. Here's the plan. You go over to that balcony over there," I whisper, pointing to the adjacent balcony on the right-hand side, "and I'll go over to that balcony over there," and I point to the adjacent balcony on the left-hand side. "We will then climb up onto the balconies above us from the side furthest away from the slaveboy's flat. We will then jump across to the slaveboy's balcony together." He nods his head and turns to face his target balcony. I cannot help but add, "If you had climbed straight up to the slaveboy's balcony and the General was on it, or had a view of it from inside, he would have blown your

154

head off without hesitation." He has his back to me, so I cannot see his facial expression, but I hope I have removed the smirk.

I walk over to the balcony wall and hear him make his jump behind me. There is approximately a one-metre gap between the two balconies, which I can make from standing. I step up onto the wall, bend my knees, and pull my arms back. I execute the perfect standing long jump and land on the wall of the target balcony. I slap my palms on the side of the balcony above me to stabilise myself. I peer inside the flat and there is a young boy inside, but he is too absorbed by his video game to notice me walking past the patio doors. Again, I lift myself onto the balcony wall with my left foot before jumping up to the balcony above.

Kevin is stood waiting for me on the balcony that I had told him to wait on as I lift myself up. I peer inside the flat; it is empty. I walk to the balcony wall closest to the slaveboy's flat keeping myself as close as possible to the tower block's wall. I launch myself onto the balcony wall using my left foot. I pull out my gun, flick off its safety, and cock it. He mimics my actions. I signal three fingers to him. Two fingers. One finger. We both jump simultaneously across to the slaveboy's balcony.

My knees buckle painfully when I land. I try to minimise the pain by executing the perfect roll, making it look intentional. Both Kevin and I are up against the patio doors peering into the small open-plan living space, which has the living room closest to patio doors and the kitchen along the wall on the far side as well as the front door. No one is around. Kevin goes to open the sliding patio door, but I knock him to one side. I grab hold of the handle and start opening it very slowly.

There are only two internal doors, two-metres apart, on the left-hand side of the living room. The nearest door is closed; the furthest door is ajar and behind it a television plays loudly. I step across the threshold and dive against the wall on the left-hand side.

I am halfway past the closest door when it is thrown open. I am confronted with a young, pale, and naked boy, who is drying his hair with a towel. The surprise encounter startles us both. Even though he is paralysed with fear, I jab my fingers into his throat to stop him alerting the General. He grabs his throat with both hands, dropping his towel onto the bathroom floor. His body is covered in bruises, but I only look down as far as his midriff. Kevin accidentally knocks me as he rushes past to cover the boy's mouth.

I hurriedly proceed to what must be the bedroom. I kick open the bedroom door and it flies off its hinges onto the bed. The General, who is lying on the bed wearing only his boxer shorts, moves his feet to avoid the falling door whilst reaching over for his gun on the bedside table with his right hand. With expert judgement, I aim and pull my trigger before he has a chance to grab his gun. My gun releases an almighty kickback. His index and middle fingers explode off his right hand; an eruption of blood sprays over the wall. He screams in pain and rolls off the bed.

I narrowly avoid being sprayed with blood as I follow up with a hard kick to his genitals, immobilising him further. He tries to scream, but he is too winded to make a noise. I punch him in the face as hard as I can. He is knocked out before his head collides with the bedside table.

Kevin and the boy are now tussling in the bedroom doorway. Kevin has managed to keep his hands covering the boy's mouth. The boy spins himself around harshly and Kevin loses his grip. They both disappear from sight, so I run after them. Kevin dives and tap tackles one of the boy's legs so that it hits the other one, causing him to trip over. He collides with the kitchen cabinets, several feet away from the front door. Kevin jumps on his naked body in an attempt to pin him down, but he isn't going to stay down without a good fight.

I drag the unconscious General into the living room by his ankles. I hoist him up and sit him on one of the dining chairs. I bound his wrists behind his back before tying them to the chair with the television's power cable. I wrap the cable tightly around his right wrist to stop him losing any more blood.

The front door is heavily fortified, and I doubt that I would have been able to kick it open, at least not before the General had armed himself and fired at me through the door. Kevin and boy continue to wrestle; they both look increasingly pathetic as fatigue kicks in. I push the sofa past them and use it to block the door.

The General stirs. I slap him hard across the face to expedite his return to consciousness. The boy reverses his predicament. He manoeuvres himself on top of Kevin and punches him in the face. Kevin manages to block some of the punches, but most of them get through—although, they do not inflict much damage. In a different setting, it would be a humorous spectacle to watch. The boy increases his intensity and starts causing Kevin some real damage.

"Help me," he shouts repeatedly in between punches. If we were back in my boxing gym, then I would leave him for a bit longer to toughen him up and see what he was made of; however, I currently cannot afford for him to be too hurt as I may need him later. I reach down, grab the boy's arm, and launch him onto the sofa. Without looking at his naked body, I throw his towel to him.

"Cover yourself up." I extend my arm to Kevin. He grabs it with both hands, and I lift him to his feet.

"He's a vicious bastard," he says, embarrassed.

"I thought you'd be dead by now," the General croaks, with a deep Russian accent. He has turned very pale.

"There's no need for the accent—I know who you are. I'm sorry to disappoint you. I doubt I've got long left. Although, it is probably longer than you've got!" He turns his head to discover that his exit is blocked but is relieved to see that his slaveboy is safe and sound. Cogs turn in his head, trying to formulate an escape plan. "You're not going anywhere, my friend." I do not need to check his restraints.

"Go and get the boy dressed." I motion to the bedroom with a sideways nod of my head.

Kevin grabs him roughly by his right arm and drags him to the bedroom. As he is guided past us, he breaks free from Kevin's grip and throws his arms around the General. He hugs him as passionately as a couple that has been separated by a long operational deployment overseas. They kiss each other hard on the lips. His grip on the General is loosened by Kevin's grip on him until it is broken. As he is hauled away, he rips the General's gold crucifix necklace from his neck with his fingertips, securing it tightly in his fist. Kevin shoves him harshly into the bedroom.

I turn to face the General, who now has a large devious smile on his face.

"Why are you so happy, my friend?"

"I behold one of Mikhail's most trusted assassins here with the Chinese Mafia." He tries to tease information out of me, but I ignore him.

"Why are you invading Chinese territory?" I walk over to the kitchen area and flick on the already nearly full kettle. This gets his attention; he sits upright.

"Why not? Mikhail was always too scared to take on the Chinese. Now he is going legit, I am going to take ownership of his territory, as well as that of the Chinese. If I don't act quickly, then the Albanians will get it all to themselves."

"I doubt he was scared. Have you not considered that he is more experienced and savvier than you! Did you not expect the Chinese to retaliate?"

"Yes, but we will squash them," he states, matter-of-factly.

"Does Mikhail know about your extracurricular activities?"

"Of course not. I expect that he'll hand over his empire to either Vitali or Yosef. They're all too weak, lazy, and unambitious to control this city. It's time that this country's citizens take back control of our city," he says patriotically.

"Do you realise what you nearly started?" I say, expressing my annoyance. "The Russians and Chinese were working harmoniously together, and you nearly sabotaged it."

"What can I say?" He tries to shrug. "This business is survival of the strongest. If you're not strong then you'll be killed."

The kettle clicks off and begins to shake on its powerbase. I walk slowly to the kitchen area and pick it up. As I walk back to him, I shout to Kevin in the other room, "Have you finished yet?

"Nearly."

"Well, hurry up—bring the boy back in here when you've done." The General's smirk is wiped off his face as I approach him. "I've got a few questions that I need you to answer in front of Mr Li," I say as Kevin and the boy enter the room. "Is that OK with you?"

"As long as you release the boy," he growls. He is beginning to panic that I'm going to hurt the boy—which I won't, of course.

"I am sorry, but I cannot do that. I can promise that he'll not be harmed."

"Mikhail mocked you for being weak."

"I hope he did. People like him never understand the meaning of principles. Their own overwhelming arrogance blind them to the skills, abilities, and capabilities of people that they consider inferior to them. Anyway, my principles got me where I am today and yours got you where you are," I gloat. He clenches his jaw.

Kevin sits the boy on the sofa. The crucifix necklace is still clutched tightly in his fist. I walk over to Kevin and whisper in his ear, "Please grab a tea towel and cover the General's mouth when he screams."

He obediently walks over to the kitchen area and picks up a tea towel off the kitchen worktop before positioning himself behind the General. He rolls the tea towel long ways and the General tries to see what he is doing, but his restraints don't allow him to turn his head. I pour a splash of boiling water onto his mutilated right hand.

When he opens his mouth to scream, Kevin throws the tea towel over his head and pulls it tightly into his mouth with both hands. The General moves his head forward and down, causing Kevin to temporarily lose his balance.

However, he reacts quickly and maintains the dominant position by thrusting his knee into the General's back. The General screams again, but the tea towel muffles it.

The boy screams in protest at the violence directed towards his master. He jumps off the sofa and runs over to him. I put my arm out a bit too quickly to stop him and his head collides with my knuckle. He drops the General's crucifix necklace on the floor so that he can clutch his face with his hands. The resultant shockwave created across my body causes several drops of boiling water to escape from the kettle's spout and land on the General's bare foot. He screams out in pain, but it is inaudible. The boy walks backwards and collapses back onto the sofa.

The anger in the General's eyes has now turned to fear as they flicker between the kettle, the boy and me. He tries to shuffle and wriggle free, but to no avail. I sprinkle a small quantity of boiling water onto his lap to regain his undivided attention. He goes berserk from the pain; Kevin controls the situation well. The skin near his boxer shorts goes bright red, some of it begins to peel.

"What have you been planning?" I ask, hoping that this torture will be over quickly.

The General starts to talk, but I cannot make out any of the muffled sounds. I nod at Kevin who loosens his strain on the tea towel. As I step forward to listen to his whisper, he narrowly misses my shin as he tries to kick me. Kevin is shocked by his actions and jerks his head back with the tea towel.

I angrily pour more boiling water onto his right knee. The water scalds his knee and continues it scolding journey as it trickles down his shin onto his foot. He goes even more berserk. I punch him firmly in the stomach with my free hand; he immediately stops moving. He takes in deep breathes through his nose.

There is a loud bang on the front door. Everyone jumps. It sounded like someone had tried to ram it open. Everyone goes quiet. I cannot hear any movement outside. Kevin and I look at each other; he is petrified. There are then more bangs in quick succession, but the door does not budge.

"I am guessing that these are not your men?"

"No, definitely not," Kevin replies.

The front door cracks as an axe blade partially makes its way through it. The General's eyes change from that of prey to predator. The person outside begins to ferociously hack at the door with the axe. Wood splinters are hurled into the boy's face, who screams out in more pain.

159

"Quick Kevin, we need to get out of here."

He releases the tea towel.

"Fuck you, Mr Smith—I am coming for you," the General shouts, foaming at the mouth whilst panting.

Kevin grabs a kitchen knife off the counter and rams it into the General's left shoulder blade. The General screams loudly. Kevin follows me as I step back towards the balcony. Something hits the wall on my left-hand side. I turn as a grey metal canister—a stun grenade—bounces off it and lands in the middle of the room. I face the General, who is the closest to it.

"I forgot to mention, I am also an undercover police officer, you piece of shit!"

The explosion from the stun grenade releases a blinding flash of light. This, combined with an unbearably loud bang, causes me to drop the kettle as I fall back against the wall. I slide down the wall into a slumped sitting position on the floor. I have gone blind and loud noise has damaged my earing. I can only hear the ringing in my ears; I have trouble balancing myself. I find it harder getting to my feet than when Extra Arm knocked me down.

My vision starts to come back, but it is still very blurry. The General is lying on the floor still attached to the chair. The boiling water has spilt out onto the floor and he is lying in it. The skin on his face has melted in certain places. His mouth is moving, but I cannot hear what he is saying. I turn to escape via the balcony, but trip over the boy and land next to him. My face is inches from the General's crucifix necklace; the crucifix part is in two pieces. A flashing red light is emitted from the end of one of the pieces.

The General wasn't lying: he is an undercover police officer. I suspect he has gone rogue. The boy must have activated his necklace, sending out a distress signal. The sofa pushes up against me as the opening front door moves it back against me.

I spring up onto my feet and zigzag my way to the balcony. When I reach the balcony, I accidentally bump into Kevin, knocking him over. He seems to be struggling more than me. Bullets start striking the concrete balcony wall, so I dive to safety at the side of the patio doors. Without thinking, I pick him up off the floor, turn, and launch him across to the adjacent balcony. I jump up onto the wall and jump. My balance hasn't fully returned to me, so my legs give way partway through the jump. I try to grab hold of the adjacent balcony's wall, but I fail.

The skin on my face, midriff, and hands scrapes against the wall. My feet land on the balcony wall on the floor below my target balcony. I fall forward, roll, and land sprawled out on my back. I look up at the boy's balcony and two firearms officers come into view; they fire at Kevin. I go to grab my gun, but it isn't there. One of the firearms officers jumps across to the adjacent balcony and the other one is about to do the same when he notices me. I sit up just in time for the above balcony to provide me with cover. Bullets penetrate the floor inches away from my hands.

I open the sliding patio door, step into the flat, close the door behind me, and lock it. On the sofa is a very young mum breastfeeding her baby whilst smoking marijuana; she doesn't notice me. She takes the joint out of her mouth and laughs at something happening on the television until she coughs harshly. Her baby falls off her nipple and starts crying, which is nearly loud enough to drown out the sound of gunshots outside.

Still unnoticed, I rush past her as she tries to settle her baby. I grab the empty beer bottle off the coffee table. I study the floorplan on the back of her front door whilst unravelling the clear bag of white powder. I dip my right index finger into it and bring it up to my nose. I close my right nostril with my right thumb and offer the powder to my left nostril. I breathe in deeply. My body instantly loosens up and my pain disappears. I feel like I've gained a lot more energy and power. Looking through the peephole, I confirm that no one is outside in the corridor. I open the front door and also confirm that the far ends of the corridor are clear before sprinting to the stairwell.

I open the fire door to the stairwell and am confronted by three firearms officers running down the stairs to my landing. The first officer does not have time to shoot before I grab hold of his gun and point it to the side of me. Whilst holding his gun, I smash the bottle across his face and helmet. The other two officers do not have clear shots on me.

I ram the broken glass bottle into the first officer's thigh. As he falls to the ground, I fall down with him so that he continues to provide me with cover. Whilst I continue to hold the gun, he pulls its trigger until the ammunition runs out. I pick him up and lie him across my shoulders. I use his legs to kick the second officer's gun away from me. I let go of his gun and grab his baton out of its holster before dropping him on the floor. I smash the baton against the hand of the second officer, causing it to hit the wall.

The third officer holds an axe in one hand and lifts it high whilst reaching for his thigh-holstered handgun with his other hand. I smash the baton against the side of second officer's knee. He collapses onto me, and I push him out of my way. He lands next to the first officer. The third officer nearly has his gun pointed at my chest, but I knock it out of his hand with the baton and it disappears over the side of the stairwell. His axe starts coming down, aimed at the centre of my forehead. I turn my body to the side and feel a breeze against my face as it passes by. It keeps falling until it collides with the second officer's foot; chopping off all his toes. The side of my head is sprayed with blood.

I kick the axe out of his hands and take custodianship of it before it falls to the floor. I spin around and thrust it between his legs. I rotate the blade horizontally and pull at an angle. The blade gets behind his right calf and pulls his foot off the step. He falls backwards, and his helmet collides with the corner of the concrete step, cracking loudly on impact. He falls down the remainder of the stairs and lands on top of the second officer.

I finish tying the plastic handcuffs around the second officer's ankle, as three more firearms officers appear on the landing above. I duck for cover behind the landing wall moments before one of them starts firing. With a short round of bullets, they carelessly riddle the three firearms officers on the floor next to me. The now dead second officer's gun is next to me.

Without looking, I throw the axe down the stairs. I pick up the second officer's gun and confirm that it is fully loaded. I pull his deceased body towards me using the handcuffs that are secured around his ankles and relieve him of two magazines. I store them in my trouser pockets, making sure that I do not rip the bag containing the white powder in the process. I am crouched in a thin layer of blood, which has now spread across the landing and has started to flow down the stairs. I grab one of his smoke grenades, remove its pin, and launch it over my head into the stairwell.

I keep firing above the heads of the officers at the top of the stairs to keep them at bay until the smoke from the smoke grenade provides me with cover. Frustratingly, they force my hand by putting me under heavy fire as they descend the stairs. I grab another smoke grenade, remove its pin, and throw it at the bottom of the stairs next to me. It releases bright blue smoke that quickly rises and consumes them. I grab his stun grenade, remove the pin, wait two seconds, and launch it over my head in the direction of the top landing.

I place my fingers in my ears and close my eyes. BANG. The light does not affect me this time, but the sound causes my ears to start ringing again—albeit more tolerably this time. I stand and fire above the heads of the officers again.

I sprint down the stairs and fire intermittently into the underneath of the concrete stairs above me. I reach the landing below and as I pick up the axe, one of the officers materialises out of the blue smoke. Before he can aim at me, orange smoke rises in the stairwell, providing me with enough cover to roll to safety behind the concrete wall. He starts firing so I stay low behind the wall and disappear down the next flight of stairs.

The ringing in my ears gets drowned out by the loud fire siren. I fire a couple of shots—which are loud enough to be heard over the fire siren—at the wall in front of me, before running down the next flight of stairs. I continue this practice down the next flight of stairs as the orange smoke gets denser. I reach the landing on the second floor and stop as a group of firearms officers ascend to it. I fire a shot at the wall next to the leading officer, forcing them to all duck behind the staircase wall. I open the door on the landing as the leading officer pokes his head up and applies pressure on his trigger. However, he releases the pressure when residents run into the stairwell from the corridor in response to the fire alarm. Once the last person passes me, I dive through the door.

I sprint down the corridor, trying doors as I go, but they are all locked. A man and woman exit their flat; I manage to get around them and catch their door before it closes. The officers enter the corridor but cannot fire at me as the man and woman are in between us. Even so, the second officer fires over the first officer's shoulder, mowing them both down. I step back into the flat as bullets spray across the doorway. They continue firing in my direction, so I bend down low, hold my gun around the corner, and fire at them until the magazine is spent. I rest the axe against the wall whilst reloading.

A guy living in a flat a couple of doors down the corridor, but on the opposite side—the side that faces the minibus—opens his door. He looks at me and freezes; he is petrified. I shout at him, "Go back inside." I also gesture with my gun for him to go back inside. He looks at me and understands what I tell him but steps out into the corridor anyway. On his second step, he is shot dead. His corpse falls back into his flat, wedging his front door open. A screaming woman runs to him from inside the flat. I hide the gun behind my back before she looks at me. With the axe in my hand, I point it down the corridor, and mouth the words, "Stay back!" The officers fire a couple more shots at her doorway. She falls backwards, seeking refuge in her flat.

I poke my gun around the corner again and fire several more shots to hold them back. The woman runs back to her front door cradling a shotgun. I fire several more shots at the officers before dashing across the corridor, jumping over the deceased man, and tackling her to the ground. She hits me on the head with the barrel of the shotgun and tries to wriggle free. I drop my weapons and snatch the shotgun out of her grasp. I use the butt of it to knock her out. I turn around as an officer comes into view.

I pull my trigger first. His head is mostly blown off; fragments of brain, skull, and facial matter, as well as lots of blood, cover the wall behind him. Whilst keeping the shotgun pointed at the corridor, I grab the deceased man by his chin and pull him into the flat next to me. The door automatically swings to a close once his body is out of the way and the latch engages its lock.

I grab the woman by her jumper's collar with one hand and drag her into her bathroom, leaving her in the middle of the floor. I go back into the living room, throw the shotgun on the floor, and shut the bathroom door behind me. I grab the deceased man under his arms, drag him to the bathroom door, and drop him across it. The officers in the corridor shoot at the front door's lock. I roll and grab my gun and axe. I fire a couple of bullets through the door as I run around the sofa to get to the patio doors. I throw back the sliding patio door and dive across the threshold as they enter the flat and start firing. I wave at the driver, who immediately pulls out into the road.

In the middle of the street, between myself and the minibus, are two more firearms officers. They both look up at the source of the gunshots and broken glass. They do not notice the accelerating minibus behind them as they take aim at me. Before the minibus hits them, they both notice it, and try to move out of its way—but they are too late. It hits them both; forcing one of them up onto the windscreen of a parked car, and the other one across the road and down a grass verge.

I am now safe to start making my way down. I leap onto the balcony wall and see Kevin jumping down from a first-floor balcony onto the minibus' roof. The officer on the grass verge starts firing at the minibus. I return fire in his general direction; I cannot see him clearly enough from this angle. Kevin lies down on his back looking up at me; he is exhausted. I wave my gun forward and shout, "GO, GET OUT OF HERE!"

He slaps his hand twice on the roof of the minibus and the driver accelerates the minibus away. Without thinking, and already out of breath, I jump onto the adjacent balcony wall. The other officer has rolled off the windscreen and his feet are back on the tarmac. He sees me and starts firing. I jump down onto the balcony and take four steps before leaping onto its wall and jumping across onto the adjacent balcony wall.

I take another four steps on this balcony and leap onto its wall. The officer's bullets smash the glass in the patio doors behind me. My hood is blown back off my head as I take a leap of faith into the abyss. As I fall, the minibus and Kevin pass by underneath me.

I bring my axe down and manage to ram its blade into the rear edge of the minibus, between its roof and the rear doors, inches from Kevin's feet. I hold onto the axe with all my strength and swing into the minibus' rear doors. My left elbow goes through a rear window and both of my ankles hit the rear step.

I manage to maintain solid grips on both my axe and my gun. I clamp my elbow on the inside of the broken rear window to support myself; the broken glass tries to penetrate my hoodie, which thick enough to not let it through. I let go of the axe, which remains firmly embedded in the minibus, take my gun out of my other hand, and try to grab the windowsill while holding it. I unclamp my elbow and grab hold of the middle headrest on the back row of chairs.

Now fully supported, I lift my feet up and place them on the rear step. I turn and start firing at the officer on the grass verge, who rolls behind a tree for safety. The officers appear on the balcony of the unconscious woman and the murdered man; they only notice us as we turn a corner, heading back to the safety of Chinatown.

Chapter 17
The Race Back to Chinatown

The orange and blue smoke escapes from the tower block and rises into the atmosphere; it can be seen for miles around. We hit a deep pothole which causes my right leg to slip off the minibus' rear step. I am still holding onto the middle headrest on the back row of seats, so I easily recover the situation. I try to open the back doors, but they're locked. I could probably just fit through the broken back window, but there isn't enough space between it and the back seats. I put my right arm through the window to try and unlock the door, but the handle doesn't move. The minibus moves sharply around a bend and my elbow catches a piece of glass. My elbow begins to drip blood.

I shout through the broken window to our driver, "Can you unlock the back door or pull over?"

"I'll take the next right and pull over," he shouts back. At least, that's what I think he says: my ears are still ringing.

As soon as he indicates to turn right, a machine gun begins to roar behind us. I squint my eyes, hold on tightly, and brace myself for impact. A bullet screams past my ear and slams into the minibus' metalwork. Two massive black SUVs race up behind us. They both have heavily blackout-tinted windows, so it is impossible to see who they are. Our driver knocks the minibus down a gear and slams his foot down on the accelerator pedal. Despite the initial aggressive jolt, its rate of change of speed is infuriatingly sluggish. Kevin taps on my head.

"Quick, get up here." A man wearing a balaclava leans out of the front SUV's front passenger window, waving his machine gun in our direction. I fire at him until my magazine is spent.

"Move back, Kevin," I shout. He moves back out of view. I throw my gun onto the row of back seats and rip the axe out of the metalwork. I let go of the headrest, grab the upper part of the windowsill, put my left foot on the lower part of the windowsill, and launch myself up. The minibus is now travelling at more than forty miles per hour, so the wind makes it difficult for me to clamber onto the roof. I smash the axe into the roof and haul myself up onto it with both hands. I lever the axe out of the roof only to smash it back in again, but this time closer to the middle of the roof. The machinegun roars again and the rear of the minibus is sprayed with bullets. Kevin and I both lie on our fronts, clutching the axe handle tightly.

Judging by the speed of the other cars, we are now travelling faster than the national speed limit. Our driver expertly weaves between the cars across all three lanes of the outer ring road. We lightly graze a small car as it hesitates before committing itself to change lanes. The minibus barely moves off course, but Kevin and I are thrown to the side. His legs swing around and off the side of the roof; his arms spaghettify as they hang onto the axe handle for dear life. I grab his collar and pull him back onto the roof. Bullets narrowly pass over our heads.

His t-shirt is blown up by the wind, revealing his gun tucked into the back of his jeans. Our driver aggressively swings us into the inside lane, providing us with a clear shot of man hanging outside of the SUV in the outside lane. I pull Kevin's gun out of his jeans, release its safety, and fire at the man twice. The first bullet hits his chest; the second bullet hits his face, blowing his head back. The upper half of his body dangles outside of the SUV, but his lower half remains on the inside of it.

A person inside of the SUV opens the front passenger door to try and rid themselves of the body. The door opens a bit, before swinging violently shut. They try again, but this time a car pulls into their lane in front of them, forcing the driver of the SUV to slam on the brakes. As the SUV slows down, a lorry in the middle lane removes the open door with the body still attached. The SUV becomes trapped in the outside lane. Our driver keeps his foot on the accelerator pedal; the SUV falls into the distance.

The other SUV flies down the empty inside lane towards us. I aim for its tyres, but its body shape makes a clear shot from this angle impossible. Another man wearing a balaclava tries poking his head out of the front passenger window; I fire at him, obliterating their wing mirror in the process. The traffic lights ahead are on red and there is a lot of traffic passing across the junction. They have been on red for a fair while, so they should change at any moment. There is a build-up of three cars in both the inside and middle lanes, but only one car in the outside lane, which is indicating to turn right.

Our driver is forced to apply the brakes and the SUV knocks us gently from behind before they start to also apply their brakes. The cars stop passing the junction and the traffic lights, which are one hundred metres away, turn amber. The minibus' engine screams in pain when our driver downshifts, causing the exhaust pipe to cough out a heavy black plume.

The traffic lights turn green and the car in front of us is quick to pull away. Although, it fails to turn quickly enough, and we clip its back bumper, causing it to spin around. The minibus shakes slightly; Kevin and I barely notice the impact. We fly over the junction. The road we are now on has a long, clear stretch.

The SUV is hot on our tails. It tries to come up on the inside of us, but our driver swings us into its path and blocks it. Although, he is too aggressive and nearly loses control of the minibus. He regains control and we find ourselves in the outside lane, kissing the barrier. The SUV races up next to us in the middle lane before ploughing into us. I lose my footing; my legs swing around uncontrollably and I unintentionally kick Kevin quite hard. His left hand loses its grip on the axe handle, and he rolls onto his side. I am forced to drop my gun, which is instantly blown away, and grab hold of his right wrist, before he falls off the roof. Despite him shaking from panic and exhaustion, he effortlessly swings himself back around and grabs the axe handle with his left hand.

As we are about to go over a long bridge, I slide my way up the minibus, stretch my arm over its side, and knock on our driver's window.

"Yes, Mr Kulikov," he shouts. I do not respond quickly enough. "MR KULIKOV."

"Push them towards the wall," I scream.

"OK. Take my shotgun." He holds his shotgun out of the window; its barrel is pointed directly at the centre of my forehead.

"I can't now—but I'll be back for it shortly." I push it back down.

I crawl back over to Kevin, who is now as white as a ghost.

"It will be over shortly, my friend." I put my hand on his shoulder, which does little to reassure him. Our driver starts moving us closer to the bridge wall. I keep an eye on the lampposts. "Can you swim?" He looks at me with curiosity. He tries to reply, but he is too scared and the words don't come out. He settles with a nod of his head.

As we approach the middle of the bridge, I stand, grab his collar and belt, and heave him up, ripping his grip off the axe handle. I take one step forward

The SUV's driver has no choice but to fall back slightly. My driver struggles to keep the minibus driving in a straight line. The guy with me on the roof notices that my right foot slips ever so slightly, so he tries his luck by attempting to kick my legs away from me. He is successful—as I try to move, my feet slide from under me and I fall onto the roof. It is a soft landing as the roof bows to absorb weight. As I land, I try to kick his legs, but he jumps out of the way. Whilst he is in the air, the minibus swings wildly to the right to go around a car, resulting in him stumbling when he lands.

Crouching, I rush towards him with my arms wide open. He turns and tries to duck out of the way, but I rugby tackle him sideways on. I land on top of him and squeeze him as hard as I can. He elbows me in the back multiple times; my back is tensed so he simply hits solid slabs of muscle. I keep squeezing until I snap a couple of his ribs.

I let go with my left arm, and use it to punch him in the ribs, breaking even more of them. I loosen my grip, bring my knees up, and launch him off the roof. He tries to grab my axe as he flies past it, but it moves out of his way when the minibus hits a pothole. He hits the road, bounces a few times, and rolls. A car violently swerves to avoid him but is unsuccessful and hits the car next to it in the process. Both cars then hit other cars, causing a small pileup. The pileup is not too violent as the people behind us had all slowed down to watch the show.

We are fast approaching Chinatown. My driver tries to push the SUV out of the way, but we are pinned in the middle lane by the surrounding cars. I grab my axe and brace for impact. My driver turns violently, forcing the SUV against the safety barrier. We bounce off the SUV and narrow avoid ramming into a large lorry; however, we clip the back corner of it, which causes the minibus to rock. The rocking quickly gets progressively more violent and the wheels start lifting off the floor.

Once we pass the lorry, we begin to topple over. I reach over the side of the roof and grab hold of the upper windowsill of the side passenger window that I smashed earlier as my body is lifted into the air. Once the minibus passes the point of no return, I ram my axe into the side it—which is now nearly the top—and pull myself over.

I hold onto my axe tightly as the minibus grinds along the rough road surface into Chinatown territory. The SUV skids sideways towards us; the man in the front passenger's seat can clearly be seen reloading his gun. I push up with my arms and get to my feet. I grab my axe with my left hand and swing it back across my body.

As soon as I release my axe, I take a step forward and jump. He sees it flying towards him and puts his right arm up to protect himself. It slices through the upper half of his arm and goes into his neck. His arm is stuck to his neck. He and my axe both fall out of the SUV, which slides over them. My hands slap the SUV's roof and my feet land on the front passenger door's sill. I dive into the front passenger's seat moments before it smashes into the minibus. On impact, the airbags are deployed. The front air bag slams into my face, pinning me back into the seat.

I am in a daze and it takes me a couple of seconds before my bearings return to me. My airbag reduces its stronghold on me as it deflates. I punch the disorientated driver in the face. I throw my upper body through the gap between the two front seats and confirm that the two goons in the back have lost possession of their guns. I punch the goon on my right-hand side in the face and I go to punch him again but the goon on my left-hand side punches me painfully in the ear. I rocket my whole body into the back by using the dashboard as a launch pad.

The goons sat either side of me are now punching me relentlessly. The goon that punched my ear, now on my right-hand side, receives my right elbow to his face, busting his nose. I headbutt the goon on my left-hand side; his head is knocked back, but it is cushioned by deflating airbag attached to the door. The goon on my right-hand side gets me in a headlock. I throw my head back, but I only hit his shoulder. This gives him an opportunity to crush my head against him. I punch the guy on my left-hand side several times and quickly get out of breath. I quickly become uncomfortably weak from the lack of oxygen. I throw my right elbow back against his stomach, but he doesn't loosen his grip. I twist my body across, kick the goon on my left-hand side, dislocating his jaw with my heel.

I begin to feel sleepy but am pulled away from my journey to unconsciousness by a gunshot; the driver has shot his airbag. He forces his airbag out of his face and turns to face us. As he turns, he swings his gun around. I initially think that he wouldn't shoot me due to the risk of hitting my strangler; however, the pressure that he has already applied to the trigger indicates this is a risk that he is willing to take. I throw my elbow back and hit my strangler hard in the groin. I am instantly released. I lunge forward and get my right index finger behind his overhanging trigger finger.

The driver's eyes open wide in shock; he squeezes the trigger hard against my unmoveable finger. I duck down, withdraw my finger, causing him to shoot the goon that was previously strangling me. Blood sprays over my back and drips down my t-shirt. He is momentarily frozen with shock and I use the opportunity to snatch the gun out of his hand. By the time that I have flipped the gun around, he has opened his door and has started to fall out of the SUV. I fire one shot into his back before he disappears.

The goon on my left-hand side clutches his unhinged jaw. I fire a bullet through his windpipe, which penetrates the already deflating airbag on the other side of him. I lean across him as blood spurts out of his neck and open his door. I kick him out of the SUV through his unlocked door and throw myself after him. As I fall, I fire another shot into the escaping driver's back. My neck compresses awkwardly as I land on the goon.

Chapter 18
The Unwavering Loyalty

The residents of Chinatown start to coalesce around the wreckage, and the traffic is building up behind it. Three more massive black SUVs join the end of the queue of traffic over one hundred metres away. Several armed men immediately vacate them, disperse, and head towards Chinatown. I grab the man closest to me.

"Get this message to the Dragon Master: Tell him Mr Kulikov says that he needs to get here right now to protect his people," I shout in his face.

He is momentarily taken aback but nods his head obediently. He gets his phone out of his pocket and, as he walks away, he begins to speak loud and fast Chinese into it. The minibus' windscreen is severally cracked but remains as one piece. Through the cracks, I can make out the outline of the driver crunched up in a ball on his door. The armed men weave in and out of the parked cars towards me. It has become difficult to tell where they all are, especially as the growing crowd starts to surround me. I turn to leave the driver, but something inside of me stops me from walking away.

I run over to the closest clothes shop and steal a couple of jumpers off the stand outside. The old woman at the counter sees me stealing them but does not complain. I wrap them around my hands as I barge my way back through the crowd. I repeatedly ram my fists into the windscreen and pull out the glass. Someone gets that close to me that I accidentally elbow them in the face; I do not apologise. In my haste, many shards of glass fall on the driver. Some of his face has been scraped off from grinding along on the tarmac. I pull a fair amount of the glass away, but there is no suitable way of pulling him out as he is lying in an awkward position.

I step over the remaining pieces of glass and place my foot on the driver seat headrest. He holds up his right arm, which I take hold of with my right hand and

174

pull him up in front of me. Once most of his body is off the floor, I wrap my left arm around his back and pull him up to his feet. I keep hold of him because I know that he'll collapse in a heap again without my support. I manoeuvre him closer to where the windscreen used to be. Several outreached arms grab hold of him and help to pull him out. His feet knock off the bottom shards of glass that remain embedded in the windscreen as they are dragged over them. I push off from the headrest and pass back through the windscreen onto the street.

People pour out of the surrounding shops and building onto the street, which has now become very busy. Only a handful of people pay me any attention; everyone else concentrates their attention on the armed men approaching Chinatown. Behind a row of parked cars, that are well scattered, they have formed a human wall, which is at least three people deep. More people hastily join the great wall. All their backs are straight, and their heads are held high. There is a look of pride on all their faces as they stand steadfast.

My helpers keep the driver upright as they move him away from the minibus. The armed men are now uncomfortably close. I grab hold of him and hoist him up onto my left shoulder. The old woman, who was at the counter of the clothes shop, now stands at the threshold of her shop motioning with her hands for me to seek refuge there. She says something in Chinese, but I do not understand.

I run as fast as I can with the driver on my left shoulder towards the clothes shop. He grunts every time one of my feet hits the floor because it unavoidably causes my shoulder to dig into his stomach. The reflection in the clothes shop's window, reveals the armed men approaching the wall. Multiple gunshots crackle through the air and I automatically duck. I try to run faster, but to no avail. The driver's body thuds against my back. There are more gunshots, which seems to attract more people to run faster towards the sound of the noise.

I am not going to make it to the clothes shop, so I hide behind a Land Rover. I shout at the oncoming stampede, "GO BACK, GO BACK!" But no one pays me any attention.

I grab a teenage girl by the arm as she passes. She tries to pull away, but my grip is too strong. Bullets penetrate the Land Rover's bodywork, so I drag her behind it next to me. I lay the driver on the pavement and rest his head on the curb. She is horrified when she sees the state of his face. He barely moves or makes a sound, but he is still alive. Blood pours out from his body and flows along the gutter to the drain. I roll him onto his side and reveal a bullet hole in his left shoulder blade, which is also leaking blood. She takes off her jacket and tries to put it under his head before I stop her. I rip it out of her hands and force it onto his gunshot wound.

"You need to apply pressure here," I say, demonstrating what she needs to do. She takes over from me and applies pressure to the wound with both hands. My hands are covered in blood. I wipe it away on his trousers.

Several more gunshots are fired; I don't know where the bullets go. I poke my head up and look through the back window of the Land Rover. The human wall is doing a fine job of impeding their journey into Chinatown, but they are slowly making their way through it. They have probably stopped firing because they have realised that they do not have enough bullets to take out everyone, and the fact that the more people they shoot the more people that come to join the wall. One of the goons hits a weathered old woman in the face with the butt of his gun to get her out of his way. I cannot allow this carnage to continue whilst I wait for the Dragon Master and his army. A crippled old man slowly makes his way to the wall. I put my hands on his arms and drag him next to me behind the Land Rover.

"I am sorry, mate, but I am going to have to commandeer this for a short while," I say, snatching his walking stick from him. "You'll have to hold onto the car for support." He doesn't understand what I say, but he naturally has to put his hands on the Land Rover for support. I crouch low, get on the pavement, and run along it, hiding behind the row of parked cars.

One of the armed men is several metres in front of me; he doesn't notice me as there are about three rows of people between us. I remain low and force my way around so that I can come up behind him. Everyone seems to be aware that I am there to help them, but I still have to push some of them quite hard to get them out of my way.

I pop up behind him, throw the walking stick over his head, and get him into a stranglehold. I kick the back of his knees and pull him to the floor. He fires his machine gun and the bullets are absorbed by a man's torso. His dead body collapses onto the floor next to us. Several people grab the gun and point it at the floor. He puts up a good fight and a couple of people trip over the corpse whilst trying to keep the gun pointed at the floor. I get my hands on his head and quickly twist it around. His neck snaps in several places and his body immediately goes limp.

A man with sheer desperation in his eyes takes ownership of the gun. He stands up and points it at what I suspect is another armed man. I don't know if he is desperate to genuinely help or he wants the reward and respect that he'll get from Dragon Master if he kills one of the armed men. Either way, I cannot let him proceed as there are too many people around, and he will not have a clear shot.

I push the corpse off me and jump to my feet. Several people are now between me and the resident with the gun. He aims the gun at the next closest armed man, who stands, like me, a good shoulder height above everyone else. I throw the walking stick up to try and point the barrel of the gun upwards to avoid risking anyone's life; however, the stick gets knocked off course when it hits the elbow of a person stood between us. The man fires as a woman tries to jump on the armed man's back. The bullet goes through the woman's neck and hits his bulletproof vest. The woman falls from view.

The resident with the gun takes aim again. I shove the people stood in between us out of the way, and successful use the walking stick to direct the barrel of the gun to point into the air this time. He pulls the trigger and the bullets are discharged above the crowd and into the windows and walls of the surrounding buildings. He slides the barrel of the now empty gun off the end of the walking stick. He tries to aim it at the armed man again, but he has now disappeared below the canopy of heads. The resident looks back at me with venomous eyes.

I head towards the armed man, who is upright again and searching for the person that shot at him. I pop up at the side of him, swing the walking stick around, and force it at the bridge of his nose. His nose splits open and blood explodes from it. He cups his nose with both of his hands. The gun is still in his right hand, and is now pointing at the sky. I thrust the walking stick into the hands of the man stood next to me. I slap both of my hands against armed man's ears.

Whilst he is disorientated, I shove the palm of my left hand into his face and I rip his gun from him with my right. The people around him pull him to the ground. I poke the gun through the gap between the people and move his helmet back off his forehead. His look of shock immediately disappears once I fire. The two people either side of the gun fall off him onto the floor, clutching their ears.

The next armed man is only a couple of metres away from me. He is facing away from me, so I run towards him, ploughing people out of the way as I go. A couple of people already have their arms around him and are attempting to pull him down to the ground. One guy is doing a particularly good job of strangling him. I do not have a clear shot, so I place the barrel of my gun in his right armpit and fire down into his torso. Everyone around him now manages to get him to the ground. People continue to pile on him, and I cannot tell if he has been killed. Even if he hasn't, the man strangling will finish him off shortly.

I turn my attention to the next armed man, who is again a couple of metres away. He is a big man and he is hurting a lot of people around him. I crouch low and out of his sights as I manoeuvre my way through the crowd towards him. I pop up at his side and fire into his thigh at a steep angle towards the floor. Despite his facial features not showing any emotion, it would have inflicted serious pain and damage. However, I do not get a chance to assess the level damage because he moves his gun towards me. I fire into his right foot, and, this time, he screams in pain—but continues swinging his gun towards me. I do not get a clear shot under his chin.

I drop my gun and sweep his legs together in my arms. My back twinges, but it doesn't stop me from lifting him and the two people attached to him, up high into the air before slamming them all down onto the floor. The people around us start stamping on his helmet and face. He fires his machine gun and the bullets hit the legs of the people around us; many of the victims collapse onto the floor.

Numerous people pile on top of him in my place. I get on my knees prior to getting to my feet. His machine gun is still tightly held in his left hand. I stamp hard on his left hand, breaking a finger or two. He releases his gun, but it gets kicked out of my reach and disappears behind a forest of legs.

The combination of me tiring and the crowd gaining energy makes it a slow journey to the next armed man. Someone toughly pulls on my collar and I instinctively turn to elbow them in the face. A fat man dressed in a chef's outfit winces as I stop my elbow about an inch away from his face. His face relaxes, and he holds up his cleaver knife for me to take. I nod my head and mouth the words, "Thank you," as he passes it to me.

I start putting in extra effort to get to next armed man once I get close enough to him to notice that he is mercilessly stamping on a teenager's face. It will only take another couple of stamps before he kills him. I get up behind him, tilt his head to one side, and hack at his neck below his helmet's strap. After several hacks, his head is barely attached to his body. This cause some of the people around me to scream as they are showered in blood; I manage to avoid getting much of his blood on me. He falls on top of the teenager on the floor. His head becomes detached from his body on impact with the tarmac, and it gets kicked about between everyone's feet.

Many people cheer when three of the Dragon Master's G-Class Mercedes-Benz race towards us. I nearly have the situation under control: there are only three armed men left. As soon as the Dragon Master's men get out of their cars, this place will become a bloodbath. I sprint towards the closest armed man, who has already started firing at the cars. He doesn't notice me come up next to him. I bring the knife down on his wrist. His hand, which still grips his gun, falls to the floor. He screams in pain as blood sprays from his arm and blasts an old lady in her face. The quantity of blood that hits her causes her to start choking. I swing the knife towards his neck. Just before I strike him, he looks down at his arm. The knife slices his cheek and philtrum and is abruptly stopped by his cheekbone. He falls to the floor; I let the crowd finish him off.

The Dragon Master's men get out of their cars and strategically position themselves around us. The next closest armed man begins firing at the Dragon Master's men as he retreats. The desperate nature of the situation forces me to risk throwing the knife at him. It cuts his helmet strap and lodges itself in the side of his face, inches in front of his ear. Before he falls to the floor, I run up next to him and hold him up.

I use him as a human shield as I make my way to final armed man, who is also shooting at the Dragon Master's men. I get within a couple of metres of him before he notices me. He fires his final bullets into my shield. He drops his machine gun and reaches for his thigh-holstered handgun. I rip the knife out of my shield and let him go. I step over my shield and slam the knife in between final armed man's neck and shoulder. I use that much power that it drives him to the ground. He ends up in a praying position in front of me.

I try to pull the knife out of him, but it is stuck. Everyone around me begins to cheer and pat me on my back and shoulders. A couple of people get carried away and try to pick me up, but they quickly desist when they realise how heavy I am. The crowd parts in front of me, leaving a clear path to the Dragon Master, who is surrounded by ten of his security guards. His security guards do not look as intimidating as Mikhail's, or even the Sheikh's, but they are just as deadly.

One of his security guards passes him a gun; he snatches it from him and points it at the big man, who I shot in the thigh and foot. He says something before he pulls the trigger. He is never one to miss out on a publicity stunt. He returns the gun back to his security guard. He goes to embrace me with open arms until he realises that I am covered in blood and sweat.

"Thank you, my friend. I cannot explain how grateful I am to you."

I do not reply; I am too out of breath. I remember that the teenager girl will still be attending to the driver and that I took the old man's walking stick. I jog back to the Land Rover, dancing around all the people, including dead, that are scattered on the floor. A person holds out the walking stick; I snatch it out of their hands and say, "thank you."

I have no choice but to jump over the woman who was shot in the neck because people are either side of her trying to help up those that are injured. The teenage girl is still applying pressure to the driver's gunshot wound. I pass the walking stick to the old man, who takes it with a shaky hand, smiles, and walks away as if nothing happened. The Dragon Master sneaks up behind me, making me jump.

"We need to get him to the hospital."

"Don't worry about the hospital; we take care of our own." He beckons over two of his security guards with his hands. Without asking the girl to move, one of them moves her off the driver with the palm of his hand. As soon as she stops applying pressure to the wound, blood spews from it. She dives back to cover the wound. He tries to push her off again, but I grab his hand. He looks at me ready to attack then looks at the Dragon Master for the order. The Dragon Master puts his hand on my shoulder and shouts an order at him in Chinese. He drops his head in shame and speaks to the girl in Chinese. The two security guards pick up the driver and all three of them sidestep to one of the cars.

"Where is Kevin?" the Dragon Master asks.

"We were chased here by Mikhail's men—well, the General's men. Actually, in fact, I am currently not sure whose men they were. Anyway, I had to throw him into the River Wynn for his own safety." He nods approvingly whilst surveying the flipped over minibus and the surrounding chaos. He lifts up one of his eyebrows momentarily.

"Come on, Mr Kulikov, I'll take you back to my office." He motions to his car with his hand. Even though I am covered in blood and I've got too much adrenaline pumping around my body to take a car journey, I do as he commands. I am putting people's lives at risk by being on the street.

"One more thing," I say, as we make our way to the car. The sombre crowd silently stares at me. Every person we pass, even those that are seriously injured, bows their head. "There should be a police-issued gun somewhere in the minibus, unless it has fallen out. You need to get one of your men to find it and plant it in one of their SUVs." He tilts his head back and whispers into the ear of the security guard next to him, who nods his head before running over to the minibus.

"Consider it done."

He helps me step up into the back seat of his car. I collapse onto the seat and he closes the door behind me. He walks around the rear of the car and gets in beside me with his finger outstretched, balancing a small pile of white powder on it. I nod my head, lean over, and sniff it off his finger. I sit back in my chair and relax, letting the powder perform its magic.

Two of his best, and most trusted, security guards get in the front of the car and we accelerate hard back to the office. There are many people on, or at the edges of, the roads, but they all move out of our way. The cars move out of our way to allow us to pass and we do not even stop for traffic lights. In no time, we take a hard right and fit snuggly between the two buildings at the entrance of the underground carpark.

Chapter 19
The Safety of Chinatown

The Dragon Master leads me to the back of his restaurant after he only gave me fifteen minutes to use his washroom and put on a fresh set of clothes. He sits me down in his usual seat at the middle of a very long and beautifully detailed oak table, which sits on a platform in the back right-hand corner of the restaurant, directly below his office. We overlook all the other tables and the bar area on our left-hand side.

Despite the restaurant being quite busy with people who were not part of the carnage that only finished less than half an hour ago, there is an uncomfortable atmosphere of melancholy. It would be even worse if we could see the full figures of the people that run, limp, or are carried past the front of the restaurant; however, the restaurant is partially underground, and the front windows only extend about one foot above the pavement level.

"I think your privacy has well and truly been blown," he says.

"Yep." I am extremely annoyed about what has happened today, but I don't let it show on my face. I also hold no regrets. "How is Talia?"

"I've heard that she is doing well." He puts his hand on my shoulder. "May-ling will be over shortly; you'll be able to get more from her."

"Thank you. And how is Kevin?"

"Yes, he is good. He has just called us from a payphone; some of my men are rushing pick him up now. He also wanted me to thank you for saving his life." He smiles. "I am also very grateful to you for saving his life. Trust me when I say that Kevin is a good guy. I believe that he'll be a great asset to this organisation and your cause." I nod my head.

"He did well today." I say, deliberately not giving too much away.

"The surgeons believe that Qingquan will pull through."

"Who?"

"Oh, he was your driver. He is still in a bad way, but they have managed to remove the bullet at least."

"Good. He also did very well today. They've both done you proud." He nods.

"I never expected anything less." He grips my shoulder tightly. "For now, you are safe here. Take your time and enjoy our hospitality." He looks around the room proudly. "If there is anything you need, then please do not hesitate to ask. I'll be back shortly." He takes his hand off my shoulder.

"I don't know what happened to Hiromi and the other guys." His smile disappears.

"Neither do I—leave it with me."

He leaves the restaurant via the side door on the right-hand side, next to the kitchen's double doors. This side door leads to a private foyer that contains the stairs and the lifts. The three security guards that were positioned in the furthest three corners of the restaurant away from the side door follow him; the one in the closest corner repositions himself next to side door.

As soon as they've disappeared, his waiting staff rush over to me and start placing numerous, impressive-looking food dishes all around me. They don't know who I am, but they would have been told to treat me like royalty. Everyone bows to me after they've put down their dishes. At the front of the restaurant, on the left-hand side, there is a set of double doors behind which are the stairs that lead to the main entrance. There is another a set of double doors on the left-hand side towards the middle of the restaurant that lead to the stairs and lifts for the underground carpark. The bar area is at the back of the restaurant, also on the left-hand side.

I lean forward and take some of the aromatic crispy duck off the large pile of it and place it on my plate. It is piping hot, which makes it even more delicious. I ignore the complementary ingredients—cucumber, spring onions, hoisin sauce and pancakes—as they will slow me down.

Without asking, a quiet, dispirited waitress brings me over a drink of what looks like a pint of Coke. She places it on the table without saying a word. She doesn't bow before she turns to leave. Before she gets chance to walk away, I catch her name badge as it swings past me.

"Thank you, Betty," I say. She doesn't look back.

I wash the duck down with the very cold and refreshing soft drink. The sugar gives me much needed energy, but I would prefer a cold water right now. I am in quite a bit of pain now, and it is getting worse as my muscles begin to stiffen up. The last time an airbag was blown into my face, it took me two days in bed to recover from it. I discreetly pull the bag of white powder out of my pocket.

I wish Madame Grace was around to look after me, but she is out on the street helping people. I dip my finger into the white powder and confirm that the security guard isn't watching me before I bring it out from under the table and sniff it off. I put the bag back in my pocket and I get an itch in my left nostril where some of the powder has got lodged. As I wipe it away, the security guard glances at me. Luckily, I don't think he notices; he doesn't know how much pain I am in.

After nearly fifteen minutes of eating, as I put the last pieces of the duck onto my plate, Betty arrives with a fresh plate of it and swaps it for the empty, old one. She still looks as dispirited as she did when she delivered my drink; however, her facial expression, demeanour, and posture all immediately change when the Dragon Master re-enters the restaurant. Only her sad eyes give her true feelings away.

"Thanks, Betty." This time she bows to me before she leaves.

The Dragon Master is absorbed by an intense phone call as he makes his way over to me. He has put on a black tie to complement his black suit and white shirt. His three other security guards also enter the restaurant and all four of them resume their original positions in each of the restaurant's corners. Whilst still on his phone, he picks some of the duck up off my plate and says, "You not hungry, my friend?"

My only response is a quick smile before I begin shovelling more duck down my throat. He puts down his phone after two minutes of intense discussion and returns it to his inside jacket pocket. As he pulls open his jacket, he unknowingly reveals his gun, which is holstered on his left-hand side. It also looks like he is wearing a bulletproof vest under his white shirt. I start to internally question how truly safe I am here if he thinks that he still needs his gun and bulletproof vest.

He beckons the now gleeful Betty over. Before she gets too close, he says, "Two more pints of Coke please." She bows to him after his command and rushes over to bar like her life depends on it.

"You've caused quite a bit of a mess, my friend."

"Yes, well—it does appear to have become a slightly messy situation. It gets worse. The General not only works for Mikhail, but he is also an undercover police officer. It appears that he enjoys the work that he does for Mikhail a bit too much and is looking to take over from him when he turns legit." His phone vibrates, and he immediately answers it. After ten seconds, of a quiet, yet very heated conversation, he puts it down.

"It appears that the armed men who entered Chinatown were Mikhail's men. This is exactly what we did not want." He bangs his right fist on the table whilst he reaches over me for a spring roll with his left.

"That does not surprise me. Whilst they were Mikhail's men, I do not believe they were following his orders." At the slaveboy's flat, it was the armed police that came to the General's aid after the boy had activated his hidden distress alarm. Mikhail's men must've only caught up with us once we had escaped and were a fair distance away from the flat. Therefore, they were waiting nearby but not at the flat; they probably didn't even know exactly where the General was.

"The General must have called them once we had escaped. He will tell Mikhail that we ambushed him. Mikhail won't know that he is a dirty cop either. He now has no other choice than to start an all-out war."

"I agree. But we'll have to wait. That is the only information I've got at the moment. My men are going to continue extracting information from the survivors." I do not push the subject further.

"I cannot believe the loyalty of your people; I've never seen solidarity like it."

"Yes, we look out for one another. I will not lie though: some of them did it out of fear and/or desperation. Some people assume that I am the same as my predecessor. If they had walked away from the situation under his rule, then they would've been severely punished; he may have even killed some of them himself." He grabs the last spring roll. "However, I am not ruling out that those who walked away will not be punished. I am only saying that it won't be as severe. But rest assured, those that stood up to Mikhail's men today will be greatly rewarded."

Two men enter the restaurant and head straight to our table. The Dragon Master straightens his back as they approach. They bow to us both when they reach the table. They do not sit down and he does not invite them to.

"There are more casualties than we thought. Our private medical staff and those that are volunteering cannot manage it all," the more confident looking of the two says.

"Get the word out to all the restaurants, shops, hotels and casinos, etc. that we need to borrow the people in their employment that have medical experience to provide assistance at once. Do not pull our people from the hospital unless it is absolutely necessary; we need to try and keep this one away from the outside world as much as possible. But inform them that as soon as they've finished their shifts, they will need to help out here. Overtime at the hospital is banned for today." The two men turn to leave, but he has not finished with them. "Also, call in all our tradespeople to repair all of the damage that has been caused. We need Chinatown presentable and operational again by the morning. People pay us to protect them—and that is what we will do. Do you understand?"

"Yes, Dragon Master," the same man says. They both bow their heads to us again. The more confident one turns and walks away, but the less confident lifts his head up and says, "What do you want to do about the dead bodies, Dragon Master?" His hands start to visibly shake.

"They are to be cremated immediately." He glances at me in the corner of his eye. "Also, close all the surrounding restaurants and tell them to bring their food and staff here. Get all the grieving families to come here as well so that we can all grieve together. Whilst I remember, get all the tapes from the CCTV cameras in the area and destroy them. Also, find all the persons not loyal to us that got caught up in the mess. Bribe them to be quiet and pay them for any photographs or videos that they took. If you have any issues with them then bring them to me."

We continue eating our food in silence as the staff, including the staff from the other restaurants, busy themselves around us, preparing the restaurant for the arrival of the grieving families. The first of the grieving families trepidly step into the restaurant and quietly find a place to sit. They all avoid eye contact with the Dragon Master. Realising what is happening, the closest bodyguard to the door starts directing everyone to him first. The Dragon Master listens intensely to everyone's story and is genuinely sympathetic to each one.

Over the course of thirty minutes, the restaurant gradually fills with people and food. There is an awkward atmosphere; people want to mourn, but this is not the place to let out their true feelings. No one even attempts to take any of the food off the many mountains of it placed all around the restaurant. Not only do I feel guilty that I am sat here with them all, I also feel disrespectful for doing so with such a full stomach. They all quickly turn away when I catch them looking at me—the elephant in the room. They know that I am responsible for all their pain.

The Dragon Master taps his empty pint glass with his chopstick. Instantly, the whole room goes quiet—even the dishwashers in the kitchen show good manners. There is a lot of nervous energy in the room; people are desperate for his speech to be over so that they can leave and grieve properly at home. He speaks slowly and controlled; it is in Mandarin, so I do not understand most of it. Without interrupting his speech, he beckons Betty over and points at me. She walks behind me and whispers the translation into my ear.

"My family—I take full responsibility for what has happened today. As you are aware, the Russians have been slowly encroaching on our territory. In an attempt to discreetly handle this issue, we enlisted my good friend, Mr Kulikov." He puts his hand on my shoulder and turns to face me. "Unfortunately, as usual, our attempts at being discreet, generous, and respectful have been met with Russian aggression."

He takes his hand off my shoulder and turns to address the crowd again. "I can assure you that the death of your loved ones will not go unavenged. We have troubling times ahead of us; but, if we work together, make sacrifices where we need to, and be patient, then we will prevail. We will prosper. You have my word." Everyone solemnly bows to him.

I sense a subtle change in the atmosphere and my heart starts racing wildly. All the security guards bring one hand up to cover their earpieces synchronously. They are frightened by whatever they are being told. The guard stood at the entrance to the restaurant locks the front double doors. He pulls out his gun and steps away from the doors. The other guard near the front, but on the right-hand side, closes all the curtains as he runs across the front of the restaurant. He doesn't close the final curtain; instead, he withdraws his gun and stands on a chair to peer through the window. The two guards at the back make their way towards the Dragon Master with one of their hands placed inside of their jackets.

A low hum from some kind of motor fills the room. This makes everyone look around and become tense; the Dragon Master stops talking. The cutlery, plates, and glasses clink together as they vibrate on the tables; once they gain enough energy they start bouncing around. A swarm of bullets rips through the middle set of double doors on the left-hand side, blowing them to smithereens. The bullets fly around the room, decimating the Dragon Master's colony with their sting. I lean back, grab Betty, and kick the table. As we both fall back, I put my arm behind her to stop her head from hitting the floor. I place my feet on the underside of the table and heave it onto its side.

There is an intermittent gap at the bottom of our wooden shield due to it resting on the backs of several tipped-over chairs. The motor's sound is replaced by screaming and shouting. The remainder of the double doors is kicked off the walls by two men. They carry assault rifles and professionally take out the two security guards at the front.

The Dragon Master, stood between his two remaining security guards, tower over me, directing their fire at the two men. They manage to take one of them out, but the remaining one concentrates his more dominating firepower in our direction. Our wooden shield absorbs most of the bullets; a handful gets through, but they only damage the wall behind us. Before I can kick the Dragon Master's legs away from him, bullets diagonally spray him across his body. One enters his left thigh, several impact his chest—but they are absorbed by his bulletproof vest. He falls down next to me; I dive in front of him to protect him from further damage. The security guard, who was on his right-hand side, falls down next to him—two bullets are embedded in his face. The last standing security guard drops down onto one knee and continues to return fire over the table.

I grab the fallen security guard's gun and insert it into the back of my trousers. I grab the Dragon Master under his arms and drag him over the fallen security guard towards the side door. There is no need to forage for safety because as soon as we leave the safety provided by the wooden shield, the bodies that are piled on top of one another at the top of the platform's stairs offer the much-needed cover to get to the side door. There are only two men who managed to escape the room and make it to the safety offered by the foyer. They are both holding onto each other as they cower in terror in the corner. They stop crying and let go of each other when they see me dragging the Dragon Master into the room.

The last standing security guard is keeping the enemy at bay, but he won't be able to hold out for much longer. Betty has curled up into a ball on the floor on the far side of him. She looks at me with wide eyes and eyebrows; her lips and body shake violently. She knows that death is imminent. I beckon her to come over to me with my hands, but she is paralysed with fear. I leave the Dragon Master on the floor; he is in a lot of pain but will survive. I sprint over to Betty, bend down, and grab her. As we are about the stand, the table is riddled with bullets—forcing us back down on the ground.

Over the sound of the gun battle, the motor roars back into life. There is now no time to hesitate; I grab her clothes at the back and run with her to the side door. The minigun's battle cry roars as soon as we both pass through the side door. The bullets pass through the table like it doesn't even exist; pieces of the last standing security guard splatter against the back wall. The minigun surveys the room for any survivors.

I take the Dragon Master's gun, and, along with my gun, I give one to each of the two men in the foyer. They reluctantly reach out and take them. They know what is expected of them, but I say it anyway.

"You two are to remain here and make sure that no one gets through this door. You are to protect the Dragon Master at all costs." They both nod their heads.

The minigun goes quiet again. They both relax a little bit and take one step towards the door. I throw the Dragon Master on my shoulder and head towards the security door at the bottom of the stairs.

"No, take the lift," the Dragon Master splutters. As I walk to the lift, something scratches my hand. I look down and he is trying to hand me a card. "Stick this in the slot." A red light flashes in the card slot next to the lift's doors. I insert the card and doors immediately spring open. I remove the card and step into the lift. Betty also jumps into lift. She stands against the back wall behind me. The two guys stand near the doorway looking out for the enemy. Despite them holding their weapons like experienced military personnel, I still have no hopes that they'll be able to keep the enemy back for long.

"Press the button," the Dragon Master screams. Before I can bend down to press it, Betty has pressed it. The doors close as bullets start flying into the foyer.

The lift's doors open and Betty steps out into the corridor first. Before I step out of the lift, the Dragon Master says, "Turn me towards the controls." I turn around and face away from the controls so that he can do what he needs to do. "There, that should stop them from hacking into the lift's system downstairs." The lift shaft amplifies the gunshots from downstairs.

We step out of the lift, cross the corridor, and enter the Dragon Master's office. I sit him down on his chair; Betty shuts the door. He has also been shot in the right biceps. With his working arm, he opens his top drawer, and extracts a cigar and a lighter. He offers the lighter's flame up to the cigar and repeatedly puffs on it until it becomes self-sustaining. Betty and I patiently await our instructions. The cigar hangs loosely between his lips as he reaches under his desk, pulls out the futuristic-looking gun, and hands it to me.

"Chinese secret service, my friend." He answers the question that is on the tip of my tongue. I take hold of the gun and wrap my fingers on my right hand around the handle. The LED band at the back remains on red. "Ah, wait a second." He reaches into another drawer and pulls out a black rubber band. "You'll need to wear this on the wrist of the hand you are firing with." I put the gun in my left hand and slide the rubber band onto my right wrist. I wrap my fingers on my right hand around the handle again and the LED band changes to green.

"Mr Kulikov, can you please open the window so that it looks like you've escaped through it?" he asks. I turn around and open the window as asked. There is a window ledge, which Betty and I could shimmy across, but the Dragon Master would not be able to make it. We all jump when we hear a machine gun approaching us. "We haven't got long before they get here. Right, you both need to do as I say. Mr Kulikov, please remove those books on the shelf behind you." He points his cigar at some books. Hidden behind the books is a red rotary switch.

"Turn the switch ninety degrees clockwise." I turn the switch ninety degrees and the full-length mirror swings open several inches. "Right, pull the red switch out and put it in your pocket. Now, you and Betty are to take refuge in there." He points his cigar at the full-length mirror.

The gunshots stop. I bend down and put my hands under his arms. As soon as I touch him, I make him jump.

"What are you doing?" he says with a raised voice.

"Picking you up," I reply, confused.

"No, you have to leave me here." I look at him angrily. "Don't defy my orders."

Betty walks over the full-length mirror, grabs its edge, and pulls it open. There's barely enough space for me in there, let alone all three of us.

"You two are to remain in there until the coast is clear. Do you understand?"

"Yes, Dragon Master," Betty says nervously as we both politely rub against each other as we squeeze ourselves into the secret room. My brain tries to think of a way to save him, but to no avail.

"I am fairly confident that they will not kill me. At least until Mikhail has had a chance to speak to me anyway," he states, unconvincingly. "Please tell May-ling that she is in charge whilst I am gone. She will provide you with everything you'll need to rescue me." He continues to suck on his cigar like his life depends on it.

"You have my word that I'll try my best to get you back." I commit myself to the forthcoming mission.

"If I am killed, tell her not to waste resources avenging my death." He struggles to keep his eyes open. "It's nothing personal."

"Betty, can you please pass me your phone?" I ask. She slowly pulls her phone out of her bloody waitress apron and hands it to me. "Thank you."

I sprint over to the Dragon Master and shove it into his sock. His eyes are now closed, and his cigar is held limply in his hands. I whisper in his ear, "Hold on for as long as you can, old friend. Keep feeding the Murder Squad with information so they go easy on you. Just keep thinking about Changying." He opens his eyes and there is a faint glimmer of hope in them before he closes them again.

"Make sure you kill Hiromi." He drops his cigar on the floor.

"It will be my pleasure. I'll even do it for free." The edges of his closed mouth briefly twitch.

The Russians noisily approach the Dragon Master's office. I wipe my hand over the blood spilling out of his thigh, wipe it across the windowsill, push the books back in place, and dive back into the secret booth. Betty pulls the bar on the back of the full-length mirror. The mirror door quietly locks shut as the office door is kicked open.

Yosef rushes into the office with his assault rifle in hand. He is swiftly followed by the other four members of the Murder Squad. The office seems to have shrunk now that it contains these Russian monsters. Boris and Viktor search the room then go over to the window and look out. Boris goes to climb onto the windowsill, but Viktor grabs his jacket and pulls him back down. Viktor dips his finger in the blood on the windowsill, sucks it off and seems satisfied with the taste of it. Yuri stands by the door, guarding it.

Toothless walks up to the full-length mirror with an open mouth, revealing his bare gums to us. They are grotesque and are covered in scars where his teeth used to be before they were ripped out. His face is covered in tattoos. At this distance, one can see that these tattoos cover up very deep and thick facial scars; in fact, his face seems to be completely made up of scars. I keep my gun pointed at his head, even when he turns and walks away.

Yosef walks up to the Dragon Master and puts his hand on his chest. Upon contact, the Dragon Master's body shakes violently.

"This was a lot easier than I had expected," Yosef declares. They all chuckle. The Dragon Master lets out a defeated whimper. "You win, let's get out of here." Yosef nods at Yuri and Viktor. Their guns are strapped to them, so when they let go of them, they fall and dangle at their sides. Viktor grabs the Dragon Master's arms; Yuri grabs his legs. The Dragon Master screams in pain when his limbs bear his full weight.

When the Dragon Master is halfway to the door, the sound of footsteps on the stairs enters the office. Yosef, Toothless and Boris get themselves into a fighting stance; their weapons are fixed on the doorway. Despite their appearance and behaviour, they become a well-structured, efficient, and deadly military unit when the situation commands it. Boris signals with his hand that the noise is not a threat. Boris and Toothless leave the office first and they are swiftly followed by Yuri and Viktor, who carry the Dragon Master with ease.

Yosef takes one last look around the office. His eyes linger momentarily on his own reflection in the mirror. My heart rate quickens noticeably and I apply more pressure to the trigger. When he makes it to the doorway, Hiromi runs into the office and clips his arm.

"Watch what you are doing, little man!" he barks.

"Did you get him?" Hiromi asks, panicking.

"We only got the Dragon Master," Yosef grumbles.

"Where is Mr Smith?"

"He must have escaped through the window. He has probably gone to the roof."

"But we need to kill him."

"That's your mission. My men and I have only been sent here to capture the Dragon Master. You promised Mikhail that it would be you who'd kill Mr Smith first." Hiromi's head drops. "Our priority now is to get the Dragon Master out of here. You deal with Mr Smith! Our services will be required later if you fail to kill Mr Smith, or he kills you first. He smiles. "If I were you, I'd get myself to the roof, pronto." He vacates the room.

Hiromi walks over to the window and looks outside. He also dips his finger in the blood on the windowsill, but he does not lick it off—instead, he wipes it on his trousers. He then turns around to face the full-length mirror and freezes. My gun is pointed at his forehead. Betty has been very still up until now but she begins to shake. She knows who he is and that he is responsible for all the death and destruction. I wrap my arm around her and put my hand over her mouth.

He knows that I am here, but he doesn't dare do anything on his own. He looks over at the bookshelf, which looks untouched, and then back at the mirror. His fingers start to twitch. He knows if he makes the slightest movement that indicates he is going to grab his gun from inside his suit jacket then I'll have no choice but to shoot him.

I wish I could shoot him now but am very reluctant as the Murder Squad may double back at the sound of gunfire. I cannot take on the Murder Squad on my own in these circumstances. Considering what Yosef just said, I doubt they will double back, but I cannot risk Betty's life. He stares at where my eyes are as he sidesteps towards the door. I keep watching his hands until he sprints out of the office.

Chapter 20
The Reclamation of Chinatown

When Hiromi's footsteps go quiet, I take my hand off Betty's mouth and my arm off her shoulder. I push down on the bar and the mirror door springs open. We both step out of the secret room. We both stretch out, glad that we've each got our own personal space back. She collapses into the Dragon Master's chair; I pace the room whilst working out what our next steps should be.

Gunfire erupts outside; both Betty and I run to the window. Kevin and several of the Dragon Master's foot soldiers are engaged in a firefight with the Russians, who are blocking the entrance to the underground carpark. Many spectators stand around the war zone, waiting to pounce on the Russians when the opportunity arises.

"Right, I need to use this opportunity to get the Dragon Master back," I say, focusing on the door. She nods her head. "You stay here." She jumps up off the chair and gets behind me. Her eyes tell me that she isn't going to stay here—no matter what I say or do. "You need to stay behind me and be no more than an arm's length away from me at all times." She nods her head.

My right eye is aligned with the gun's sights and I approach the door sideways on. I poke my head around the door and confirm that the corridor is clear. As I step across the threshold, my t-shirt gets caught on something. I turn around; Betty is holding onto it.

"If we do not make it, I want to thank you for everything that you've done for us." She has tears in her eyes.

"What do you mean?" I whisper back, keeping an eye on the stairs.

"My mother called to tell me that my brother was killed earlier in the firefight on the outskirts of Chinatown. I didn't catch any more details because the Dragon Master and you entered the restaurant, so I had to put down my phone—as did many other members of staff who were having similar phone conversations with their friends and family. I will not lie: we were initially planning on poisoning your food because we thought you were responsible for it."

"Unfortunately, I was." She turns her head to the side, confused.

"What do you mean?"

"It was my fault; we brought them here. In hindsight, we should have headed in the opposite direction to Chinatown."

"No, it is not your fault. You could not have expected those Russian savages to have acted how they did. A lot of people in Chinatown are here because they had to flee criminals, persecution, and many other bad things in China. For the most part, there is peace and prosperity here. But now, the Russians want us as their slaves. It's like we've swapped one enemy for another, possibly an even more ruthless one. However, our strength is derived from our solidarity, and no one will beat us—no one."

I nod my head and smile. I like her determination; even as innocent people are being killed outside. She looks at me with serious eyes. "You were trying to help us, which we will be forever grateful for. If you help rescue the Dragon Master and bring peace back to Chinatown, then you'll be worshipped as a god."

"Thank you for your kind words." I chuckle and try to generate energy from her motivational words. "Please make sure that no one worships me like a god; in fact, don't tell anyone about me—it is safer for everyone that way."

"With all due respect, Mr Kulikov, or Mr Smith, or whatever your name is. You risked your life to save me, which already makes you a god in my eyes."

The rapidity of the gunshots increases so I decide to let her win the argument.

"I hope I continue to live up to your expectations. Anyway, let's get a move on."

I quickly scan each room adjacent to the corridor as we make our way down it. I do not want anyone sneaking up behind me. I also do not want Betty watching out for people behind us as I need her to concentrate on following me.

As we proceed down the stairs, the smell from the already decomposing bodies begins to abuse our nostrils. The security door at the bottom of the stairs lies on the floor; it has been mutilated and ripped from its hinges and locks. We step over the door and back into the foyer. One of the two men that formed the last line of our defence is slumped against the back wall with a bullet through his forehead; the other lies on his front near the lift with the back of his head blown out. A feeling of guilt briefly attempts to challenge my pragmatism; I doubt their sense of honour would have allowed them to escape with us even if I had begged them to.

Several people are talking quietly in the restaurant, but I cannot make out any of their words. I can only distinguish Hiromi's voice. With my back against the wall, I edge towards the restaurant. A pool of blood sits around the side door and in the middle of this pool is someone's hand that has been separated from their wrist. I peer into the restaurant but can only see as far into it as the edge of the raised platform that I was eating on before the ambush.

I step around the pool of blood to get a better view of the restaurant. Betty tries to follow me; but I put my hand on her shoulder, push her back, and shake my head. She does not question me. The reflection from what remains of the mirror behind the bar, displays Toothless, Boris, and Hiromi in a heated discussion. Hiromi is making wild hand gestures in my direction, but the Russians are not interested in his pleas and try to walk away.

There are so many bodies around that I need to work out the steps that I need to take so that I am not tripped up by any of them. I take a few deep breaths and start running towards the bar. As I enter the restaurant, I glance at my targets. From this angle, Boris' huge body shields Toothless and Hiromi. I barely apply pressure on the trigger and a shot is fired. Boris' body shakes from the impact.

There is minimal kickback from the gun so its sights broadly remain on the original target. I fire two more shots at Boris: the first hits his right shoulder blade; the second hits him in the back of the head. The upturned table has been obliterated. It offers me near zero protection from machine gun fire, whilst hindering my view of the restaurant greatly; therefore, I am forced to keep running towards the bar. When I reach the gap between the table and the bar, I aim in the direction of my two remaining targets. Unfortunately, I have afforded them both with enough time to escape through the gap where the double doors that led to the underground carpark used to be.

Betty steps into the restaurant, but I wave for her to go back. I struggle to walk over all the dead bodies as I approach Boris. Every step I take, I must step on at least one part of a dead body. A dead man's head is barely attached to his body; his eyes calmly look up at me. I have no choice other than to put one foot on his face to avoid stepping on a little girl.

As I step on his face, his head detaches from his body. His skull cracks a couple of times as it bears my full weight. I keep my gun pointed at the vacant space where the double doors used to be when I reach Boris. I stand over him and kick his machine gun out of his hands. I bend down to check his pulse; there isn't one. I grab his gun and stand back up.

The gun battle continues to rage on the street outside. The main front doors remain locked; no one has used these doors since the security guard locked them. I head to the underground carpark. There are no bodies that I need to step over here, only thousands of empty cartridge shells that litter the floor. A tide of blood creeps in from the restaurant, collecting the cartridge shells as it moves. I check that the stairwell to the underground carpark is clear before beckoning Betty over to me.

She initially tries to get down the platform stairs, but there are too many bodies in her way, so she is forced to follow the path that I took. Once she reaches the bar area, she hesitantly begins stepping over the dead bodies. She speeds up when she gets a bit more confidence. Unfortunately, she tries to go too fast; she ends up tripping over someone's arm and falling face first in someone else's bullet-ridden stomach. She lifts her head up; her face is covered in thick blood. She tries to wipe it off, but her hair becomes even more matted with it. When she moves her head, her hair paints a thick layer of blood over her face.

She spots Boris and takes a detour over to him. She looks scary; she towers over him covered in blood, which drips off her onto him. She looks at me expressionlessly then back at him. She stamps on the back of his head repeatedly. She walks towards me and stops about one metre behind me. I nod, and she reciprocates as she bunches up her hair and tucks it into the back of her shirt. I lean forward and wipe some of the blood away from her eyes with my sleeve. She reaches for Boris' gun, but I pull it away from her.

"Give me the gun so that I can help you—I am ready," she says, desperately. I look at her with an annoyed expression. She ignores me and goes to grab the gun again. I pull it away from her again. She looks at me with the same eyes that I used on people whose help I was deprived of when I was younger. Against my better judgement, I flick on the gun's safety and hand her the gun.

"Only flick off the safety," I say, pointing to it, "if you need to. Do not waste bullets, and, most importantly, do not shoot me. The recoil on this gun will be immense. So, even if you think you have your target in your sights, you'll likely miss it." She nods her head and holds the gun like a professional.

We make our way down the long and exposed flight of stairs to Level One of the underground carpark, which according to the displays above the pair of lifts is where they are both currently positioned. Betty and I must hold onto the handrail due to the amount of cartridge shells resting on each step. Small amounts of what I presume is the Dragon Master's blood is interspersed between these cartridge shells on some steps. When we get to the bottom of the stairs, one of Mikhail's signature black SUVs flies past the glass double doors in front of us. I kick open these doors and race onto the floorplate of Level One. I step my left foot in front of my right, bring up my gun to my eye line, and take a couple of deep breaths.

Betty screams, "Quick, they're getting away. SHOOT."

I cannot visually see the driver's headrest because the windows are heavily tinted. The SUV is at such an angle to me that the rear passenger headrests will not be in my way; in fact, I could possibly hit the side of the driver's head from here. After I pull back the trigger, the SUV's rear window smashes, but it continues towards the ramp that leads up to the street. I fire another two shots at where I calculate the driver's headrest to be. Instead of going up the ramp, the SUV veers and collides head-on into the wall. I expel my breath.

Betty slaps my shoulder. "I've never seen anything like that in my life. Now I see why the Dragon Master favours you." I smile, impressed by my achievement, and secretly glad that someone witnessed it. Betty stays close behind me as we approach the SUV.

"You should wait behind there." I point at one of the concrete pillars. She hunches her shoulders but carries out my request.

I approach the SUV at an angle from the left-hand side, trying to stay in its blind spot as much as possible. I reach the rear passenger's seat on the driver's side first. I cannot see inside properly as there is an airbag in the way. From the body's outline, I would guess that it is Hiromi. The driver's window is severely cracked from the crash; one of my bullets has exited the vehicle through it. The driver is slumped over his airbag with two bullet holes in the back of his head. I do not recognise him; his tattoos suggest that he is one of Mikhail's men.

The front passenger's door opens. I get on my tiptoes to see over the driver's airbag. I catch a glimpse of someone falling out of the SUV and out of view. I instinctively put my hand on the bonnet and launch myself up onto it. Betty was making her way towards the SUV but stops dead in her tracks. Toothless jumps up off the floor and sprints towards her. I jump onto the car's roof and crouch down in order to avoid hitting my head on the underground carpark's roof. Betty is too close to my line of sight to risk taking the shot. I take two steps forward and dive at him.

Whilst I am flying towards him, Betty tries to shoot him, but no bullets are discharged—she has panicked and forgotten to release the safety. Thankfully, I put the safety on; otherwise, she would have torn me to pieces.

My right elbow smashes into the back of his head and I drive him to the floor. I land on top of him but immediately roll off him. He swipes his blade at my torso before I am fully upright. I lift my gun-wielding left arm up and arch my midriff over. His blade swings across me, cutting only my t-shirt. Betty has her gun pointed down whilst she figures out how to turn off its safety. She has stood still long enough for blood to drip off her and form a pool around her feet.

He repeatedly jabs the blade powerfully at my heart, forcing me to keep stepping back out if its way. He doesn't give me chance to point my gun at him. After one jab, he is too slow to retract his arm, so I grab hold of his forearm. I drop my gun and grab his wrist with my other hand as well. I twist his arm by moving my body under it until it twists out of its socket. He releases the blade and I easily push him to the floor. I get over him and drop my full weight on him.

Even though his arm is out of its socket and my full weight is on him, I still have trouble keeping him pinned down. As I headbutt him, he lifts his head up, which reduces the power that I can get behind it. Both of our foreheads collide, causing each other a similar amount of pain. I go to headbutt him again, but a cold and wet piece of metal rubs against my left cheek. He stops fighting me when he eyes Betty's gun. Two drops of blood drip down from it onto the side of his head.

"NOT YET," I scream. I need to ask him some questions. BANG. His face explodes; my face gets blasted with his blood. My left ear rings loudly and I am once again disorientated by a close-range gunshot. I roll off Toothless onto the floor, clutching my ear. Luckily, I don't think my eardrum has ruptured.

Whilst I was rolling on the floor, Betty has made her way over to the SUV. As she opens the rear passenger's door, Hiromi kicks the gun out of her hand. She stumbles back and falls on the floor. He jumps out of the SUV and lands on top of her. Over the ringing in my ears, I hear her shout, "HELP ME!"

He punches her in the face as hard as he can and her whole body goes limp. He takes hold of her gun. He helps her back to her feet. Pointing her gun at her head, he starts talking to me, but he is too quiet for me to hear.

"Stop right there," someone commands. Kevin emerges from behind the SUV at the bottom of the car ramp with two other men. "What is going on here?" He directs the question at Hiromi but looks at me.

"These two are traitors. They let the Russians in and handed them the Dragon Master," Hiromi says.

"The Dragon Master was in one of those SUVs?" The two other men keep their guns pointed at my head as they make their way over to me. "Is he still alive?"

"Yes, they took him. He was alive though—but only just. These two set him up." He points at me. Kevin eyes me suspiciously. He looks at Kevin and can tell that he is not falling for his lies. "He has been working for Mikhail the whole time. The competition that they set up was an elaborate ploy to capture the Dragon Master."

"And what has Betty got to do with this?" Hiromi subtly tightens his grip on his gun. Before he answers, May-ling appears from behind the SUV with several more men. She ignores me and looks at Hiromi and Betty.

"Do you know where they have taken the Dragon Master?" She glances at me. I nod my head but am too slow for her to see it.

"Yes, May-ling," says Hiromi.

"Good. Our number one priority is getting the Dragon Master back."

Hiromi relaxes, letting the gun fall away from Betty's face. As soon as its muzzle is pointed at the floor, May-ling throws her gun up and fires it without aiming. Everyone except myself jumps. The bullet goes straight into the middle of his forehead; his head is thrown back followed swiftly by the rest of his body. Kevin throws his gun up, points it at the side of her head and shouts, "What the fuck!"

"Why don't you ask Mr Kulikov?" Betty replies vehemently.

Everyone turns to face me; they all project their anger at me. I struggle to get to my feet to address them.

"Hiromi was working for the Russians," I state, struggling to gauge the volume of my voice due to the ringing in my ears. Kevin enters a state of deep shock. "He abandoned us when we visited the General. He also told Mikhail's Murder Squad where the Dragon Master and I were. As you can see, there is Toothless." I point at Toothless' deceased body on the floor. "Betty was the one that actually killed him."

May-ling turns to face her and says, "Impressive. Thank you."

Betty bows her head.

"When you go upstairs to the restaurant, you'll see that it is a bloody massacre," I continue. "The Murder Squad was not messing around; they brought a minigun to the party." Everyone shakes their head in disgust. "Boris is dead upstairs—I killed him."

"Oh my," May-ling cries. "How many?"

"Everyone—a couple hundred people. We were cornered; the Dragon Master sacrificed himself for Betty and me." Everyone except May-ling looks shocked. I look at her. "He has put you in charge whilst he is aware. Betty can testify to that."

"Yes, I did—Dragon Mistress," she jokes. But it falls on deaf ears.

I walk over to May-ling and pull her to one side.

"I'll rescue the Dragon Master," I whisper, "but under one condition." She nods her head. "That you'll do all that is in your power to help Emma rescue Nataliya from Mikhail if I am killed." She looks at me with fierce eyes.

"After all that you've done—and are going to do—for the Dragon Master, me and everyone else in this organisation, I would happily give my life for Nataliya's."

My body shakes from a mixture of happiness and nervousness.

"Thank you."

I turn and head to the ramp when Betty shouts, "Where are you going?"

"To get the Dragon Master back."

"I am coming with you." She runs to catch up with me. I let out a loud sigh; my eyes become watery.

"I need to go alone; I cannot risk your life as well."

"You have no choice; I have a life debt to repay." I shake my head. I am not falling for that rubbish. "We also make a very good team."

No, we don't, I say to myself in my head. I stop and turn to face her.

"You are more valuable to the Dragon Master if you stay here and help May-ling sort all this mess out." She shakes her head. She has now killed someone and thinks that it is always that easy. She thinks that she is invincible. "You are to protect May-ling at all costs. Do you understand?" I put my right hand on her shoulder for extra reassurance. She becomes ecstatic at gaining this new responsibility. She looks at May-ling, who bows to her.

"Don't worry—I'll get the Dragon Master back," I address everyone.

"No, not on your own you won't," Kevin states. "You may need Chinese help."

"I can assure you that I won't." I say, unconvinced by my own statement.

"Well, I am coming with you, whether you want me to or not. Even if I am only your driver."

"OK then, but you best stay out of my way." He bows his head. I turn to Betty and pass her my phone.

"Actually, I do need you. Can you please type your phone number into my phone?" She takes my phone and starts typing in her number.

"See, I told you that you'd need me." She is annoyingly smug. I do not respond.

"You'll need a weapon," May-ling shouts.

She flicks her finger in my direction. One of her men responds to the command. As he runs to me, he releases his handgun's magazine and replaces it with a fresh one. As he passes it to me, I recognise it as an out of production Browning Hi-Power handgun. They do not want me leaving with a Chinese weapon. He also hands me two magazines.

Betty passes back my phone and says, "Good luck!"

I do not respond. Instead, I turn to walk up the ramp.

"Do you want to take a G-Wagon downstairs, or the minibus upstairs?" Kevin asks excitedly.

I send Betty's phone number to Emma.

"We'll take the minibus." He is disappointed with my decision.

Chapter 21
The Butcher's Shop

"Right, so where are we going?" Kevin asks me as he drives us out of Chinatown on the opposite side that we need to go. I want him to drive around randomly first so I can confirm that no one follows us.

"Head towards Old Town. I've not had the Dragon Master's location confirmed yet, but I suspect that I know where he is."

"What! You said you knew where he was?" He becomes distressed.

He seems oblivious to the speed limit and is forced to cut someone up as a result.

"Yes, and I do—although, I've not had it confirmed yet. Can you please keep to the speed limit?"

He takes his foot off the accelerator pedal a little but remains slightly over the speed limit. He smiles smugly to himself.

"Why are you helping to rescue the Dragon Master?"

"What do you mean 'helping'? I'm the one doing the rescuing. Anyway, stop asking personal questions. All you need to know is that we have a special relationship and we are both invested in each other."

He pulls a face as he tries to work out what I mean by 'special relationship'. He doesn't ask me to elaborate—I wouldn't elaborate even if he did ask. He pulls out in front of a speeding car. It honks its horn at us several times, but it doesn't faze him.

We reach a side street that runs parallel to Main Street. On one side of this street is the back of the shops that face Main Street; on the other side is a row of terraced houses. Both sides of this street are fully lined with parked cars. We have to drive about halfway down the street before we find a fairly large space on the side with the terraced houses. I would have no problem parking the minibus in this space, but it takes him several attempts to reverse park it. Its rear wheels on the passenger's side ends up on the pavement but he doesn't notice—or he doesn't care. I get out of the minibus and shake my head at the quality of his parking when an annoyed pedestrian looks at me. We cross the road and walk down the street towards the back of the butcher's shop.

Kevin tries to appear to be cool, calm, and collected; but his eyes dart around looking for cameras and Russians. I walk casually as I know that there are no cameras around and that there won't be any Russians—at least not on this side of Main Street. We reach the butcher shop's yard and I open the back gate. We walk down the stairs to the back entrance of the shop and let ourselves in.

As I enter the back room, the shop's owner—Wayne the Butcher—is on the other side of chain fly screen handing meat over the counter to a customer. He spent a fair amount of time in prison after the police raided his parent's farm and found numerous illegal activities going on. He did whatever made him money, including providing barns for human and animal traffickers to temporarily store their goods; storing and selling red diesel; and burying asbestos. The police also suspected that he disposed of people and animals in his pigpens, but they didn't find any evidence to underpin this suspicion.

I first met him when he came to my boxing club straight after his release from prison about five years ago. He not only provided me with valuable information on the human and animal traffickers that he used to work with, but also gave me the contact details of pig farmers that have been disposing of bodies for me ever since. He wanted to become a butcher, but he had no money. His parents had bankrupted themselves fighting to free him; they died without a penny to their names.

I provided him with this shop so that he didn't have to return to a life of crime, and so that he could keep an eye on the Murder Squad's pawnshop on the opposite side of the road. He has worked hard to make this business a success. He has paid me back in full and contributes a fair share of his profits to my boxing club's coffers.

His smile disappears when he sees me. He doesn't acknowledge me, instead, he turns to serve his next customer. We walk through the back of the shop, which is pristine. It doesn't matter how clean a butcher's shop is, the smell of rotting organic matter makes it feel dirty. I open the door that leads to the stairs and we both make our way up them to the front room. I type in the required sequence of numbers into the combination lock. I open the door and step into what I call the

'Observation Tower'. The camera is set back from the window so that no glare from the camera lens can be seen from outside.

The Observation Tower is also kept very dark. The only light source comes from the monitor when it is turned on; there isn't even a bulb in the ceiling light. I grab the remote control next to the monitor and turn it on. Wayne has been keeping an eye on the pawnshop and reporting back to me. This is the closest I have ever dared get to it. I have managed to identify most of the people that the Murder Squad have taken into their pawnshop, both directly and indirectly. However, in the last month or so, there have been eight people that I have not been able to identify yet. Ironically, the Murder Squad has been especially busy over the last few months now that Mikhail is trying to go legit.

I sit down at the desk and start rewinding the recording. I only need to rewind about half an hour before I observe them reversing their SUV down the alleyway at the side of the pawnshop. Yuri gets out of the driver's seat; Viktor get out of the front passenger's seat; and Yosef gets out of the rear passenger's seat on the passenger's side. Viktor opens the pawnshop's side door whilst Yuri opens the SUV's boot.

Yosef makes his way around the SUV and removes the licence plates. Another licence plate sits underneath each one. He stands guard at the door with the licence plates in his left hand and his right hand tucked into the inside of his jacket. He looks around. At one point, he looks directly into the camera. The boot closes and Yuri walks out from behind the SUV carrying someone on his shoulder. It is not possible to 100% confirm who it is because they've placed a black bag over their head.

I convince myself that it must be the Dragon Master because the person is wearing the same clothes that he was wearing when he was kidnapped. They are only out in the open for less than a couple of seconds before they all disappear into the back of the shop. I replay the footage once more to study the person's dimensions to confirm that it is him, and not a decoy.

I fast-forward the recording to confirm that they haven't left the building— they haven't.

"Right, let's get moving." I stand up. Kevin sits looking at the monitor, a tear rolls down his face. I put my hand on his shoulder. "We need to move now; they will be torturing him as we speak."

He shakes his head and jumps to his feet. As I step through the doorway, Wayne steps across it and stops me. His huge farmer's frame fills the doorway.

"Is it time, Boss?"

I put my hand on his shoulder.

"Yes, I'm afraid it is, my friend." A flicker of fear flashes in his eyes, but he remains steadfast. "But not for you. I appreciate your offer, but Kevin is here to help." I nod at Kevin. He steps back from the doorway, leaving a gap for us to exit through. "However, I do need you to do something more important for me."

"Anything."

I step back and flick off the camera.

"If we are not out of the Pawn Shop in half an hour, I need you to get all the information and recordings," I look at the four-drawer safe in the corner of the room, "to Superintendent Emma Payne." He nods his head. "Her details are in the safe."

"No worries, Boss. You can rely on me." He straightens his back and stands proudly.

"I know I can. Thank you for all your help."

He thrusts his hand out and I slap my right palm against it. He wraps his large sausage-like fingers around my hand before he firmly shakes it. I put my other arm around him and we embrace each other. My head rubs against his gold necklace.

"Good luck, my friend. Make those bastards suffer!"

I nod my head and smile.

"They will. Actually, do you mind if I borrow your necklace?"

Before he has a chance to respond, I hold out my hand.

"Not at all, Boss."

He removes his necklace and places it in my hand.

Chapter 22
The Pawn Shop

Kevin and I cross the mostly deserted street. I lead the way into the pawnshop. A bell rings when the door opens. It startles the shop assistant, who was engrossed in his phone at the counter. He looks like a typical, unwelcoming Russian foot soldier, especially with all his tattoos and shaved head.

"Good afternoon, sir," I greet him.

He grunts something back; he is probably lacking proficiency in English. He looks at Kevin with interest as he begins to browse the jewellery display unit. His left hand is on the counter; it slides back closer towards him the closer that I get to him. I look over his left shoulder at the camera, which is directed at my face. I step to the left and use his body to shield me from it. He slides his left hand under the counter when I put my right hand into my back pocket. A relief washes over him as I pull Wayne's chunky gold chain out of my pocket. I feel more relaxed now that he has relaxed. He brings his left hand back up onto the counter.

"How much for his?" I dangle the chain in front of him. He quickly glances at Kevin again before snatching it out of my hand. He pretends to weigh it on some scales before looking at me and saying, "Twenty."

"Try again."

He smiles. He deliberately goes very low first with his first offer; he is trying his luck. Drug addicts do not have the time to barter if they are desperate for their next fix. I pick the gold chain out of the scales and present its trigger to him.

"Look, it is 18ct gold." I point at the engraving on the trigger.

The door on my right-hand side opens and Yosef steps through it. Kevin jumps out of his skin—instantly giving himself away. When Yosef pans around to me, he also jumps out of his skin. He rapidly withdraws his gun from inside of his jacket. My reflexes take over; I sidestep, kicking the door back onto him before he lifts up his gun. The door slams into his arm, causing him to drop his gun. The shop assistant brings his gun up from under the counter with his left hand. I whip the gold chain against his right hand, which rests on the counter holding his phone. He also drops his gun and screams in pain. He clutches the back of his right hand with his left hand. I spin around and whip it across his face. Kevin leaps over the counter and tackles him to the ground.

Yosef charges at me without a weapon. He gets low and puts his arms out to tackle me as he approaches. I drop the necklace and attempt to uppercut him, but he tackles me before I can connect. Instead of falling back, I manage to step back with him attached to me, absorbing some of his energy. I elbow his back, but he doesn't loosen his grip. I elbow him twice more. I bend over and wrap my arms around his waist as he forces me back towards the jewellery display unit. I grip him tight and lift him up so that he is upside down. I fall back and his legs smash through the glass display unit.

His upper body rests on top of me. I push him off and get back to my feet. He stays on the floor moaning in pain and clutching his left calf, which has shards of glass embedded in it. The shop assistant has his left hand around Kevin's neck and punches him in the head repeatedly with his right hand. He pins Kevin up against the wall. Kevin manages to grab his left index finger, which is around his windpipe. He forces the finger back until he breaks it. He uppercuts him on the chin, freeing himself from his restraint.

Yosef pulls the largest shard of glass out of his calf, and lunges forward, trying to stab me with it. I step back out of his striking range. This gives him enough space to properly get back to his feet. He jabs it at me again, but I easily dodge it. He quickly slows as his left leg struggles to bear much of his weight due to the shards of glass that remain embedded. I do not drop my guard; he might be trying to lure me into a trap.

I grab someone's once beloved iPad off the side and throw it at his head. It hits the bridge of his nose and forces him to step back uneasily. I jump up and kick him with both feet. He flies back and collides with another glass display unit—but he doesn't break the glass.

He gets back to his feet straight away; he comes back stronger and with more determination. He wildly alternates between trying to punch and stab me. I keep stepping back out of their way. Stab, stab, punch. I try to move my body back further, but I am stopped by a display unit, which is positioned next to the wall. He stabs me; the shard of glass clips my stomach.

Before I have a chance to turn the situation around, he has pulled the glass out of my stomach and has it rocketing towards my neck. I punch him hard in the face, but it doesn't stop the glass. The glass grazes the lower part of my neck; I feel it tugging against my skin as it rubs over it. He swings the glass at me again; I grab his wrist and terminate its trajectory. I hook my foot around his left calf and drive pieces of embedded glass deeper into it. His left leg buckles painfully as the glass cuts deeper into his muscles and tendons. I throw my right shoulder into his chest and knock him back. Before he can stand up straight, I headbutt him awkwardly—it feels like I've hit a bowling ball. As he falls, he grabs my jacket.

I land on top of him and he releases the glass dagger. I attempt to roll off him, but he grabs hold of me. The harder I fight to get away, the stronger he pulls me back. He spins me over and forces my face into the floor. Tears involuntarily fill my eyes. He grabs my right arm with both hands and tries to bend it behind my back. It takes all my strength, but I manage to stop him—although, I nearly snap my shoulder out of its socket in the process. I am now on all fours.

He repositions himself on top of me and gets me into a firm headlock. I throw my head back against his face. I feel a couple of his teeth enter the back of my head as I knock them away from the gums. Blood drips onto the back of my head, rolls down the side of my face, and drips off my chin onto the floor. Blood from the small cut in my neck also drips onto the floor, but with less flow. The two pools of blood coalesce. His grip on me tightens as he tries to take advantage of the situation. I throw my head back again; this time it doesn't make contact. I can feel myself falling asleep. I grab one of his arms and momentarily prise it away from my neck. This gives me a chance to take a deep breath.

Kevin is lying on his back whilst the shop assistant stamps on him. This doesn't stop him from reaching for the shop assistant's gun on the floor with his foot. The shop assistant is not paying Yosef or me any attention when Kevin kicks his gun in my direction. He attempts to stamp on Kevin again, but Kevin grabs hold of his foot and kicks his other leg away from him. Kevin then gets on top of him and punches him repeatedly in the face.

The shop assistant's gun stops within reaching distance of Yosef and I. Yosef goes for the gun with his right hand, but keeps his left arm around my neck. He puts all his weight on me as he leans forward. As soon as his fingertips touch the gun, I grab his arm with my left hand and bring it across my body. At the same time, I lift up my lower back and throw him over my head. We roll across the floor grappling each other until I manage to get behind him and lock my arms around his head.

We are both lying on our left sides; I am the big spoon. He tries to reach for the gun again, which is in front of us. I manage to pull him back, outreach him, and take ownership of it. I bring it back towards him whilst positioning my index finger on the trigger. He grabs hold of the gun's barrel with both hands. His left index finger is covering the muzzle when I fire a shot.

He screams in pain and I feel him grow stronger as he pushes the gun further away. After about ten seconds of struggling, his strength starts to disappear faster than mine. I position the gun under his chin, aim it away from me, and pull my head back as far as possible away from his. As I squeeze the trigger, he accepts his fate and releases the gun.

I roll his corpse off my left arm and get back to my feet. My ears do not ring this time. I keep an eye on the door, making sure that none of the remaining members of the Murder Squad take us by surprise. I hope their torture room is soundproof. Kevin is still on top of the shop assistant, but the shop assistant's hands are now around his throat.

Kevin keeps throwing punches, but they don't have enough power to cause much damage. I don't risk firing another shot. I put the gun into the back of my waistband and pick a piece of glass out of a broken display unit. I get on my knees with the shop assistant's head between my legs. I ram the piece of glass into his throat; blood sprays onto Kevin's face. He tries to scream in pain, but only the sound of blood gurgling in his throat escapes. His arms fall onto his body then down by his sides. Blood pours out from his throat and mouth, down his neck and cheeks, and forms a pool around him. I feel my trousers soak up the blood around where my knees are.

Kevin stands up straight and puts his hands on the back of his head as he tries to get his breath back. Movement in the corner of my eye catches my attention. A teenager boy with Down's syndrome is at the window shadowboxing. An old woman comes up behind him; the colour drains from her face when she sees the horrifying scene inside the shop. She doesn't scream; the look on her face suggests she knows better than to call attention to this scene.

Before I get a chance to turn away, she looks deep into my eyes. Both of our faces are covered in blood, so she would not be able to provide an accurate description of either of us. She pulls the reluctant boy away from the window and out of sight. I look at Kevin.

"Go and lock the door," I command.

He picks Yosef's gun up off the floor before going over to lock the front door. I walk over to Yosef, grab his left leg and drag him over to the shop assistant. I bend down, grab the shop assistant's right leg, and drag them both out of view behind the counter. I search Yosef and extract his phone from his trouser pocket and pocket it. Wayne's gold necklace is on the floor next to me so I pocket that as well.

Kevin has his gun pointed at the back door; he is in the full view of the camera behind the counter. I face the camera towards the wall. Kevin notices the camera and looks ashamed. I shake my head. With an opened palm, I direct my left hand to the door as I retrieve my gun. He nods his head, brings his gun up to his face, and proceeds cautiously to the door. He opens the door wider before storming across the threshold. I wait in the shop, giving him time to clear what I suspect is an empty room.

I step across the threshold into the kitchen. Kevin closes the door behind me and locks it.

"Keep your gun pointed at that door." I point at the large single door on the back wall, which has a clock attached to it. He turns, points his gun at the door, and gets down on one knee.

It is a fairly large kitchen with an eight-seater table in the centre. The whole kitchen is spotless. The table looks clean enough to eat food off—despite the numerous people killed, or dead bodies stored, on it. There are a set of double doors on the right-hand side that lead to the alleyway. The frosted glass in the double doors presents a blurry image of their SUV on the other side of them.

I grab a load of kitchen roll off the side and wipe all the blood off my face, neck, and hands. It turns out that there is in fact a cut on my neck; however, it has already stopped bleeding. I throw the bloody sheets in the bin and rip off a couple of fresh ones. I look in the mirror and wipe the blood away from the cut on my neck, which is much sorer than I was expecting. It weeps after I've finished wiping the blood away. This time, I put the used sheets in my pocket. I point my gun at the large single door and offer Kevin the kitchen roll. He knocks my hand to the side.

"Thanks, but I'll be OK. Let's go and get the Dragon Master."

I put the kitchen roll back on the side, and, keeping close to the back wall, I head to the single door. I spot the SUV's car keys on the side, behind the fruit bowl. I grab them and throw them at Kevin; he catches and pockets them. When

I reach the door, I notice that the clock has a hidden camera in it. I grab hold of the clock and lift it up off the nail that it is attached to. A cable is attached to it through a small hole in the door. I rip the clock away from the door and rip the cable away from it. I throw the clock in the sink.

Kevin remains at the other end of the kitchen with his gun pointed at the door. I nod at him and he reciprocates. I grab its handle and throw it open. I prepare myself for an exchange of gunfire. Kevin gives me the 'all clear' nod. I poke my head around the door frame; I am faced with nothing but blackness. My eyes adjust and I see dim flicker of light at the bottom of the stairs. The cable at the back of the door is attached to the wall and goes down into the darkness. I head down the stairs; I sense Kevin walking behind me.

"You wait here," I whisper sternly. I take a few more steps down and he continues to follow me. "I need you to wait here!" I do not turn around to face him as I keep my gun pointed at the light source at the bottom of the stairs.

"I am coming with you. I am not letting you rescue the Dragon Master without me," he spits.

"Yes, you are. You need to make sure that we have a clear escape route. Once I get him, we are getting straight out of here."

I think he receives the message because as I continue down the stairs, I do not sense him following me. When I reach the bottom of the stairs, I am startled by several gunshots; however, they are not real gunshots. They sound like they came from a television. My hands shake from the shock. I crouch down with my back against the wall on the opposite side to the door; I am cast in darkness.

I peer into the room and see Viktor sat on the sofa in the centre of the room. He is playing a first-person shooter video game whilst eating food off a plate on his lap. He has a headset on and is talking into it. I cannot hear what he is saying over the sound of his virtual machine gun. I peer further into the room and see a naked man hanging upside down. His feet are bound by a rope, which is attached to a hook on the ceiling. Despite him facing away from me, I can still tell that it is the Dragon Master.

His head is only an inch or two off the floor. A man sits in a chair on the other side of him, but I cannot see his face. It must be Yuri. I continue to survey the room. Along the wall on the right-hand side is a row of jars. I cannot see what they contain as it is too dark over there. Further along from the jars is a small metal cage but I cannot see what's encaged within. On top of the cage is a machine gun. Behind Yuri is a row of CCTV monitors that display the various camera feeds. One of the CCTV monitors displays static; he hasn't noticed because he is too busy questioning the Dragon Master. The only light source in the room is from all the CCTV monitors and the television.

Yuri pokes his head out around the dangling Dragon Master and looks directly at me—but he cannot see me in the darkness. He does something to the Dragon Master, which causes him to scream and swing around. I dive into the room, but I cannot shoot Yuri as the Dragon Master swings in the way. Yuri notices me and he dives for his gun; I turn my attention to Viktor, who isn't aware of my presence. I fire into his temple, blowing his head to the side.

I dive onto the sofa and aim at Yuri, but I still don't have a clear shot. I land on top of Viktor and my head hits the game controller and a pile of large crisps that are on his lap. Yuri fires into the back of the Viktor. I feel his body absorb several bullets. Yuri moves the gun along the back of the sofa; bullets explode through the sofa, and the throw resting on the back of it.

One bullet grazes my trousers near where my kneecap is before smashing into the television. The room goes quiet and dark. I roll off the sofa onto the floor. Looking under the sofa, I see the top of the Dragon Master's head, which is about two inches off the floor. On the other side of the Dragon Master's head is Yuri's boots. It is a risky shot, but I have to take it. The bullet flies under the sofa, through the Dragon Master's hair, and drills itself into the gap between his big toe and the rest of his toes.

Yuri stops firing and lifts his foot up. I am tempted to shoot his other foot; however, I am conscious that if I wound him too much then he may start firing wildly—and I cannot risk the Dragon Master being killed. I jump up and step on the sofa between Viktor's lap. I shout, "Lift your head up."

I step on the back of the sofa and leap into the air. I fire at the rope holding up the Dragon Master. The bullet cuts the rope; he falls to the floor. I grab the remaining rope with my free left hand, swing, and force my heel into Yuri's face. He drops his gun as he flies back into the metal cage. A large rat jumps up and tries to bite and claw at his exposed neck skin. I drop to the floor; he bounces off the cage and falls onto my signature right uppercut. His head snaps back and his whole body is lifted into the air. He lands on the floor awkwardly in an unconscious heap.

I pick the Dragon Master up, put my arm around him, lift him up, carry him over to the sofa, and place him next to Viktor's dead body. His head wobbles all over the place like it is not attached to his body. He tries to speak to me, but he doesn't make any sense. I look behind me and there is a small kitchen area. I run over to the kitchen and grab the kitchen knife lying on the work surface.

The knife is covered in blood and leaves a pool of blood behind when I lift it up. I return to the Dragon Master, who has slumped against Viktor's corpse. I grab him by his shoulders and put him back into an upright position. I cut the rope binding his feet together first. The knife is very sharp and cuts through it like butter. Kevin quickly scans the room before entering it. He is overcome with emotion when he looks directly at the Dragon Master. After I finish cutting the rope, I ram the knife into Viktor's thigh.

"Quick, we need to get the Dragon Master dressed and out of here," I say.

I walk around the coffee table, I believe the smashed phone on it is Betty's. I find the Dragon Master's clothes in a pile on the floor, next to a white sheet. I pick up his clothes, except for his underwear, and throw Kevin his t-shirt. Kevin and I put his t-shirt and trousers on him, respectively.

"Quick, let's get him up. You need to get him out of here now whilst I finish up down here." He doesn't move fast enough so I yank his arm. "NOW!"

He struggles to lift up the Dragon Master, who is a deadweight. I lightly push him out of the way and place my hands under the Dragon Master's armpits and lift him up. Once he is up, Kevin puts his right arm under his left arm. I let go of him and Kevin bears his full body weight. They slowly make their way to the stairs.

I walk over to the CCTV monitors, take the hard drive out of the digital video recorder, and put it in my pocket. I also pocket Betty's phone, well the big pieces of what's left of it. Kevin and the Dragon Master leave the room and start to ascend the stairs. I look closely at the jars on the walls; they all appear to contain pickled human organs as I had anticipated. There must be over one hundred jars on the shelves. The large black rat looks hopelessly at me from inside of its metal cage. A shiver runs down my spine; I look away.

Rats have been very useful to me, but I still hate them—I hate them with a passion. Yuri stirs and murmurs as his consciousness returns. I should shoot him, but it doesn't feel right—it would be too easy. If his victims were in my position now, then they would not let him off so lightly. I walk over to the table in the far corner of the room. As I approach it, I realise that it is shaped like a crucifix. It has straps on it to tie a person down. At the centre of the crucifix is a gold crucifix necklace. It might have been Toby's bodyguard's necklace. I knock it onto the floor and kick it away.

I pull the table over to Yuri, pick him up, and throw him onto it. I strap down his arms, head, and torso. He only realises what is happening to him when I start strapping down his legs. He starts kicking his legs around wildly, and I have trouble keeping control of them. I let go of his legs, reach over the sofa, and pull the knife out of Viktor's leg. I turn around just as his right leg barely misses my groin.

I ram the knife into the outside of his right thigh. I leave it there to restrict his leg's movement whilst I push it down easily with one hand and strap it down using my other hand. His left leg nearly clips my face. I put my full-body weight on it and strap it down overly tight.

Once fully strapped down, Yuri calms down and lies still. His eyes glaze over; he doesn't say a word. A shiver runs down my spine as I walk past the watchful rat. Damn, I hate rats. I walk back over to where the torture table was. It is too dark in this corner of the room to see much. I get my phone out of my pocket and turn its torch on. The torch reveals an array of medieval torture weapons and surgical tools. The medieval flail particularly captures my attention—I have never used one before. I scan the beam of light across the wall until I come across a glass display unit like the ones used upstairs.

Sitting on top of it is a strange container; it comprises a metal box attached to the top of a hollow-based Perspex cube. It's about the size of a microwave oven resting on its side. I think I understand what it's for. It is the perfect end for Yuri—I am sure his victims would agree. I scan it with my touch and see that an electrical cable is attached to its metal box. The rat starts going berserk.

I walk over to Yuri with the container, which is much heavier than it looks. Its plug trails behind on the floor. I place it on his chest; he tries to move violently but the straps do their job. I walk over to the rat; we look each other in the eyes. I shine my light on it and open the lid on the top of its cage.

I expect it to start attacking my hand as I reach down to grab it, but it remains motionless. I pick it up by the scruff of its neck and carry it over to the container. I lift up a side of the container and place it under it. It looks around at me and I feel a strange connection with it. It looks down and starts scraping at Yuri's t-shirt; it is getting a head start.

Yuri neither makes a noise nor tries to escape; he knows his fate has been sealed. I bend down, pick up the plug, and ram it into an electrical socket on the wall. The room lights up with a soft orange glow from the heat lamp. The rat instantly picks up its pace. I turn off my touch and put my phone back in my pocket.

When I reach the door, I cannot help but look back to see how much progress the rat has made. It has already started to churn the top layer of Yuri's skin. Yuri remains quiet and motionless. As I step across the threshold to leave, there is an almost silent whisper, "help me?"

I stop dead in my tracks. It wasn't Yuri, and it certainly wasn't Viktor. The room is eerily quiet apart from the rat's movements and the electric static from the CCTV monitors and the heat lamp. Kevin and the Dragon Master reach the top of the stairs. The person whispers again, "help me!"

I cannot work out where the voice is coming from. There must be a hidden room. I get my phone out and flick on its torch. I search for a hidden door, but I cannot find one. The rat has now dug through the outside layer of skin; its paws and face are covered in blood.

"Help!"

I pick up the pace of my search. I walk around the broken television to the kitchen and frantically throw open the cabinet doors. I get to the tall upright fridge and, as I walk past it, I notice that it is padlocked shut. I do not need to pick the lock or shoot it off as both the hasp and staple are poorly attached. I grab the staple and yank on it; the whole fridge rocks around. The person inside starts to cry.

"Don't worry, my friend. I am here to save you. Hold on." They do not respond; their crying gets louder. I put my phone back in my pocket. I place my now free hand on the side of the fridge and pull harder. The screws start to give way and bend. After not much more effort, two screws spring out at the same time. I bend the staple back so that the door is clear to open.

I take a deep breath before opening the door. As I open the door, the light inside flicks on. A naked man has been forced into the tight confines of the fridge. Blood flows out of the fridge onto the floor. His knees are butted up against his face and he cannot move his head to see me. He carries on crying and his body, which has gone blue, shakes uncontrollably.

"Don't worry, you're safe now. I've got you." I put my right hand on his cold right shoulder that is against the back of the fridge and put my left hand under his cold knees and try to slide him out—but he is stuck. I start wiggling him out and he screams in pain. Some of the skin on areas of his arms and legs has been heavily flayed. I do not have time to assess his condition as I am concentrating on not snapping one of his feet as I pull him out. As soon as his body is free from the fridge, he stops screaming and his body goes limp. The door closes, plunging the kitchen area back into darkness.

As I carry him over to the sofa, Yuri cannot help but let out a short whimper. The sound gives the man in my arms some energy. He lifts up his head, looks at Yuri momentarily, and goes limp again. I place him on the sofa next to Viktor's dead body. Despite him being blue, I instantly recognise him—he is Sheikh Latif.

He curls back up. He shakes violently. I grab Viktor's collar and throw his dead body onto the floor. His head collides with coffee table; the game controller and bowl of crisps fall onto the floor next to him. The bowl smashes and the crisps spill out across the floor. The crisps are like nothing I've seen before. They intrigue me, so I pick one up. Its texture is strange; it feels like thin piece of pork crackling. I drop the crisp when I make the connection. They are not crisps at all: they are human crackling. Viktor must have cooked skin flayed from both Toby's bodyguard and the Sheikh, as well as possibly from other victims, and has been snacking on them.

After I've wrapped the sofa throw around the Sheikh, I pick him up and rest him on my left shoulder in a firefighter's lift. I step across the threshold again when Yosef's phone starts vibrating in my pocket. I look back at Yuri. I am very impressed by his self-control; he's a true warrior—a true Russian. In fact, I may never have come across someone with such good self-control before.

I place my left hand on the Sheikh's lower back whilst awkwardly getting the phone out of my pocket with my right hand. The caller ID says, 'Boss'. I walk back to Yuri; his eyes are wide open, staring at me. I tilt my body to one side and balance the Sheikh on my shoulder. I take my left hand off the Sheikh and place it over Yuri's mouth. I smile evilly at him. I casually flip the phone open with my thumb.

"Bring over the Dragon Master; my brother is on his way," Mikhail commands. I watch the bloody rat frantically dig for its survival whilst I leave Mikhail waiting for a reply. "Yosef, are you there? I cannot hear you. The signal in that basement of yours is starting to get on my nerves." He is always impatient.

"No—the signal is fine," I respond, calmly.

"Ah, Mr Smith. You're still alive then, my friend?" he responds, instantly.

"Of course, my dear friend. Although, the same cannot be said for any member of your Murder Squad."

"You bastard! You are good, my friend. I'll give you that. However, you cannot keep running. I'll get you in the end."

"Maybe you will, it doesn't matter."

"I'm afraid, my friend, that everyone has something to lose. If you'll just bear with me for one second."

I do not have a spare second; I need to get out of here. I'm about to end the call when I hear Nataliya screaming. A high voltage shock of anger electrifies my body. I clamp my left hand around Yuri's face and ground this anger through a crushing force on his face. He still doesn't make a noise. The rat has its full head burrowed inside of his chest. Mikhail comes back on the phone.

"You see, my friend. We all have something to lose. We are reasonable men. I'm sure that we can come to some type of arrangement."

"I'll be in contact tomorrow. I've got to get the Dragon Master out of here." I scream internally. "Also, I've got to get Yosef's bullet out of my shoulder," I lie. He chuckles to himself. "Oh, say 'hi' to Vitali for me."

I slam the phone shut. I scream internally again. I'll destroy him.

"AAAAHHHHHH," I scream out loud.

When I take my hand off Yuri's mouth, he spits on my elbow. I put Yosef's phone back in my pocket. I balance the Sheikh more securely on my shoulder and clench my right fist tightly. I smash the bottom of my hand into his face and crush his nose. I repeatedly smash my fist into his face using the same hammer motion. When I've finished, his face is completely caved in. He is well and truly dead.

Immediately after the last punch, the adrenaline begins to rapidly wear off. I feel a sharp pain in my little finger. It hurts a lot, but it was worth it. The rat has stopped digging and is looking at me. A strange emotion runs over me and, despite hating rats, I feel sorry for it. Its job here is done so I push the container off Yuri and onto the floor. The light smashes when the container hits the floor. The silhouette of the rat jumps off Yuri onto the floor. It disappears into the darkness.

Chapter 23
The Sheikh

The screech from car wheels spinning over the alleyway's tarmac infiltrates the kitchen through the ajar double doors. I dart through the kitchen with the Sheikh still resting on my left shoulder. He groans on every step as my shoulder digs into his abdomen. I dive through the double doors as a police car turns into the alleyway from Main Street on my right-hand side. The Murder Squad's SUV is reversing out of the alleyway on my left-hand side. It squeals to a halt after it has blindly reversed into the side street. Kevin glances emotionlessly at me before accelerating away.

"Stop! Hands in the air," a police officer instructs me as he jumps out of the front passenger's seat. He withdraws his stun gun. I am forced to reveal the Sheikh's face to them as I rotate my body around to hide my face and body from him. "Hands in the air. NOW."

I put both of my hands in the air. A car engine growls loudly on my left-hand side. It is Kevin reversing the SUV back down the alleyway towards me. The boot is open, and the Dragon Master is sat across the back seats looking between the headrests at me. He throws his right arm over the backseat and beckons me to get in the car.

Wayne runs up behind the police officer with the stun gun and hits him behind his right leg with a metal meat tenderiser. He hits him harder than he probably should have; the officer crumbles onto the floor. The air cracks loudly and Wayne immediately starts to shake violently. I jerk forward and start running towards the reversing SUV.

The Sheikh barely slows me down; I run nearly at top speed. When a distance of ten metres separates us, I throw him off my shoulder and cradle him in my arms. At a separation distance of five metres, I feel a couple of pinches on my back. All my muscles start to involuntarily spasm simultaneously, forcing me to a slow walk, and then to a stationary wobble.

I launch the Sheikh into the SUV's boot when it is one metre away. I try to jump after him, but my leg muscles seize up, and start to give way. As the SUV grinds to a halt, it hits my legs and scoops my upper body into its boot next to the Sheikh. It accelerates away, causing me to roll back with the Sheikh. The Dragon Master leans over the back seats and grabs my jacket before I fall out onto the tarmac.

He screams loudly as he musters all his energy to pull me back into the boot. Once I am safe, he jumps into the boot with us. His knees land on the Sheikh and his right elbow lands on my temple. The electrical shock has now ceased. He rips the two dart-like electrodes out of my back and throws them out. He closes the boot as the SUV drifts around the corner.

As the Dragon Master clambers over the back seats, he kicks off the throw that was wrapped around the Sheikh, exposing his naked body. The Sheikh's colour has almost returned to him, but he is still very cold. I flick the throw back over him. I fling my arm around him, pull him close to me, and hug him tightly. We are both violently thrown into the side of the boot as Kevin throws the SUV around a corner.

"Slow down," I order.

"Slow down," the Dragon Master repeats my command.

"We need to get back to Chinatown quickly," Kevin responds. He slams on the brakes at a set of traffic lights and everyone jerks forward.

"No, we don't," I explode. "Look what happened last time. For now, we simply need to get off the streets. Keep driving down here and turn into the Flowery Hill multi-storey carpark. Do you know where it is?" He doesn't respond. Instead, he looks at the Dragon Master through the rear-view mirror.

"Do you know where it is?" the Dragon Master repeats my question impatiently.

"Yes, it is down here on the right."

"Good. Now slow down," I shout. "You are drawing unnecessary attention to us." He does not slow down. It takes someone to direct the sound their horn at him in order for him to ease the pressure applied to the accelerator pedal.

The Sheikh remains cold, so I hug him harder. He winces in pain as I put pressure against his cuts, but he welcomes my efforts to warm him up. The Dragon Master leans over the back seats and asks, "Who is this?"

"Sheikh Latif. He is the latest person to have the misfortune of dealing with Mikhail." I pull out my phone, unlock it, and call Emma. She answers after only one ring.

"I wondered when you'd be needing my help again. The whole police department has been tasked with finding you." I cannot help but smile as soon as I hear her voice.

"Hi Emma," I say slowly in the tone of a schoolboy saying sorry for something that they are not sorry for, not in the slightest.

"I'm guessing that Wayne Sutcliffe is Wayne the Butcher?" she asks, frustrated.

"Yeah. To cut a long story short: the Murder Squad captured the Dragon Master and were torturing him in their pawnshop. He has now been rescued and the Murder Squad has been eliminated."

"What? No way. All of them?"

"Yup."

"Oh, my. Well, well done. That's going to make life a lot easier. It means that I can also relax as I was worried about them one day being tasked with torturing me. Anyway, are you OK?"

"Yeah, I'm hanging in there. I'm with the Dragon Master now trying to find a safe place to hide. Wayne sacrificed himself so that we could escape. As his file shows, he already has a record. I need you to make sure that he gets off lightly."

"I'll try my best, but he is the least of our worries at the moment."

"Unfortunately, it's not over yet."

"Yes, unfortunately. I'll stay away for now whilst I try and contain some of your other messes." Her tone suggests that she wants me to give her information on my next move.

"Ah, yes. I've been busy. By the way, don't waste your time with Chinatown. It will be cleaned up soon."

"Chinatown! Chinatown is a fucking mess. Don't get me started on Chinatown. We cannot even get in. The police officers on the ground are getting increasingly infuriated by the sheer amount of people blocking their path and impeding their entry into Chinatown. Even though it hasn't even turned violent—and probably never will—preparation of the riot police has been ordered by my superiors. I don't think approval will be given for their deployment though." The Dragon Master, who is listening to our conversation, forces an unfazed smile and the rise of an eyebrow.

"As I said, don't waste your time with Chinatown." She mumbles something, but I don't catch it. "I don't know if you've been watching the news recently, but Sheikh Latif has been in the city."

"Yes, I've seen him on the news throwing his money around."

"Well, he was also in the basement of the pawn shop. He was locked in the refrigerator."

"Really?" Her voice goes high-pitched.

"Yeah. He is in a very bad way. Anyway, the reason I called is that I need you to find out the contact details of his people."

"Not a problem. I'm good friends with the person who has been liaising with his security detail."

"Good. It is urgent. I am hugging him to warm him up as we speak."

"Not a problem. I'll get the contact details for you now. I'll need to end this call first though."

"Thank you."

"Before I go, I should say that there has been no progress on the Nataliya front." I become so overwhelmed by the thought of Nataliya that I struggle to reply.

Instead of telling her my plan to get her back, I say, "I've got Yosef's phone. I'll text you his number shortly." I end the call before she has time to respond.

Kevin scrapes the side of the SUV against a concrete pillar at the entrance of the Flowery Hill multi-storey carpark. The scraping sound is unbearably loud and irritating. He pulls up alongside the ticket machine but is too far away from it to press the ticket button whilst seated. To compensate for his error, he opens his door, stands, and leans across to press the button. After he presses the button, the machine's internals churn loudly for several seconds before spitting out a parking ticket. He snatches the ticket out of the machine before shutting his door. He accelerates forward, barely missing the slowly rising barrier. This carpark has particularly tight parking spaces and thoroughfares. He picks the first available space, a space allocated for disabled people.

The Sheikh has started to warm up.

"You're OK. You're safe now," I whisper in his ear.

"Damn, that was close. I cannot thank you enough," the Dragon Master cries, his adrenaline has started to recede. "The hardest part was keeping Yuri distracted from looking at the monitors whilst you and Kevin were fighting in the shop."

"Yes, thank you for that." I keep rubbing the Sheikh's back, but he is still nonresponsive. My phone vibrates in my hand, making me jump. *Unknown Caller* is displayed on the screen.

"Hello," I answer.

"I understand you have Sheikh Latif?" the man on the other end asks with a posh English accent.

"Yes, that is correct. Whom am I speaking to?"

"I am afraid I cannot disclose my personal details. All you need to know is that I'm the Sheikh's Head of Security." He acts cool, calm, and collected—but I can sense his desperation.

"Well, you've not done a very good job—have you?"

"I am fully aware of the situation and I expect to be severely punished by the Sheikh when he has been returned to me," he says seriously. "My only concern at the moment is retrieving the Sheikh."

The Dragon Master moves his head closer to me so that he can better hear the conversation.

"OK. I have the Sheikh, but he is not in a good way—he needs urgent medical care."

"Do not concern yourself with the well-being of the Sheikh. We already have a team of medical experts assembled and waiting to deal with any situation." I am impressed. "Where are you?"

"We are currently parked on the ground floor of the Flowery Hill multi-storey carpark."

"OK. Good, you're off the street. Does the carpark have an open-top roof?"

"Yes, I believe it has."

"Good. Go there now. We've got your location. Our ETA is four minutes. Go now." He ends the call.

"What does he mean go to the roof?" the Dragon Master asks. "Surely, they want us to meet them somewhere."

"I am not too sure. We need to offload him though: he's going to slow us down."

"Where did you find him?"

"In the refrigerator."

"No way. I had no idea." He suddenly goes quiet as the thought of being back in the basement has scared him. He turns away.

"Take us to the roof," I order Kevin.

He spins around and looks directly at the Dragon Master, who nods his head. He reverses out of the disabled parking space and slams his brakes on, causing the Sheikh and I to be thrown against the boot's door. The Sheikh groans loudly on impact. Kevin accelerates forward. He tries to drift the SUV around a concrete wall to go up the ramp, but the rear end hits it. We are all thrown to one side. The Sheikh groans in pain again but this time it is because I bear too much weight on him.

Unbelievably, Kevin doesn't hit any more walls or pillars as he races to the roof. Once we reach the roof, he parks the SUV in the middle of two car parking spaces. I am relieved that that was the last time he drives me anywhere. He turns to face me with a very large, smug smile on his face.

"Now what?"

"We wait."

I pull Yosef's phone out of my pocket, retrieve its number, and send it as a text message to Emma on my phone. I tap my phone on the Dragon Master's shoulder and he turns around. "I think you should call May-ling."

He nods. I bring up her number and start the call. As he takes my phone out of my hand, the dull thumb-thumb-thumb sound of a helicopter's rotating blades roars into life. I shout, "Open the boot."

The boot opens, and the thumb-thumb-thumb sound grows in intensity. I jump out of the boot, grab the Sheikh, pull him out of the car, and cradle him in my arms. I walk around the side of the SUV and stand next to the Dragon Master; Kevin stands on the other side of him. We all scan the sky for the helicopter, but it is not in sight. About thirty percent of the car parking spaces on this level are full and, fortunately, there appears to be no one else around.

The helicopter's roar deafens us when it swings around the skyscraper in front of us. It is a large, black military-style helicopter. I have never seen anything like it before. The helicopter comes to a sudden halt, hovering in front of us. The force from the propellers blows us all back against the SUV. Many of the car's lights start flashing, but I cannot hear their alarms over the sound of the helicopter. The helicopter turns sideways as it lowers itself down, revealing several soldiers all pointing guns at us. Large metal canisters rain down on the carpark from the side of the helicopter. Instantly, large plumes of smoke rise up from them. This smoke is whisked around and thrown in all directions by the helicopter's rotor system.

The helicopter descends until it is hovers about a metre above the roof of the cars. Numerous soldiers leap out of it onto the cars below, spread out, and disappear behind the cars and the smoke. A final soldier jumps out of it and centres me in his assault rifle's crosshairs. Naturally, I presume he is the Sheikh's Head of Security. He keeps me in his crosshairs as he leaps from car to car towards us. The helicopter launches itself into the air and begins to circle us. The other soldiers search inside and under all the cars as they 'secure' the area.

An identical helicopter swings around the same skyscraper and circles us as well. The door gunner scouts the area. The sound coming from both helicopters is incredible. The Dragon Master is blown into the side of me. When the Sheikh's Head of Security reaches the car in front of us, he leaps off it without hesitation. He continues towards me until his gun is millimetres from my forehead. He is the guy at the golf course who I assumed was in charge of the Sheikh's security. I look into his eyes and there is something in them that I have not seen for a long time. It is the look of someone who is willing to do whatever it takes to get the job done—even if it means sacrificing themselves. There have been many occasions when I've had the same twinkle in my eyes.

His assault rifle is high tech, bordering on futuristic. Special operations forces do not even use this type of weaponry. Despite the strong winds, his rifle barely moves. Two other soldiers appear out of nowhere and point their weapons at Kevin's and the Dragon Master's foreheads. The Head of Security glances down at the Sheikh in my arms to confirm that it is his boss. It was only a quick glance, but it was enough time for me to have ended his life if I had wanted to.

He is satisfied that it is the Sheikh. Another soldier comes up behind him and throws a large black holdall at my feet. I only glance down at the bag, but in that time, he has also targeted his gun on my forehead. The Head of Security drops his own gun. Its strap keeps it suspended at his side. He steps closer, revealing all the small scars that cover his face. I have even more respect for him now. He bends forward and puts his hands underneath the Sheikh.

"We cannot thank you enough. Please accept the money in the bag as your reward," he shouts as he bears the Sheikh's bodyweight.

"You're welcome."

"We'll be in touch." He nods at each helicopter. "We've been informed that the police are on their way. Unfortunately, we cannot take you with us. But,

Asim," he glances at the soldier pointing his gun at my forehead, "will help you escape."

He nods at Asim before turning around and walking towards the car that he jumped off. He puts his right foot on its bumper and launches himself and the Sheikh up onto its bonnet with ease. He glides over the cars towards the helicopter, which lowers itself before coming to a rest on top of four cars. As soon as he steps into it, it lifts off the now crumpled cars and rockets into the air. The remaining helicopter continues to circle us. A man and a woman step out onto the floorplate. They take several steps before realising the situation that they've walked into. The man immediately pulls his phone out of his pocket, but one of the soldiers runs over to him, grabs it out of his hand, and launches it over the carpark's wall.

Asim, whose build is similar to Head of Security's, lowers his weapon and reveals similar facial scars. It looks like they've all been assembled on the same production line.

"Right, we need to get you guys out of here," he commands. "We'll distract the police and make sure that your path is clear. We have a guy controlling the traffic lights and cameras. He has already sanitised all the traffic camera footage since you picked up the Sheikh." He puts his hand to his ear. "We need to move; the police will be here in one minute." I grab his large shoulder as he turns to leave, causing him and his men to jump. All his men point their guns at me.

"No one gets hurt," I say, holding onto his shoulder with a vice-like grip. He smiles.

"Naturally." I take my hand off his shoulder. I offer him Yosef's phone, but he doesn't take it.

"This phone belonged to one of the men who kidnapped the Sheikh." He eyes it cautiously. He snatches it from me and secures it in a pouch attached to his wristband. He and his men walk towards the carpark's wall.

"Right, let's get going then," Kevin says, turning around and stepping up to get back into the driver's seat. I grab his jacket and pull him back down.

"I don't think so, my friend."

"Get in the back, Kevin," the Dragon Master orders as he picks up the black holdall. He walks around the SUV to the front passenger's side and gets in. I jump into the driver's seat and smash my knees painfully against the steering wheel. It always frustrates me much more than it should when small people have used a car before me. I lift the lever at the bottom of the seat and slide the seat back. I close my door and put on my seatbelt. The Dragon Master also puts on his seatbelt. Kevin closes the rear passenger's door and sits behind the Dragon Master.

The SUV's wheels spin as I accelerate it towards the exit ramp. When I reach the next level down, I have to slam on my brakes to avoid hitting an old lady, who is trying to reverse her very small car out of a relatively generous parking space.

Regrettably, I do not have time to wait for her. I am pretty sure that she doesn't even notice when my front bumper lightly touches her back bumper. I slowly increase my foot's pressure on the accelerator pedal and push her back into her parking space. She fails to turn her steering wheel so her car scrapes down the side of the car in the adjacent parking space. She looks at me in her rear-view mirror and I mouth the words, 'I'm sorry'.

I put my foot down hard on the accelerator pedal again and race to the ground level. As I exit the bottom ramp and head to the ticket barrier, I shout to Kevin, "Pass me the ticket." I press the button on my door to lower my window. He thrusts his ticket-wielding arm into the front. I snatch the ticket out of his hand and snap, "Thank you."

I take my foot off the accelerator pedal and barely touch the brake pedal when the Dragon Master says, "Look, the barrier arm is lifting. The Sheikh's man must be controlling them."

I toss my ticket into the back and slam my foot back down on the accelerator pedal. As we approach the road, I prepare myself to turn left. However, Asim and his men have dropped smoke grenades on the left-hand side, stopping all the traffic. Two police cars have been blocked by this traffic. I pull the steering wheel down hard with my right hand and we drift into the road. Kevin flies across the back of the SUV and into the door behind me. I take the second gear all way to the red line on the rev-counter. I am harsh with the clutch as I change up to third gear. A plume of dense black smoke is expelled from the SUV's exhaust pipe when I smash the accelerator pedal into the floor.

One of the police cars mounts the pavement to get around the traffic blockade and takes up the pursuit. We travel to a set of traffic lights that are on red. There is not much traffic at the crossroads so I continue to gather speed, hoping for the best. As we get closer, the traffic lights switch to amber and then green moments before we pass by them at thirty miles per hours faster than the speed limit.

I pull out into oncoming traffic and swerve around them; however, the SUV is too sluggish to respond to my demands, and its front bumper clips the corner of someone's rear bumper. The SUV shakes on impact, but it neither bothers the Dragon Master nor I; however, Kevin flies face-first into the back of my seat. We lose vital momentum; the police car closes the distance between us. The helicopter takes off from the multi-storey carpark and disappears behind some buildings.

The next set of traffic lights are on green and a lot of stationary traffic quickly forms on the crossroad, which is a major artery into the city. I take the third gear all way to the red line before shifting into fourth gear. We start to pull away from the police car. At about forty metres away from the traffic lights, they switch to amber. We fly through the traffic lights moments after they've switched to red.

Immediately, traffic on the crossroads moves forward. The police car manages to stop just before hitting the side of the stream of heavy traffic. I take a hard right down a side street and out of view. I drive around randomly. All the sets of traffic lights that we approach are on green and they remain that way as we pass them. After about ten minutes, we approach a set of traffic lights that are on red. They continue to stay that way as we come to a halt. We are now safe and on our own.

Chapter 24
Zea Graze

The Dragon Master ends the phone call to May-ling and turns to face me.

"They're still a fair way off sorting out the mess in Chinatown, but they're making good progress. All hands are on deck." He turns his head and looks at Kevin. "She has told us to go to the supermarket. They'll use one of their delivery lorries to smuggle us back into Chinatown."

"OK, where's that?" I ask.

"You'll have to turn around and head back towards the cinemas."

I am not quite sure where he means. I turn right into a side street and execute the perfect three-point turn. I reach the main road, wait for a break in the traffic, and turn left. The set of traffic lights up ahead are on red. I flick my indicator down to signal that I intend to turn left. I move into the left-hand lane and pass the queuing cars in the right-hand lane. As we come to a halt, we pass a police car that is second in the queue.

"Keep looking forwards," I say, as both of my passengers twist their heads to look at the police officers. It doesn't help that the right-hand side of the SUV that is facing the police officers is covered in deep scratches from when Kevin scraped it in the Flowery Hill multi-storey carpark. In the wing mirror, I can see the police officer in the passenger seat talking into his radio. "I suspect we've been spotted." The Dragon Master suspects the same thing and starts to panic.

"What are we going to do?" he asks.

"The police station isn't far from here; they'll have more police here in no time. I'll lead these guys away to give you a chance to escape." The police officer in the passenger seat steps out of the police car. "Before you take the wheel, I am going to need you to give me two bundles of cash." I look at the Dragon Master.

"You don't need to do this; we can lose them." His eyes betray him. I do not respond. I know for certain that it's not possible. "Here, you take the holdall," he tries to pass me the holdall. I undo my seatbelt and push open my door.

"I only need two bundles." I hold out my hand. He passes me two thick bundles of cash. "Remember, I need about six of your men to be spread out, discreetly surrounding Mikhail's mansion at twenty-three hundred hours tonight." I slide out of the SUV and pocket the bundles of cash.

"After everything you've done for me, I give you my word that my men will be there." He steps over the gearstick and handbrake into the driver's seat. I nod my head and slam the driver's door shut.

As the police officer takes his second step towards me, I withdraw Yosef's gun from my back and fire one bullet into his right thigh. He screams in agony, clutching his wound. His right leg goes weak; he collapses onto the tarmac. The traffic lights change to green and the Dragon Master races the SUV away. I walk in front of the car at the front of the queue in the right-hand lane. There is a family in the car and they all have their heads down. The dad peers at me through the gap between the steering wheel and the dashboard.

I step onto the pavement as the police officer in the driver's seat opens his door. I fire two bullets into his door, forcing it closed. Before I turn to run, I fire one bullet into the police car's front tyre.

Whilst running at about fifty percent full speed, I insert the gun into my back waistband and withdraw my phone. I call Emma, who answers on the third ring.

"Yes," she answers, frustrated.

"Where are you?" I take a very deep breath.

"I'm leaving the police station now." Police sirens sound in her background. "My task force and I are the only police officers left at the station and we've been ordered to get to the Hampton junction. A police officer has been shot."

"Yes, I know—I shot him."

"You what?! Are you mad?" She is beside herself with rage.

"I had no choice. I had to do it so that the Dragon Master could get away. I am on foot and running away from the scene." I glance over my right shoulder. The police officer that I didn't shoot is following me. "Can you get to the 'Zea Graze' coffee shop opposite the police station?"

"Well...Jesus Christ. Yes, OK. OK. I am looking at it now through my window. I'll tell my team to go on ahead without me."

"Thank you."

"I'll be there in about two minutes. But I cannot stay long. I'll have to catch up with my officers."

"Thank you. Get a table and order two coffees. I'll be there in less than five minutes." I end the phone call. I put my phone into my back pocket so that I can use both hands to run at about seventy-five percent full speed.

About four minutes later, I am on the street containing both Zea Graze and the police station. I turn and see the police officer who is chasing me enter the street that I have just stepped off. He is a good two hundred metres behind me. I dive around the building on the corner and out of view before he sees me.

As I sprint to Zea Graze, I nearly knock over a woman, who blindly steps out of a posh clothes shop. I step to the side, but not quick enough to avoid clipping one of her many shopping bags. It is getting very dark and cold. People don't want to be outside for too long so they are rushing to either get home or to the next shop; they are in too much of a rush to care about me weaving in and out of them. I stop when I reach the alleyway next to Zea Graze.

Thankfully, the homeless man who has been living in this alleyway for the last few weeks is there; he has his head inside one of the Zea Graze's bins. I know about his presence because I frequently use Zea Graze whilst I wait to follow certain people as soon as they've been released from the police station. I quickly scan the alleyway to confirm that there are still no cameras around before approaching him.

"Excuse me, sir," I say. He doesn't turn around as he probably thinks I am someone going to ask him to stop raiding the bins. "Would you like to earn some money?" This gets his attention. He drops the bin's lid and turns around. He studies me curiously.

"Hello again." He checks my hands to see if they contain any food. He does this because I gave him a bag full of sandwiches the last time I was here.

"I didn't get a chance to ask you last time because you ran off once I gave you the food, but can I ask why you're here?" He shrugs his shoulders.

"PTSD. I've struggled with civilian life since I left the army—this is why my wife and kids have left me. It is a good thing though. I don't want to hurt them when I have one of my episodes." I raise my eyebrows in surprise.

"I appreciate your service. There are a couple of guys at my boxing club that have, or have had, PTSD. They would be more than happy to help you." He isn't giving me his full attention so I talk louder. "Go to 'One Hit' gym on Weston Street when you get a chance and ask for Big Stan. Trust me, it will change your life." He nods his head, but he is not convinced. "Anyway soldier. I've got a mission for you." His back straightens.

"Go ahead." He says, looking at me curiously. I reach into my pockets, pull out the two bundles of cash, and hold them out for him to take. He is desperate to take them but restrains himself. He looks me in the eyes. "What do I need to do?"

"Take it," I command.

He reluctantly relieves me of the cash; he crams a bundle into each of his front trouser pockets. I take off my jacket and pass it to him. "I need you to give me your coat and woolly hat." He nods his head. He puts my jacket between his legs, takes off his coat and woolly hat, and passes them to me. I put on his coat and woolly hat; he puts on my jacket.

"Is that all?" he inquires.

"Not quite." He is not surprised. He exhales loudly anyway. "I need you to run through Zea Graze next door and create as much commotion and chaos as you can. I also need you to steal the CCTV digital video recorder in the cupboard under the coffee machine on the back counter. There will be a police officer hot on your tail, so you'll have to move fast. Got it?"

"Roger that. Is that all?" He raises an eyebrow.

"Yep."

"You want me to do it now?"

"Yes, I need you to do it right now," I say with desperation in my voice.

"Consider it done." He heads to the main road before looking back at me over his right shoulder. "I was worried you wanted to sleep with me."

"You think you're worth that much money?" He laughs as he jogs around the corner.

I open the bin that he was searching for food in and act as though I am now searching for food. Moments later, the police officer is gasping for air on the pavement outside the alleyway. I keep my head down in the bin. Zea Graze's front door opens, and the sound of complete pandemonium enters the street. He rushes to Zea Graze; I drop the bin's lid and follow him.

Emma is seated on a two-seater table on the right-hand side with her back against the wall. I jog past the front window and slip through the front door as it closes behind the police officer. I dance around people and the tables, one of which has been flipped on its side, until I get to Emma's table. I sit opposite her, but she doesn't acknowledge me; she is absorbed by something on her phone.

Emma has long, natural brown hair and bright, crystal-blue eyes. Her hair glistens under the wall light above her; it comprises numerous shades of light brown. Even though she doesn't need to, she wears minimal make-up to cover up the scars on the right side of her face. She is physically fit and strong, as well as a very capable fighter.

Every now and again, a new recruit will ask to spar with her, but they quickly regret their decision. I do not know anything about her personal life—and I do not pry. I respect the required boundaries of our personal relationship. I also respect her need for privacy. To the extent that I don't know where she's from, or even if she's in a relationship with someone.

I first met her when I was overseeing a museum robbery. Mikhail, at the behest of the Kremlin, commissioned three men to steal several Russian artefacts. These artefacts were believed to have been stolen from the Russian state during the dissolution of the Soviet Union. They were only in the city for a couple of days as part of a Russian-themed exhibition. Mikhail had never used any of the three thieves before so ordered me to watch them closely to ensure they didn't run off with the artefacts once they had them in their possession.

Unbeknown to the thieves, I was sat in the car behind their getaway car, which was parked opposite the museum, whilst they were stealing the artefacts. Annoyingly, but unsurprisingly, they triggered a silent alarm. Emma had only been a qualified police officer for a few days when she and her partner arrived at the museum as the thieves were running down the stone steps towards their getaway car. There was a quick tussle before a fight broke out. Her partner was a big guy so two of the thieves fought with him and the remaining one concentrated on her.

It didn't take them long to knock her partner down. He quickly got back up but was immediately knocked back down again. This time, he remained on the ground motionless. Emma bravely fought on and managed to land some hard punches. Inevitably, she also got knocked down. The two thieves ushered their partner in crime to leave with them, but he wasn't finished with her. Before she could stand up, he knocked her back down and kept her down by stamping on her. She tried to spin onto her front to protect herself, but he stamped on her forcing the right side of her head into the tarmac. Now vulnerable, weak, and tired, he repeatedly stamped on her; he wasn't going to stop until he killed her.

The two thieves in the getaway car slowly started to drive away to encourage their accomplice to join them. However, he was too preoccupied to notice them, so they drove off with their artefacts, leaving him and his artefacts behind. I planted my house key firmly between my right index finger and middle finger as I exited my car and stormed up behind him. I placed my left hand on his neck and smashed my right fist against the other side of his neck multiple times in different places. His blood rained down over Emma. He collapsed on the floor next to her, clutching his wounds.

It didn't take long for him to bleed out. I tried to find her partner's pulse but to no avail. I was tempted to just call her an ambulance and leave, but something inside of me stopped me from doing that. She was barely conscious and her broken ribs made it difficult for her to breathe. If the thief had carried on much longer then he would have killed her. I picked up his holdall, placed it on her, and cradled them both in my arms back to my car. When I placed her on the back seat of my car, she momentarily grabbed my arm before passing out. Sometimes when I close my eyes, I recall the image of her face as her tenacious expression slackened when she passed out. I raced to the hospital and left her outside of A&E.

I visited her in the hospital the next day. I waited outside her room whilst her colleagues interviewed her. Looking through the slit in her bandages, she recognised me as soon as I crossed the threshold of her room. She welcomed me into her room and we exchanged generic pleasantries. I brought up the topic of the previous night's events; she smiled trustingly when she said she'd told her colleagues that she couldn't remember what had happened. I knew then that I could trust her.

I gave her a file that contained information on the two thieves that had escaped and enough evidence connecting them to other criminal activities to lock them away for a long time. Despite being in agonising pain, she beamed with excitement as she flicked through the pages. I only stayed with her for less than five minutes, but it was enough time to both develop a strong bond with her and come to the realisation that she would be a great asset to my cause. As I was leaving, I told her to visit me one afternoon at the 'One Hit' boxing club if she really wanted to tackle crime and make a difference.

A few days after she was discharged, she had tracked down the two thieves and had them convicted of the crimes that I had given her evidence on. However, she couldn't, and still hasn't managed to, pin neither her colleague's murder nor the robbery on them—she'll struggle pinning the robbery on them now because

I stole the stolen artefacts from them on the night of the robbery and gave them to Mikhail.

A week after her discharge, when she had still not recovered enough to leave her house, she visited my boxing club. We have been working as a formidable unit ever since. We have mostly concentrated on capturing perpetrators involved in human trafficking, including several of her superiors, and rescuing those being trafficked. We have saved many lives. We gather the evidence together and, depending on the situation, I either deal with it my way or she deals with it the legal way.

She jumps when she looks up from her phone. A cheeky smile spreads across my face. No matter how bad I am feeling, she never fails to cheer me up. She smiles back at me.

"Impressive," she says in an unimpressed tone.

"Thank you." I ignore the sarcasm.

The police officer helps a waitress turn the table back upright. I cannot hear what they are talking about because there is still quite a bit of commotion. He walks towards the kitchen and asks, "Was he wearing a black jacket?"

"Yes," the waitress answers. "After he stole the CCTV recorder, he ran into the kitchen, and out through the fire escape.

"Well, this is going to be difficult to explain if we're spotted together." She raises her eyebrows.

"Yes, I know. I'm sorry. These are exceptional circumstances. Besides, as you've heard, the ex-serviceman that ran through here took the CCTV recorder with him so the CCTV cameras are not recording."

"And who is this ex-serviceman?" She watches the police officer disappear into the kitchen.

"He's currently homeless. He was searching for food in the bins in the adjacent alleyway. I have a feeling he'll be a valuable asset to us in the future." She does not respond.

A flustered waitress places our coffees down on our table without saying a word and rushes off to continue cleaning up the mess that the ex-serviceman left in his wake. All the customers have gone back to staring at their phones. I keep my voice low.

"Mikhail has a party at his house tonight and I am going to use the opportunity to get Nataliya back. You want to come?" She doesn't hesitate.

"Of course." She looks around to see if anyone is listening in on our conversation. A tear involuntary forms in my left eye and I immediately wipe it away with the back of my right forearm. "Don't worry, we'll get her back." She puts her hand on my clenched fist—which I wasn't aware I had formed. I smile, and she reciprocates.

"I'll not stop until Nataliya is safe. I'll annihilate Mikhail and anyone else who has touched her," I say more to myself than to her. I clench my fist even more tightly.

"Don't worry, you're not alone." She tightens her grip on my fist. "We will get her back!" She takes her hand off my fist and uses it to bring her coffee up to her lips. She doesn't look at me as she takes a deep swallow of coffee. I copy her. I feel and hear the lukewarm liquid slide down my throat into my stomach.

"All I want is for her to be safe."

"Well, let's go and get her then."

Chapter 25
The Rescue

Momentarily, I have the head of one of Mikhail's security guards in my sniper's crosshairs before everything goes black again. As soon as we have travelled over the wave, I painfully land back on my elbows and my crosshairs drop back onto his head. The river is very choppy tonight and the waves aggressively attack our speedboat. The moonlight disappears behind a cloud, making everything around us even darker. The bitter wind relentlessly blows the life out of my head; it doesn't attack the rest of my body as it is below the sides of the speedboat.

Emma is freezing though because she is sat up in the driver's seat at the back. My crosshairs go black again when a large fishing trawler passes in front of us as close to the shoreline as it dares. This is the third fishing trawler to have driven past in the last hour; this cost us a lot of money to arrange.

"Keep going," I command as I feel Emma decreasing the pressure on the throttle.

"But we're going to hit the trawler." She panics.

"No, we won't. Full speed ahead." The front of the speedboat rises as she increases the pressure on the throttle.

I become nervous that we will hit the trawler as we quickly approach it. I take my left hand off my sniper and grab hold of the side of the speedboat at an angle that Emma cannot see and brace myself for impact. The trawler passes by with a good foot to spare and we race through its wake.

"Kill the engine." I position my left hand back on my sniper.

She kills the engine and we glide towards the shore. The naturally occurring waves and those generated from the trawler make it difficult for me to keep the security guard's head in my crosshairs. I jump to my feet, crouch down, and use my knees as shock absorbers. He collapses as soon as I've pulled the trigger. He rolls down the grassy embankment towards the river.

Even with the suppressor, the sniper is still quite loud. At least it is to me; no one else should be able to hear it over the sound of the chugging trawler and the soft, welcoming music coming from Mikhail's super-yacht, which is moored on the other side of his mansion next door. I swing the sniper round and fire again as soon as I get the next security guard's head in my crosshairs. The sniper has only stopped moving for a split second before I target the next, and final, security guard that is in view.

Emma directs the speedboat to the left-hand side of the small wooden pier. Mikhail's speedboat is on the right-hand side of it and is pointed out into the river to allow for a quick getaway. The cages filled with stones at the bottom of the embankment reflect the waves back into the river; these waves rapidly slow us down. I hold the sniper rifle in my right hand and pick up the mooring rope with my left hand. As the speedboat begins to be pushed back into the river, I step on its side and jump onto the pier.

Another security guard casually walks around the left-hand side of the mansion, looking out across the river. I lift my sniper rifle and get him in my crosshairs. As I apply pressure on the trigger, the speedboat tugs my left arm back and throws me off balance. I manage to stay upright and fire in the direction of him. The bullet hits his chest, causing him to collapse—however, it doesn't kill him. Lying on his side, he reaches for either his weapon or phone—I cannot tell as he is cast in darkness. Whilst still playing tug of war with the speedboat, I fire at him again. This bullet hits the mark; it ploughs through the centre of his forehead.

I put my right arm through the sniper rifle's strap, throw it over my right shoulder, and take hold of the mooring rope with both hands. My wet feet slide along the floor of the wet, wooden pier as I pull the speedboat closer to it. Emma withdraws her gun and jumps off the speedboat onto the pier. She runs onto the embarkment and positions herself against the fence on the left-hand side. I walk down the pier with the speedboat and wrap the rope around the mooring post closest to the embankment. I turn around and look at Mikhail's speedboat. His is significantly more expensive than the one that we managed to get our hands on. It has its key in the ignition; it is fully prepared for a quick getaway.

As I turn around, Emma's suppressor pops. I duck down low and see another security guard drop a couple of metres back from where I shot the last security guard. I run and get behind Emma. The upstairs curtains are all drawn but shadows of the captives are cast onto them as they walk around their bedrooms. The downstairs curtains are all open and all the lights are turned off.

"Quick, we need to get up to the side of the house and out of Mikhail's sniper's visuals." I withdraw my handgun. I scan the area for CCTV cameras, but there are none. People like Mikhail prefer to use their own people for security rather than rely on CCTV cameras; it is much easier to remove a person than a digital footprint. We both sprint alongside the fence towards the house. "You keep your attention on the house and look out for anyone coming around the far side; I'll focus straight ahead."

I come to a halt outside the side door. As far as I can tell, there are only three security guards left outside. They are all stood along the front fence watching the expensive cars pass by on their way to Mikhail's party.

"You stay here and keep guard. If any of them comes back towards the house then take them out," I instruct.

I keep my gun pointed at the closest security guard, who is leaning over the wall to get a better look at a particular car, as I dart to the side door. Before I reach the door, I bend down, grab the dead security guard's earpiece, and throw it at Emma; she catches it with one hand. When I reach the side door, I crouch down, and place my gun on the floor. I pull my lock pick gun and tension wrench out of my bum bag.

Before I offer my tools up to the door's lock, I pull the door handle down to make sure that it is indeed locked. The handle doesn't move. I place the tension wrench in the lock with my left hand and apply a small amount of pressure. I place the lock pick gun's steel rod in the lock below the tension wrench with my right hand. I keep pulling the gun's trigger. I think I feel the lock give way a little bit after I've pulled the trigger around ten times, but it is hard to tell with gloves on.

After I've pulled the trigger approximately twenty-five times, the lock finally gives up the fight and allows the cylinder to rotate. I return the lock pick gun and tension wrench to my bum bag. I pick up my gun, pull the door's handle down, and crawl into the house.

The kitchen is empty. I quickly close the door behind me to minimise the draught and block the sound of the music coming from Mikhail's super-yacht. I rest on my knees for a few seconds and try to pinpoint the origins of the different noises coming from inside the house. They all seem to come from people talking and moving around upstairs. I stay low and proceed through the kitchen into the hallway.

From studying a schematic diagram of the house early, I confirmed that the tunnel to his mansion was most likely located in the cellar. I wipe my right glove across the floor near the door under the stairs before holding it up to the dim green light being emitted from the house alarm's keypad. There is a thin layer of dirt on my glove. I walk back into the kitchen and look for some glasses. The kitchen is spotless and there isn't a thing out of place. I peer into the cabinet with glass doors and see that the drinking glasses are stored in them. I open one of the glass cabinet doors, pull out two glasses, close the door, turn around, and head back to the hallway. I place a glass upside down a couple of inches away from the door under the stairs and place the other glass upright on top of it.

I reach the bottom of the stairs and slowly make my way up them. Each time a step creaks, I stop and listen for any movement downstairs, or a change in movement upstairs, before proceeding. I reach the top of the stairs and scan the two corridors, one either side of me. These corridors are mirror images of each other; they both have doors about halfway down on either side and one at the end. All the doors are closed and sounds only come from behind the closed doors on my left-hand side. I slowly walk down this corridor until I reach the two doors opposite each other.

The door on my left is the noisier of the two, but it is hard to distinguish any particular words over the sound of a small child crying. I try its door handle, but it is locked. The key is in lock. I step back and prepare myself to throw the door open with my shoulder as I begin to turn the key in the lock. I start to shake with nerves at the possibly of Nataliya being on the other side of the door. I turn the key, turn the handle, and shoulder barge the door open.

I rush into the bedroom and am faced with a woman and little boy lying in a single bed on my right-hand side, and a topless woman lying on a double bed with a little baby on top of her and a man stood next to them on my left-hand side. The baby has just been sick all over her, and the man towers over them trying to wipe it off them both. Everyone jumps when they see me, except the baby, who continues to cry, and the little boy, who remains asleep. The baby screams even more loudly when its mother stops paying it any attention. My heart sinks at the thought of not seeing Nataliya.

"Mrs Kallinski?" I ask the woman who is now sat bolt upright in the single bed. I believe I recognise her from when she was sat at the ringside of one of her husband's fights. Her face gives nothing away. "Do you speak English?" Her eyes shoot open in panic.

"Yes. Yes, I am Mrs Kallinski," she croaks, rubbing her little boy's hair with a very shaky hand.

"Good. I am here to get you both out of here." Her facial expression doesn't change; she doesn't move a muscle. "You'll be with your husband shortly." Without hesitation, she throws the bedsheet back and jumps up.

"When" She is excited at the prospect of seeing her husband, but she eyes me suspiciously.

"He'll be here to collect you shortly. But we need to move now." The couple with the baby is petrified of me. "Come on, let's get out of here, everyone." I beckon them out, but I seem to confuse them even more and they do not move. The man eyes my weapons with desperation.

"They don't speak any English," Mrs Kallinski tells me. Her little boy starts to stir.

"Well, tell them to get ready to move. I am getting them out of here as well." I spin around and exit the room.

As I turn the key in the door on the other side of the corridor, Mrs Kallinski talks to her roommates in Russian. I burst through the open door into a pitch-black room. The light from the corridor pours into the room and my eyes adjust themselves; five old ladies are asleep in five separate single beds. They all look up at me confused.

"Quick, get up, I'm getting you out of here." They all look at me frightened and try to hide under their bedsheets. Mrs Kallinski rushes up behind me and shouts at them in Russian. They immediately jump out of their beds.

I sprint down the corridor to the door at the far end; there is an awful racket coming from behind it. I turn the door key and shoulder barge it open. This is the largest bedroom that I've come across and is lined with bunk beds. There are approximately ten children: five are lying in their beds, and the other five are playing the board game Twister in the centre of the room. They all jump when they see me; those playing Twister fall into a heap on the floor. Everyone is paralysed with fear. I try to give them the friendliest smile I can muster whilst I place my handgun into my thigh holster. I place my right index finger against my lips and say, "Shh!"

The curtains are drawn. I switch off the light, throw my sniper rifle off my shoulder, and sprint to the window. I crouch down when I reach the window and lift the curtain from the bottom. I adjust my scope and survey the roof of Mikhail's mansion. The mansion and the surrounding grounds, including the super-yacht, are well lit. I scan the mansion's roof for the sniper, but its slant is too steep for him to be on let alone hide on. I also scan the bedrooms and surrounding areas, but I do not spot him.

I scan the mansion one more time to satisfy myself that he doesn't have visuals on this property's grounds. I step back from the window, letting the curtain drop back down. I throw the sniper rifle on my shoulder and withdraw my handgun. I rush back over to the lights and as I switch them on, Mrs Kallinski steps across the threshold and shouts at all the kids in Russian.

"Are my parents here?" the youngest-looking girl in the room asks.

"Yes." I smile at her and nod my head. "Everyone's parents are waiting for them, but we've all got to be very quiet and move very fast."

They all hurriedly jump up and follow me out of the room. The liberated people from the previous rooms line the corridor and I run between them with the children hot on my tail. I poke my head and gun around the corner and point it down the stairs. The coast is clear. I run past the stairs and to the first door on the right-hand side. I turn the key, but the door is already unlocked. I open the door and am faced with blackness. I turn on the light, which reveals an unoccupied bedroom. There are three single made-up beds in this room.

I turn around to open the door behind me when Mrs Kallinski says, "What are you doing, sir?"

"I am trying to find Nataliya." I turn to face her, but she avoids eye contact.

"The girls who sleep on this side of the corridor are working tonight."

"What do you mean, 'working'?" I spit angrily and instantly realise my mistake. Mrs Kallinski and the rest of the crowd that has gathered nervously at the top of the stairs cower away from me.

"The girls are entertaining Mikhail's guests on his yacht tonight."

An unquenchable thirst for blood and death rises inside of me. I had sniffed two piles of Chinese medicine before I boarded the speedboat and it has caused my anger levels to rise to a height that I've rarely experienced before.

"OK then. Let's get you all out of here." I get my phone out of my pocket and call Big Stan.

"Hello," he answers before the first ring.

"Send Extra Arm now." Mrs Kallinski's eyes light up and she brims with joy. I squeeze through the crowd so that I can lead them out of the building. "Follow me."

After I take a couple of steps down the stairs, I realise that no one is following me. Mrs Kallinski's son has his right leg in a cast, and he is struggling to step down the first step. I walk back up the stairs, pick him up, and cradle him in my arms. It is quite difficult to walk down the stairs with him whilst keeping my gun pointed forwards ready to fire. We reach the bottom of the stairs and follow the hallway around to the kitchen. When I reach the glass cups, I gently move them closer to the door with my foot so that they are out of everyone's way.

I step through the side door and stand next to Emma, who has her gun pointed at one of the security guards at the front gate. I keep close to the building as I head to the front gate. I shuffle the young Kallinski in my arms so that he is supported by only my left arm. I wave my right hand at the closest security guard on the left-hand side and whisper to Emma, "Yours." She nods her head.

A minibus taxi pulls up at the front gate. The three security guards straighten their backs as they get themselves back into character. I fire two shots in rapid succession at the security guard on the right-hand side; Emma does the same with the security guard on the left-hand side. I swing my gun across to aim it at the security guard manning the gate, who is waving for the taxi driver to keep moving along. Before I get a chance to fire at him, Emma has put two bullets in the back of his head.

Emma reaches the gate first, grabs the dead security guard, and drags him to the side out of our way. I try to open the gate, but it is difficult with the gun in my hand. Someone shoves me to one side.

"Out of the way," Mrs Kallinski demands.

"Catch these," Emma says, throwing her the keys that she has taken out of the security guard's belt. She snatches them out of the air. She jabs a key into the lock and turns it. The lock clunks loudly. She grabs the gate's metal bars with both hands and uses her whole-body weight to lever it open. Emma dives in front of me and throws the minibus' side door wide open. The minibus' interior light turns on.

Extra Arm is in the driver's seat. He turns his head and beams when he sees his son in my arms. His right eye is still really swollen from when I elbowed him; I doubt he can see much out of it. I throw his son on the closest passenger seat and step out of the way, allowing all the other captives to board the minibus.

243

Mrs Kallinski sees her husband and **dives into the** front, puts her arms around him, and kisses him hard. All the **minibus' seats** quickly become occupied, so I start throwing the remaining children **on top of the** people sat down.

"Get in, don't worry about getting **a seat. You** need to get out of here now," I command forcefully. When all the **captives are in** the minibus, I grab its side door. "Extra Arm, get out of here now."

I pull the door across and let go **of it. Before** it slides to a shut, he shouts back, "Thank you."

Emma puts her hand on my **shoulder and says,** "Where is Nataliya?" I turn to face her and start guiding her to the **front of the** minibus.

"Unfortunately, Mikhail has her **with him on** his super-yacht." I hold open the front passenger's door for her. "**You need to get** out of here."

"I told you that I'll help you get **Nataliya back**—and that is what I'll do!" She grabs the front passenger's door **below where** my hand is, pulls it from my grip, and flings it shut. She bangs **on the side of** the minibus twice with her knuckles and its wheels spin as it **accelerates away.**

Chapter 26
The Tunnel

I step back behind the gate as a Ferrari roars its way to Mikhail's residential mansion. Emma pulls the gate shut, locks it, and pockets the key.

"Come on then," she orders.

I watch the minibus drive away and think of how happy I would be if Nataliya and I were also on it. The minibus disappears behind a hedgerow, forcing me back to reality. I spin around and run back to the house with Emma. She dives through the side door and I am hot on her tail. She surveys the kitchen and I dart around her. She follows me to the hallway and I lightly move the two glasses—which have remained where I placed them—out of the way.

I am faced with pure blackness and a chilling draught when I pull open the door under the stairs. Emma taps my left shoulder. Instead of using the light switch, I grab the torch out of my bum bag with my left hand. I throw my left hand up in front of me and rest my gun-wielding right hand on top of it. I turn on the torch with my thumb; a steep, narrow flight of stairs made of bricks materialises in front of me.

"You're going to need your torch," I say, stepping down onto the first step. I descend to the bottom of the stairs and survey the large, nearly empty cellar before declaring, "Clear."

She closes the door and rushes down the stairs to join me in the cellar. The house was built with a cellar, but it looks like the Roldugin brothers have recently lined the floor and walls with stone. It doesn't look like they've finished with this room yet as the only thing down here is a simple wine rack that hosts about 30 bottles of wine.

"Where's the tunnel?" she asks.

"I'm not sure. There must be a hidden door to it down here somewhere."

I convince myself that I have found the outline of the door as I rub my hand across the wall that faces Mikhail's residential mansion, but I cannot see a way of opening it. I force my shoulder into it but it doesn't budge. Emma scans the wine rack, which is on the wall on the far side from where I am. She tries to pull out a bottle of wine on the far left-hand side, but it won't shift. I stop what I am doing and watch her.

"Don't watch me, help me."

She lets go of the bottle and stands aside. I pass her my torch and she points it at the wine bottle she was trying to pull out. I grab hold of it with my left hand and notice that it is made of metal. I try pulling it and yanking it, but it doesn't move. I holster my gun and grab hold of it with both hands. I put my right foot on the wall. I slowly start to straighten my right leg and feel it moving with me—this door has been designed to not be opened easily from this side. There is a loud mechanical clunk and the tunnel door, which I had found the outline for early, partially opens into the cellar.

Emma hands me my torch and I unholster my gun. As we walk over to the door, she glances nervously back up the stairs.

I pull open the tunnel door just wide enough for me to slip through. Emma is the first one through it. We are faced with a stone-lined tunnel, which is cast in darkness, but there is a source of light at the far end. It is approximately fifty metres in length. There are lights positioned at regular intervals along the wall on the right-hand side but they are all turned off. We both automatically turn our torches off.

"Wow," Emma whispers. "The Roldugin brothers have outdone themselves." I nod my head whilst also admiring the impressive tunnel.

I position myself in front of Emma as we make our way through the tunnel. With each step, Emma's breathing rate increases. When we are approximately twenty metres away from the source of the light, two security guards come into view. They are sat side by side on boxes of champagne and are not paying attention to the tunnel. In fact, they appear to be quite drunk. One of them brings a bottle of champagne to his lips. He takes a big swig from it before passing it to the other one. Whilst the other one takes several gulps, he cracks a joke, causing the guy to splutter champagne everywhere. They both start howling with laughter.

Emma storms forward. I grab her arm and pull her back; she hasn't seen that they are both cradling machine guns on their laps. From this distance, it is likely that she'd miss her target, giving them chance to return fire, or worse, escape.

"Stand on the left-hand side," I whisper, stepping back towards the captives' cellar.

I holster my gun and slide my sniper rifle off my shoulder. I walk back to the cellar, stand sideways on, and pull the stone door to a close. I leave a gap just big enough for my sniper's barrel and scope. I place my left leg in front and lean into my rifle. I have the closest security guard's head held firmly in the middle of my crosshairs. They are both still giggling and throwing their heads around quite a bit. Once both of their heads are aligned, I fire. Their heads snap to the side and their bodies are thrown off the champagne boxes. The gunshot echoes loudly off the cellar's stone walls. I put my sniper rifle back and retrieve my handgun whilst sprinting down the tunnel.

"Quick, get to the bottom of the stairs," I order, sprinting past her.

We both reach the bottom of the stairs and aim our guns up them. It is eerily quiet. The only sound comes from a champagne bottle glugging its contents onto the floor. We both jump when a floorboard above us creaks. If this mansion has the same layout as the captives', then it sounded like someone has walked down the hallway and into the kitchen.

"Keep watch whilst I change my magazine," Emma says.

I keep my gun pointed at the top of the stairs and say, "It sounds like there is only one person on the ground floor. We'll take them out first then proceed upstairs. I suspect that Mikhail's sniper is in the bedroom at the far end of the corridor on the left-hand side when you reach the top of the stairs. We can work out where to go from there." She nods her head, snaps the new magazine into her gun, and leads the way up the stairs.

She steps out into the hallway and turns left. I quickly follow her but turn right. No one is there. I turn around, close the door under the stairs, and follow her to the kitchen. The top half of the security guard is covered by the top door of the tall standing fridge as he raids it for snacks. Emma enters the kitchen first, but I pull her back.

"Do you have the black bags?" I ask her.

"Yes, you told me to bring them!"

"OK, good. Right, your job is to turn the kitchen lights off when I reach the man then quickly shut the kitchen door behind you. You are then to come up behind me with an opened black bag."

As I head over to the man, I stay below the level the kitchen island in the centre of the room. His machine gun is resting on the island; it is resting at such an angle that he cannot efficiently use it against me. The fridge's power supply is on the wall next to it. When I am one metre away, the kitchen lights go off; however, the kitchen remains quite bright from all the exterior light sources and the fridge's internal light.

I dive forward, slam the fridge door shut with my left hand, and wedge his body in it. I poke my gun around the door as Emma shuts the kitchen door. He throws his head back into the barrel of my gun. I fire. Awkwardly, I use my gun's grip and right palm to keep his head inside of the fridge. I reach back with my left and flick the power switch off. The black bag rustles as she rushes up behind me.

"Throw it over his head," I say, pulling the fridge door wide open. She throws it over his head and tightens it around his neck. "Thank you. You keep a watch out whilst I drag him to the cellar." She darts back to the hallway ahead of me. I get him under the armpits and drag him to the hallway. She has already opened the door under the stairs for me and is crouched in a firing stance at the bottom of the stairs. He is quite a heavy guy, but I manage to lift him up, turn around, and launch him down the cellar stairs. As I close the door, I check the floor to confirm that he hasn't left a trail of blood behind.

I walk up the stairs slowly; Emma is behind me guarding our rear. About halfway up the stairs, we both stop when we hear the faint sound of someone moving around upstairs. As we proceed up the stairs again, the person stops moving and coughs several times. We reach the top of the stairs and I confirm that both corridors are clear before moving down the corridor on the left-hand side.

All the doors are closed except the door on the left-hand side, which is ajar. Someone behind it coughs twice. We slowly approach it and peer inside. A security guard is leaning back in Mikhail's large leather chair with his feet on the grand oak desk. He has left his gun on the desk near his feet whilst he relaxes, smoking a big, fat cigar. A large glass of whiskey is on the desk next to the ashtray. Even though I could shoot him through the gap in the door, I would risk informing Mikhail's sniper of my presence.

We both holster our guns simultaneously. She withdraws her combat knife from her calf strap and pushes me gently to one side. With her right palm held upwards, she waves it twice at the door at the far end of the corridor whilst mouthing, "Go, I've got this."

I twist my body around and hold the door handle. As the security guard exhales his cigar's smoke, I mouth the words, "Three, two…" I pause for a couple of seconds until he starts to inhale again. "One!" I push the door back and she sprints past me.

The security guard shouts, "FU—" but ends up choking on the smoke and cannot finish what he wanted to say. I catch her pounce over the table like a lioness bringing down her prey before I shut the door.

I walk down the corridor with my gun pointed at the door at the end. The ceiling light closest to the door is not working. I stop to consider my approach and something catches my eye. A small, black button-like object is stuck against the skirting board on my right-hand side. It is placed about six inches above the floor. There is also another one on the skirting board on my left-hand side. As I step over the line between the two button-like objects, several quiet bangs originate from Mikhail's office.

When I am a couple of steps away from the door, my body tenses painfully. I break into a run and use my left shoulder to rip the door from its restraints. The light from the corridor infiltrates the bedroom, exposing the sniper, who is hunched over his rifle—as expected. As he tries to spin around with his gun, I shoot him in his thigh. He drops to the floor. Once his head drops below the level of the window, I fire all my remaining bullets into it. Even though he is obviously dead, I keep running at him. I smash the sole of my boot into his skull and crush it against the wall.

I insert a fresh magazine into my gun and holster it. I slide my sniper rifle off my shoulder and place the barrel of it through the three-inch gap at the bottom of the open sash window. I scan the super-yacht for Nataliya. The DJ is on the top floor, projecting his sounds and lights down onto everyone on the deck below. It is quite busy, but not as busy as I was expecting. I recognise quite a few of the faces in between the senior comrades of the Harkov crime family. There are lots of vodka bottles and half-naked women dotted around. The party currently seems quite civilised; the vodka has not had chance to take full effect.

I nearly break down in tears when I catch a glimpse of Nataliya. She sits down and goes out of view behind Mikhail. She is sat between Mikhail and the police commissioner at one of the many private booths. On the other side of the booth is Vitali along with three topless women. Nataliya leans forward again and takes a sip of her drink. She is the only one in her booth not laughing.

A small, round Jacuzzi is positioned behind them; it contains four naked women who seem to be overly enjoying themselves. Two of them simultaneously splash Mikhail but end up mostly wetting Nataliya. She wipes the water away with annoyance; Mikhail turns around and launches the contents of his drink at them, jokingly. He stands up and walks over to them.

He throws all his clothes off and parades his naked body around the Jacuzzi before entering it. All the women immediately start rubbing themselves up against him. From what I can see, he only has two of his security guards with him on the yacht. They reposition themselves to get a better view of him in the Jacuzzi. Vitali's bodyguard is sat at another table and seems to be more preoccupied with the woman sat on his lap than protecting Vitali.

I only have a limited view of the grounds from this position, but it is enough to confirm that there are more security guards walking around than I was expecting. Each security guard cradles a machine gun but seems to only be walking around with the purpose of trying to catch a glimpse of the women on board the yacht.

I put my sniper rifle away, withdraw my handgun, and exit the bedroom. I put my ear up against Mikhail's office door; no sound comes from within. I throw the door open and dive inside. Emma is sat on the floor, resting against a bookcase; she is covered in blood. The security guard is lying on his side on the floor behind the desk.

"Some of these Russian bastards are as hard as fuck," she says, trying to catch her breath. I smile at her.

"Yeah, you've got to put them out of their misery quickly; otherwise, you'll be in a world of trouble."

"At first, there were no opportunities to stab him in a fatal location; therefore, I kept stabbing him in various places until a fatal location presented itself. It was like I was poking a bear; he grew angrier and stronger with each penetration."

I extend my left hand down to her. She grabs it with her bloody right hand and I struggle to hold onto it as I pull her to her feet.

"Are you cut?"

"Oh, nope—this is all his blood. The only thing that really hurts is my pride. Look, there is a safe." She points at the wall behind me, which backs onto the stairs.

I turn around and there is a small safe on full show in the middle of the bookcase that covers the whole wall. I walk up to it and try to move it, but it is attached to the wall. I tap the wall around it; it is only plasterboard.

"The wall behind the safe is only constructed from plasterboard. This safe is only a decoy, a distraction."

"His desk drawers are locked." I walk over to her holding out my tension wrench and lock pick gun.

"Do you have a rake instead?"

I nod my head, put my lock pick gun back in my bum bag, withdraw a rake, and pass it to her. Whilst she is trying to pick the lock, I step back into the corridor and check that it, the stairs, and hallway downstairs are all still clear. I re-enter Mikhail's office and start pacing the room to put her under even more pressure. As I peer through the gap in the curtains, my phone rings. I answer the 'Unknown Caller' on the second ring, "Hello."

"Patrick, the Albanians are on their way. They'll be with you in a couple of minutes," the Dragon Master says. I begin to panic; I need to get Nataliya and Emma out of here quickly. I close my eyes and take a deep breath.

"Shit. How many?"

"I understand there are at least two vans heading your way. It was not possible to see how many people were loaded into each. Do you still need my men?" I do not respond quickly enough. "They're yours—if you still want them."

"Yes, tell them to stick to the original plan, but only once the Albanians have entered Mikhail's grounds. Also, I need to call in another favour."

"Anything." He sounds excited.

"I need you to call the emergency services and inform them that the police commissioner has been kidnapped, and that he is caught in a firefight between heavily armed Russians and Albanians."

"Sure—of course. Anything else?"

"And make sure you fire some gunshots in the background while you are on the phone. I would do it here, but I risk exposure."

"You've got it. I'll do it right away."

"Thank you." I struggle to end the call with my shaking hand. My brow, armpits, and lower back are all now covered in sweat.

"Jackpot," she exclaims with delight. She holds up several accounting ledgers and waves them in the air; she looks like a football player holding up the World Cup. "These contain everything. The amount he has sold each bar of gold for, the people he has on his books, the transport companies he uses. Everything—"

I interrupt her, "Quick, you need to get out of here. The Dragon Master has just informed me that the Albanians will be here in a couple of minutes."

"Shit, what about Nataliya?" she asks.

"She is on the yacht with Mikhail. The police are also on their way here so I'll use the ensuing chaos to extract her. I need you to get back to the Mikhail's speedboat and bring it around to his yacht—but keep your distance. Only come and get us once we've jumped overboard." She nods her head. She pulls out a black bag and starts throwing all the accounting ledgers into it.

I pull the curtain back slightly. The front of the property is littered with vacant luxury cars. The front gates are closed and guarded by approximately ten men; they all look professional and ready for action. Emma jumps up from behind the desk and throws the heavy black bag over her shoulder.

"Come on then, let's get on with it."

She dashes out into the corridor and disappears down the stairs. I release the curtain and follow her.

Chapter 27
Car Crashing

Emma and I walk down the stairs and part ways; she goes through the door under the stairs, and I proceed into the kitchen and go through the door on the far side into the garage. I switch on the light and the fluorescent lights flicker several times whilst warming up. The garage has brilliant white walls and a polished purple concrete floor. A row of five very expensive cars fit comfortably next to one another; it feels more like a showroom than a residential garage.

The longest car is the Rolls-Royce Phantom. I slide off my sniper rifle and position it on the passenger's seat. I slide into driver's seat. I sit still for a couple of seconds, embracing the luxuriousness of it. I press the button on the door, and it shuts automatically. I lay my handgun on my lap and start the ignition.

The dashboard lights up, and the car barely vibrates as the engine murmurs into life. I press the Up arrow on the black device stuck in the middle of the dashboard and the garage door begins to lift.

The car is an automatic; I select the 'D' option. I place my foot on the accelerator pedal and press it down slowly. All the security guards at the front of the property are distracted by two sets of highlights approaching the property. I force my foot down on the accelerator pedal and wheel spin out of the garage. I pull the steering wheel down clockwise and drift sideways until the wheels grip the damp grass and hurtle me straight towards Mikhail's yacht.

I initiate the cruise control, and ramp it up to eighty miles per hour. The car accelerates autonomously to meet its target. I aim the car at the yacht about one-quarter of its length from the back. This should be far enough away from Nataliya to not impact her too much, but short enough away for me to get to her rapidly. It should also take out the aft gangway ladder.

I grab my sniper rifle and handgun, open the driver's door, and jump out of the car. I hit the grass and roll. Whilst I roll and slide on the grass, I accidentally let go of my sniper rifle. The car crashes into the side of the yacht with an awfully loud bang. As soon as I come to a stop, I reach back, and my sniper rifle slides into my hand. I dive behind one of several red Ferraris.

Gunfire erupts at the front gate. I sling the sniper rifle over my shoulder and firmly take hold of my handgun. I lift my head up over the Ferrari's bonnet. The two security guards near the yacht watch the gunfight with extreme nervousness; they begin to retreat back towards the yacht. I put a bullet in each of their heads as I sprint towards them. The bonnet of the Rolls-Royce, including its front wheels, are lodged into the side of the yacht; its back wheels hang over the sea wall, but its boot sits firmly on land.

When I place my right foot on the Rolls-Royce's roof, one of Mikhail's bodyguard's body leans over the side of the yacht. A bullet enters his head as soon as he makes eye contact with me. His body falls over the side of the yacht and takes off the driver's wing mirror as it drops onto the broken pieces of gangway ladder that float in the water. I take another step on the roof before launching myself up onto the side of the yacht. I pull myself up and over into the yacht. As I hit the deck, a burst of bullets pulverises the side of the yacht where I've just been.

Mikhail's last remaining bodyguard is knelt by the side of the Jacuzzi firing at the front gates. Mikhail is half out of the Jacuzzi when he sees me. He freezes; his jaw drops and the colour drains from his face. His bodyguard catches me in the corner of his eye and spins around. I fire a bullet into the side of his head, giving Mikhail enough time to fall back into the Jacuzzi.

The four naked women scream as they get out of the Jacuzzi. He grabs one of them and pulls her across him. As he drags her across his body, her legs open and expose his heart. Even though the yacht is rocking slightly, I take the shot.

The bullet lightly grazes the woman's upper thigh before going into the side of his heart. Another burst of bullets from the front gate is directed at the yacht, forcing me to the floor. All three of the standing women are blasted with these bullets and forced back into the Jacuzzi. I look for the last surviving woman in the Jacuzzi, but she is hidden under all the dead bodies. She should be safe under them for now.

Nataliya screams as Vitali drags her by her arm towards the front of the yacht. His bodyguard is positioned between Nataliya and me. I take aim at his head, but the police commissioner tries to sit up from a lying down position next to me. He looks extremely infuriated and has his right hand inside of his jacket.

"Do you know who I am?" he demands. I respond by firing a bullet into his left foot. He yelps in pain and grabs his foot with both hands.

I fire at the bodyguard's back, but a senior comrade's head moves in front of the bullet. As the bodyguard steps over two women, who are embracing each other on the floor, I shoot him in the head. Vitali stops and turns around.

When he sees me, he grabs Nataliya with both hands and places her directly between us. A sinister smile spreads across his face. Several other senior comrades dive in front of us and push them back as they all head to the front of the yacht. As they all try to squeeze through the door at the far end, I run towards them, firing bullets into the back of their heads.

"Stay down. Stay down. Stay down," I shout at the women, peering up at me from underneath the tables. I eject my magazine and reload a fresh one. A senior comrade slams the door shut behind him. I leap over two dead bodies, sprint as fast as I can, drop my left shoulder, and ram the door open before he manages to lock it. The door flings open and smashes him in the face. I put a bullet in his forehead as he slides along the floor on his back.

Vitali drags Nataliya to a door on the far right-hand side and there are three senior comrades hot on their tail. I put a bullet in the back of each of their heads before shouting over the sound of approaching gunfire outside.

"Vitali—STOP!" He stops immediately, spins Nataliya around, and ducks down behind her.

"Mr Smith, very impressive." He peers through a window and sees the Albanians approaching outside. Nataliya looks petrified; my presence has done nothing to comfort her. He puts his hand over her mouth.

"They're not my men. They're Albanians—and they're here for you and Mikhail," I answer his yet-to-be-asked question. I glance across the water on my left-hand side. Emma is waiting for us; she is closer than I would like her to be. I look back at Vitali. "Slowly withdraw your gun and throw it on the floor."

As he slowly withdraws his gun from his front waistband, I tighten my grip on my trigger, even though I do not have a clean shot on him. I am not in a position to return fire if he shoots at me.

Whilst keeping my eyes on him, I fire four bullets into each of the corners of the window on my left-hand side in quick succession, before swinging my gun to point back at his head. I grab a chair with my left hand, bring it across my body, and launch it at the window. The chair smashes the glass, and flies straight through the gap. A very cold gust of wind smashes against all three of us.

"Release Nataliya," I demand. He shakes his head. He catches Emma on the speedboat.

"Only if you let me come with you?" he counters. "I'll make you a very rich man." He smiles, mischievously. I stare into his eyes and conclude that there is no time to waste on this stand-off—his time will have to come later.

"OK," I say, holstering my gun. "We need to jump." Emma sees us and starts approaching; however, she gets interrupted by gunfire from multiple machine guns. She is forced to take a hard right away from us. The gunfire follows her as she disappears into the blackness. "Shit!"

Bullets impact the side of the yacht near where we are, forcing us all to duck down.

"Quick, follow me," Vitali says. He removes his hand from Nataliya's mouth as he tries to reach for his gun.

"Steve," she starts talking but I ignore her.

"Leave it." I point my gun at his now exposed forehead.

He eyes me venomously. He withdraws his hands and grabs Nataliya's right arm. We all crouch low, making our way to the door on the far right-hand side. He keeps hold of her, trying to keep as much of her body between us as possible. I stumble when my right foot slips on some of the blood that is pouring out of the head of one of the senior comrades. I quickly recover it but catch Vitali trying to work out if he could have turned the tables with that opportunity if he had his gun.

Vitali and Nataliya walk through the door first and disappear down the stairs. I check that no one is behind us before following them closely. The stairs lead to a floating garage that houses a bright green Lamborghini speedboat. He violently pushes her across the water gap into the speedboat. She lands awkwardly on her high heels, slips over, and bumps her head on the side of the speedboat. She lies motionless and my heart stops.

After a second or two—which feels like an eternity—she starts to move again. My heart goes into overdrive. I make a promise to myself that he will suffer an even more painful death than I had originally intended for him. He jumps into the driver's seat and starts the engine.

"Press the button," he commands, pointing at the black switch on the wall. I follow his command and the hydraulic-operated hatch slowly starts to open up the side of the yacht's hull. Emma attempts to approach the yacht again.

"Nataliya, get out of the speedboat." I point my gun at Vitali's head.

She looks at Vitali expressionlessly. She tries to stand but slips back down onto her buttocks. Emma comes under fire again—but this time it is from someone who is directly above us. Bullets impact the front of her speedboat, forcing her to swing around and disappear back into the darkness.

"If you want Nataliya to get out of here safely, you're going to have to clear the deck for us. And you're going to have to do it quickly" He smiles cruelly. I hate to admit it to him, but he is not wrong. I desperately want to lodge a bullet in his head, but Nataliya's greatest chance of survival is to escape with him—assuming he knows how to skilfully drive the speedboat.

"Shit," I shout. I take one last look at Nataliya, who is rubbing her head where she banged it.

"Don't worry, I'll keep her safe," he says, matter-of-factly. I nod my head.

"Give her to the woman on the speedboat," I say, pointing in the direction of Emma.

"Only as long as you promise to rescue Mikhail." I nod my head again and don't give away the fact that I've already killed him.

"Only drive out of here when a body falls into the water." I turn and leap up the stairs, two at a time.

There are two Albanians firing at Emma through the broken window. I run at them and fire a bullet into the back of each of their heads. Unfortunately, the man on the right-hand side, who received the first bullet, was leaning out of the window too much and his body falls out of it. His body bangs against the hydraulic-operated hatch before splashing into the water.

"Shit," I scream.

When I step back outside, an Albanian is in mid-step over a senior comrade's corpse. His body collapses on top of the corpse when I put a bullet in his forehead. Two more Albanians are stood around the Jacuzzi, emptying their magazines into Mikhail's body. One of them spots me and swings his gun around to me. I dive into a booth. I land awkwardly on my wrist; my gun is ripped from my grip and disappears under the table. A woman, who was ducking down on the other side of the booth with her back facing the shooter, screams when bullets pummel her. Her blood rains down on me.

I flick my sniper rifle off my shoulder and wait for him to reload. As soon as he stops firing, I jump up. Whilst incorrectly holding the rifle at my midriff, I fire at him. The bullet hits his chest, but it doesn't kill him; it only forces him to step back. As the other Albanian turns to see who was firing, I bring the scope up to eye level. I fire into the side of his head, blowing him into the Jacuzzi. The remaining Albanian slips on a mixture of blood and water and falls off the yacht. There is a loud splash when he lands in the water.

Another Albanian jumps up off the Rolls-Royce below and grabs hold of the side of the yacht. As he lifts himself up, I blow a crater in his chest. There is a bang when his body hits the Rolls-Royce, but it isn't followed by a splash. Emma comes back into view and flies past the yacht, drawing multiple machine gun fire away from Vitali and Nataliya as they leave the confines of the floating garage. I crouch below the yacht's sides and walk on all fours to the Jacuzzi. When I reach the Jacuzzi, I get on one knee. Three Albanians are firing at Emma from the shoreline. I take them each out with a headshot before any of them is aware of my presence. Mikhail's bullet-ridden corpse floats in the Jacuzzi with the other corpses.

Gunfire erupts at the front gates as the armed response vehicles arrive. The Albanian drivers try to turn their vans around but quickly realise that they are cornered; they are forced to abandon their vehicles and jump over Mikhail's front gate onto his property. As the armed police officers exit their vehicles, an Albanian, who is hidden behind a tree, guns two of them down. He only appears in my sights for a split second but is long enough for me to take him out.

The armed police officers start scaling the front wall, forcing the Albanians back towards me. One of them tries to jump into the sea, but I take him out mid-air. Emma heads back towards the yacht and I am about to jump overboard when an armed police officer starts firing at her. She swings wide and attempts come back for me, but I wave her away—I don't want her risking herself for me.

The armed police officers take out the remaining Albanians and get the situation under control. There is movement behind me. A woman has taken ownership of the unconscious police commissioner's gun.

"Put that down," I command, throwing my sniper rifle into the sea. She eyes me suspiciously. "The armed police are here, and they won't hesitate to shoot you if they see you holding that." She panics and drops the gun. "Get on your front and put your hands on the back of your head." I take my handcuff key out of my bum bag and slide it into the waistband of my boxer shorts before copying what I told her to do. She lies down next to me. "Don't worry, you'll be fine." I have no emotion as I stare at Mikhail's corpse whilst waiting for the armed police officers to arrive.

It takes several minutes for them to board the yacht.

"Stay where you are," one of them orders. The woman next to me takes her hands off her head. "STAY WHERE YOU ARE, GOD DAMN IT!" An officer steps over me and crouches down. He violently yanks down both of my arms and handcuffs them. Another officer does the same to the woman.

"Let's get you up." Each officer places a hand under one of my armpits and they both lift me to my feet. One pat-downs my front; the other pat-downs my back. My bum bag is unclipped and cast to the side.

One of them holds my arms up whilst the other pushes my head down. They guide me over the dead bodies and through the door. They navigate me around the dead bodies in this room. Instead of going towards the door that leads to the floating garage, they push me through the door in front. We pass through several more rooms before we reach the gangway ladder.

An officer sprints over to me.

"What the fuck is he doing here?" he shouts, turning his gun around. He smashes the butt of it into my nose, busting it open. It really hurts, but I do not reveal that I am in any pain. "This is the fucker that was in the tower earlier— the piece of shit." He hits me with the butt of his gun again, but this time I move my head down so that he hits my forehead.

"Fuck off, Rogers. You shouldn't be here. The boss told you to go home after your fuck up earlier," one of the men behind me shouts. "Get the fuck out of the way."

They manoeuvre me around all the sports cars—many of which have been pulverised with bullets and sprayed with Russian or Albanian blood. The front gates have been opened and a police van reverses a couple of metres onto the property before coming to a halt. An officer runs past me and opens the back door. Without stopping, I am forced up the steps into the back of it and positioned at the far end. An officer reaches behind me and clips my handcuffs to the chair's lock. As soon as he steps out of the van, another officer forces the woman into the van. He clips her to the seat opposite me and exits the van. As he closes the back door, Rogers grabs it and stops him.

"I'll ride in the back to the station with these two."

"Don't you fucking dare touch them," replies an officer.

"Of course, I won't."

Rogers closes the back door behind him. He sits next to the woman. Someone outside hits the side of the van twice.

After a minute or two of driving, Rogers takes his helmet off and looks at me. I do not recall him from earlier.

"You shot my friend in the face with a shotgun earlier, didn't you?" he spits.

"I think you've got the wrong guy, my friend," I reply, looking away. He currently has the upper hand and I don't want to anger him any further.

"Yes, it was you," he hisses. He smashes the butt of his gun in my face again and the woman next to him screams. He hits her in her face with the back of his hand, forcing the back of her head to hit the wall. Her nose starts to bleed, dripping blood all over her. She begins to cry, but we both ignore her.

"You are going to die for what you did." He stands up. "If it wasn't for Jackson, I'd have killed you in the corridor." I look up at him. Now I remember— he was the one that killed the innocent couple. He begins to smash the butt of his gun into my head repeatedly. Whilst he is hitting me, I release myself from the handcuffs. I am just about to grab his gun when the police van screeches to a halt. We are all thrown forwards. He collides head first into the van's front wall. He bounces off it and falls onto the floor. I remain in my seat, pretending that I am still his captive.

I can sense a lot of commotion outside, but I cannot hear any voices. Three gunshots are fired in quick succession, causing us all to jump. Rogers sits up straight and looks at me, terrified.

"What's going on?" he screams, pointing his gun at me.

"I wouldn't point that at me if I were you," I say, nodding my head at his gun. Blood drips painfully into my eye. "The people outside are here to either save me or kill me. Either way, they will kill you if you kill me before they get me." As he gets to his feet, I smile at woman opposite. I wink at her with my right eye, so Rogers cannot see it. Nervously, she smiles back.

"What the fuck is going on?" Rogers speaks into his radio that is attached to his bulletproof vest in front of his heart. There is no response. "Hello. Is anyone there? Hello."

A key enters the lock in the back door and it is turned until the lock is undone. Rogers spins around and points his gun at the door. The door is flung open and we are faced with about twenty men, all wearing balaclavas and pointing their machine guns at us. Kevin pokes his head around the door and says, "Can we interest you a lift, sir?"

"Certainly." I stand up and leave my handcuffs on the seat. Both Rogers and the woman look at me in shock. I kick Rogers in his face, snatch his gun out of his grasp, and ram the butt of it into his head. It doesn't knock him out, but he is severely dazed.

"What about the woman?" Kevin asks.

"Why were you at Mikhail's party?" I ask.

"I was told that I would be killed if I didn't attend the party and ensure that the guests had a good time," she says with an American accent. "I was kidnapped and transported here. Even though my dad has a lot of money, they were asking for more cash than he could get his hands on quickly. I was told that he was going to hand over the money for me in a couple of days."

"I don't know what trouble your dad has gotten himself into, but it must be bad. Mikhail would've taken his money then killed you anyway—and most likely your dad as well." She gasps loudly.

"How do you know?"

"He would never have let you see all those people tonight and hear their conversations and still let you keep your life. No chance. Every woman on that yacht tonight would've been killed once they had served their purpose. Are you warm enough?"

"I was fine when the wind wasn't blowing on me."

A cold shiver causes her body to shake violently. I take my jacket off and throw it over her.

"OK, we'll leave her here for the authorities."

"Please, take me with you?"

"If we take you then the police will think you've either escaped or been kidnapped again," I state. "Throw me your gun." I hold my hand up to Kevin. He lifts it up, showing it to me.

"It won't work for you," he says.

"Of course." I immediately feel stupid for asking. "Can you please shoot this man in the kneecap?" Kevin looks at the officer then back at me, confused.

"He was one of the armed police officers that killed innocent people in the tower block earlier."

Kevin smiles and nods his head.

"With pleasure then." He jumps up into the van as I step out of it.

I turn around and say, "The quickest and safety way back to your dad is to wait here. The police will be here shortly."

Kevin fires a bullet into each of Rogers' kneecaps. Rogers' high-pitched scream fills the night and scares the cattle in the field next to us into running away. His screams are replaced by approaching police sirens. Kevin jumps out of the van. "Maybe sooner than I would like." I smile at her and throw the door shut.

Chapter 28
Loose Ends

Kevin runs into the wall on the other side of the door and nods at me. I swing the heavy battering ram at the door with all my strength. The door feels like it is made of cardboard as I smash it away from its lock and hinges. Before I get a chance to throw the battering ram on the ground behind me, he is through the door and firing his assault rifle. I withdraw my handgun and step across the threshold. He runs down the middle of the room to the door at the far end in what can only be described as a makeshift hospital ward. Sedated patients lie in their beds on either side of the ward.

Two security guards now lie slumped up against the blood-splattered wall at the far end of the room. Kevin stands by the door waiting for me. Several gunshots are fired in the adjacent room, which makes me jump. As I sprint down the corridor to him, I scan all the patients to see if any of them are Changying.

All the patients are connected to machines that keep them sleep whilst they wait for their turn to have their organs harvested. Before I reach halfway, I am covered in sweat. There is no air conditioning, so the room is like a sauna. I try not to breathe too much to avoid the repugnant smell of hot, sweaty, and putrefying flesh.

I run past Kevin and kick the open door that he is guarding. The door swings open and narrowly misses the Sheikh's Head of Security, Aziz. I momentarily point my gun at his head before lowering it to the floor near the head of a nurse that he has just killed. This hospital ward is similar in size to the previous one, but several of the beds are empty.

Asim runs up behind him and says, "She is not here, sir."

"Shit," I exclaim. "Let's hope that we are not too late then."

I dart to the door on my right-hand side, but Aziz is quicker than me and he reaches it first. He kicks it open with ease and I am right behind him as we storm into the operating room. He shoots the three doctors leaning over the organ donor and I fire over his right shoulder at the doctor standing over the transplant recipient. The recipient sits up and I put a bullet in the middle of his forehead. Asim directs the two screaming nurses out of the room.

Changying is lying naked on the operating table. She is unconscious and is connected to several machines. Jalal, the medical officer, runs into the room with a wheeled stretcher and announces, "Hostiles are approaching. We've got to get her out of here, NOW." He runs around her and disconnects her from the machines. "Thank God. We arrived without a second to spare." I shake from the overwhelming relief. "Right, I need help transferring her." I holster my gun and grab her upper back. Asim and Jalal each take a leg. "Three, two, one, lift." Simultaneously, we lift her up and onto the stretcher. Jalal runs around to the top end of the stretcher and has trouble getting it to the door.

"I'll take it from here, Jalal. You get in the van. Aziz, you and your men provide me with cover." They all rush out of the room. On my way to the door, one of the doctors grabs my leg with one hand. His other hand is covering his throat as he unsuccessfully tries to stop the bleeding. I kick his hand away and run out of the operating room. I grab the blanket off the first unoccupied bed, and, despite the sweltering heat, I cover Changying's malnourished body with it. Loud gunfire erupts outside; it is only Aziz and his men firing warning shots to keep the hostiles back.

I push Changying into the unbearably intense sunlight, which blinds me temporarily when I step into it. The medical van reverses towards me on my left-hand side with its back doors wide open. Jalal stands in the back, beckoning me over. Aziz and his men are on my right-hand side; they occupy two Jeeps, each of which supports a Browning M2 .50 calibre machine gun. Aziz and Asim direct these Browning guns at the three Jeeps snaking their way down the mountainside towards us.

The medical van stops a couple of metres in front of the stretcher. I hit the back of it with the stretcher and rest the far end of it on the van's floor. I press the button on the stretcher with my right thumb and its wheels automatically fold up. I push it into the back of the van and Jalal takes hold of its handles. I jump into the back of the van and throw one of the doors shut behind me; he presses the button on the stretcher and it springs up again.

As soon as he applies the stretcher's brakes, he shouts, "Go, go, GO."

The van's wheels spin on the muddy track before it thrusts itself forward. The unshut back door swings open further and smashes into the side of the van before being flung back. I grab the side of the van with my left hand and grab the closing door with my right hand. I slam it shut and the pane of glass in it falls out. We drive up a steep slope and out of the remote village into the rainforest.

The Jeep at the back keeps firing at the hostiles but they are gaining on us. They start returning fire, but it doesn't cause us any issues. Jalal desperately tries to check over Changying as we are all violently thrown around. The van hits a pothole and she is thrown up off the stretcher. I lean on top of her to keep her pinned to it. I look through the glass partition between ourselves and the driver's cabin; our driver is managing to maintain a speed of around fifty miles per hour through the narrow, winding roads. Huge rainforest trees line the road and we narrowly avoid them as we skid around tight corners.

After several minutes, a Jeep races down the hillside onto the road in front of us. It also has a mounted Browning, but it is pointing forwards. Our driver struggles to keep up with the Jeep, but it is much easy to navigate now that the Jeep leads the way. The hostiles continue to gain on us. When we reach a wide section in the road, the Jeep directly behind us pulls to the right and slows down to allow the Jeep at the back to overtake it and reload.

The entrance to the private airstrip is about two kilometres up ahead. The sound of a hovering helicopter penetrates through the Browning fire, but it is not visible. We drift around a corner too fast and our driver only just manages to stop us from sliding over the edge of the road into a fast-flowing stream. A military helicopter stops and hovers about fifty metres above the road between the airstrip and us. Our speed drops as the helicopter's rotor system push us back and rocks us viciously from side to side. Once the final Jeep passes under the helicopter, the 'dakka dakka dakka' sound from its minigun deafens us. It obliterates our enemy's three Jeeps as well as a vast proportion of the vegetation and wildlife surrounding them. All three enemy Jeeps catch fire and blow up.

The security guard lifts the barrier and we hurtle past into the private airstrip. We drive up to a sparkling white, medium-sized private jet. We screech to a halt. I grab both door handles and throw the doors open. Jalal tries to unlock the stretcher's brakes and move it, but to no avail.

"We don't have time for that." I politely push him out of the way.

I put my left arm under Changying's back and my right arm behind her knees. I lift her up and jump out of the back of the van. I sprint as fast as I can to the jet.

The Dragon Master appears at the entrance of the jet with his hands on his mouth. I reach the steps and jump up them two at a time.

Before I barge the Dragon Master out of our way, the Sheikh wraps his arms around him, and pulls him back into the jet. Blood seeps out from the wounds on his arms and is absorbed by his brilliant white thawb. Changying's hair whips each of them in the face as I squeeze us both past them.

The Sheikh's medical team has created a makeshift medical unit at the back of the jet within a soft wall enclosure made of clear PVC. The head surgeon opens the curtains as we approach him. I basically throw her at him, but keep hold of her blanket. He catches her and retreats to the operating table, which is already surrounded by other medical professionals. The self-sealing PVC curtains close. The Dragon Master runs up to me and throws his arms around me.

"Thank you."

The Sheikh pats me on the shoulder. "Well done, my friend."

Aziz, Asim, Jalal and two other men enter the jet. One of the remaining men pulls the stairs away from the jet whilst the rest of them stay with the Jeeps. Asim locks the jet's door. The Sheikh turns around and shouts at the pilots through the open cockpit doors, "What are you waiting for? Get us out of here!"

Ingram Content Group UK Ltd.
Milton Keynes UK
UKHW020354210623
423772UK00005B/85